24 HOURS TO KILL

They were bringing in Jack Kelty. Though young, he had killed two men during a botched robbery. Thanks to reporter Martin Hillary, he is now something of a hero. Hillary is pursuing the caravan, followed by Kelty's young gang. But as the police caravan drives Kelty to justice, a savage storm floods the area, stranding them all in the small town of Blue Valley. Most of the men of Blue Valley are fighting the flood elsewhere. Only a handful are left in town to deal with Kelty's arrival. There's Steve Michaels, engaged to Mayor Ben Blake's daughter Sue; and Ben himself, who quickly appoints Steve sheriff as the flood cuts the town off from the rest of the country—and Ben's younger daughter Gretchen, who is very curious about this renegade in their midst....very curious indeed.

BLUE MASCARA TEARS

Jack Cummings is a San Francisco cop, an honest cop. Which is why he resents the way Knocko Cutter gets away with murder. Oh sure, nothing can be proved. But Cummings knows who killed the prostitute a few weeks ago, just like he knows who's behind the killing of a small time gambler in a downtown hotel. But Knocko has got the fix on his side. Cummings can't even trust his own partner. He doesn't even know if he should trust his captain. But one thing's for certain—he knows what he has to do. Cummings is an angry cop, a desperate cop, and he is going to get Knocko no matter what it takes.

James McKimmey Bibliography
(1923-2011)

CRIME NOVELS

The Perfect Victim (1957; expanded from "Riot at Willow Creek," *Cosmopolitan,* 1957)

Winner Take All (1959)

The Satyr (1960)

Cornered! (1960)

24 Hours to Kill (1961)

The Wrong Ones (1961)

The Long Ride (1961; expanded from "The Long Ride," *Cosmopolitan*, 1960)

Squeeze Play (1962)

Run If You're Guilty (1963; expanded from "Death Trap," *Cosmopolitan*, 1962)

Blue Mascara Tears (1965)

A Circle in the Water (1965)

Never Be Caught (3 novelettes, 1966: Never be Caught, And Then She Was Dead, Kill Him Again)

The Hot Fire (1968)

The Man With the Gloved Hand (1972)

JUVENILE FICTION

Buckaroo (1979)

As Benjamin Swift

Playoff (1981)

As Dewey Daniels

The Martindales' Nightmare (1981)

24 HOURS TO KILL

BLUE MASCARA TEARS

James McKimmey

Introduction by Nicholas Litchfield

Stark House Press • Eureka California

24 HOURS TO KILL / BLUE MASCARA TEARS

Published by Stark House Press
1315 H Street
Eureka, CA 95501
griffinskye3@sbcglobal.net
www.starkhousepress.com

24 HOURS TO KILL

BLUE MASCARA TEARS

“Idolatry and Playing God to Cure ‘The Fix’” copyright © 2023 by
Nicholas Litchfield

ISBN: 979-8-88601-036-7

Text design by Mark Shepard, shepgraphics.com
Cover design by James Heimer, jamesheimer.com
Proofreading by Bill Kelly

First Stark House Press Edition: August 2023

Idolatry and Playing God to Cure "The Fix"
by Nicholas Litchfield

The suspense novel *24 Hours to Kill,* issued by Dell Publishing Company in May 1961, featured cover art by renowned painter Robert McGinnis and carried this impressive back cover blurb by iconic author John D. MacDonald: "This man can manipulate tension and character in ways that are beginning to frighten me."

After reading the novel, *New York Times* book critic Anthony Boucher was inclined to agree. Considering the author an adept practitioner of MacDonald's vein of crime writing, he rated him "the brightest recent newcomer in the field of paperback crime originals" (Boucher, 1962). However, though comparable to the innovative MacDonald, this author had "his own likable individuality," and Boucher especially appreciated his "smooth storytelling" and ability to create tense, credible situations (Boucher, 1961b).

The exceptionally disciplined James McKimmey (1923–2011), who strived to hit 1,000 words per day (sometimes 5,000), and once wrote a novel (*Winner Take All*) in ten days and sold it to Dell (McDonald, 1962), was an accomplished full-time fiction writer who forged a fruitful career while in his twenties. As a student at the University of San Francisco, he frequently wrote columns for the *San Mateo Times* and his college newspaper, *The Foghorn* (Guthrie, 2004b), as well as little magazines like *The American Pen* (*The Commercial Advertiser,* 1948) and *Skyline* (*The Commercial Advertiser,* 1951). When he graduated, he intended to work for newspapers in the Bay Area but couldn't find an opening (McDonald, 1962).

After a brief spell of work at an electronics plant, he managed to support himself through his writing by focusing on commercial fiction. He was encouraged by Pulitzer Prize-winning author John P.

Marquand, who became a kind of "patron saint" for McKimmey, to devote full-time effort to the pulp markets rather than take part-time work and attempt literary fiction in the evenings (McDonald, 1962). The science fiction genre most appealed to McKimmey, and so he targeted those publications, selling a number of stories to *Planet Stories* and *If*, among other SF digest magazines (Crider, 2016). Then, with some hesitancy, he accepted a position at Fiction House, contributing formulaic novelettes to the Ki-Gor series for *Jungle Stories* under a house name, "John Peter Drummond" (Guthrie, 2004a).

Although the market dried up, McKimmey profited greatly from the experience, becoming more adept at plotting lengthier yarns. He subsequently placed stories with *The American Magazine* and the *San Francisco Chronicle* (*The Commercial Advertiser*, 1954) and "slick" magazines like *Collier's* and *This Week* (*San Mateo Times*, 1954). His attempt at a crime novel, titled *Riot At Willow Creek*, resulted in a sale to Dell (who released it as *The Perfect Victim* in 1958*)*, with *Cosmopolitan* acquiring first serial rights and issuing an abridged version under the original title in 1957 (Guthrie, 2004a).

As a crime/mystery novelist, McKimmey became highly prolific and particularly marketable. During his lifetime, he wrote seventeen books (of which fourteen were crime novels) and contributed close to four hundred stories and articles to periodicals, such as *The Saturday Evening Post, Good Housekeeping, Alfred Hitchcock's Mystery Magazine, Omaha World-Herald*, and *Redbook*. All of his paperback novels were optioned for films, but none of these books were ever made into a movie (Guthrie, 2004a).

Of the author's novels, Boucher ranked *24 Hours to Kill* above McKimmey's others, lauding it as "an explosively effective combination" of character and tension. (Boucher, 1961a). Anthony Award-winning author Bill Crider, who, in a previous Stark House collection, provides a careful examination of McKimmey's novels *Cornered!* and *The Long Ride*, discusses the author's "shifting points of view" technique and his efforts at offering insights into all the characters, noting: "it's evident that he drew from all sectors of society and that he enjoyed writing about what makes people tick." (Crider, 2017). In *Cornered!*, the reader delights in discovering which characters will act in the ways we anticipate and which will surprise us. "Some will be cowardly, some will perform little acts of heroism, and some won't survive," writes Crider. "McKimmey makes us care about all of them."

The same might be said of *24 Hours to Kill*. Set in the Midwest, Ashford County Sheriff Fred Whitehall and ailing Police Detective Al Druggan take charge of high-profile killer Jack Kelty, intending to transport him over state lines from Colorado to Nebraska to face trial. Kelty is responsible for killing a warehouse guard, formally of the Ashford Police Department, while committing a robbery.

Awkwardly, public sympathy for the boyishly handsome Kelty is running high, thanks to influential newshound Martin Hillary, a feature writer for the *Ashford Times*. A harsh critic of the Ashford PD, committed to exposing police corruption and brutality, Hillary sees Kelty as a great opportunity to severely damage the police force and further his own career as a crusading reporter. His defense of Kelty, "built up in the public eye as an innocent victim of a slum environment" (*Buffalo Evening News*, 1961), and his inflammatory accusations against the dead warehouse guard and the Ashford PD, endanger the transportation of the prisoner. In an effort to circumvent the angry public mob Sheriff Whitehall anticipates encountering on the journey to Kelty's hometown, he deviates from the scheduled route, making an overnight stop at a police precinct in smalltown Blue Valley.

Things go horribly wrong when a severe storm hits the area, causing riverbanks to burst and taking out a couple of crucial bridges. Sherriff Whitehall and two of his police force perish in the flood, and the town becomes isolated from the outside world, with the townspeople divided on about how best to protect themselves against the dangerous forces rapidly converging on their community. What threatens their safety is not the raging flood but the five teenage hoodlums targeting the precinct, aiming to rescue the hero killer from lockup before police assistance arrives.

Stacked with a whole range of interesting citizens, from the volatile and the vulnerable, the cowardly and the predatory, to the antagonistic and the easily misled, McKimmey succinctly details character backstories and long-lasting friction between the various residents. Ultimately, relationships are tested, allegiances are broken, and valor and villainy battle it out. Exciting and atmospheric, with a decent number of surprises, the story rumbles along at an agreeable pace, drawing to a fitting conclusion.

Favorable reviews back up the impression that the novel was a high point for McKimmey. His books weren't always winners, but he was the type of writer who dropped something of substance into every one of them. As John Henry "Jack" Russell, columnist and editor at the *San Mateo Times*, said of *Blue Mascara Tears*: "You won't remember the characters or the actual plot, but you will recall certain scenes; they are so well handled" (Russell, 1965). He was referring to the death of the gambler in the opening scene and the weary detective's cross-examination of the fourteen-year-old girl who claims to have been raped by a black man in an alleyway. Declares Russell: "The language rips the fabric of civilization apart as the facades crumble."

That novel, included in this twofer, was a Ballantine paperback original published in 1965. When it first hit the shelves, it featured alluring cover art, this time by Ron Lesser, one of the more accomplished illustrators of the mid-century period (Pulp International, 2023). The bold text beneath the title proclaims impishly: "She was gorgeous—and her curves spelt death!" Amusingly, when *San Mateo Times'* photographer Ray Zirkel asked, "Who does the front pieces on your paperbacks?", McKimmey replied, "I don't know, but if I did, I would kick him to death" (McDonald, 1962).

Dissimilar to *24 Hours to Kill*, this novel is a grim and seedy, old-school hardboiled gangland crime story with a main character who's a hard-bitten San Francisco law enforcer with something of a Messiah complex. Widowed and devoted to his job, the tough, honest Inspector Jack Cummings admits to being "Christ-like within his own mind and heart." His ambition—waking fixation, in fact—is to arrest well-connected gangster Knocko Cutter, a powerful crime lord involved in gambling and prostitution rackets. However, bribery and corruption at the police department protect Knocko from capture and make Cummings' goal near-impossible.

In the neatly written opening chapter, in which gambler Robert Lundstrom dies from his bullet wounds in a hospital, Cummings immediately sets out to establish a connection between Knocko and the shooting, figuring he must be involved, if not directly responsible. The theft of $65,000 from Lundstrom's hotel room brings into play a cluster of varied suspects and keeps the action concentrated around the hotel workforce, and a contentious side plot involving a teenage rape victim proves to be more than merely a philosophical exploration of racial divides. As Cummings digs into scandal and sleaze, battling his supervisor, Captain Otto Blane, and those on the take at city hall, he realizes that he will need more than hard-found evidence and frank testimonies from felons to put a hole in the crime syndicate and "kill the fix" that impedes the long arm of the law.

Dark and gritty, this is a lean but punchy tale with occasional dashes of welcome introspection to break up the author's unembellished strands of dialogue. A compelling start sets the tone for what's to come, and if the middle sections get a little rutted at times, a superior final chapter mends the narrative, drawing attention to McKimmey's flair for formidable, expressive prose.

Jack Russell was a journalist with much to say about McKimmey's work. Though not always content with the stories, he was continually drawn to his books and appreciative of the author's succinct prose and characterizations. For him, McKimmey was "a master of the quick, incisive probing into a situation" (Russell, 1965), able to "depict a character or an event in just a few, choice descriptive passages" and make "a line of prose do what he wants it to" (Russell, 1963). The author's resourcefulness, refined by years of writing commercial short stories, made him "adept at setting a mood for a place with an economy of style" (Russell, 1968). He viewed McKimmey as one of those rare crime fiction writers who had "the knack of George Simenon in reaching a crucial point in human relations and then laying it bare with the resulting exposition". (Russell, 1965).

Skillfully weaving the lives of residents into his swift-paced tales, McKimmey proved capable of bringing humanity to his characters and authenticity and familiarity to their situations and daily struggles. The result is that you care about the fate of Inspector Cummings and want him to triumph against the odds. You're curious to see the community dynamics at play in Blue Valley and learn who will rise to the occasion to protect the town against disruptive outsiders. You may rail against the actions of irresponsible citizens like the newspaperman Martin Hillary, but you understand their motives and empathize with their desire to thwart police corruption and enforce change.

Sixty years on, both novels are still relevant and challenging and worth examining. Fleshed-out protagonists, crisp descriptions, and proficient plotting are McKimmey's hallmarks, and in keeping with previous Stark House reprints, *24 Hours to Kill* and *Blue Mascara Tears* spotlight the professional crime author in prime form.

—May 2023
Rochester, NY

Nicholas Litchfield is the founder of the literary magazine *Lowestoft Chronicle*, author of the suspense novel *Swampjack Virus*, and editor of ten literary anthologies. His stories, essays, and book reviews appear in many magazines and newspapers, including *BULL: Men's Fiction*, *Shotgun Honey*, *Volume 1 Brooklyn*, *Daily Press*, and *The Virginian-Pilot*. He has also contributed introductions to numerous books, including fifteen Stark House Press reprints of long-forgotten noir and mystery novels. Formerly a book critic for the *Lancashire Post*, syndicated to twenty-five newspapers across the U.K., he now writes for *Publishers Weekly* and frequently contributes to Colorado State University's literary journal *Colorado Review*. You can find him online at nicholaslitchfield.com and on Twitter: @N_Litchfield.

Works cited:

Boucher, Anthony (Jun 25, 1961). "Criminals at Large." *New York Times*, p. 1

Boucher, Anthony (Nov 12, 1961). "A Roundup of Current Criminals at Large: Large." *New York Times*, p. 2

Boucher, Anthony (Apr 15, 1962). "Criminals at Large: Criminals." *New York Times*, p. 2

Buffalo Evening News (Jun 3, 1961). "From the World of Crime," *Buffalo Evening News*, p. 20

Crider, Bill. "James McKimmey." *Cornered! / The Long Ride*, by James McKimmey, Stark House Press, 2016, pp. 7-11.

Guthrie, Allan (Feb 2004). "James McKimmey: Part 1." Allan Guthrie's NOIR ORIGINALS, February 2004, http://web.archive.org/web/20140422225940/http://www.allanguthrie.co.uk/pages/noir_zine/profiles/james_mckinney_1.php

Guthrie, Allan (Feb 2004). "James McKimmey: Part 2" Allan Guthrie's NOIR ORIGINALS, http://web.archive.org/web/20140422231916/http://www.allanguthrie.co.uk/pages/noir_zine/profiles/james_mckinney_2.php

McDonald, Hugh (Jan 20, 1962). "Story of a Successful Writer." *San Mateo Times*, p. 27

Pulp International (Feb 11, 2023). "Vintage Pulp: Hue and Cry." Pulp International, https://www.pulpinternational.com/pulp/entry/Cover-for-Blue-Mascara-Tears-by-James-McKimmey.html

Russell, Jack (Sep 14, 1963). "Books: Run If You're Guilty." *San Mateo Times*, p. 36

Russell, Jack (Jul 10, 1965). "The Book Corner." *San Mateo Times*, p. 38

Russell, Jack (Mar 30, 1968). "Books: The Hot Fire." *San Mateo Times*, p. 40

San Mateo Times (Aug 30, 1954). "M'Kimmey Gets Story in Slicks." *San Mateo Times*, p. 5

The Commercial Advertiser (Dec 14, 1948). "James McKimmey, Jr. Headed For The Big Time." *The Commercial Advertiser*, p. 7

The Commercial Advertiser (Oct 30, 1951). "'Skyline' Carries Story By James McKimmey, Jr." *The Commercial Advertiser*, p. 1

The Commercial Advertiser (Dec 7, 1954). "James McKimmey's Story In San Francisco Chronicle." *The Commercial Advertiser*, p. 4

24 HOURS TO KILL

James McKimmey

Chapter I

The lead car of the sheriff's caravan was speeding its way sixty miles beyond Colorado, just below the south border of the sheriff's home state.

The sheriff, with his entourage, had picked up Jack Kelty at Fort Morgan where Kelty had seriously wounded a deputy sheriff. But because Kelty had done his other killings in Ashford County, the Colorado authorities had been willing to hand him over to the Ashford County Sheriff.

Now they were taking Kelty home. In the front of the lead caravan car were two of the sheriff's officers, in the back seat Kelty sat with wrists handcuffed to Sheriff Fred Whitehall and an Ashford police detective, Al Duggan.

"Real treatment, huh?" Kelty said. "Latched on to the sheriff on one side and Inspector Duggan on the other. No lousy patrolmen but the hierarchy itself!"

"Shut up, Kelty," Sheriff Whitehall said.

The sheriff looked at Jack Kelty as the prisoner smiled and tipped his head back against the seat. The midafternoon light was sunless, gray and murky. It cast its illumination so that Kelty's face was unshadowed and seemed unlined and extremely youthful. Kelty had neat blond hair, almost crew cut. His face had the clean-lined look of a college junior, though he'd quit school in the tenth grade and was now twenty-eight years old. He wore a neat blue Paisley sport shirt and gray slacks over a compact six-foot, one-hundred-and-eighty-pound frame.

Sheriff Fred Whitehall, slim and white-haired, tried to figure it out. Somehow Kelty should not have wound up this way. Maybe that was why he had appealed to the public. He'd had some tough breaks, but not many. Perhaps a lot of people could project and think that this, but for a twist of fate, might have happened to them. It might be that, along with the effective work of the *Ashford Times* and its expert feature writer, Martin Hillary, who had defended Kelty from the beginning, which made Kelty a hero to some.

The sheriff turned his head, looking out at the gently rolling countryside. They were perhaps fifteen miles south of the raging Soshone River that ran along the south border of the sheriff's home state. But you could continually see signs of the flood that was tearing up the countryside.

They sped over a concrete viaduct that crossed a tributary creek swollen to the size of a small river. Water sprayed away on either side as the tires hissed through the spillover. The water of the stream flowed swiftly between newly created banks, the grass soaked and driven flat at the edges. The flow was muddy from topsoil torn away with the force of the current, a miniature version of what the Soshone, bloated with melted mountain snow and days of heavy rain, must look like now.

In a way, the sheriff thought, there must be some parallel between a river like the Soshone and a man like Jack Kelty. You could know a river to be dependable, trustworthy—then it suddenly became a killer. Kelty, the sheriff didn't doubt, had once been as innocent as a quietly flowing stream.

But how could you know what went on now behind the college junior façade, the bravado manner? Jack Kelty had started his blood bath by killing a warehouse guard just outside Ashford during an attempted small-scale robbery. Before that he'd been just an average product of a tough city neighborhood with a few minor trouble skirmishes to his credit.

What had made his finger squeeze the trigger and release that first killing bullet? Fear? No doubt. And there had begun the history of a killer.

But the savageness had come with the desperate attempt to escape from an angry, tough Ashford police force, one of whose members had fallen before Kelty's gun. No doubt it was the reputation given to the Ashford force that had contributed heavily to the unusual public sympathy for Kelty.

For a long time now, the *Ashford Times*, represented well by the sharp pen of Martin Hillary, had been working on the brutalities, the corruptions, the heartlessness of the Ashford police force. That the history of the Ashford force contained defects was, no doubt, a fact. Human foibles were as common among law officers as other human beings. The valid possibility that there might be less fault in the Ashford force than in a great number of other big-city departments went unnoticed by a statewide *Ashford Times* readership. The *Times's* circulation-loving publisher knew that circulation was not increased by proclaiming virtues.

Somehow, then, Jack Kelty had become an underdog, glamorous in his role because of his soft manner and collegiate good looks. And though not one soul who might have been subconsciously rooting for his successful escape would willingly have wanted to find himself in Kelty's path, there still had been a strange and strong public sympathy for one frightened young man in a life-or-death conflict with a dangerous Ashford police force.

The sheriff turned his eyes from the soaked countryside and looked at a tired and nervous Inspector Al Duggan. The public was wrong, of course, and a good hard cop like Duggan was right. Eventually it made no difference how a man had come to be a killer; all that mattered was that he had become one. Al Duggan, a cop clear through, knew you didn't risk anything when that had happened.

"How about a cigarette?" Kelty asked.

This time Al Duggan said it: "Shut up, Kelty."

Sheriff Whitehall watched Al Duggan roll his window down to relieve the muggy interior of the car. Duggan was fourteen years Kelty's senior and twenty pounds heavier. The murky light was not so kind to his heavy features as to Kelty's. He looked older than forty-two and, the sheriff knew, he felt older. It had taken five days to flush Kelty into flight out of Ashford, another five days before he was captured in Colorado. The sheriff knew that Al Duggan had not relaxed in those ten days; he knew that Al Duggan would not relax until Kelty was locked behind bars in Ashford.

"I've got rights," Kelty said.

Al Duggan brought his eyes from their abstract study of the countryside. "When did dead men have rights?"

"You think I'm dead, Inspector?"

"I know it."

"You may be surprised."

"You're dead, Kelty."

"Maybe I am at that. Maybe this is heaven, huh?"

"Maybe this is hell. You'll think so pretty soon anyway. You're going to scream before this is over."

Kelty laughed softly. "How can a dead man scream?"

"In time, Kelty. In time."

The sky remained a gloomy steel-gray. They crossed another creek swollen over its banks so that once more the tires whirred through a thin stream of water pouring across the highway. Kelty leaned his head back again. Al Duggan resumed his staring at the countryside. The caravan rolled swiftly on.

Just above the border midway across the sheriff's home state, Sue Blake drove eight miles west of Blue Valley, population fifteen hundred, to pick up Steve Michaels in the neighboring village of Hampton Mill where flood damage created by the angry Soshone River had been the heaviest.

Weary after hours of placing sandbags to strengthen the flood wall on the southeast corner of town, Steve Michaels watched her drive up the short main street. He stood in front of the Hampton Mill Community Hall that had been serving as headquarters for the volunteer flood workers. Hampton Mill had a population of three hundred people, but there were now four times that many persons in and around town helping secure the levee that acted as a buffer for the valley running to the east. That land to the east rose to a hump where the town of Blue Valley rested.

Steve, a dark and lean twenty-eight, tanned and well-muscled in sport shirt and old slacks, stood at the curb and admired the clean beauty of his blond fiancée as she swung the yellow convertible expertly up beside him. She had been just nine years old and very distant and untouchable when Steve had been sent from Blue Valley to the boys' home on the outskirts of Ashford.

Over the years before he'd returned to Blue Valley, he'd carried a picture in his mind of a prim and sweet little girl, face haloed by the young, soft blond hair, eldest daughter of the most respected man in town, Ben Blake. Somehow he had not thought she would change, because nothing had changed in his memory. When he got out of the Marine Corps and came back to the University sixty miles from Ashford to earn his teacher's certificate, he had found the first day on campus that she had indeed changed.

She was no longer the little girl, no longer, he'd discovered, remotely untouchable. They'd talked all afternoon; that evening he'd kissed her at the door of her sorority house. He'd realized that she had become as much a woman as any he'd ever known. Beneath the calm, nearly sweet exterior there was, he knew, great perception, strength and passion; it would take equal capacity for a man to return her love.

He opened the door of the convertible. She gave him her smile that made him feel comfortable and secure, as though the rather tumultuous boyhood of Steve Michaels had been buried once and for all, so that now he was on the kind of solid ground not even a rampaging flood could reach and destroy.

"You look really tired, Steve," she said, leaning across the seat to kiss him briefly.

"An illusion. I feel great."

"Everything all right?" She made a swift U-turn and drove back to the graveled road that would return them to Blue Valley.

"Under the circumstances."

"Damn this river."

"No," he said, smiling grimly, looking at it.

The Soshone was just to their right, a vast stream of rolling water. Near the edges, trees stood in water that had half submerged their trunks. Other trees, uprooted upstream, had become floating leaf-stripped logs. A roof of a chicken coop bobbed along. With the sun trying futilely to get through the fine film of rain clouds, the water had taken on an eerie color, touched here and there with silver, deepening into brownish black, constantly rolling so that streaks of mud and silt blended visibly with the currents.

"It's turned into a killer, Steve."

"It's not human. It has no soul. We create the soul in our own minds, because we've grown so familiar with it. If it's gone crazy and if we blame it, we've got to blame God. If you say damn the river, you're saying damn God."

She looked at him quickly. Her blue eyes flashed with a sudden smile. "I can't get used to you as the philosopher, Steve."

He leaned back, the smell of the killing river still in his nostrils. "I'm a teacher now. I've got to be musty sometimes, don't I?"

"Sometimes, I suppose," she agreed. "But not all the time. Save a little of the old swashbuckler for me, won't you?"

He grinned.

"Steve," she said, suddenly serious, "I do love you. You know that, don't you?"

He looked at her. She took her foot from the accelerator, a cool-looking girl in a simple blue dress, bare legs tanned and good, line of face clean and firm. She braked.

"Steve—"

He reached for her and kissed her long and hard. She was trembling a little. "God, I do love you, Steve."

"I love you, Sue," he said, almost perfunctorily. In a moment she had started the car, and they were at full speed again.

"You won't mind talking to Rod for Daddy?" she asked.

"Why would I? It was my idea, remember." In the moment of contentment, he was not at all concerned about the reappearance of a subject that had caused more havoc in the Blake household than the flooding of the Soshone. "I think it's fair to ask for his side of it."

"Personally, I think my little sister needs the hard hand of my father applied to her backside for ever allowing the boy to get her into a compromising situation like that."

"I haven't heard Rod's side yet. But man is always the pursuer, isn't he?"

She looked at him quickly, eyes sparkling, "Of course!"

It was raining again when they passed the city limits of Blue Valley.

Chapter 2

The caravan taking Jack Kelty home was coming now into a small town labeled Bennington by a white sign on the outskirts. A roadside service station and café came into view. Sheriff Whitehall leaned forward. "Pull up."

The lead car led the others to a stop beside the café. "Let's go inside, Al," Sheriff Whitehall said.

Within seconds the prisoner had been unmanacled, then handcuffed again to two patrolmen. Officers from the other cars bristled up smoothly. The car containing Kelty was efficiently covered with a dozen guns. Kelty, again between two men in the back seat, said, "Hell of a lot of trouble for one man, isn't it?"

Both Al Duggan and Sheriff Whitehall checked the placement of the officers. Sheriff Whitehall said, "Make a move, Kelty. We'll save ourselves all this trouble."

"You'd like that, wouldn't you?"

The sheriff and Al Duggan walked toward the café as rain again began to spatter against the grease-stained concrete in front of the entrance.

A man in a white shirt wearing a white apron waited at the door, blinking at them. He backed as they entered. "That Kelty?" he asked, incredulously. "Jack Kelty?"

The sheriff shook his head. "No." The sheriff looked back at the end of the caravan. Three cars came to a stop, one by one. Newsmen, the sheriff knew. As the result of the *Ashford Times's* stand, no newsmen were welcome. But you couldn't keep them from following; and an automobile had been the only solution for returning Kelty—

transporting him on a train would have endangered too many people. The one thing the sheriff had accomplished before they left Fort Morgan was to make an agreement with the newspaper people that they would leave him and everyone else in the caravan alone during the trip back. They had also agreed, in order to ensure security, not to do anything that might make a circus out of the caravan on its return. Fortunately, Martin Hillary of the *Times* was not among them. The sheriff had been waiting for him to show up, but happily he had not yet appeared.

The man in the white apron insisted, "Thought I saw Kelty in that car. You look like that sheriff from Ashford. Seen your pictures in the papers. And your license plates—"

"He's a con who broke out of our state prison two years ago," the sheriff said. "Picked him up in Fort Morgan. We sent Kelty back by plane. That's not Kelty."

"Well, it sure looked like him!"

"How about some coffee?" Al Duggan said.

The man continued to squint outside, stubbornly curious.

"I said how about some coffee!" Al Duggan snapped.

The man jumped, then hurried around the single counter.

"Take it easy, Al," Sheriff Whitehall said gently.

Al Duggan nodded. "I will."

"You look tired. You don't look good at all."

They sat on stools nearest the window. Al Duggan kept his eyes on the car where they'd left Kelty.

"Easy, Al. They're good boys. They're all watching him."

Al Duggan nodded again, feeling his pulse keep up its incessant hammering. He was very tired. But he couldn't relax. Lately it had been that way all the time. For years he'd been able to keep up a hard work routine, sometimes sleeping no more than three or four hours a night for weeks on end. It had never bothered him, until recently. A month ago, he'd seen his own physician, even though he had a department physical coming up soon. Hypertension, the doctor had called it. The doctor had prescribed a drug to reduce the overaction of the brain and so reduce the strain on the heart. "You've been working that heart overtime, Al. You've got to give it a rest, or one of these days it'll just quit." Well, he'd run out of the pills just before Kelty started his spree, and there had been no time to buy more or to find an ounce of time to relax. These last days, while the hunt was on for Kelty, seemed to have ruptured an energy vein. But he would worry about that when Kelty was returned....

The man wearing the white apron put two mugs of coffee before them. Sheriff Whitehall put down a fifty-cent piece. "I need a dime or two in the change. Do you have a public telephone?"

The counterman pointed his thumb toward the rear of the narrow steamy room. "Ain't a public telephone, but you can use it. Don't need no change, but don't make no long-distance calls unless you do it collect. I can check with Lois on the switchboard."

The sheriff nodded. He said to Al Duggan, "I'm going to check the office in Ashford. That river's in a hell of a way. It's lousing us up."

"It better not," Al Duggan said.

The sheriff disappeared around the partition. The man in the apron drifted in that direction, as though trying to hear.

Al Duggan said, "How about filling up my cup again and sliding down that newspaper?"

The man, irritated, shot the newspaper, the *Ashford Times* down to Al Duggan and brought over the coffee container.

"Good story on Kelty by this Hillary. I swear that looked like Kelty out there."

"Maybe you need glasses," Al Duggan said. "This guy's up for forgery. Broke out of the state pen. Just like the sheriff told you."

"You're a cop, ain't you?"

"They're taking me back too. Armed robbery. Shot a man. Restaurant in Hollyvale."

The man was blinking again. "You a prisoner?"

"Now you've got it."

"But—how come the sheriff lets you sit here alone?"

"He trusts me. We're old friends. This is my third trip."

The man swallowed. "You'd shot a man in a restaurant in Hollyvale?"

"That's right. I shot the counterman. He talked too much."

The man took a sudden step backward. Then moved sideways down to the middle of the counter where he stood staring silently at Al Duggan, blinking rhythmically.

Al Duggan began reading the front page feature under the by-line of Martin Hillary:

> So at last, like the fox condemned at birth for being a fox, inevitably to be hunted down by the hunters and hounds, Jack Kelty has been taken prisoner in Fort Morgan. The police

are to be applauded in the way those who ride to hounds are to be applauded. There is something spectacular about hunting down a tiny fox, who is defenseless except for …

Al Duggan had begun to sweat as he read. He'd been fighting Martin Hillary for a long time, but this last was the worst.

… and so the count on Jack Kelty is now undeniably the count of a man going to his death. One guard killed in a suburban warehouse just outside Ashford while Jack Kelty was attempting robbery—undeniable. One city detective killed while Jack Kelty was trying to find cover in Ashford. One deputy sheriff shot and in serious condition when Jack Kelty was captured in Colorado. All undeniable. Now Jack Kelty faces death in the electric chair.

But as I have asked in this column before: who really started this trail of blood?

Was it not the police of Ashford itself? Was it not because that warehouse guard had once been a policeman on the Ashford force—a man dismissed because of crookedness? Was it not because that guard, in the grand tradition of the Ashford force, elected to shoot first and ask questions later? So that Jack Kelty was forced to fire, in order to save his life? No one would attempt to deny that the guard's gun had been fired, and this was precisely Jack Kelty's explanation when he was captured.

So then, when one of its own former members died in such a fashion, and despite the fact that this member was no longer a member as the result of personal corruption, did not the Ashford force, as a unit, make up its mind? Did not, at that time, the whistle blow in the squad room of the Ashford police headquarters, a room with a noble record of bloody brutalities, and the order go out, "Kill Jack Kelty on sight"? And did that not start the chain of reactions, resulting in even another death of an Ashford police officer, forcing Jack Kelty into blind and terrified flight? Dangerous, of course, as all hunted animals are dangerous. But only because the hunters following were even more dangerous?

I do not condone Jack Kelty. But let us look once again into the facts of the case. I have interviewed Jack Kelty's mother. Yes Jack Kelty has got into minor trouble previously. But perhaps you who are familiar with the Berry Street neighborhood will find it difficult to be too harsh on Jack Kelty for that, especially when you consider that Jack Kelty's father was killed just twenty years ago in an accident while employed by the Hareford Grain Company in South Ashford, an accident caused by faulty company equipment.

I have previously reported that Jack Kelty's mother is a sick woman in need of expensive medical attention. Due to the generous hearts of many readers, donations have come in. Mrs. Kelty is now getting the treatment she needs. But the one who wanted to do that for his mother was Jack Kelty himself. Yet it is on record that the very company responsible for the death of Jack Kelty's father would not hire Jack Kelty when he was desperately in need of a job. And it is a fact that the major stockholder in that incorporated company is none other than Harold Adams Hareford, presently the police commissioner of this city.

With that fact in mind let me reiterate the cold, sadistic code blindly adhered to by the police, despite its medieval overtone the code that states, "A cop killer is the worst killer ...!"

Al Duggan, face flushed, slammed the newspaper down. Sheriff Whitehall returned to the counter.

"That sonofabitch Hillary," Al Duggan said.

"He's still at it?"

"We ought to put him away with Kelty. Put them in the same cell."

"Easy, Al."

Al Duggan stared at the newspaper for a moment longer, then pushed it away. "What did you get from home?"

"Maybe this is Hillary's fault too. There's a rumble your headquarters gave my people. A bunch of Ashford punks want to spring Kelty. Some clerk released our plans to lay overnight at Broken Rock. Probably Hillary got him to talk. So these punks want to spring Kelty at Broken Rock."

Al Duggan shook his head in amazement. "What are we going to do because of this Hillary—butcher a dozen people?"

"I've got a report from the office that the bridge at Walnut Springs is weak. That's where we'd cross over to hit Broken Rock. They tell me the bridge at a little town called Blue Valley is still in pretty good shape. What do you think?"

"That's a county seat, isn't it?"

The sheriff nodded.

Al Duggan was silent for a moment. "Why don't we skip Broken Rock? The rumble may be phony, but you can't tell. Some of these kids think Kelty is God Himself. I'll lay odds Hillary'll show up there. We can pass up the Walnut Springs bridge and keep on going to Blue Valley. Cross the river there and hole up in Blue Valley until tomorrow morning. We'll miss both the punks and Hillary that way. We don't want to be driving at night anyway when you can't see who's in front and back of you. They'll have a good jail there, and the sheriff can help us—just in case." Al Duggan looked down the counter at the man in the white apron and saw that he was too far away to have heard. "I don't see any need to let the Blue Valley sheriff know we're coming. The more security the better. And tell them to keep it quiet in your headquarters in Ashford this time. Otherwise Hillary'll smell it out and broadcast it to every delinquent in the state. How does it sound?"

The sheriff considered. "All right."

When the sheriff had returned to the telephone, the man behind the counter again edged toward the partition. Al Duggan said, "More coffee." The man reluctantly came up front again.

As Sheriff Whitehall and Al Duggan walked back through the increasing rain to the car containing Jack Kelty, the sheriff said, "It's important to all of us to get Kelty back to Ashford. It's lucky he didn't hurt more people than he did. But you feel pretty strongly about him, don't you, Al?"

"Yes," Al Duggan said.

"Because one of the men he killed was your friend?"

"That's not the only reason. Inspector Lacy was mainly a man, not a cop. This bastard's killed two men. Another's shot up bad enough he may die. Yet somehow he's gotten to be a hero. Partly because of the way he looks. Mostly because Hillary started the ball rolling and it snowballed. Now Kelty's a hero to a lot of kids and even a lot of adults. I want to see him back safe and sound. So he gets the proper trial. So people can get the unbiased story of how it is when a killer like this is on the loose. I know Kelty. He got into this of his own free will. And that's all of it. To me, he's a willing killer, and I want to see him stripped of all that goddamn angelic college boy front of his. I want the public to see that, so they'll think twice about shoving all their frustrations into making a hero out of a tough like this. When they get ready to burn him, he'll show up for what he is. I want the whole world to see that. I've got a lot of reasons for wanting to see Jack Kelty brought back to Ashford. They're all good."

The sheriff nodded as they reached the car. "Well, we've only got about four hundred and fifty miles to go. I don't know what can go wrong now."

"I'll take a breath," Al Duggan said, "when we know it didn't."

Chapter 3

Ben Blake's house was built on a knoll on the north edge of Blue Valley. It was a rather massive-looking, white-frame house, properly aged to have become symbolic, in local terms, of dignity, money and position. From its broad porch facing south you could look over almost the whole of the town. You could see the dark column of the water tower and the more distant silhouette of the grain elevator; the gray courthouse and jail with the surrounding kept-up lawn; the sprawling green rectangle of the Municipal Park containing the tennis courts, the new swimming pool, and the bandstand where the Blue Valley High School band performed its spring concerts on warm Saturday evenings. You could also see, from the front porch, the irregular profiles of Blue Valley's business buildings lined stolidly along the main street.

From the back of the Blake house, you could look north, over the Blue Valley power plant, and see the gentle bluffs which, beyond the now-roaring Coyote Creek grown nearly as large as the normal Soshone, ultimately flattened into the broad plains that dominated most of the balance of the state.

Ben Blake, Steve knew, had not lived here as a boy. He'd come from a small town in Indiana at the age of twenty-two with a nondescript past rarely talked about. But he'd shaped his life firmly in Blue Valley, starting with a small grocery store and industriously expanding so that now he owned three large farms, the Blue Valley Produce Company, the grain elevator, and had, just a year ago, been elected mayor of Blue Valley for the second time.

Blue Valley was Ben Blake's adopted home. But he had lived here for exactly thirty years now, and, in the way of most converts, had a loyalty to his community matched by no one.

Sue Blake put the convertible in the wide garage. She and Steve hurried across the rain-swept breezeway into the Blake house. It was a few minutes past four-thirty. Ben Blake was waiting for them in a room recently converted to a library, freshly paneled in pine and lined with books, featuring a cupboard-style bar and a liberal placement of leather furniture.

Ben Blake was the kind of man who would have looked impressive in any society. He was as tall as Steve, but, at fifty-two, considerably heavier, though he did not look paunchy. He'd once owned hair as dark as Steve's, but now it was completely white. His eyebrows, however, had remained mostly dark, and the contrasting shades gave him a commanding look. He wore now a very neat gray tropical suit.

Ben Blake turned. "Hello, Sue—Steve. How's the work going?"

"Pretty good," Steve said. "We think the worst is over."

"Let's hope so." Ben Blake lit a cigar. "I've got more equipment—trucks, jeeps, more boats—coming up from Parisville. If that doesn't guarantee it, we'll demand the National Guard. If we can keep that levee at Hampton Mill we're all right."

"Sure," Steve agreed.

"Hell, Steve—excuse me. You're probably dead tired. All I've been doing today is talking on the telephone. You've been breaking your back. Mix him a drink, will you, Sue?"

Steve smiled. "Without your organizing things, Ben, all we'd have would be three-quarters of the county's population milling around like hogs in the sale ring."

"With the sheriff over there directing things? Hell!" Ben Blake said it in a self-derisive attempt, but his pride was obvious.

He could feel pride, Steve knew. Without Ben Blake's organizational abilities for getting equipment to the right place at the right time, the Hampton Mill levee might very well have gone by now. That would have meant that the waters of the Soshone would have poured over into the northern flat of the valley where the rising Coyote Creek would have met it to form a solid body of water west of Blue Valley. Such a catastrophe would probably have made an island out of Blue Valley, because the Coyote ran into the Soshone only a few miles east of the town. But Ben Blake was a doer. He wasn't hoisting sandbags, but he was forty times more valuable in the emergency than any single laborer.

Katherine Blake and her youngest daughter, Gretchen, came into the room. Katherine Blake was tall like Sue, and, in fact, looked more like Sue than she did Gretchen, though she was dark and had only recently begun to turn gray, a fact that seemed to add more beauty to her looks. She stood quite straight and smiled very intimately, so that you had a compellingly odd effect of warmth and reserve at the same time. With Ben Blake's good looks and his wife's prettiness, the attractiveness of the Blake daughters was no surprise.

Gretchen was just sixteen, black-haired, and very well shaped. In contrast to her mother's simple yellow dress, she was wearing a rather tight white blouse and white tennis shorts. She was sunned almost to the color of an acorn. She was a natural athlete, but there was nothing tomboyish about her. Her every pose, every motion was somehow attractive to the male eye.

Katherine Blake said, "Hello, Steve. I'm so glad you could come back and get some rest."

Steve took the drink offered him by Sue. "Everybody thinks I'm worn out. I'm supposed to stay in as good shape as members of my basketball team, remember?"

"Better put that drink down then," Ben Blake said, grinning.

Steve tasted his drink. "What I'm supposed to do and what I do are generally separate things."

Gretchen walked up to him, back turned to Sue. "Give me a little sip, Steve."

Ben Blake boomed, "Give me a little sip! I'll give you something, young lady, if you don't watch your manners."

Gretchen cocked her head, doing things with her eyes that Steve kept telling himself were only innocently natural to her. "Are you listening to Daddy? Or to the lady's request?"

"Watch her, Steve," Sue said, a faint bite going into her voice. "She's not a little girl anymore."

"I wish *I* were allowed to say anything I wanted to when I felt like it," Gretchen responded. "Steve?"

Steve smiled. "Maybe not a little girl anymore, but when the lady grows up completely, I'll listen to her. In the meantime I'll listen to her father."

"Hell!" Gretchen said, turning away.

"Don't swear," Sue said.

"*You* do. And I might say that you and Steve—"

"Enough, little sister."

"That's right!" Ben Blake said. "Your sister's completely grown up, Gretchen. And she and Steve are engaged, I remind you."

"You don't need to remind me, Daddy," Gretchen said sweetly. "When the lights go out in the living room—!"

"I'm being patient," Sue said, a definite edge in her voice.

Ben Blake looked at his wife. "Kate, how about everyone letting me talk to Steve alone?"

"At least I'm not that rude," Gretchen said.

"You'll find out how rude I can be in a minute," Ben Blake said.

"I wonder what you and Steve are going to talk about?"

Ben Blake's face flushed. Sue said, "Gretchen?"

Gretchen turned to her mother. "Mother?"

Katherine Blake nodded.

Gretchen flounced from the room, followed by Katherine Blake. Sue paused to kiss Steve lightly on the cheek. In her eyes was still a faint anger, but that disappeared as she touched him. She whispered, "Thanks for talking to Daddy, Steve."

Then she was gone and Steve was thinking that she still didn't understand how much it meant to have finally been accepted not only in Blue Valley, but in this very house. If she did, she wouldn't think it necessary to thank him for talking to Ben Blake; she would know it was his privilege.

Ben Blake was silent for a moment, then he walked over to the bar. He mixed a drink carefully. In a way, even this matter of a late-afternoon highball pleased Steve. In Blue Valley such a thing denoted sophistication. In Blue Valley only the respected could afford any sort of sophistication. If you were on the bottom of the ladder and drank, you were a bum. If you were on the top of the ladder and served highballs in the late afternoon, why, you were simply demonstrating your earned rights in the community.

"Steve, I'm relieved you're going to talk to that Newall kid."

"Glad to, Ben."

"I'd personally like to do more than talk to him."

"I can understand."

"I doubt that. You'll be marrying Sue month after next. Then maybe you'll have a daughter. Wait until she's sixteen and a thing like this happens, then you'll understand how I feel."

Steve nodded. "I suppose you're right."

Ben Blake sipped his drink, then seemed dissatisfied with it. He put his cigar between his teeth and walked to a window overlooking Coyote Creek. He stood silent and grim. Steve tried to project to how he felt.

When Gretchen and Rodney Newall had accidentally been discovered by Ben Blake in the sun porch the night before, Steve realized that Ben Blake had suffered the unhappy emotional experience of knowing, finally, to what extent his daughter had become the object of male attention. If Gretchen had been in a state of near disattire and Rodney had done the crazy thing of bolting straight off the sun porch and into the night, who could blame Ben Blake, having unwittingly switched on the hall light and partly illuminating the porch, for thinking murderous thoughts about Rodney Newall?

"The truth is," Ben Blake said darkly, "that kid needs his ass kicked out of town."

"Ben, there are some things to take into consideration. His mother—"

"I know Fay's had it rough. But her damn kid is no good!" Ben Blake turned around. "Look at you, Steve. Not a break in the world! I remember well enough when you were a tough, grubby little bastard hanging around Harry Bell's saloon. I'm not insulting you, am I? No, because I'd be proud, if I were you, of the fact I'd done something with my life. So you didn't have an old man either. I'll tell you something— neither did I. My old man was run over by a train engine when I was twelve years old. My mother turned into a recluse when that happened. I had to get out and make enough dimes to keep us eating. I did it until she died. Then I picked up and came out here and found myself a nice little town—Blue Valley.

"I'm not apologizing for what I've done with my life. And look at you. Goddamn it, Steve, I'd stake my life on you. So where does that snot-nosed Newall kid fit in? Frank Newall dropped over with a heart attack owning enough life insurance to amount to a fortune, and what good has it done Fay Newall and that kid of hers? He comes swaggering around here and then starts that stuff with my daughter. Then he hasn't even got the guts to face the music when—"

"Ben," Steven said, "you're just working yourself up. I'm going to talk to him at my place in an hour. I swear I'll do my best with him. You're heated up right now. It's hard to tell black from white."

Ben Blake sighed, relaxing a little.

"I'll tell you, Steve. I had to be convinced about you. I guess you know that. I think a lot of my daughters. But Sue always had good sense, and she proved it with you. Now—well, I like this world around me. I've been in Blue Valley thirty years. Outside of my wife and kids, there's nothing in this world I love more than this town. This town, my family, working to keep it all going.

"When something comes along like this flood and threatens the very town I live in, I get edgy. When someone comes along like this kid Rodney Newall and threatens my baby daughter, I get more than edgy. If I had him right now in this room, I think I'd break his face in.

"But you're handling it for me, Steve. I appreciate that. I'm trusting you to do the right thing. The main thing is, Steve, I don't want anything to change, you see? I like you, and you're a part of this family and a part of Blue Valley again. That makes things pretty complete. I just don't want things changed—either by this flood, or by some smart kid, or—" He stopped, shrugging apologetically. "Why am I complaining? Gretchen told me nothing actually happened. We've got the flood in control. How would it be if we'd gotten in the way of this Jack Kelty? Maybe we would have had something really to cry about, eh, Steve?"

Steve smiled. "Well, that's one thing we don't have to worry about, Ben."

Chapter 4

Martin Hillary, thirty-eight years old, a bony-looking man in a conservative dark suit, drove his new Plymouth sedan swiftly down the flat highway. The carefully kept car, its press card tucked neatly behind the right side of the windshield, was heading west. At the moment it was two hundred miles west of Ashford, almost in the center of the wide state, precisely forty miles north of Blue Valley.

Martin Hillary glanced in the rearview mirror. The low-riding Mercury was still behind him. Hillary smiled, a performance of mouth muscles that created what Ed McCabe, day editor of the *Ashford Times*, had once described as the splitting of a mummy's face. The Mercury had been behind Hillary ever since he'd stepped out of the Times Building and gotten in his car. Hillary did not know exactly who was in that car, but he knew generally; he also knew pretty well what they were after. He had been careful not to shake them in the two hundred miles so far covered.

Hillary glanced at his wrist watch. He mentally calculated. The afternoon was wearing thin; the caravan ought to have reached Broken Rock by now.

In another mile Hillary moved into the outskirts of a typical midland town called Central Junction.

He pulled off into a service station that offered, additionally, a restaurant and bar. He left the car beside the pumps to be serviced and walked inside. He paused, just inside the door, to look back and see the Mercury roll to a stop on the opposite side of the pumps. There were five youths in the car. The one thing they weren't, Martin Hillary told himself, was subtle.

The restaurant was divided into two sections; one contained a counter and tables, the other a bar and booths. There were two men at the counter, obviously drivers from the trucks parked outside. There was but one ill-clothed man at the bar. A juke box rested silently in the dimmer light of the bar section. A red-haired waitress was working the lunch counter. An ageing man who used armbands on the sleeves of his shirt was behind the bar.

There was a combined odor of fried restaurant food and a musky smell of tap beer that annoyed Hillary, but he was too exhilarated now to bother with incidental irritations. He bought a bottle of orange pop and got a pocketful of change from the waitress. He would have preferred a cold Gibson. However, he thought, the ass at the bar undoubtedly would have mixed it wrong no matter how carefully he instructed him. Besides it might have a slowing effect, and Hillary could relax later when he reached Broken Rock. He had a fifth of good Scotch in the car.

Inside a telephone booth Hillary put in a call to the sheriff's office at Broken Rock; in a moment he was speaking to the county sheriff. "This is Martin Hillary. The *Ashford Times*. I fully realize that secrecy must exist in this matter, but I'm sure you'll give me full cooperation. You may have followed my recent features on a certain case very much in the news lately. Am I understood, sheriff?"

Hillary was only mouthing formalities. There remained nothing secret whatever about the plans for the caravan to lay over at Broken Rock; the news had been released on television and radio, and Hillary had been the one to pry loose the information in the first place in order to keep the caravan steadily in the spotlight. Hillary's strategy so far had pleased himself. By not appearing at Fort Morgan, he had no doubt confused Sheriff Whitehall and Al Duggan. Any defense against him they might have worked up certainly had fallen apart as the result of his failure to appear. There was a personal satisfaction in keeping the sheriff and Duggan on their heels. Hillary had nothing particular against Whitehall, but he liked to cut at Duggan; and Duggan, Hillary was certain, was actively advising the sheriff. Moreover, when Hillary did show up at Broken Rock, the layover town would be the center of attention as the result of Hillary's own effort. It would be a clear opportunity for fine publicity, both for Kelty and so for Hillary himself. But now Hillary was only trying to impress the Broken Rock sheriff with his good intentions.

"Yes, sir," the Broken Rock Sheriff replied. "You're understood."

"Well, then. I'm merely checking to find out if the plans made regarding this matter have worked out so far."

"I'll put it to you bluntly, Hillary. I can't give you any information."

Hillary's face suddenly flushed. "Now, look here, Sheriff. You may be under the impression that, because of certain city police prejudices established against me in Ashford, I am not in the fullest cooperation with all law agencies. I assure you that's not true. I have the utmost respect for what you people are doing everywhere. I have criticized only the law enforcement of my own city. No more, no less. And that because I am conscientious about what I consider gross miscarriages of justice. Now if anyone has been telling you that I—"

"I've got no ax to grind with you, Hillary. I'm simply telling you I can't give you any information. The plans were changed."

"Let's put it bluntly," Hillary snapped. "Is that caravan there or not?"

"No. And it won't be. That's all I can say!"

The sheriff hung up. Hillary swore bitterly, then put in a collect call to the city room of the *Ashford Times*.

In a moment Ed McCabe was on the line. Hillary said, "I'm in some little dump called Central Junction. I just called the sheriff in Broken Rock. He tells me that caravan isn't there and won't be!"

"Right," Ed McCabe said. He was a quiet-spoken editor who respected Hillary only for Hillary's inherent reporter ability and the dogged dedication to follow a story through. He did not approve the assumed ethics of Hillary. But he was not the publisher.

"Where the hell are they taking Kelty now?"

"I don't know, Martin. We've got a UPI report they passed up the bridge that would take them across the line and up to Broken Rock. Maybe the flood's weakened the bridge."

"Well, is that all you know? How many wire men are behind that caravan anyway?"

"They're not getting cooperation. You ought to know that. You're mostly responsible."

"I don't want a sermon, Ed," Hillary said. "I want to know where that caravan is!"

"All I know is they're traveling somewhere below the state line. They stopped in a little town called Bennington. Then they took off again full tilt straight east. Right now they ought to be about a hundred and fifty miles east of Bennington. Where exactly, I wouldn't know."

Hillary snapped the receiver down. He returned to the counter and got more change. He noticed that two of the occupants from the Mercury had come in. They were drinking beer at the bar, one dark and very big, the other sandy-haired and smaller but with the face of a tank fighter; neither was older than eighteen, Hillary judged, though they might look older to a less practiced eye and that was why, no doubt, they had been served. They kept their eyes away from Hillary with studied nonchalance. They had fed the jukebox, and it was now thumping mightily with rock 'n' roll music.

Hillary returned to the booth. This time he put in a call to the sheriff in Bennington. The high voice of the switchboard operator in Bennington informed him there was no sheriff because Bennington was not a county seat. Hillary swore silently again, then asked for the local newspaper office. In a moment, a woman's voice enunciated in rather pretentiously formed syllables, "*Bennington Weekly Bugle.*"

"This is Martin Hillary of the *Ashford Times*. I'm calling from Central Junction."

The woman gasped. "*The* Martin Hillary?"

Hillary relaxed instantly. He smiled very faintly. "Well, my name is Hillary. I write for the *Times*."

"Of course, Mr. Hillary. I never miss it!"

"With whom am I speaking, please?"

"This is Miss Grace Abbot. I'm the editor of the *Bugle*."

"Why, certainly!" Hillary said suavely. "One of the few ladies running a very excellent newspaper in our section of the country." He had, in reality, never heard of the newspaper.

"Why, thank you, Mr. Hillary!"

"Miss Abbot, I wonder if you might give me some assistance concerning the caravan taking Jack Kelty back to Ashford. I understand the caravan stopped in your town earlier today."

"Well, it certainly did! There's been ever so much excitement since!"

"I'm picking up the caravan as it heads home to Ashford. But I'm trying to get all the intimate color I can, since I wasn't able to start out with them at Fort Morgan. Now if you might possibly—"

"Well, I've just come back from Luke Dirk's café, as a matter of fact! That's where they stopped, you see. And ..."

Hillary listened in bored silence. Finally he said, "That's wonderful,

Miss Abbot! I can certainly use all of that. I'll be directing my office to issue a small check to you for your trouble, and I wonder if you'd mind our using your name?"

"Why, Mr. Hillary!"

"One thing more, please. Could you repeat the name of the café? It might help to talk to Mr. Dirk personally."

"You just wait a minute, Mr. Hillary!" In a moment, the excited Miss Abbot had rattled the receiver, brought in the switchboard operator, and had the call switched to the café where Luke Dirk's voice finally sounded. "Yes?"

"Mr. Dirk, this is Martin Hillary of the *Times* calling long distance. Miss Abbot of your newspaper just referred me to you. I've been covering the Jack Kelty case. I understand the caravan stopped at your place."

"Mr. Hillary, you're the man I want to talk to! I've been reading your pieces right along. You've drawn up a pretty good picture of that police department in Ashford. I wouldn't argue with it for a minute. No, sir!"

"You had some trouble, did you, Mr. Dirk?"

"Well, let me tell you this. This caravan pulls up, and these two big-shot city fellows get out. One of them I knew right away was the Ashford County Sheriff who was sent to pick up this Kelty. I knew that from the pictures in the papers and television, see?"

"Yes, Mr. Dirk."

"Well, I said to him is that Jack Kelty out there in that car? And that sheriff said no it wasn't. Now what do you think of that? Lied to me right off, and there was ten people that saw that caravan pass on through town and got a look inside the car. They'd swear on ten stacks of Bibles that was Jack Kelty. Do you see what I mean? Lied to me in my own place, all full of big-city smartness. Only I didn't care so much about that, it was this big fellow that was along with the sheriff. I said to him are you a cop? You look like a cop. And you know what he told me?"

"I'd have to guess at it, Mr. Dirk."

"Well, I'll tell you. He said he was some prisoner being took back to the state pen. Now some of the folks here in Bennington seen him too when the caravan passed on through. And they said he was the very same cop who had charge of the search for Kelty there in Ashford. I described him to Miss Abbot, and she said it was that very same cop name of Dugan or Dergan or some such. What do you think of that, Mr. Hillary?"

"I think that's very interesting, Mr. Dirk."

"Now I'll tell you, I asked two questions off two men supposed to represent the law in Ashford, and I got two lies in return. What is somebody supposed to make of that? I got a right to know things, ain't I? Right here in my own home town?"

"I'll go along with that, Mr. Dirk."

"Well, I'll say this. I can't blame that Kelty for being more scared than a cottontail rabbit running from a good pair of beagles. Except these fellows didn't look so gentle as beagles to me, especially that big fellow who lied about being a cop ..."

The man's voice was rising in volume, and Hillary held the receiver away from his ear a little until the man had finished. The thing you didn't want to do with Mr. Dirk, Hillary thought, was withhold information from him in his own home town, especially if you were full of big-city smartness.

"Well, that all very interesting to hear, Mr. Dirk," Hillary said finally. "But there's one thing more. I've found out there was a change of plans. Unfortunately the gentlemen you're talking about have not seen fit to cooperate with me any more than they did with you. I'm wondering if you might happen to have overheard anything about those plans of theirs?"

"Just hold on a minute, Mr. Hillary. Lois, are you on the line?"

The switchboard operator's high-pitched voice came in. "I was just checking on the length of the call, Luke."

"Lois, you get off for a minute. I don't want to get you involved in anything you shouldn't."

"Well, all right, Luke."

"There. Heard it click. Now, I'm not saying it was Lois who told what that sheriff had to say when he called up his headquarters in Ashford, Mr. Hillary. That's for anybody to guess. Only you just don't print where you got it, that's all. All right?"

"Mr. Dirk, I have a sacred respect for my sources."

"Well, sir, what it was that sheriff phoned in was that he was taking the caravan on down the road to the Blue Valley bridge to hold Jack Kelty overnight in the county jail there...."

When Hillary stepped out of the restaurant and walked toward his car, the faint smile was still on his mouth. Blue Valley. Hillary had an accurate memory, and he remembered the map well enough to know that Blue Valley would be forty miles straight south. With any luck, he ought to beat the caravan there.

He paid his bill and watched the two youths who had been in the bar trot toward the waiting Mercury. Then he drove off, glancing in the rearview mirror; the Mercury was right behind him.

Jack Kelty's fan club. They might be obvious, but they were still smart, knowing he would not fail to pick up that caravan and trusting him to lead them to it rather than following news reports. Well, what harm could they do? None, Hillary was certain. Yet their presence would add considerable color to a situation that had already enhanced his own career measurably.

As a student in the journalism college of the University of Missouri at Columbia, Martin Hillary had been an intellectually inclined idealist with an ego substantial enough to be certain he was going to do something about the wrongs committed in this world just as soon as he got actively into his chosen profession.

Martin Hillary, upon graduation, went to work for the *Ashford Times.* In general, and like a lot of newspapermen who begin with idealism, Martin Hillary found himself quickly disillusioned. He saw more abuse of human values in a month than an average citizen witnesses in a lifetime. An idealist like Martin Hillary was excellent material for becoming a cynic.

At the time Hillary began to graduate into being a cynic, he promised himself that he would eventually divorce himself from journalism and write a play, a novel, or perhaps even actively engage in theatrical work as an actor. Dormantly ambitious then, and becoming the reporter who personally interviewed every great or near great who passed through the city of Ashford, Hillary began to find himself in an extremely paradoxical position.

Greatness was within touching distance, but Hillary tasted none of it. Unlike a good business executive who could compensate a lack of fame with money, Hillary had, on a reporter's salary, neither money nor fame.

But in the meantime, Hillary was finding a substitute ego satisfaction. By turning to his early police-reporting experience, he had found an avenue through which he had begun to develop a name. By working on the Ashford police force he discovered public response. His stock rose. He became a specialized feature writer with a constant byline. And the eventual championing of Jack Kelty had brought him closer to satisfaction of his frustrated ambitions than he had dreamed was possible while still a newspaper reporter.

By now Hillary made little distinction between fame and infamy. The only thing that mattered was that Jack Kelty's name had become the best-known name developed between Chicago and the Rocky Mountains in years. Martin Hillary, whose name was growing right along with Kelty's, was sticking close on Kelty's shirt tails.

Hillary lit a cigarette and put his foot down harder on the accelerator. He was wondering just how the tired face of Inspector Al Duggan would look when he found Martin Hillary waiting in Blue Valley to greet the caravan. Hillary inhaled his cigarette pleasurably. He was pretty certain he knew exactly how Al Duggan would look.

Chapter 5

The trailing Mercury contained five blue-jacketed youths, a rundown of whom would have sounded like the call of names over the loudspeaker when a professional football team runs onto the playing field: Norman Teller, Richard Rajeski, Thomas Marcelli, Louie Harlan, Nicolas Cowley. They were not, however, very athletic.

Three of them were eighteen: Teller, Rajeski and Cowley. Louie Harlan was seventeen. The youngest was Marcelli, who was sixteen and the largest of the group. Each had yet to do anything notable with his life, with the possible exception of Nick Cowley, who claimed reasonably accurately that he had fathered four children with four different girls, only one of which resulted in an abortion.

It was true that Norman Teller considered himself an excellent handler of guns, though any high school R.O.T.C. student would have known more about nomenclature. Richard "Cut" Rajeski considered himself an expert knife handler and always carried one; still his was not particularly a skill but rather an unhesitancy to use it on his fellow beings. Marcelli's major claim to fame was his great size and strength, which he liked to demonstrate on others as often as possible.

The smallest of the group, Louie Harlan, did not pretend to be good at anything, but only tagged along as a flexible, self-effacing buffer for the others' jokes. A good psychiatrist might have noted a masochistic tendency in Louie Harlan and made a new individual out of him; but Louie was not employing an analyst at present.

At the moment all five were speeding along in the Mercury through territory they had never seen because of the simple fact that not one of them had ever been out of the city limits of Ashford before in his life.

But it was not an educational tour to investigate the merits of their home state. None had given more than a fleeting and occasional glance at the countryside. Rather they carried their own world along with them, on the tail of Martin Hillary. They were well supplied with liquor, knives, guns and ammunition. The radio was tuned to a rock 'n' roll station with a volume that would break the eardrums of someone not used to it. It was Berry Street on wheels, in essence, and every youth in the car, no matter how he covered it with an outward façade, was a fraction more excited than he had ever been in his life. They were on their way to do something, and none of them had ever really done anything before.

Large and blond Norman Teller was driving, mainly because the car was his, and he was a leader who had not yet learned to trust his lieutenants even to driving the car. Cut Rajeski, Teller's first lieutenant, was beside him; Rajeski was the soberest youth in the car next to Teller, who had thus far drunk nothing. In the back seat sat Nick Cowley, Louie Harlan and Tommy Marcelli. The one who had drunk the most so far was Louie Harlan, small and dark and given to periodic laughing. Marcelli, dark as Louie Harlan and three times as large, had been in the Central Junction bar with sandy-haired Cut Rajeski, who was built and looked like a professional welterweight fighter.

At the moment Nick Cowley, fair-skinned with dark red hair, had propped his feet upon the seat ahead of him, smiling with the pleasure of delicious thoughts. "I'll bet this country stuff is wild, huh?"

Marcelli laughed harshly, then rammed a heavy elbow into an uncomplaining Louie Harlan who sat with a bottle of red wine in his lap. "Hey, Louie, huh?"

Louie, no doubt the handsomest youth of them all, laughed too. "Crap."

"What do you mean crap?" Marcelli asked, taking the bottle out of Louie's hands. "What do you mean crap?"

"I mean crap!" Louie said, giggling now so hard tears formed in his eyes.

"Crap!" Marcelli said and banged his huge left fist lightly but tellingly into Louie's right arm. Louie laughed with pain, and Marcelli wrestled him forward like a one-armed bear, tickling him brutally, then shoving him back and down in the seat, so that Louie was left lying half on his back. Marcelli poured the wine over his face. Louie got some of it down his throat, choking and giggling. Marcelli roared.

In front, Teller snapped, "Tell 'em to knock it off."

Rajeski turned around. "Knock it off, for Christ's sake!"

"Shut up, Cut," Marcelli said, grinning and continuing to pour wine down Louie's throat.

Rajeski leaned back and slapped Marcelli's face, then yanked the bottle out of his hand. Marcelli flushed. He brought his hands up threateningly. Rajeski slapped him again. "Quit the screwing around."

"Screw you, Cut."

"I mean it."

"He means it!" Marcelli laughed meanly.

Now Norman Teller yelled from behind the wheel, "Shut up, Marcelli!" They all had to yell because of the loud thumping music.

Marcelli finally shrugged. "Who cares?"

Rajeski's eyes flickered faintly. His hand had been inside his jacket, fingers closed around his knife. He relaxed and turned around, facing the front. Louie Harlan wriggled up to a sitting position, giggling again.

"Crap," Marcelli said, smiling once more.

"Crap!" Louie said, closing his eyes and laughing, the tears streaming down his cheeks now.

Up front Rajeski balanced the wine bottle between himself and Norman Teller. "Wonder what Jack's thinking about right now?"

Teller shrugged. Kelty, for a long time now, had been the glamour boy of Berry Street. For the past days he had been the only topic of conversation in the neighborhood. The fact that everyone in the car had a nodding acquaintance with Kelty had an importance transcending being a long-time, personal, bridge-playing friend of the President of the United States. "Countin' on us maybe."

"How about that?" Rajeski smiled happily. "We really gonna bust him out, Tell?"

Teller's eyes were narrow, dedicated to his driving. "If we can keep this stinking group from springing to pieces."

"They're just having fun! They've got the guts, huh? I mean who else volunteered?"

"Bottom of the bag, maybe."

"Better'n just you and me, man."

"We'll see," Teller said doubtfully.

Rajeski stretched. Lack of specific plans, lack of any kind of plans at all, was hardly alien to the group's methods. The main thing was to point in the right direction and hope for the best. "That Hillary just goes and goes, huh? You sure your idea's gonna work out, Tell? You sure this newsboy's taking us to Kelty?"

"He'd better be," Teller said.

Rajeski slumped a little in his seat. "Where you suppose he is now?" he said dreamily. "I mean, I wonder where old Jack is right now anyhow?"

Chapter 6

The sheriff's caravan was now rolling near the swollen Soshone River, heading for the silver-painted bridge that would take it across the state line into Blue Valley. At the moment, there was less than a hundred miles to go. For the past hour flood reports had been sounding on the car radio.

"Shut it off," Al Duggan said finally. "We know there's a flood by now." The radio was turned off.

Jack Kelty smiled. "Real edgy, Inspector."

Al Duggan did not answer. It was true. He was getting more and more nervous. He lit another cigarette. The miles went under them. Every minute they were closer to putting Kelty safely behind bars in Ashford. But Al Duggan couldn't relax, couldn't even breathe normally. His pulse pounded. Twice he'd felt lightheaded, as though he might pass out. But what, he asked himself, could go wrong now?

The afternoon was waning by the time they neared the bridge. The rain had stopped again; it was still and muggy outside. They were right on the river now, and there was the stench created by dead animals floating bloatedly downstream.

Finally Sheriff Fred Whitehall said, "Well, there's the bridge."

Fortunately the Blue Valley bridge had a long wooden approach on either side that led into the main metal structure covering what was once the normal stream. The approaches spanned the extra width of the river, and so the bridge was still usable.

There were two men in work clothes standing at the end of the south approach. The lead car slowed and stopped. Sheriff Whitehall lowered his window. One of the men, skin burned from season after season under the hot Midwest sun, ambled over. His eyes skimmed the interior of the car, settling on Jack Kelty for a long moment, then on the handcuffs linking Kelty to Sheriff Whitehall and Al Duggan.

He rubbed his chin, then self-consciously brought his hand down, assuming an air that he'd seen about all there was to see anyway.

"How's the bridge?" the sheriff asked.

The man shrugged. "She's holding."

"Can we use it?"

"She ain't as strong as she ought to be."

"I've got an idea," Jack Kelty said. "Let's swim it."

Al Duggan felt more anger. But why fight it? Get him back, that was all that mattered now.

"What do you think, Al?" Sheriff Whitehall asked.

Al Duggan watched a tree limb jar into one of the round wood under-supports of the near approach. The approach trembled. "Anybody use it recently?" he asked the man standing outside the car.

"Emil Dome took his pickup over ten minutes ago. Main thing we're here for is to tell people it ain't as strong as it ought to be. You're the law, ain't you? It's going to be your decision, I reckon, ain't it?"

"I reckon," the sheriff said wearily. "Let's take it, Al."

Al Duggan nodded grimly. The car moved forward, leading the caravan slowly down the road toward the approach.

An hour earlier, the neat, new Plymouth driven by Martin Hillary had sped into Blue Valley, followed by the low-riding Mercury.

Hillary drove into Stu Halper's Conoco service station two blocks from the business section. Stu's wife, temporarily running the pumps while Stu sandbagged at Hampton Mill, directed Hillary to the courthouse three blocks away.

A few minutes later he parked at the edge of the broad courthouse lawn and strode up the walk toward the gray building, big and entirely square but for the annex wing of the jail extending from the northeast corner.

At the top of the stone steps, Hillary paused to look back. The Mercury had come to a stop beneath a large cottonwood near the southeast intersection. Nobody got out.

The interior of the courthouse was tomblike. Hillary took the marble steps up to the main rotunda, his footsteps echoing hollowly. The doors of all the offices but the County Clerk's were closed. Hillary stepped inside to the wooden counter. A neat woman with graying hair and a pencil carefully tucked above her right ear walked up with an arthritic limp.

"This seemed to be the only office open," Hillary said.

The woman looked at him as though he'd just stepped in from another world. "Well, there's a flood."

"Everyone's working to relieve the situation, I take it."

The woman looked at him closely. "Isn't that what they ought to be doing? I've got relatives above Hampton Mill I haven't heard from yet! You must be from somewhere pretty far away if you haven't kept up with this flood!"

Hillary decided not to announce who he was for the simple reason that he suspected she would not appreciate it. Instead he smiled apologetically and said smoothly, "I just didn't realize how difficult the conditions had become here. I wonder if you might tell me where I could find the sheriff, madam?"

"My name is Mrs. Corpler. Most every man and quite a few of the women are over at Hampton Mill seeing to the levee. Working very hard, I might add. The women cooking and making coffee. The men loading sandbags. I don't know what all. If I wasn't crippled up, I'd be over there too. The rest of the country seems to be asleep. We've got the worst emergency we've had since nineteen thirty-nine. It seems to me—"

"And the sheriff is now at Hampton Mill, Mrs. Corpler?"

"Of course! He's directing things with his deputy. Where else would he be?"

"Yes, ma'am. But when do you expect him back?"

"When the flood goes down!"

"Thank you very much, Mrs. Corpler. I wonder if you could tell me where the jail is?"

"It's the wing extending toward Apple Street. You go downstairs and take the door to the right. It's open because there's nobody down there but Mr. Potter. He keeps his cleaning supplies there."

"There are no prisoners at present, in other words."

"In any kind of words there isn't anybody there but Mr. Potter. He's too old to work over at Hampton Mill or I'm sure he'd be over there! He doesn't keep this building altogether too clean either, but he tries hard!"

"Thank you, Mrs. Corpler." Hillary smiled and walked out of the office, feeling a peculiar excitement.

A few moments later he was opening a heavy metal door on the lower level of the courthouse and stepped into the Blue Valley County Jail. There was the smell of pine-scented disinfectants in the small room that preceded a row of four barred cells, two on each side, facing each other. The anteroom served as a jailer's office, Hillary guessed. There were several barred windows letting in a dim light. A single light bulb hung from the ceiling. There was a worn light-oak desk with a telephone on it and a swivel chair beside it. Four straight-backed wooden chairs were scattered about the room. The walls and ceilings were dark gray. There was a deep yellow-stained porcelain sink and a small cracked mirror above it. All the cells were empty. Sitting beside the desk was an old man wearing overalls and a blue work shirt buttoned at the neck. He turned, blinking watery gray eyes at Hillary.

Hillary said, "Mr. Potter?"

The old man stood up with effort. A bucket of water was beside his feet. He'd been running a mop through the rollers attached to the top edge of the bucket. "Yes, sir?"

Hillary smiled, looking at the jail very carefully. Then he stepped to a window and looked through the bars at the Mercury parked at the end of the block beneath the large cottonwood. "I'm Martin Hillary, Mr. Potter, of the *Ashford Times*."

Mr. Potter blinked, obviously impressed. "Is that a fact?"

"Yes, sir, Mr. Potter. That's a fact. Now I'm told that neither the County Sheriff nor his deputy are in Blue Valley right now. I'm told they're directing flood operations at Hampton Mill, which, if memory serves me, is a small hamlet a few miles to the west. I'm to infer, I believe, that almost every able-bodied Blue Valley man is over there working with the sheriff to hold the levee. Is that correct, would you say, Mr. Potter?"

"Yes, sir. I'd say that was about correct. Everyone's over there but the youngsters and the oldsters like me. I'm seventy-six, Mr. Hillary." Mr. Potter peeled back his lips to display badly fitted false teeth. "What do you think of that?"

"Well, sir," Martin Hillary said, "I'd say that's really something, Mr. Potter. You're the janitor of the courthouse, I take it. And that would leave you pretty much in charge here, wouldn't you agree, Mr. Potter?"

Mr. Potter considered, then said proudly, "I reckon you're about right, Mr. Hillary."

Hillary laughed softly, then sat down and put his heels up on the corner of the desk.

"But," said a puzzled Mr. Potter, "what are you expecting to do around here, Mr. Hillary?"

"Well, I'll tell you, Mr. Potter. If it's all the same to you, I'm just going to sit here very quietly with my feet up on this desk and see what happens next."

Chapter 7

The most important thing that happened next occurred upstream on the Soshone River.

The Alhurne County Dam, under more pressure than its engineers had suspected it ever would be, slowly weakened. With the continuing rain, the pressure became too much. That late afternoon, with sudden defeat, the Alhurne Dam gave way. The released waters rolled down in a wall that tore the Hampton Mill levee out at the east end and poured water across the land between Hampton Mill and Blue Valley.

There was no way to send a warning downstream. Five people were drowned. Telephone lines were ripped down. Coyote Creek took on the fury of the river, as the two blended waters. The water separated with the spine-like higher ground upon which Blue Valley was built. But on either side of the town, destruction came sweeping like a tidal wave.

The concrete viaduct north of Blue Valley was driven out as though with a huge armored fist. The Soshone hit the Blue Valley bridge its final and deadly blow, then swept on, to meet again the waters of the Coyote downstream. But not before the lead car of the Kelty caravan, alone on the bridge to avoid excess strain, had been tumbled into the water just before it reached solid land on the Blue Valley side.

Chapter 8

An hour before the flood wave ripped past Blue Valley, Sue Blake had driven Steve Michaels to the small white house he rented five blocks east of the business district. While he got under the shower, she started coffee in the kitchenette.

"I'm beginning to feel alive again!" he called from the bath.

"Need any help?" she called back.

"Sure." He grinned, scrubbing himself furiously.

"I think you'll have to wait a month and a half, Mr. Michaels."

"Why be a prude?"

"Why be anything?" she replied.

But she was not a prude, he knew. The waiting had somehow become his responsibility. They had almost not waited at least a hundred times since he'd come back to Blue Valley. She would not have stopped anything. But somehow he could not visualize the rightness of it. On sober reflection, he'd told himself it might have been because he was not yet wholly in love with her and so could not take advantage of her obvious total love. But he'd forcibly dismissed that thought. Of course, he was in love with her. You just didn't go to bed with a girl like Sue Blake before you married her—not the eldest daughter of Sam Blake.

He put on a robe and found her in the bedroom. She had gathered his clothes, folded them, and arranged freshly laundered green dungarees Steve had owned in the Marine Corps. The heavy work shoes soaked working at Hampton Mill were replaced by the combat boots that had also been worn in the Corps.

"I've got to run, darling. More coffee and sandwiches to be made and delivered. Do you want to have dinner with us and ride back to Hampton Mill with me?"

"I'll eat something here. Then I've got to get straight back. I'll drive my car."

"All right."

He put his arms around her. "You're the best, Sue."

She looked up, straight into his eyes. "That's pretty damn romantic." She smiled very faintly.

"Sue, listen— "

She patted his cheek, kissed him lightly and was gone.

Rodney Newall appeared a half hour later as Steve, dressed and surprisingly rested from the short break, began his dinner.

Rodney was a very tall boy of seventeen. He had carefully combed black hair and very fair skin. He was dressed in a red sport shirt and dark slacks. He was well-coordinated and would, in a year or two, fill out to match his large frame. At the moment, however, his slacks seemed to be hung on a miracle. Steve knew that he wore size thirteen shoes; this fact, along with the lean waist and tremendously long legs, gave him a shambling look when he walked. It was an illusion. Rodney was very fast and good on a basketball court, and he could dance better than any other youth in Blue Valley.

"Hello, Rod. A pretty good spread. Cold beans. Soup. Ham sandwiches. Want to join me?"

"No, thanks."

Rodney walked once around the room, swaggering a little, as Steve returned to his dinner.

"Sit down, Rod."

Rodney came over and sat down.

"What's new? Been helping with the flood work?"

"I was at the river all day. I'll be over at Hampton Mill tomorrow. That's where we really need the work. I guess."

"It's under control, I think." Steve tried the cold beans. In the dungarees and boots, he looked cool and capable. He'd been a sergeant in the Marine Corps. He'd handled his authority quietly, but effectively. Rodney Newall's eyes flickered over Steve's clothes. A note of appreciation showed in his eyes, but he seemed to quell it self-consciously. "What else is new?" Steve asked.

Rodney shrugged. "I've been keeping up with Jack Kelty in the newspapers."

"Good thing they finally got him."

"Oh, I don't know."

Steve paused, fork in air. "I don't follow you, Rod. The man's a killer."

"You've been reading Martin Hillary in the *Times?*"

"Well, there's always something to be said for both sides, I suppose." Steve was silent for a moment. He liked Rodney Newall. But Rodney, it appeared, could go any number of directions right now. A good reason for that, Steve was certain, was because his mother desperately needed him close to her. The loss of her husband had been shattering. Too many times since, Fay Newall, in an effort to keep Rodney close, had allowed him to have his own youthful way. That youthful way was too often misguided by immature values—for example, his obvious sympathy for a killer like Jack Kelty. Steve said, "Hillary's written a lot about Kelty's background. Maybe you've heard about my youthful background in Blue Valley."

Rodney shrugged noncommittally. "A little. Not much." But now he was interested, Steve could see.

"I'll be frank with you, Rod. I was the town's star delinquent until I was thirteen and Harry Bell got me into the Ashford Home. That was a favor, and they took the swagger out of me pretty quickly. I've always been grateful to Harry. You see, my father deserted my mother and me when I was very young. Then my mother started drinking. Did you know that?"

Rodney shook his head. "I didn't know that."

"We had this little house down on the south edge of town. My mother, nobody, really gave a damn what I did. I used to hang around the guys at the pool hall, because they'd give me nickels and dimes when they got a little drunk. Harry fed me a lot of the time. But I wasn't above stealing now and then. I remember once when I stole two bottles of whisky. My mother asked me to get some liquor for her. I did."

"Pretty rough," Rodney said.

"Sure. Pretty rough. I was a good junior bum. But the thing is, Rod, a person still learns something about right and wrong. I knew, for example, who was giving me the breaks. It was Harry Bell. But I stole that whisky from him. It was for my mother and she asked me to get it. Only I still knew it was wrong. You see, no matter how rough you have it, you still get exposed to the good things along with the bad. Even if the bum breaks outweigh the good ones, you still know what it's like to deal with someone who treats you squarely. Not everybody on this earth is bad. You're bound to meet some good ones. Take your case, for example. You had a lousy break when you lost your father."

"I'm not complaining," Rodney said grimly.

"I'm not saying you are. But you've got your mother, remember. And she's a very good woman, Rod. You've got a lot of people in town who know you and are interested in you, including me. You've got a good brain and good athletic ability. You're not starving. So you tell yourself these things, like losing your father, just happen. They do. But you keep right on living. You live in society the way you know you have to."

"I suppose. But this Jack Kelty—"

"This Jack Kelty had some bad breaks. We've all had them. Does that give him a free ticket to start shooting up civilization?"

Rodney was silent for several seconds. "In the first place, I see what you mean by your own example. I guess you had it a lot rougher than a lot of the rest of us. You're doing all right, so—"

Steve put his fork down. "I don't mean that, Rod. All I mean is that you have to live up to your own conscience. If a man's true to himself, he's displaying real honesty. We've all got a conscience. If you answer to it, you're all right, see?"

Rodney was silent again. Then finally he shook his head and stood up. "I don't see all that with Jack Kelty. I mean maybe he didn't have any tougher breaks than you did. But you wound up in the Ashford Home, and Kelty wound up with the whole Ashford police force on his back. You say you stole when you were a kid. So Kelty was only trying to steal when he ran into that warehouse guard. And this guard was a crook himself, wasn't he? And where does a conscience fit in after that? I know how I'd feel if I'd been Kelty. This Hillary says those Ashford cops would rather break you up in little pieces than breathe. So they bunch up and go for Kelty. But Kelty just tells them to shove it! He tells the whole Ashford force that! And busts his way out. That takes guts, doesn't it? It's a lot better, in my opinion, than lying down and screaming. And Jack Kelty hasn't done that!"

Steve realized by the look in Rodney's eyes that the boy genuinely thought of Jack Kelty as a hero.

"Look, Rod. We *all* have a conscience. But I'll admit this—against enough pressure and if you're weak enough, you can beat it up and finally kill it so you don't hear it anymore. But in the end it's just as though you ripped out all the instruments of a plane while you're flying blind in a storm and threw them out the window, just because you can't stand the pressure of the worry. You're going to crash pretty damn fast, I'll tell you that."

Rodney started to speak, then did not. He sat down again, his face resuming its youthfully bored expression. Steve knew he'd lost him. Kelty had achieved too much glamour. You couldn't argue logically with someone like Rodney when you were dealing with glamour.

"Okay," Steve said, pouring himself a cup of coffee. "We've all got a right to our own opinions, I guess."

"I wonder if we could get it over, Steve?" Rodney said finally.

"About Gretchen?"

Rodney suddenly looked very sardonic. "About Gretchen."

Steve's eyes flickered with sudden anger. "I'm not going to play holy father with you, Rod, so you don't need to use that sarcastic tone with me. Ben Blake is ready to have you thrown out of town. I told him I'd hear your side of it and try to keep everything straight."

"So what's to hear?"

Steve compressed his temper. "I just want you to give me your side of it."

"Okay," Rodney said, smiling meanly. "I was out there on the porch diddling her, and—"

Steve snapped the flat of his hand across Rodney's left cheek.

Rodney flushed, blinked once, then sat staring down at one clenched hand.

"I don't like that kind of cocky attitude, Rod, and you know it. As far as Gretchen is concerned, the least you can do is respect her for being a woman."

"I never respected her for not being one."

"I mean it, Rod. I mean you'd better start acting like a gentleman. Have you got that?"

"Yes, sir."

"Now what, exactly, happened? Give it to me in gentlemanly terms."

Rodney was silent for a moment. "If I'm going to be a gentleman about it, I'd better not give it to you."

"It was like that, in other words."

"In other words, yes."

"It was entirely your idea, as Gretchen said."

"Did she say that?"

"Yes."

"Then that was the way it was."

"It didn't go too far?"

"How far is too far?"

"I'm warning you, Rod."

"The lady said it didn't go too far?"

"That's what she said."

"Then it didn't go too far."

"How much forcing did you do?"

"Did the lady say I forced it?"

"Yes."

"I forced it then. I'm a gentleman all the way. I regret my previous ungentlemanly conduct."

Steve slowly lit a cigarette. "Okay, Rod. Thanks. I'm sorry for cracking you."

"Forget it."

"The main thing was that it didn't go too far. You can understand what that would mean. Why Ben has been about to lose his mind."

"I know all about the birds and bees."

"You ought to by now. One thing, Rod. And I'll quit. How do you feel about Gretchen?"

"She's very attractive." The boy looked up and stared Steve straight in the eyes. "Wouldn't you say so?"

"I would say so, yes," Steve answered coolly. "You feel a strong physical attraction toward her, is that it?"

"That's about it."

"Anything more?"

Rod shrugged.

"If you happen to think you're in love with her, it's a compensating factor. But I've seen you out with several of the others girls lately. Certainly Gretchen has been very popular."

Rod opened and closed his hand. "I don't think I'm in love with her."

Steve studied the boy for a moment then put a hand on his shoulder. "Okay. Maybe you figure this is none of my business. Maybe you're right. But I think you've got a very solid core, and I didn't want Ben to go to work on you. The way it looks to me, Gretchen's attractions simply got you into the wrong situation. I'm not going to tell you how to live, Rod. But remember what I said about living up to your own values. I don't care how attractive a girl sixteen years old might be or if she seems a little wild. You've still got your own conscience to check on your values. All right?"

Rod nodded at last. "It was my fault. I'm sorry about it."

"I'll tell Ben that. I'll tell him you didn't mean to get into it in the first place. I think that'll help as far as he's concerned. But I'm afraid you're through with Gretchen for the moment. He'd kill you if you tried to see her again. But in time, if you're really interested in her—"

"I won't try to see her."

"Good." Steve stood up and smiled. He offered his hand. The boy stood up and took it.

The telephone rang, and Steve walked over and picked it up.

"This is Ben, Steve. The goddamn river's gone crazy again! It just came down with a wave the size of a mountain. Knocked the bridge out. It must have broken through the levee at Hampton Mill. Sent water clear across the west to meet up with the creek. The creek's gone wild too—pushed out the viaduct south of town. No telling how much damage, how many people lost. We've got an ocean of water around this town right now. A couple of miles of dry land on the east and the west and the power plant's still on dry ground, thank God, but that's all. We're an island, Steve. Everybody who was over at Hampton Mill, which means damn near everybody, is cut off. I've talked to Reuben at the power plant, and he says there's enough diesel fuel to get us through the night. Alice Stritt's staying on the switchboard, and she's got us switched into reserve power so we can dial and use the telephones in town. But we've lost communication with the outside— the lines around town are down. We're isolated, in other words, so we'd better get organized. I doubt if we can make contact with anyone outside until tomorrow morning. I'll meet you in my office downtown in five minutes. Hell, you and I are damn near the only able-bodied men in town!"

Chapter 9

When the sheriff's car rolled slowly onto the bridge approach, the following cars in the caravan waited behind, to minimize the strain.

There was barely any tremor in the lead in approach, none as they crossed slowly over the metal bridge itself, but again a faint tremble as they were coming off in the direction of Blue Valley, the water rushing perhaps six inches beneath the planking.

Then the flood wave created by the break of Alhurne Dam struck.

They saw the wave coming as high as a house. Sheriff Whitehall yelled for his driver to speed up. But then there was a blinding crash, followed by a sickening roll as the car was pitched over and pushed into the churning water. It happened so fast that Al Duggan had no time to realize what had happened.

All he knew was that the car had been bounced into the water as though it were weightless. He knew the door on his side had been sprung open. Then he was torn into the sucking currents. A blinding, whirling rush of water encompassed him, filling him with sudden panic, as he fought desperately to free himself. Finally he got control of his wits, holding his breath, feeling his arm, the one linked to Jack Kelty, nearly torn off his shoulder.

The force of the river swept all three of them, Duggan, Kelty, Sheriff Whitehall, out of the car and downstream. They were hurled and rolled as though they were puppets tangled together by their own strings.

Fortunately, downstream, the north bank rose in a shale cliff that had, with one of its crevices, collected trees and other debris. Even with the sudden rise of water, the top surface remained unflooded and ran into the higher ground supporting the town of Blue Valley. It was Al Duggan who was flung against that debris, so that he was able to hook an arm around a tree branch.

With superhuman effort, he pulled himself up enough to gasp for air, then securing his hold, crawled up and onto that wedge of debris in the crevice of the cliff, dragging Kelty behind him. By that time the car they had exited had been rolled through the water a half dozen times, leaving the two patrolmen, who had been unable to free themselves, quite dead in the water-flooded prison.

Duggan held onto his gained perch desperately, fighting the tearing pull of Kelty. Kelty, in his own effort, was strong. Choking and coughing, he grasped Duggan's wrist with his locked hand and fought against the drag of Sheriff Whitehall on his other wrist. Sheriff Whitehall's head bobbed to the surface just once, and that was in time for a swiftly floating telephone pole to ram and crush his skull.

Finally Al Duggan found his breath and shouted, "Pull him in, Kelty!"

"He's had it! That pole—!"

"Pull him in!"

Swearing, coughing against the water, Kelty began climbing onto the tree trunk that had caught Duggan. He was hampered steadily by the dead weight of Sheriff Whitehall's body being pushed by the force of the current.

Finally Kelty made it almost all the way onto the trunk, one arm still pulled by the body attached to it. "Goddamn, he's dead! Goddamn it, Duggan, cut me loose!"

Duggan, nearly exhausted, realized the failure of Sheriff Whitehall to surface. He drew out the key for both handcuffs from a trouser pocket.

"Hurry up!" Kelty screamed. "He's tearing me in two!"

Leaning over the struggling Kelty, Duggan inserted the key and snapped the lock, releasing the body of Sheriff Fred Whitehall.

At the same instant, Kelty, with his just-freed hand, grabbed for the key. But his arm was too numb. And Al Duggan had anticipated. He flipped the key into the racing river.

Kelty swore, muddy water sliding down his handsome face.

Duggan, drenched, face set like a death mask, said, "Let's get it straight, Kelty. I'll dive in the river and pull you with me before I'll let you get away. You can't do anything but cooperate if you want to get to dry land. Have you got that?"

The look of hatred on Kelty's face destroyed the handsomeness.

"All right," Duggan said harshly. "Let's move."

Oddly, the dripping sun appeared now, washing its light over the water-ravaged countryside. Far on the other side of the vastly spread river, only one car from the caravan was in sight. Its nose was tipped up at a crazy angle from the water, where it had been lodged into a pair of now-flooded trees. The land rose beyond that, and there was the motion of those who had survived the flood wave, moving up the ascent. Duggan had looked over once, and only long enough to realize he was totally cut off from the others.

Like corpses suddenly come alive and crawling to light, Al Duggan and Jack Kelty, linked together by steel, made their precarious way over piled-up logs and branches toward solid ground.

They arrived at last at a plateau of shale that dipped a dozen yards beyond, then rose again to the small hill that bordered the southeast corner of Blue Valley. There was a small road there used mainly by a farmer named Roy Hawkins.

On solid ground, Al Duggan and Jack Kelty faced each other. Blue Valley was cut from sight by the hill on the southeast corner. Neither knew they were now standing on an island.

"This is the end of the line, Duggan."

Duggan stood stubbornly erect and ready, fighting the blackness that insisted on washing over his eyes. "You're crazy, Kelty. I'm taking you in now."

Kelty laughed without humor. "How? You're half dead, Duggan, You can't use your gun, it's soaked. This is it."

"You're still hooked to me."

"So I'll get unhooked."

"Wrong," Duggan said stubbornly. "Wrong—"

Kelty's fist chopped up against Duggan's chin. Duggan instantly sagged. When they both went down, rolling, Kelty was suddenly confident that he was going to win and go free. It was a desperate, silent battle, as the men rolled, the fresh late sun glinting periodically off the handcuffs holding them together. But it was no even contest....

Chapter 10

Lean, sunburned Roy Hawkins was in a daze. It didn't show in his manner nor in the set of his face—only in his eyes. He drove his jeep slowly up the hill road that led to Blue Valley, then suddenly stopped. He was a tall man of thirty-five. He wore a cowboy hat, a checked blue shirt and overall trousers. He also wore a pair of good boots, and around his waist was a webbed cartridge belt and a leather holster that contained the P38 pistol Roy Hawkins had taken from a German officer outside Minden, Germany.

He was a very neat man, ruggedly handsome, and one of the best-liked men in the Blue Valley area, although there were some, like Emil Dome, who resented his good war record. Roy Hawkins had gone through a year and a half of almost steady combat with a tank outfit.

He'd remained unwounded, through luck and skill, but he'd once suffered battle fatigue after forty-seven straight days on line, when he'd been pulled off for three weeks' rest.

He'd married a German girl he'd met in Kulmbach after the war. His dedication to her was total. He'd bought his land on the GI bill; in the years following he'd produced two daughters, aged three and five now, one of the most prosperous farms in the country, and a deeply matured love between himself and his extremely loyal, hard-working German bride.

Roy Hawkins's farm was just behind the point where he now sat in his jeep. The day before, when sixty acres had gone under water during the first flooding, he'd started to evacuate. But by noon on this day, when the flood seemed to be under control and the water was yet no nearer than a quarter of a mile to his house, Roy Hawkins's great desire to return to his home overrode caution. He had returned his wife and children to the farm from Allen Borney's house, where they had stayed overnight. He'd also started to return the loads of household goods he'd moved into the Blue Valley sale barn the day before.

An hour ago he'd gotten almost all of their possessions back to their house, killed with the pistol one rattler and one coyote driven to higher ground by the flood, and was returning toward Blue Valley for the final load of blankets and dishes. He had driven away from the house, his wife and two children standing outside in the yard to see him off. When he had driven up the rise of the hill road, he had heard the strange roar upstream.

He stopped the jeep and turned his head. In the next moment, the wall of water came crashing by. He sat transfixed, watching it sweep straight across his farm. He saw it knock down his wife and daughters, then uproot the house and send it sliding a dozen yards, half turning it around. He blinked and thought it must be a dream, because his entire family disappeared before his eyes. He waited for the water to evaporate and leave his family standing down there on dry land.

But the water did not evaporate, and his wife and daughters did not reappear.

Roy Hawkins sat unmoving for some time, a peculiar look going into his eyes. Then finally he frowned, started up the jeep once again and drove forward, thinking that he ought to drive into town and tell someone that his family had just disappeared.

It was when he reached the top of the rise that would lead him into Blue Valley that his eyes caught the flash of metal on the shale.

Calmly, he stopped again. He saw two men struggling, saw the flash of metal. He got out and walked coolly up the shale. In the struggle, the men did not hear him approach.

Roy Hawkins removed the pistol from its holster. "All right."

The men suddenly froze. "Get up," Roy Hawkins said.

He watched them get to their feet, the larger of them doing so with great difficulty. He looked at the handcuffs linking wrists, then at the mud-streaked clothes and faces. His stunned mind told him: escaped prisoners, caught in the flood fighting between themselves. His thinking was simple and orderly. There was one thing to do. Take them in.

Roy Hawkins said, "This way."

The slighter of the two men shook his head, eyes blazing.

"Move," Roy Hawkins said.

The slighter man changed his mind. The two men moved toward the jeep ahead of Roy Hawkins.

At the jeep, Roy Hawkins looked at the way they were manacled together. He said to Duggan, "You drive with your left hand?"

Duggan nodded, breathing with great difficulty.

"All right," Roy Hawkins said, "get in."

The two men climbed into the front seat of the jeep. Roy Hawkins got into the back and pointed his pistol. "Drive."

Al Duggan, barely alive, drove the jeep one-handed over the rise and into the town of Blue Valley.

Everyone remaining in town who was on the route to the courthouse stared in amazement as the jeep went by. This included Ben Blake, who saw the strange sight pass below his office window as he was talking to a just-arrived Steve Michaels. It also included, when the jeep reached the courthouse, Jack Kelty's fan club parked beneath a cottonwood tree in the low-cut Mercury. In fact, the five were so surprised that for a full minute not one of them realized he was looking directly at his hero.

By that time Roy Hawkins was marching his two prisoners up the walk toward the jail's outside door.

Behind him, there was a sudden flurry of action. A half dozen cars had followed the jeep, once it had gone through the business district. One of these contained Ben Blake and Steve Michaels. As Roy Hawkins ordered the men ahead of him to open the jail door, the following crowd was right behind.

The door was opened, and Roy Hawkins took his captives inside.

There, Inspector Al Duggan, trying to keep from blacking out, stared at the thin conservatively dressed man standing up beside the worn light-oak desk. The thin man suddenly smiled. Al Duggan started swearing.

Those who had followed the jeep were coming into the room, Steve and Ben Blake among them.

Ben Blake, taking immediate authority, said, "What the hell is going on, Roy?"

Roy Hawkins looked at Ben Blake. "Found them out by the river, Ben." Then his eyes found Steve Michaels. He handed Steve his pistol. "I got to go back and see about my family and farm, Steve."

"Listen, Roy—" Steve began, but Roy quietly walked out of jail. Ben Blake swung his head one way, then the other. "What the hell!" he said, completely bewildered.

The thin man in the conservative suit stepped forward, still smiling. "May I introduce myself, sir? I'm Martin Hillary of the *Ashford Times*."

"Well, for Christ's sake! What's going on here? I'm Ben Blake and I'm the mayor of this town! I want to know!"

"Allow me to introduce these two gentlemen, sir," Martin Hillary said happily, motioning at the manacled men. "The larger of these gentlemen is Inspector Albert Duggan of the Ashford police force. The other—"

"Goddamn it!" Al Duggan exploded. "This is Jack Kelty! Keep that gun on him, do you hear? And get somebody in here to cut these handcuffs so we can throw this bastard in a cell!"

Roy Hawkins, who had just brought Jack Kelty in, did not hear that, however. He was instead driving his jeep back through town and over the hill road toward the river. He drove quite calmly, finally stopping just exactly at the point from which he'd seen his family disappear. He stared at the rolling waters for quite a long time. But there was not a sign of his wife or his children.

Finally he put the jeep into gear and drove down toward the water. He drove right into the water until the current tipped the jeep over and pulled him into the river. In a moment, Roy Hawkins was being swept downstream, the water drowning the life out of him.

But Roy Hawkins didn't protest. He didn't care. He and his family had always done everything together.

Chapter 11

For a moment, after Al Duggan had snapped out the name of Jack Kelty, the Blue Valley citizens froze in stunned surprise.

A faucet of the deep yellow-stained sink had a worn washer; you could hear the sound of drops striking the porcelain bottom. A slight breeze had lifted outside; it blew across the green courthouse lawn, rustling the slick, shiny cottonwood leaves above the parked Mercury sedan. The recent appearance of the late sun had brightened the sky, and sunlight spilled in through the single barred west window of the jail, creating a collection of light shafts coming between the steel bars and alighting on the concrete floor at the feet of Jack Kelty. River water from Kelty's soaked clothes dripped onto the rectangular white patterns. A small fly darted through the light shafts, golden and humming, thumping against the glass pane of the west window.

Suddenly Al Duggan said, "Didn't anyone hear me? Where's the sheriff here anyway?"

Ben Blake came alive. "There isn't any sheriff."

Al Duggan motioned angrily to Steve. "Come over here and put the gun on his head." Then, as Steve moved behind Kelty and put the muzzle against the base of Kelty's skull, "Let's have it again, Mayor. What do you mean there isn't any sheriff?"

Martin Hillary said pleasantly, "Do you want me to explain, Duggan?"

"Shut up, Hillary." He nodded at Ben Blake.

Ben Blake said, "We've had most of our men over at Hampton Mill helping hold the levee. The sheriff and his deputy were running things. We've been cut off from them by the flood. This town's surrounded by water right now, and practically every good man we've got is on the other side. We don't have communication out of here. How did you get in?"

"The wave knocked our car into the water when the bridge went. I got out with Kelty, but Sheriff Whitehall and two patrolmen are dead. The rest of the caravan, whatever's left of it, is on the other side. Here we are."

Hillary laughed softly. "And here we are."

Duggan's face was gray, his breathing heavy and difficult. "Can't we get out? Can't anybody get in?"

Ben Blake shook his head. "Not until tomorrow morning. It's going to be dark before long. Nobody can cross that water in the dark."

As though in response to his words, the light shafts from the west window disappeared as the sun, reddening and suddenly cool, slipped beneath the horizon.

"Well, we'd better get something organized," Duggan said tightly. "Let's get these cuffs cut. Let's get Kelty into a cell."

"Steve," Ben Blake said, "I think you'd better take over."

Duggan looked at Steve and nodded. "How about that cowboy who brought us in. I liked his looks too."

Steve watched Ben Blake look about the room evaluating the help available. There was Martin Hillary. There was Mr. Potter. At the doorway was Harry Bell, thin, ageing, almost clown-looking with his large, protruding, vein-broken nose. Standing beside Harry Bell was Tim Crawford, owner of Tim's Lunch Counter, an equally thin man, middle-aged, eyes staring out from flour-white skin.

"Harry," Ben Blake said. "Tim. You're both on the city council. We're the only authority in town now. I'm appointing Steve as sheriff."

"All right," Harry Bell said. "That's fine."

"Tim?"

"Yes! I don't care!" He looked nervous, suspicious, afraid. Though he was able enough to have been working at Hampton Mill, he'd offered instead to set up his lunch counter around the clock as a feeding center for the workers when they returned to Blue Valley. He'd offered a discount of ten per cent on all meals served anyone who had legitimately worked on the Hampton Mill levee.

Ben Blake nodded. "All right, Steve. You're appointed acting sheriff. Take charge here."

"I'll help Inspector Duggan all I can," Steve said. Then he added, "Someone bring a chair over here for the inspector." It was obvious that Al Duggan was barely alive.

A chair was shoved across the concrete; Al Duggan slumped into it.

"How about me?" Jack Kelty asked; he too was given a chair. His voice had risen in pitch, as though he sensed that he was no more than an animal being viewed by a curious group of passers-by. Steve could sense his fear; but Duggan had told him to put the gun on his head, and that was what he continued to do.

"Mr. Potter," Steve said, "see if you can find something to cut these handcuffs with. Have you got a key for the sheriff's office?"

"Yes, sir," Mr. Potter said.

Steve noticed Rodney Newall now standing among the women clustered around the door. He said to Mr. Potter, "Take Rod with you and have him bring down any guns and ammunition he can find. Is there a cot around?"

"In the sheriff's office," Mr. Potter said, moving excitedly from one aged foot to the other.

"This is a circus is what this is," Jack Kelty said.

Martin Hillary smiled. "Shall I quote you on that, Jack?"

Steve said, "Get the cot in here too then. As fast as you can." Mr. Potter hurried off. Steve looked at Harry Bell. "Harry, drive out and see if you can get Roy Hawkins back in here."

"Right, Steve." Harry Bell disappeared.

"You can handle this all right, Steve?" Ben Blake asked.

"With Roy, Harry, Rod and Mr. Potter, we'll be all right. It's just one man, isn't it?"

"Okay," Ben Blake said briskly. "Everybody else clear out of here. Tim, you come with me. We've got to start patching together some kind of system until we get some help."

"I've got to get back to my lunch counter!" Tim Crawford said angrily.

"Well, who in the hell are you going to serve?"

Grumbling, Tim Crawford followed a quick-stepping Ben Blake outside. The door was closed. Hilary got out a cigarette. "As a member of the press, I've got an interest in this. You don't mind if I stay, do you, Sheriff?" He enunciated the word sheriff with careful emphasis.

"It's up to you," Steve said.

"Thank you, Sheriff," Martin Hillary said dramatically.

"This is just a goddamn hick town circus is what this is," Jack Kelty said. "You can quote me ten dozen times."

As the curious scattered from the courthouse, Jack Kelty's fan club decided to awaken from their lethargy and find out what had happened. Red-haired Nick Cowley was selected to perform the mission. Stepping out of the Mercury in the path of a thirty-year-old Blue Valley mother and housewife named Lou Ann Bordly, he switched his eyes up and down her plump figure encased in a light summer cotton dress; he gave her his most brilliant, experience-tested smile.

"Ma'am, we're just passing through. What's all the excitement?"

Lou Ann Bordly frowned. "Don't you know this town's surrounded by the flood right now?"

"Surrounded by the flood?" Nick Cowley said, blinking stupidly.

"A wave of water came down and took out the river bridge and the creek bridge, and I don't know how much damage it caused. Of course, we're surrounded! Now they've brought Jack Kelty in. And we don't even have a sheriff in town. We don't have any men, practically! Just Steve Michaels and Ben Blake. And just about nobody else, except that detective from Ashford. And he looks about half dead. I don't know who you are or what you're doing here. But you look young and healthy, and I'd think you'd want to help out in our little town. I've got to go! My husband's on the other side of the river. So is Doc Renley. Now my boy Douglas has got the measles, and I'm very upset!"

She hurried down the sidewalk. Nick Cowley stared after her, still blinking. Finally a slow smile crept across his broad face. He opened the back door of the Mercury and sprawled in beside Louie Harlan.

"What was she yakking about?" Norman Teller asked.

"Man," Nick Cowley said, shaking his head, laughing. "Oh, man, oh, man!"

"What's going on?"

"Man," Nick Cowley said, roaring with laughter as he finally realized everything. "Douglas has got the measles!"

Chapter 12

Inside the jail Steve Michaels listened to the steady clicking of Martin Hillary's typewriter as Hillary readied the material to be released the next day when contact was made with the outside. After the handcuffs linking Duggan and Kelty had been cut, Hillary had carried in his portable machine and set it up on a packing crate found in a lower courthouse hallway. Also on the crate was a large glass ash tray resting beside a bottle of Teacher's Scotch; Hillary had immediately offered everyone a drink—the only takers had been Jack Kelty, who had been denied the privilege by Al Duggan, and Mr. Potter, who had gulped down a third of a glass, then gone instantly to sleep on one of the cell bunks. Harry Bell, Steve noticed, had looked at the bottle several times since he'd returned from a futile attempt to find Roy Hawkins, but in respect for his assignment, had not yet taken a drink.

On the corner of the oak desk beside which Steve sat, a portable radio brought in by Rod Newall hummed softly with music. They had heard, now, a half dozen news reports on the flood. The general area had been declared a disaster area by the governor. Additional help was being rushed to the valley. Helicopter contact would be established at daybreak. Large boats were being trucked in to cross the swollen waters when light again appeared. There was a general description of how the flooding had come about and a notation of the lives estimated lost up and down the stream. There had been special time given to a report on the caravan that had been carrying Jack Kelty to Ashford. At least seven members of the caravan were presumed lost in the flood; they included Sheriff Fred Whitehall, Inspector Albert Duggan and Jack Kelty.

The telephone on Steve's desk sounded. "Yes?"

"Steve, this is Ben, How is it going?"

"Fine Ben,"

"Well, everybody's very confident with you on the job. We've had a meeting up here in my office. Si Metcomb. Tim Crawford. There's a salesman here from Parisville, Bud Celt. And big Emil Dome got stuck in town—he's got the dairy farm on the other side of the river."

"I know Emil, Ben.

"Well, there's nothing much we can do. We've telephoned around and told everyone—women mostly—just to remain quiet. I've got some of the oldsters keeping watch on the river. Tim's got his lunch counter open. He's going to keep it open all night, in case anybody gets nervous and wants some place to go. His wife's helping him. There are some kids over there right now who were driving through. Tim's checking to see if they're okay."

"That's fine, Ben."

"I'm going to stay right here in my office. Grab a cat nap once in a while. I'm here in case anybody wants or needs anything."

"Good idea. It'll give people confidence to know they can come to you."

"You're sure you're all right there?"

"We're all right."

"Sue's coming over with the food pretty soon. It's safe, isn't it?"

"He's locked up securely, Ben."

"That's fine, Steve. I'm just glad you were around to take over. Is that goddamn Newall kid still there?"

"Don't worry about that, Ben. Let's worry about that later."

"You're right, Steve. I'll call you again."

Steve put the telephone down. Hillary had stopped typing and was looking at him curiously. Al Duggan lay very quietly. Jack Kelty continued to lie flat on his back in his cell, lighting a new cigarette from the stub of one still burning.

Hillary said, "I can't get over the way this little town's taking this, Michaels. Very cool."

"They've got a lot of things to worry about besides Jack Kelty."

"I suppose. But there's no panic."

"What did you expect?"

Al Duggan swung his feet slowly over the side of the cot and straightened with effort. "It's not what he expected, it's what he wanted. What he'd like to see is a small riot, some shooting, a few people killed."

"Great sense of humor," Hillary said, smiling.

"How did you know where we were headed?" Duggan asked, rubbing his gray face with his palms.

Kelty said from his bunk, "He's got a magic crystal ball."

"That's right," Hillary said.

"How do you feel, Inspector?" Steve asked.

"Okay, Michaels."

"He looks good, doesn't he?" Hillary said sarcastically. "He'll have his brass knuckles back on and swinging in no time."

Duggan took away his hands from his face, looking at Hillary with steel eyes.

"Can you use some coffee, Inspector?" Steve asked smoothly. "The food'll come in any minute. But we can get some coffee in the meantime."

Duggan started to stand up, then changed his mind. He was dressed in a pair of slacks and a sport shirt brought in by one of the Blue Valley housewives living nearby. Both he and Kelty had cleaned up in cell sinks and put on fresh, borrowed clothes. But though Kelty looked neat and crisp, Duggan still appeared to have just come out of the river. "I could use some coffee, all right."

"Rod," Steve said, "run over and pick up a couple of large containers of coffee from Tim Crawford, will you?"

Rodney Newall took one more look at Jack Kelty and Al Duggan, then left. Martin Hillary stood up, stretching. "I'm leaving for a while myself. I want to look this town over a little."

"See if you can fall in the river while you're doing it," Al Duggan said tightly.

"If anyone wants a drink," Hilary said, putting on his jacket, "go right ahead."

Hillary left. After a while, after Duggan had asked a few brief personal questions about his position in Blue Valley, Steve nodded at the bottle of Scotch. "Why don't you take a drink, Inspector?" He did not like the look on the man's face. If Doctor Renley had been in town, he would have called him instantly; but Doctor Renley was not in town.

"That's what he'd like," Duggan said, lighting a fresh cigarette. His hand holding the match was trembling. "I can see the way it would read in the *Times*. Cop gets drunk on job during siege in Blue Valley."

"I don't care what Hillary writes," Jack Kelty said. "I'll take three fingers. Make it four."

Duggan did not look in Kelty's direction. It was as though Jack Kelty did not exist now that he was locked behind bars. Steve looked at Duggan smoking silently, a detached look in his eyes, as though he were trying to look into some dark, undefinable future. The minutes went by. Harry Bell, Steve noticed, had gone to sleep sitting in one of the straight-back wooden chairs.

"I take it," Steve finally said to Duggan, "you and Hillary have had a feud for some time."

Duggan smiled grimly. "Some time, yes."

"A matter of chemistry?"

"A matter of chemistry, genes, fate, you name it. He doesn't understand."

"Doesn't understand?"

Duggan stood up with effort and walked to the empty cell opposite Kelty's. He did not look at Kelty. He seemed, suddenly, to be standing at the brink of something he himself could not define, uncertain as to whether or not he would step over that brink. He put the fingers of one hand around a bar, holding to it tightly, as though that were necessary to remain standing. "Take a look at us—you, Kelty, me."

Jack Kelty turned his head, looking at Steve through eyes half closed against the smoke curling up from his loosely held cigarette. "Listen to him, Michaels. He'll make a saint out of you. He'll lead you straight up to heaven."

Steve said to Al Duggan, "All right. I'm looking."

"Maybe we've all got something in common," Duggan said, almost dreamily. "You went through the Ashford Home, Michaels. Kelty went through the Berry Street neighborhood."

"Let's give a cheer," Kelty said, laughing softly.

"I didn't have the Berry Street neighborhood, Michaels. But I had the packing-house end of Ashford to grow up in, and it was just as bad. So've I spent my life trying to be a good cop. You, Michaels, you're a teacher. These are good things."

Kelty had begun clapping, the sound echoing through the small jail. Harry Bell lifted his chin, then let it drop again. Rod Newall came in with the coffee cartons. Mr. Potter continued to snore.

"A cop," Duggan said, paying no attention to Kelty, and letting his cigarette drop unnoticed from his fingers to the cement floor. "That's what I am today. That's all I am today." He looked at Steve. "You teach and coach kids." He motioned at Rod. "Kids like this. That's a good thing, Michaels, don't you see? It doesn't matter whatever else you don't do. If you do one big, good thing, isn't that enough?" Duggan lifted a hand, motioned toward Kelty, as though a corpse of Kelty were there instead of a live, breathing man.

"What did he do that was a good thing? I don't mean little things. Maybe he kissed his mother once. Maybe he cried when he hurt something once. Maybe he really loved someone or let someone love him, for a little while. But those were just small parts. What did he do with the big thing? Did he do anything good?"

Duggan shook his head. "Not Kelty. We all had the same coin to put down. It said good on one side. Bad on the other. Kelty put his down with the bad side up. Am I supposed to cry? Are you? Is anybody? He's a negative! Let them call me what they want to. Let them say I'm brutal, sadistic, mean, selfish. I don't care. I put the coin up the right way. So did you, Michaels. I've had to do what I've had to do, to be a good cop. I am a good cop. I've held my prisoner. I've got no apologies. My soul is clean...."

The telephone rang as Duggan's voice faded, as he tipped forward, a peculiar look going into his eyes. Steve picked up the telephone, frowning as he looked at Duggan. "Yes?"

"Michaels, this is Tim Crawford! If you're the sheriff in this town, you'd better start doing something! Those kids that were in my place. Started getting nasty with me, swearing dirty right in front of my wife. I don't know what all!"

"What kids, Tim?"

"Then they went out of here and roared around the main street in that car of theirs, running right up on the sidewalk across the street.

Saw it with my own eyes. Now, by God, they've just kicked in the front window of Harry's pool hall! By God, they've started tearing this town apart, and you'd better get started doing something and right now!"

Steve shook his head, frowning, hearing the crack as Tim Crawford hung up. He carefully put the telephone down.

Harry Bell who had awakened with the ringing of the telephone, looked at Steve curiously.

"What's the matter, Steve?" Rod Newall asked, coming forward.

Steve's eyes went back to Inspector Al Duggan. Duggan's hand had clenched around the bar of the cell so tightly that his knuckles were white. His mouth moved soundlessly, until all at once the large body loosened. The hand came away from the bar, and the large body came tumbling down as he finally went over that undefinable brink.

Everyone stood up, including Mr. Potter, who, with the sound of Duggan collapsing to the concrete, instinctively swung his stiff legs over the side of the bunk and staggered to his feet. Steve reached Duggan first, bending down beside him.

"Get the whisky!" Steve snapped.

"Michaels!" Duggan managed, in a far-away whisper.

Steve uncapped the bottle handed to him by Harry Bell, but Duggan kept trying to speak: "Michaels, listen—"

"I'm listening, Inspector."

"Michaels ... *don't let Kelty go*—"

Steve nodded. He tried to lift the man's head, tried to pour the Scotch down his throat. But he knew, suddenly, it was no good. He straightened slowly. He handed the bottle back to Harry Bell.

"What's the matter with him?" Rod Newall asked.

"He's dead," Steve said softly.

They stood around him, Steve, Rod Newall, Mr. Potter, Harry Bell. They looked at the big, unmoving body. Harry Bell suddenly lifted the bottle and took a long drink from it. Mr. Potter said, "Big young fellow like that? Dead?" The radio played softly. The telephone had started ringing again. But nobody moved. They were frozen by the sudden sound of the raw, wild laughter of Jack Kelty.

Chapter 13

The selection of Harry Bell's pool hall for a headquarters had been a natural selection by Jack Kelty's fan club. After they had left Tim Crawford's lunch counter they had driven up and down Blue Valley's main street, building up steam.

Even Norman Teller had begun drinking now, and a great hunger for action was developing in each of them.

Rajeski said tightly, "Man, here he is in this little dump with one lousy cop on him and nothing else but farmers."

"Yeah," Norman Teller said meanly. "Nothing else but farmers."

"What a stinking, lousy dump," Nick Cowley said, looking at the business fronts of Blue Valley with great disgust.

"Man," Louie Harlan said. He shook his head and started laughing. "Man, what a pig hole!" A new bottle of red wine was in his lap.

"You know what I'd like?" Tommy Marcelli said suddenly. "I'd like to tear this whole town apart with my bare hands!"

"How we gonna let Jack know we're here, Tell?" Rajeski said worriedly. "I mean, he'll flip when he hears. But how we gonna let him know?"

Louie Harlan's laughter pealed. "We just go to the old jail house door and knock. We say, 'Man, we're here! Tell old Jack we're come to get him!'" Louie Harlan roared.

"We got to let him know!" Norman Teller said seriously.

"You really want to?" Louie Harlan asked brightly.

"Hell, yes!" Teller snapped, knowing the glory of all this was nothing until Jack Kelty knew.

Louie leaned forward. "See that pool hall? Drive up on the sidewalk!"

Norman Teller frowned, squinting ahead down the deserted street.

Louie had begun giggling. "Drive up!"

"Hell …!" Teller sent the car over the curb, nosing it up toward Harry Bell's closed pool hall.

"There!" Louie Harlan yelled. He leaned across Nick Cowley and sent his wine bottle flying through the front window. "Hold it, man!"

Teller braked, eager to do anything that would start some real action.

Louie Harlan scrambled out of the car. Down the street Tim

Crawford ran outside and squinted in their direction in amazement. Louie yanked open the trunk of the Mercury, grabbed the tire iron and smashed at the already broken plate glass window of the pool hall. Sheets of jagged glass crashed inside and out. Louie ran the tire iron along the bottom of the sill, clearing the entire space of broken glass. Then he jumped through to the interior.

"Get the guns!" he yelled.

The others got the weapons from the trunk and scrambled after Louie, who found a light switch, and blazed the interior with light. "Now," he shouted, tears forming in his eyes, "old Jack'll know we're here!"

Inside the jail, all eyes were on Steve Michaels—all except those of Kelty, who continued to stare brightly at the collapsed body. The telephone continued to ring. Steve finally said, "Get a blanket from one of those cells and put it over him."

Rod Newall quietly got a blanket and put it over Al Duggan.

Steve walked back to his desk and sat down. He picked up the telephone. "Yes," he said flatly.

"Steve, this is Ben! I got a call from Tim Crawford about that bunch of kids, whoever the hell they are, breaking into the pool hall. I went down there to see what it was all about. By God, they've got guns! They fired two shots over my head! What's that all about anyway?"

"I don't know, Ben. I'll find out pretty quickly. Inspector Duggan just died, Ben."

"Died!"

"Maybe a heart attack. I don't know. I know he's dead."

Ben Blake was speechless for a moment. "Well, what are we going to do now?"

"Start telephoning, Ben. Get Alice Stritt working from the switchboard. Get everybody off the streets until I find out what these kids are after. Maybe it's got something to do with Kelty."

Jack Kelty turned suddenly, looking at Steve with alert eyes.

"We're not going to stand for it, Steve! We're going to—"

"Just get everybody off the streets, Ben. That's the only thing to worry about now."

"All right, Steve. But be careful with those kids. Tim says they're drinking."

"All right, Ben. I'll see you in your office pretty quickly."

"How about Kelty?"

"He's behind bars. I'll—" Steve looked around the room. "I'll leave someone in charge here while I'm gone. We'll straighten this out, Ben."

The outside door opened as Steve put down the telephone. Martin Hillary stepped inside. His careful eyes found the blanket-covered body instantly. He frowned.

"Duggan," Steve explained quietly, examining Hillary's face.

"Duggan!"

"He just collapsed and died."

Hillary blinked once. He rubbed his chin. "Well, what do you know about that?"

Steve stood up. "Writing the story already? Or are you too choked up with grief?"

Hillary looked at Steve, recovering from his surprise instantly. "That leaves you totally in charge, doesn't it, Michaels? You're already talking like Duggan."

Steve motioned to Rod Newall. "Let's move him out of here. Put him in one of the storage rooms in the main building. Come on, Mr. Potter. You'll have to unlock the door. Harry, do you know how to use this gun?" He motioned to Roy Hawkins's P38.

Harry Bell stepped forward. "I never shot a gun in my life, Steve."

"All right, Harry. All you do is sit down in this chair. I'm putting the pistol on the desk in front of you. The safety's off. Watch Kelty. If he tries anything, pick up the gun and point it in his direction and start pulling the trigger."

Harry Bell nodded silently and sat down behind the gun, staring at Kelty.

"Talking just like Duggan," Martin Hillary repeated.

"Mr. Potter, Rod," Steve said. "Let's get this over with."

In a few minutes they had dragged Duggan's body out of the room and deposited it in a storage room in the lower level of the courthouse.

"All right," Steve said, when they returned. "There's some trouble downtown, Harry. There are a bunch of kids who've broken into your pool hall. I don't know who they are."

"My pool hall?" Harry Bell said, blinking.

"I wondered if you'd been informed about that yet," Hillary said smoothly. "I was just down there and drove past. It seems they've knocked out the front window and taken the place over."

"Do you know who they are?"

"It's the same group that followed me from Ashford. At least it's their car in front."

"Followed you?"

Jack Kelty was very attentive now.

Hillary smiled coolly. "A car followed me during my entire journey. A rumor in the Ashford sheriff's headquarters cropped up that a group of Jack's friends might make an effort to help him escape somewhere along the route. I have no idea if this is the group, but I know they did follow me into Blue Valley. I would, of course, be very sad to think this might be that group. But—"

"What did they look like?" Jack Kelty snapped.

"They wore blue jackets. All about seventeen or eighteen, I would judge."

"What kind of car?" Kelty asked.

"A cut-down Mercury."

Jack Kelty snapped the fingers of one hand, a cunning smile forming on his lips.

"How many?" Steve asked tightly.

Hillary shrugged. "Five, I think."

Steve rubbed a palm along his jacket, trying to organize his thoughts. Harry Bell walked over to Hillary's packing case and picked up the bottle of Scotch.

"Go right ahead, Mr. Bell." Hillary smiled.

"Listen, Harry—" Steve began.

But Harry Bell had already tipped up the bottle and taken a long drink. He recapped the bottle and put it down. "I had to have that, Steve. This is a mess! Why did they break into my pool hall?"

"I don't know, Harry. But I'll find out." Steve looked at Hillary. "We're in trouble. You can see that, Hillary. Where do you stand?"

"What do you mean, where do I stand?"

"I mean, are you working with us?"

Hillary shrugged. "Well, let's look at it this way. If this were a war and I were a correspondent, I'd be a noncombatant. I might be on the scene, but I wouldn't want to pick up a gun."

"In other words, you won't help. Is that it? If I asked you to sit down here with a gun and guard Kelty while I'm gone, you wouldn't do it? Is that right?"

"It's just," Hillary said pleasantly, "that I can't see my way clear to became involved to that extent."

Steve turned away suddenly, looking at the collection of weapons that had been brought down from the sheriff's office. There was a sub-machine gun, a .45 pistol encased in a leather holster, a twelve-gauge shotgun. Additionally there was Roy Hawkins's P38. Steve examined Harry Bell again. Harry's eyes were faintly shiny; these past years, Steve knew, Harry had been drinking daily. It was showing now—how much he might have had before the two drinks of Hillary's Scotch Steve couldn't estimate. He looked at Mr. Potter. Mr. Potter smiled back courageously. He really was good for nothing in an emergency.

Steve turned to Rodney Newall, remembering the boy's attitude about Kelty. But there was no one else.

"How about you, Rod?"

Rodney Newell shrugged.

"I need your help."

"Whatever you say, Steve," he said flatly.

He was, Steve knew, covering up his nervousness, for one thing; whatever else he was thinking there was no way of knowing.

Steve strapped on the forty-five. He motioned to the shotgun. "Use it if you have to. Keep the thirty-eight in front of you on the desk. Use the shotgun first, then the pistol. Stay right at that desk, with your back to the wall. Blow the head off anybody who tries anything, and that includes Hillary."

"I'll tell you, Michaels," Hillary said, eyes thin. "I'm going to recommend you for an appointment to the Ashford police force. You're the best material I've seen since Duggan."

Someone was knocking at the door. Steve opened it, carefully now. Sue and Gretchen came in, carrying trays of food. Sue came directly to Steve. Gretchen stared at Jack Kelty, unconsciously arching her back so that the crisp white dress she wore tightened across her breasts.

"There's some trouble downtown, Sue," Steve said brusquely. "I've got to leave. I don't want either you or Gretchen in here while I'm gone. Just put the trays down and go outside, please."

Sue blinked, then nodded. Gretchen continued to stare at Jack Kelty, a faint smile showing at the corners of her pretty mouth. Jack Kelty examined her in calm, complete detail. He answered her smile with an even showing of white teeth.

"I'm leaving Rod in charge," Steve said. "Harry, you stay here too. Hillary, you said you were a noncombatant. Make sure you keep it that way. Mr. Potter, if Rod needs anything, get it for him, will you? Remember what I said, Rod. You can blow a man's head off with that gun. Don't hesitate to do it. And keep that door locked. Okay, Sue,

Gretchen—come on."

He picked up the machine gun and led them to the door. "Lock this after me, Mr. Potter. Don't let anybody in or out."

"As a newspaperman—" Hillary began.

"You'll stay in or out, Hillary."

Hillary looked at Steve, then swept a hand in the direction of Jack Kelty. "My God, he's just one individual! Is he a tiger? A wounded bull? Look at him! What kind of disease did you get from Duggan? This is laughable, Michaels!"

Steve motioned Sue and Gretchen ahead of him, then followed, slamming the door behind him. When he heard Mr. Potter turning the lock, he escorted the two girls down the walk.

It was yet a moonless night, but you could see to walk by the light of the old-fashioned, insect-circled street lamps standing on all sides of the courthouse. There was a strangeness in the look of power being turned into illumination within a small world detached from the rest of civilization.

"What's happened downtown, Steve?" Sue asked.

"Friends of Kelty followed Hillary in. They've broken into the pool hall. You'd better go home and stay there."

"I'm not afraid," Gretchen said.

"Just go home," Steve snapped. His own Chevrolet sedan was parked at the curb, ahead of Sue's convertible.

"Steve," Sue said, touching his arm, "be careful."

He did not answer. He got into his car, placed the machine gun beside him and drove off toward the main street of Blue Valley.

At the intersection bisecting the main street, he let the car coast to a stop parallel to the curb, cut his lights and stared down the silent avenue running between the main business buildings.

In the center of the nearest block on the right side of the street a bright wash of light flowed over the sidewalk from the interior of Harry Bell's pool hall. The Mercury, the only car on the block, was nosed up on the sidewalk in front of it.

All the store fronts on that side of the street were dark but that of the pool hall. A breeze blew, carrying with it a faint sound of wild laughter.

Steve turned on the car's lights and moved the sedan around the corner, letting it roll slowly onto the main street.

He could now see the pieces of broken glass glittering on the sidewalk in front of the pool hall around the front wheels of the

Mercury. He fitted his right hand around the machine gun. One-handed he drove past the pool hall, looking through the broken window at the lighted interior. He saw a single youth suddenly move down the bar to the opposite end, crouching. The flat, low-hanging disk lamps above the billiard tables lighted the quick movement of another stepping swiftly behind the partition of the small room where customers played cards.

Steve drove slowly on, down the street to the main intersection where the yellow Blue Valley flagpole rose from a central concrete base. There was no one else, Steve was certain, out on that street now. But in the next block he could see the lights of Ben Blake's office shining above the Blue Valley Clothing Store; a pickup truck was parked at the curb.

He looked back down the street in the direction of the pool hall. He remembered Jack Kelty's look when Hillary had described that Mercury parked in front—Kelty knew them, no doubt of it. Ben had said they had fired two shots over his head. Armed. Bent on freeing Kelty, if Hillary's information was right. Steve thought of those final words of Al Duggan: … *don't let Kelty go*.

He made a U-turn around the flagpole and drove back down the street. When he was almost even with the pool hall, he suddenly cut the car to the left, nosing it up at an angle to the Mercury. His hard braking rocked the sedan, then he was out and up against the brick wall to the side of the entrance, machine gun in hand. He moved swiftly along the brick, as two bullets whined into the warm Blue Valley air. He stopped to the side of the door, the broad window to the side of it demolished. Then he kicked the door open in time to see a red-haired youth sprawl in front of a billiard table flat on the floor, frozen. Steve waited at the side of the door, machine gun ready.

There was absolute silence.

Finally he heard a husky, angry voice, "Get out of here, farmer!"

He watched the red-haired youth on the floor begin to inch forward toward the protection of the bar. He fired a short burst over his head, aiming so that the bullets splattered through the back window into the trash lot behind Harry Bell's building. The crab-like figure on the floor froze again.

"All of you," he said, "up and hands free where I can see you."

There was not a sound, not a movement.

Steve waited a moment longer, then, "I'll chop the one on the floor if you don't move. I'll give you five seconds!"

"For Christ's sake, Teller!" the youth on the floor yelled.

"Okay, farmer." The voice sounded from the card room around the partition from Steve. "I'm coming—just me."

Steve waited. He was certain there was a youth behind the bar. The others—two more, if Hillary was right—could be any place.

A large blond youth with a thick-featured face stepped out from the card room. He wore a shiny blue jacket and an open-necked white shirt. He walked with a slight spring of his toes. The blond hair was clipped short on top and combed carefully on the sides. He wore black slacks, and at the waist was tucked a small pistol.

The boy rubbed a palm upward along his chin. He had a mean, shrewd look. He did not seem to be violently scared or even desperate. Steve, looking at his eyes, guessed that was because he'd been drinking; his look was more of dangerous unpredictability. The boy's hands drifted toward his gun.

"Keep your hands away from that gun."

"Sure, farmer."

"You've broken into this building, fired at the mayor of this town and at me. Do you want to explain?"

The youth shrugged, a corner of his thin mouth turning down in an inverted smile. He shook his head.

Anger flushed Steve's face. "This is a machine gun in my hand!"

"So use it, farmer."

The boy waited, eyes thin and bright.

"No? How come, farmer? Chop me, huh?"

Steve stood silent, eyes hard.

The boy laughed. "You see how it is, farmer?"

"Maybe you'd better tell me how it is," Steve said softly.

"All right. We just flew into town like a bunch of robins. This flood cut us off, so we had to have a place to roost. So we saw the pool hall here, so we roosted. You want to gun us for that?"

"You had to knock the window out?"

"The joint was closed, man. We couldn't just fade through."

"You're armed, aren't you?"

"Now that is true."

"You've fired at two people."

"Not at. Over."

"Either way, why?"

"We're strangers in squaresville, see? We don't know nothing. So we got nervous. I mean, there's this lady, and she tells us this town's cut off. She tells us there practically nothing but women left here. Now that's all right. We like women, you know. Only this lady says there's a big, bad, nasty crook in town, how about that? Some guy name of Kelty. Now we ain't stupid. I mean, anybody knows this Kelty is dangerous! That fills us full of jitters. Right away we get as scared as that lady was. So we say, man, we've got to protect ourselves. This town, this here squaresville, might be dangerous. Kelty around aching to blast somebody. Practically no men. And that includes, this lady says, the law. She said there's no law here. How about that? We're trembling now, see? So we say, man, we've got to find some sand and bury our heads. So we do, and now you come around and let go with that chopper, and we don't even know who you are, Jack. You make us nervous."

Steve looked at him for several seconds. "Are you finished?"

"Why?"

"Because I'm going to tell you a few things. First, there's law in squaresville, junior. I'm it—the appointed law. Second, I've got the report you're here to try to break Kelty out. This is where we get something else straight. You're not going to do it."

Norman Teller suddenly began to laugh softly.

"Shut up," Steve snapped. "Tell your friends to get out here in plain sight, all of them. I'm taking you in."

Teller's laughter died, his smile disappeared. "Oh, no, cop."

"I'll give you ten seconds to line up in front of me. You, on the floor, stand up."

Nick Cowley slowly got to his feet, turning to look at Steve with frightened eyes.

"Over here," Steve said.

"Just a minute, Nick," Teller said quietly.

"I'm telling you—" Steve warned.

"Louie," Teller said penetratingly. "Stand up."

At the far end of the bar, small Louie Harlan straightened and smiled wildly across the mahogany.

"See, cop?" Teller said, mouth and eyes wicked. "I want to get everybody out here where you can see them. Now you see three. That's Nick Cowley in the center. Nick is deadly with the broads, would you believe that? And Louie back there, that's Louie Harlan. He's good for nothing. How about that, Louie? What are you good for, Louie?"

"Goddamn nothing," Louie said brightly.

Teller nodded, satisfied. "Okay, Tommy—out."

There was silence, no movement.

"Out!" Teller said.

Tommy Marcelli stepped out from behind the partition of the card room.

"Now Cut," Teller said.

Richard Rajeski slowly followed Marcelli. Teller remained just in front of Steve, the rest were in a jagged half circle behind Teller.

"Now," Teller said. "The big bastard there is Tommy Marcelli. Look at those hands. Did you ever see hands like that, cop? And the guy to his right, that's Richard Rajeski. We call him Cut. You see his pants pocket bulge? Now that's a switch knife. Cut's just like a born surgeon with that knife. Man, he can cut like nobody ever cut before! That's it, cop, the whole group, except me. My name's Teller. They call me Tell, and I more or less speak for my friends."

"Are you done speaking?" Steve said grimly.

"I thought I handled the introductions pretty good, cop. You didn't like it?"

"I never liked a cheap sideshow. I'm tired of this one. For the last time, all of you line up with Teller and put your weapons on the floor."

There was a pause, then Nick Cowley took a tentative step forward.

"Stay where you are, Nick," Teller snapped.

"You're going to get one of your friends hurt, Teller," Steve said. "I'll say it once more. Move!" he waited. Nobody moved.

He lifted the machine gun a little, pointed it past Teller, firing a burst between Teller and Harlan, the bullets whining through the rear window again.

Cowley paled a little more. Marcelli's big hands opened and closed. Rajeski blinked rapidly, a muscle flickering at the corner of his mouth. Louie Harlan stared at the machine gun in Steve's hands, then put his face down on his hands and giggled hysterically.

"See?" Teller said, at last, his voice trembling a little. "They ain't going to move." Then he had control again, certain that Steve had lost everything when that burst wouldn't move them. "You might as well cut out, cop. You just ain't got the power. Tell us, were you really appointed, man, or did you just dream that up?"

"You're really aching to get hurt, aren't you?"

Teller laughed, totally confident now, his face growing meaner. "Hurt? Who's going to hurt us? You? We were just after a little shelter, just like I told you. On account of the emergency. We didn't know where to go. So we picked this. So we broke a window. So I'll tell you."

His hand suddenly went into a pocket; Steve pointed the machine gun directly at him. Teller smiled and drew out a wallet. He removed a dollar bill and let it flutter to the floor, grinning. "There's for the window, Jack. Now why are you going to go and hurt us? So we fired a couple over your head. Man, this is an open city. Man, you never know what's going to happen in an open city like this. You got to shoot a couple over people's head, just to make sure you don't run into no looters. You go along with me on that, cop?"

Steve's eyes flickered from one to another. Teller's manner was infecting all of them now; he could see the confidence rising in each one.

"And that cop business of yours. Man, we just don't know about that. Where's you star, Sheriff? I don't see no star. You see a star, Cut?"

"Up in the sky."

Teller laughed, but his eyes were gleaming, mean. "So that's the way it is. We're poor little lambs, so we found some cover. We got a little gun or two, true, but that's to protect ourselves from the looters, see? What's more, this Kelty—now he might just crawl out of this hick jail. And, man, he's a killer, right? Looters and killers around, who's going to say we can't have a little gun to protect ourselves? We're just innocent Boy Scouts, caught in the flood. So now you come up and say you're a cop and so line up and all that crap, huh? So maybe you're a looter too, huh? How do we know? Maybe you're something worse. I'd like to know how we're sure about you, Jack. So we ain't. So we don't do what you say. So what are you going to do about it? Shoot? Go ahead. Shoot me in the heart. Shoot Marcelli in the belly. Chop away!"

Louie Harlan had lifted his head at the end of the bar; now he suddenly bent over again, tears streaming down his face, roaring wildly with laughter. "Go ahead, cop!" he screamed. "Chop me!"

Teller grinned. "Get out of here, cop. Go back to your hole and see how Kelty's doing. Maybe he don't like it there. Maybe you'd be better off if you just let Kelty go, see? We're just thinking of you. You let Kelty go, maybe you've got more time to rove around the street and see there ain't no looters out there. And even other mean, dirty things, man. Who knows? You take a type like Nick here. Now Nick's all right. But he gets hungry for broads. So here's a whole town just up to its neck in broads, all pining around, lonesome, their old men on the other side of the drink. Maybe you wouldn't like a type like Nick around trying to take the edge off his hunger, huh? And then take a type like Cut there—he gets a couple of beers, and he gets hungry for using his knife, see? Sometimes he gets real nervous, and then he goes and starts cutting! And take a type like Marcelli. Now there's a type for you. Just like a goddamn bear. He's always hungry to use those hands on somebody—"

"All right," Steve said thinly. "You've had a ball. You want to play it this way, okay. You're right about one thing—this town's open. Don't count on getting anything but open-town treatment. I won't fire on a man who isn't doing anything. But if one of you does something out of line, I'll come and get you. I'll hunt you down and chop you to ribbons, I swear it. You shoot one more bullet out of here, you touch somebody, man or woman, you're dead. Have you got that? You like this place, you're staying here!"

He looked at them, from one to another. They stared back at him silently, half smiling, knowing they had won, at least for the moment.

He started backing, the machine gun held snug against his hip. He backed out and to his car. He got in, keeping his eyes on the front of the pool hall. He waited for a moment, then suddenly put the car in gear, made a U-turn and drove down the block. He pulled up in front of the Blue Valley Clothing Store. The lights of Ben Blake's office were still burning above. Ben Blake strode out from the stairway entrance, face flushed. "What the hell is going on over there, Steve? Who the hell has got the guts to fool around with our little town?"

Chapter 14

Steve led the way upstairs. "I'll explain in your office, Ben."

Ben Blake's office was cloudy with smoke. Big Emil Dome was sitting in a chair, a cigar between his teeth. Tim Crawford was pacing nervously and angrily. There was a slim, middle-aged man in a wide-lapelled blue suit who Steve did not know, standing at the corner of Ben's large desk. Si Metcomb, Blue Valley's leading druggist, sat in a chair near the wall.

When Steve strode in, Emil Dome stood up. He was a man of tremendous size. His face was shaped in round folds; from his forehead down, the skin was tanned to gold-brown; above, where his hat normally rode, the skin was as fair as a baby's. He had straight, thinning black hair. His neck was barely visible, and what was in sight blended into the great round slopes of his shoulders. He was wearing a thin, worn overall jacket and heavy twill pants. His work shoes were huge. It was a well-known fact in Blue Valley that beneath those smooth folds of fat there existed the muscle of a good dray horse.

"You take care of those kids, Steve?" he asked; he spoke in choppy phrases as though his girth were continually squeezing his breath out in bursts.

Steve picked up Ben's telephone and dialed the jail's number. "In a minute, Emil."

Si Metcomb stood up, a neat, short man who did not seem small from a distance because of the delicate proportion of his frame. His hair was a little longer than most natives of Blue Valley, curly and silver gray. He had a handsome face that had retained its good looks through his sixty-one years. He did not look sixty-one, but rather forty-seven or forty-eight. He now wore his familiar tight-necked pharmacist's jacket; he still smelled a little like his drugstore: a heavy, rich, soap-scented smell. "They're in Harry Bell's place now, Steve, they'll be in mine any minute!"

"Take it easy, Si," Steve said. Rod Newall's voice sounded on the other end of the wire.

"How's it going, Rod?"

"All right, Steve."

"You're sure?"

"No trouble."

"Nobody's tried to get in?"

"Well—" Steve heard a peal of familiar laughter. "Well, Gretchen's here, Steve."

"Rod, I told you—"

"She said you'd told her to come back and stay here. I wasn't sure that—"

"I didn't, Rod. Now see that you— Well, I don't have time now. For God's sake, don't do anything like that again. I'll be back there in a few minutes. All right?"

"Yeah," Rod said, his voice cooling. "All right."

Steve dropped the telephone on its cradle. Ben Blake put his hand on the arm of the man in the blue suit. "This is Bud Celt, Steve. He sells the Perry Food Products out of Parisville."

Steve shook Celt's hand briefly, looking at the tight, long face of the man, a man of perhaps forty-five; the face broke with a much-used smile, showing crooked but very white teeth. But the eyes, Steve noticed, did not smile.

"Any trouble at the jail, Steve?" Ben Blake asked.

"No," Steve said abruptly. "The trouble's in Harry Bell's pool hall."

All the men waited in front of him, tense, curious.

"They're apparently from Ashford," Steve said. "Hillary, the newspaperman, seems to think they're friends of Jack Kelty."

There was another silence, as though everyone had stopped breathing for a moment, then Emil Dome grunted, "Why didn't you kick their butts out of there, Steve?"

Steve looked at him quickly. "How?"

"Hell, you've got that machine gun—what have they got?"

"I don't know, Emil. At least one gun, probably more."

"Give me the tommy gun, and I'll show you how to handle them."

"On what basis, Emil?" Steve said.

"What do you mean, what basis?"

"I mean, you're going to go in there and cut them down? You'd have to, to get them to move. So you cut five kids down. How do you rationalize that?"

"I don't have to rationalize it!" Emil Dome said loudly. "They've broken into one of our stores here, so they've broke the law. Give me the tommy gun and I'll take care of them!"

"I thought I was the law now, Emil," Steve said, eyes thinning.

Emil Dome's thick head seemed to plunge a little deeper into the rolled folds of flesh around his neck. He hunched his vast sloping shoulders. "Let's not use that tone with me, Michaels—"

"Take it easy, Emil," Ben Blake said suddenly. "We're all edgy right now. Let's just get this all straight first. What do you think they're after, Steve? And what are we going to do about it?"

"What they're after is anybody's guess. There's a rumor they're hoping to break Kelty out. But they don't seem to have any definite plans."

"Well," Bud Celt, the salesman, said, "how did they know enough to come here?"

"They apparently followed Hillary in. To me, it looks like they got a big idea and fell in love with it. They're here, all right, but I don't think they know much about where they're going. Maybe it's enough for them to have gotten here, just to be around their big hero. Maybe they won't cause any more trouble."

"All right," Emil Dome said, "but what if they do?"

"We're going to have to see that they don't."

Tim Crawford, who had scurried to Ben Blake's office the minute he'd locked his wife in their house, had been pacing steadily, eyes blinking rapidly, listening. Now he stopped and looked at Steve.

"What do you mean we! You're the appointed sheriff of this town, aren't you, Michaels? Can't you handle it?"

Steve turned to him. "Yes, I've been appointed the sheriff of this town. And if I want you to do something, I want you to do it!"

"Well, by God!" Tim Crawford said. "That's up to the mayor, not you, Michaels! Where do you come off with that?"

"You don't want to let this go to your head, Michaels," Emil Dome said choppily. "Because I'm telling you—"

"Shut up, Emil," Ben Blake said. He looked around, grim-faced. "I don't blame Steve for snapping at you, Tim. Steve was around when we needed a sheriff, so I appointed him. Now don't get the idea you can start yelling at him. You too, Emil. We're all in this together, and the less arguing, the better off we'll be. Does everybody understand that?"

Emil Dome shifted his shoulders again. "This boy's practically your son-in-law, isn't he, Ben?"

Ben Blake looked at him. "Yes, he is, Emil. Is that all right with you?"

Emil Dome pulled a wooden match from his pocket and lit his cold cigar, looking at the flame, not answering.

Ben Blake turned to Steve. "What do you propose, Steve?"

"It seems to me we'd better keep a steady watch on the pool hall. Make sure nobody in town gets near them, and make sure they don't get near anybody in town. They've taken a position that they broke into the pool hall for shelter. All right, now they've got the shelter and they're going to stay there. Did they eat in your place, Tim?"

"Ate and swore at my wife and—"

"Then they don't need anything. All we've got to worry about is getting through the night. Tomorrow we'll be all right. Then we can bring in the entire state police force if necessary, to take care of them. But we'd better get started right now. Who's going to take the first shift?"

Tim Crawford said angrily, "What do you mean who's going to take the first shift? I've already said it—this is your job, Michaels! You took the job and you've got it. Why run us in?"

"I'll tell you again," Ben Blake said, "just shut up, Tim. I'll take the first shift."

"So will I," Emil Dome said. "I'll take a shift all night. I don't need any sleep."

"All right—two of you at a time. One in front. One in back. Just keep your eye on the doors. If any of them try to walk out, tell them to go back in. You'll need guns to back it up."

"How about that tommy gun, Michaels?" Emil Dome said.

Steve looked at him, then shook his head.

"All right," Dome said abruptly, "I've got my rifle in my truck. I can pick off anybody I need to with that."

"I've got a shotgun in the back of my drugstore," Si Metcomb said. "We can use that."

Steve said to Emil Dome, "Let's forget picking anyone off, shall we? You can work out your own shifts. If you want to work all night, Emil, that's fine. Just don't start anything with them. Tell them to stay in there if they start out. If they don't, warn them again. If they still won't listen, fire over their heads. If they go anyway, then shoot to hit, and not before. Keep somebody up here in this office. If a shot's fired, for any reason, call me at the jail. I'll come over fast. Remember, they're armed. The main thing, just don't incite them, just don't start anything. All right?"

"All right, Steve," Ben Blake said briskly. Emil Dome looked out a window, his cigar planted firmly between his teeth.

Steve walked to the door. Ben Blake said, "Let's go over to your store, Si, and pick up that gun. Emil and I'll go over there right now, before they decide to try to blow up the main street."

Emil Dome laughed softly and without humor. "I'd like to see that. They're going to be a bunch of dead possums if they try anything with me around, I'll tell you that."

Steve held the door open. "Remember what I told you, Emil."

"Are you ordering me?" Dome said meanly.

"As a matter of fact, yes."

"Okay," Ben Blake said. "We'll handle it, Steve. Don't worry. You just concentrate on Kelty."

Steve nodded finally. He stepped out and closed the door behind him, but not before he heard Emil Dome say, "Kind of nice, I guess, Ben, to look forward to a boy to watch over for a change when you've raised a couple of girls. It's a fact that kid's got a lot more confidence on account of being hooked up with you through your daughter. Funny thing, though, how Michaels looks at those punks in the pool hall. I reckon it's because he was no-good, south-end trash himself once, that he don't want no shooting at them trash bastards...."

Steve felt his middle tighten as he drove away. It was a feeling he'd had so many times now that he wouldn't be complete without it. Emil Dome's last words rang in his head. In that simple fashion, the words had, for the moment, stripped him of every ounce of pride he'd developed over the last years.

He turned left at the flagpole, after giving a quick look at the now-inactive pool hall area, and used the route past the newspaper office and the meat market.

The sky was clear and black now except for a vast sparkling of stars. The earlier breeze had died. Heat hung oppressively over the entire town. There was a faint but persistent smell of the river in the air everywhere now, and Steve thought about the muddy water rushing all around Blue Valley. For a moment he thought: I should never have come back. I should have stayed a thousand miles away, and the river could have washed the whole damn thing away. I could have read about it and never have given a damn....

He drove out of pure instinct, blind to the familiar houses passed. He forgot about Jack Kelty locked in the jail and the group of youths firing themselves up in the pool hall. For a moment, he was aware only of how, before he'd come back, he'd been certain that he really hated this town, knowing, at the same time, that the hate was because he'd once loved it deeply. Why, then, had he come back? Why had he given in to a stubborn insistence that he would prove himself to this town? Because what, after all, was this town? Tim Crawford? Emil Dome? Yes. And people like Ben Blake? Yes, Ben Blake represented Blue Valley to him too, perhaps was Blue Valley in many ways—the envied part. Now he was about to marry Ben Blake's daughter and make his proving-out undeniable. Who was going to argue with Ben Blake's son-in-law?

But would that change anything, really? You had something go wrong, like this, and instantly you were being fought, suddenly and instinctively, because the old feeling was constantly under the surface with people like Tim Crawford and Emil Dome. So Ben was fronting for him—but if you took Ben away, what then?

Muscles stood rigid on his jaw as he parked the car behind the jail. He looked at the yellow light flowing through the barred windows. He came back to reality, thinking once again of Jack Kelty; he thought too of those kids in the pool hall, aching to break him out....

For a moment, he felt the chill of knowing he might very well be alone if it came down to the final test. He closed his eyes, thinking of

Duggan, a cold, lifeless body in a courthouse storage room, but somehow still alive in mind. He had felt an unusual sympathy with Duggan in the brief time he'd been in his presence.

They'd all had something in common, Duggan had said: Steve, Kelty, Duggan. But Kelty had made one choice. Duggan and Steve had made the opposite one. Kelty was not going to change, no matter if they burned him. Duggan was dead, and he'd been true to his principles to the final breath. And so, he asked himself, where did that leave Steve Michaels? What would Steve Michaels prove to be before this was over? A hypocrite? No-good, south-end trash …?

The night was going to bring everything out, he was sure, as he strode up the sidewalk to the jail. Something tough and insistent told him very positively that it was going to be a bad night in Blue Valley; that when it was over, all the true colors in everybody were going to be showing, like a vivid rainbow appearing in a sky just cleared of thunder and lightning.

Chapter 15

The interior of the jail seemed at first glance just as he'd left it. Hillary was once again typing, Rodney Newall was seated at the desk with the shotgun before him, Mr. Potter had returned to a cell and was again asleep, Harry Bell was sitting in a chair beside the wall.

Then Steve saw Gretchen sitting on the cot that had been used by Al Duggan, legs crossed. There was a half-smile on her lips. Kelty also seemed amused. It was as though something had just been said between them and Steve's entrance had stopped the interchange midway.

Steve looked closer at Rod Newall and saw that he was flushed, either out of anger or embarrassment. Then Steve's eyes caught those of Harry Bell. Harry grinned at him weakly, and Steve knew what the watery, flaccid look of his eyes meant. He looked at the bottle on Hillary's packing crate and saw that it had gone down considerably.

For a moment he felt a pump of anger; Harry was fairly drunk right now, even though he sat with practiced rigidity on the chair. But then Steve thrust aside the anger. Harry had helped him once. He could not expect Harry, old now and given in to the bottle he'd once warned Steve against, to keep on providing help. He turned his attention back to Gretchen.

"You told Rod that I sent you over here?"

Gretchen looked at him for a moment, then stood up slowly. She smiled, and Steve felt the impact of all her attractiveness. She walked to him. Her white dress was belted tightly at the waist so that her breasts thrust forward sharply against the fabric.

"I got bored at home, Steve. Are you going to spank me?"

Kelty laughed from his cell. Steve looked past Gretchen and saw the shrewd, dark eyes moving over the girl's body. "If you don't want to, Michaels, I'll take care of it for you," Kelty said.

Gretchen turned, making the turn almost a pirouette, arching her eyebrows at Kelty, then faced Steve again, that half-smile returning to her lips.

The telephone rang. Rod, his angry eyes on Gretchen, picked it up. "All right." He motioned the telephone to Steve. "Si Metcomb."

Steve went over. "Yes?"

"I opened the drugstore for Ben and he's got the gun. He's in back in the alley. Emil's out front across the street. Ben said I should call and tell you that. I don't like this, Michaels. When this thing's over, there are going to be some changes made in this town so that decent citizens don't have to get involved like this."

"Where's Tim Crawford, Si?"

"He went home to see about his wife. He and I are supposed to relieve Ben in two hours, but I don't think Tim's coming back. I'll tell you this. In two hours if he isn't back, I'm not going back in that alley by myself—"

"All right, Si. We'll worry about that in two hours. If Tim hasn't shown up by then, call me. How about Celt, the salesman?"

"He's asleep. He says if he were a citizen of Blue Valley, he'd be glad to help. But this is a local matter, he says, and he doesn't want to get mixed up in it any more than any of us would want to get mixed up in something that got all twisted up over in Parisville."

"For God's sake!"

"I'll tell you this too," Si Metcomb said. "The man who started this is that detective who brought Kelty in here in the first place. What business did he have doing that anyway? Then he just goddamn ups and dies!"

"Well," Steve said angrily, "that kind of talk doesn't really get us anywhere, does it, Si?"

He dropped the telephone hard and looked at Gretchen again. If Ben knew she was here....

There was a sharp rapping at the door. Steve went over. "Yes?"

"Steve Michaels, are you in there?" The voice was high-pitched, with a hysterical edge in it.

Rodney Newall closed his eyes, flushing. Steve glanced at him, then said, "Are you alone, Mrs. Newall?"

"Yes! Is my boy in there? Is Rodney in that jail?"

Jack Kelty laughed. He sat down on his cell bunk, rubbing his palms over his face, shaking his head, laughing again. Rod's mouth tightened; his flush became deeper.

"Go ahead, boy," Kelty said, looking up. "Open the door. Your mamma wants you."

Gretchen giggled as Steve opened the door. Hillary leaned back in his chair, an amused and attentive look in his eyes.

Mrs. Newall hurried in, a rather thin, large-eyed woman whose every movement somehow seemed to be like the fluttering of a grounded bird; nervous, quick, and with an appearance of a lack of direction. She came in wearing an expensive blue dress and a recent permanent wave; since her husband's death she had spent a good deal of money on clothes and beauty efforts. Still, there was somehow an unfitted, upheavaled effect about her entire look.

Her large and worried eyes found Rod immediately. She moved toward him, then saw the gun resting on the desk. Suddenly her eyes switched to Kelty grinning at her from his cell. She stopped so hard that she gave the appearance of skidding on her high heels. Her arms came up in a fluttering motion, her eyes growing even larger. Then she turned to Steve.

"What are you doing to my boy! That man's a killer!"

"Mom, for Pete's sake!" Rod said, standing up, face burning.

"I won't have my boy in here with guns and a maniac like that!"

"Mom—"

Kelty laughed again; Gretchen giggled with him.

"Look, Mrs. Newall—" Steve paused, instantly understanding Rod's position. Hillary, he saw, was still smiling amusedly, leaning back from his typewriter.

"Hillary," Steve said, "do you suppose it would be too much to watch this shop if we step outside for a minute?"

"Glad to," Hillary smiled. "If Jack jumps through the bars, I'll whistle."

"You do that."

Harry Bell stood up with effort. "I'll take care of things, Steve." His voice gave him away. He grinned foolishly.

Mrs. Newall whirled. "Harry Bell, you're drunk!"

"Now, Fay, where did you get an idea like that?"

Mrs. Newall rotated back to Steve, sniffing. She looked at Rod and sniffed again. Then her eyes found the bottle on the packing crate. She thrust her head forward in Gretchen's direction, her eager nostrils going again. "You've been drinking, too, haven't you!"

Steve looked with surprise at Gretchen; he hadn't noticed that.

Gretchen smiled with satisfaction, turned her back and returned to the cot with a good deal of hip movement. She sat down and crossed her legs, eyes flitting to Kelty.

Mrs. Newall turned to Steve with flashing eyes. "I'm astonished at you for letting things like this go on!"

Harry Bell walked unsteadily to the packing crate and picked up Hillary's bottle of Scotch. He uncapped it and held it out to Mrs. Newall. "Why don't you take a little jolt, Fay? It might do you good."

Mrs. Newall seemed to blaze. "Right in front of my son!"

Harry Bell tipped the bottle up, drank, shook his head mightily, a shudder going through his body. Mrs. Newall gasped.

"Mom, listen—" Rod began, coming toward her.

"You get right out of here, Rodney!" she said, pointing to the door. "I don't want you in here with this sort of thing going on!"

"Come on, Fay," Harry Bell said, motioning the bottle. "It'll warm up your soul."

"You shut up, Harry Bell!"

"Sweeten your disposition."

"All right, Harry," Steve said, "Mrs. Newall, you and Rod step outside, please. Harry, why don't you sit down?"

Harry Bell straightened, looking at Steve with suddenly misting eyes. He sniffed and rubbed a hand clumsily at his mouth. "Sorry, Steve. You just can't count on me, can you? I'm no damn good, am I?"

"Never mind, Harry. Why don't you take a nap?"

"No, sir!" He started for his chair, went off course for a few steps, regained direction, then sat down very carefully and held himself rigidly. "I'm going to sit right here. I won't let you down, Steve."

"I've never been so angry in my life!" said Mrs. Newall.

"Easy, Mrs. Newall," Steve said quietly. He guided her to the door. "Come on, Rod."

The three of them went outside. Immediately Mrs. Newall said, "You didn't come home when you said you would, Rodney. And then I heard about that terrible killer being brought into town, right after all of this horrible flood around us. I've been half out of my mind! Why do you worry your mother so? I'm just about sick with a headache and you don't even tell your mother where you are. I finally telephoned Katherine Blake, and she told me you were here. Now I don't want you going back in that jail again!"

"Mrs. Newall," Steve said, trying to control his patience, "I asked Rod to help me."

She turned to him, bristling. "Did you ask him to take a drink of booze too?"

Steve took a breath. "No. And I'm sure Rod doesn't want one."

"Well, he'd better not! Now I'm taking him home."

"Just a moment, Mrs. Newall. I realize you're excited. But I need Rod here. I just don't have anybody else."

"You mean," Rod said thinly, "you'd get somebody else if you could?"

"No, Rod. I don't mean that at all. You've handled yourself very well. I just wouldn't want to lose you tonight."

"Well, I don't care what you want or don't want, Steve Michaels. Rodney's going home with me where he belongs."

"I can understand how you feel, Mrs. Newall," Steve said. "But this is a real and a definite emergency. We need everybody we can get, and I personally need Rod's help, right here, right now. That's Jack Kelty in there, Mrs. Newall!"

"That's just one of the main reasons why my son has no business in there!"

"Look. Tomorrow morning we'll be all right. But tonight we're in trouble. There's a group of toughs downtown in the pool hall who could be very dangerous. Weren't you called about that?"

"Yes, I was called! Alice Stritt called and told me to stay home because of those wild hoodlums. But my boy was gone! And—"

"Mom, you could have telephoned. If you'll just listen—"

"I'll tell you one thing, son. If your father were here, it would all be different. But your father isn't. I'm all alone in this world, but for you. I'm just a poor widow, but I try to do the best I can. I think I know what's best just now, Rodney. And what's best is for you to come home with your mother until all of this is over. I can't call on your father to help me do things because he's in his grave, God rest him. So I just ask you to mind your mother without argument. Let's go, son."

"Mrs. Newall," Steve said, "I'm not taking sides in a family discussion. I'm just telling you we're in real trouble if Rod goes. I don't say there isn't danger here, there may very well be. But there'll be a lot more to the whole town if he goes. I'll tell you truthfully I just don't want him to go!"

Mrs. Newall looked at Steve with narrowed eyes. Then she turned and started down the walk. "Coming, Rodney?"

Rod stood unmoving, staring after her.

She stopped, turned around, then said very calmly, "Rodney? We're going home now."

Rod was silent for a moment, then he said clearly, "No, Mom."

Mrs. Newall blinked. "No?" All at once her face twisted and tears were in her eyes. "No, you say to me?"

"That's right," Rod said firmly. "You go ahead home. I'll be here until tomorrow morning."

"You don't mean that, Rodney! You don't mean that you'll stand there and oppose me, son. Not the first time in your life and your poor father lying in his grave unable to help me!"

"I can't help it. I'm needed here."

Tears tracked down Mrs. Newall's cheeks. "Son, I'll just ask you again. Your mother wants you to come home now. Are you coming with her?"

"No, Mom."

Mrs. Newall seemed to stagger, then she recovered her spirit, blinked back the tears and came back, stopping straight in front of Steve. "What are you doing to my son, Steve Michaels?"

"Mrs. Newall, I'm not doing anything to him. I'm just asking for his help which I need pretty desperately."

Her mouth trembled. "You come back here to Blue Valley! You come back here and act like you're so worried about young ones here! We let you come here and teach and coach our boys, and now what are you doing?"

"Mrs. Newall—"

"I ask you! Drinking going on in there. That little Blake strut smelling like a brewery. Your old friend Harry Bell so drunk he can't even walk! The Lord only knows what effect being around that horrible Jack Kelty could have on a young boy. And you ask my son, my young, dear son, to stay with you in that sin pit, regardless of the danger to his life, let alone his morals, and— I tell you, Steve Michaels, we don't forget what you were in this town once! We don't forget you were a tough and snotty little bum they had to send away …!"

"Mom," Rod said in a very low and trembling voice.

"You let me handle this, Rodney," Mrs. Newall said, building up her fury. "You never were any good, Steve Michaels. You aren't any good now!"

"Mom, shut up!" Rod said loudly.

Mrs. Newall blinked, her mouth opening. She turned, blinked again and wagged her head in disbelief. "I heard wrong, son. I must have! You'd never—"

"I'll say it just once more. Please shut up now and go home and lock the door and stay there, please!"

Again Mrs. Newall seemed to stagger, then she regained her balance. She stood poised as though on the edge of a cliff. Suddenly she let out a yowl that was somewhere between an Indian whoop and a cry given by a man just hit severely in the stomach. Tears poured down her cheeks. She closed her mouth, swallowing, then opened it again and screamed in mortal agony.

The jail door swung open. Harry Bell staggered out.

"Harry," Steve said, "get back in there, will you?"

Harry Bell stared blinkingly at Mrs. Newall, then stepped back and shut the door.

Mrs. Newall put two tightly clenched fists to her temples, spun half around and screamed again. Then she started weaving down the sidewalk. She stumbled once, arms flying.

Rod and Steve started forward to help her.

But she regained her balance and bent in a semi-crouch. "No, you don't! Keep away from me! Both of you. I don't know you! Not even my own son! You aren't my son anymore!" She shook her head desperately, tears glistening on her face. She yelled once more, then staggered off down the sidewalk.

"Maybe you'd better help her, Rod," Steve said. "Go home with her for a while, at least. I can—"

"She'll be all right. She'll go home and stay there. I'm sure of that."

"I'm sorry, Rod. Under any other circumstance—"

"That was the first time I ever disobeyed her."

Steve nodded. "Yes."

She had reached the street now and turned for home a block away. She let out another terrible scream. Rod closed his eyes. "The trouble with her is that she gets all excited. She goes half nuts sometimes. Doc Renley says it's her change of life. He says she'll get over it in anywhere from six months to ten years. I hope to God it's six months, I really do!"

Steve watched the boy swing open the door and stride inside. He followed, smiling faintly, suddenly certain of Rodney Newall.

Between the Midwest Auto Supply building and the Farmer's Grocery building—these two structures being directly across the street from Harry Bell's pool hall—was an open space perhaps six feet wide that ran from the main street sidewalk to the alley behind. When Ben Blake had collected the shotgun from Si Metcomb's drugstore and gone down the opposite alley to wait behind the pool hall, Emil Dome had hurried along the alley on this side of the street, fat jouncing, to the gap between buildings.

He now waited behind a pile of orange crates, his .30–.30 rifle feeling good and familiar in his pudgy hands. Through slats of the top box on the pile he had a good, clear view of the pool hall. In turn, he knew he could not be seen. The stars shone above in a great sweep of scattered silver pinpoints; bits of broken glass on the cluttered surface of the ground winked back at them.

Emil Dome hunched his vast, sloping shoulders, ducking his head a little, touching a round cheek against the rifle as he pointed it across the street. He looked down the sights at a figure moving along the length of Harry Bell's bar. Come in from the city and start pushing things around, huh? All right, he thought, feeling very cool right now. If one of them so much as inched a toe out of that pool hall, that one, by God, was going to be lying right on the sidewalk kicking like a gut-shot jack-rabbit....

Chapter 16

"Where's your mamma, Rodney?" Jack Kelty asked, when Steve and Rod returned to the interior of the Blue Valley jail.

Gretchen, legs crossed, her dress riding carelessly above one dimpled knee, smiled and watched Rod with dancing eyes. Rod remained absolutely silent.

Steve said, "Take the desk again, Rod, will you?"

Rod sat down, the shotgun before him.

"What happened downtown, Michaels?" Hillary asked. "Those kids cause you any trouble?"

Kelty waited expectantly for the answer, but Steve did not give it. He put down the machine gun, picked up the telephone and dialed the

Blake house. In a moment Sue answered. "Sue, would you come down and pick up Gretchen?"

"She's in bed, Steve."

"Well, there are two of her then."

There was a moment's silence. "She must have sneaked out in the confusion—this place is a madhouse. A couple of women came over to stay with Mother and build up their mutual spirits. They called some others, now we're got an entire female colony milling around. I'll drive down right now, Steve."

Steve put down the telephone.

"I asked a question, Michaels," Hillary said.

"I heard it."

"Look. You may as well understand that I write things just the way I see them. If you fail to cooperate with me, that's the way it'll be printed in the newspaper."

"Why do you think I'd worry about that, Hillary?" Steve motioned to Gretchen. "Do you want to come with me?" He held the door open for her. She walked across the jail, turned and said, "Good night, Rod, dear." But she was smiling at Kelty.

"Come back fast, sweetheart," Kelty said. "We're going to miss you."

Steve said to Rod, "Same orders. If he tries anything, shoot. No questions asked."

He followed Gretchen outside and shut the door behind them. "What was the idea?"

"I wanted a better chance to see what he looks like."

"Satisfied now?"

She shrugged noncommittally.

Steve leaned back against the wall of the jail, and Gretchen stood close to him. He got out his pack of cigarettes, shook one out and put it between his lips.

"Me too?"

He looked at her in the streetlight illumination. "Wasn't Hillary's Scotch enough?"

"I didn't have any of Hillary's Scotch. I had a drink at home. I told Mother I was upset, and she let me."

"Did she tell you to start smoking too?"

"I'm not starting. I've been smoking for a month. I'm a big girl now, or hadn't you noticed?"

He held a match for her. She put her hand on his, taking her time lighting her cigarette as she looked at him, the flame reflecting in her eyes. "You have noticed, haven't you, Steve?"

He lit his own cigarette and tossed the match away.

"Are you angry with me, Steve?"

"You keep looking for trouble, Gretchen, you'll find it."

She moved closer to him. "Are you speaking personally? And what kind of trouble?"

"I'm talking about Jack Kelty. He isn't just a pleasant game to be played, Gretchen. He's an honest-to-God killer. Look at his eyes. He's tightening up. He knows those kids came to town to help him if they could. He knows that may be his last chance. He'll do anything he can to shake loose now. Why don't you cooperate, Gretchen? I gave Rod an order, why did you make him break it?"

"Am I that influential?"

"It's been proven, hasn't it?"

"Poor Rod."

"He's a nice kid and you know it."

"He's such a baby."

"And you aren't?"

"Do you think so, Steve?" She moved even closer.

"No, I guess I don't."

"I'm old enough to know what I want."

"And what is that?"

She tipped her chin up a little. He felt her hand touching his waist. "Steve—"

"I'm marrying your sister," he said. "Or have you forgotten?"

"You haven't married her yet—"

He stepped away from her and sent his cigarette spinning in a red-sparked arc over the lawn. "It's too bad Ben doesn't have a cell in his house. I'd escort you home personally, lock you in it and throw away the key."

Gretchen's laugh was musical as car lights whipped around the corner. In a moment, Sue was striding up the walk from her yellow convertible. Steve said, "Go out and wait in the car, Gretchen."

Gretchen turned from him sharply and walked away down the sidewalk. Sue met her halfway. "Gretchen, didn't you promise—?"

But Gretchen walked straight to the car, climbed in and slammed the door without another word. Sue came up to Steve. "Damn. I swear, I'm going to be the one who delivers that spanking. Or make it a full beating."

"I may help you." Steve smiled.

He could tell by the look in her eyes that she was angry. There was a tighter mold to her face when she was. But in a moment, she smiled a little, coolly.

"How is it going, darling? I've talked to Daddy about those boys in the pool hall. He said he and Emil Dome were going to watch and make sure they didn't leave."

Steve nodded, examining her. Gretchen may have been a slight favorite with Ben, even more than that. Gretchen might be the one who had been spoiled. But Sue was also Ben Blake's daughter, the handsome, poised, well-controlled older daughter, who called her father "Daddy" and was the select product of his created environment. Ben Blake's daughter—it was still hard to believe that he was going to marry Ben Blake's daughter.

"Are they in danger downtown, Steve?"

He took his eyes from her and looked across the lawn, reflectively. "I think those kids are mainly bluff. The only way there could be real danger is if they fight. I don't think they'll fight unless they're pushed too far. Ben won't push them. But Dome worries me."

"Why?"

He started to answer, then shrugged. "No reason, I guess."

He looked back at her, suddenly wanting to shake all worries, to take the minute, the second, and worry about whatever was going to happen when it happened. He felt a sudden and peculiar strangeness toward this town and everyone in it, as though he'd never lived here, never come back until this evening, and then as a stranger. He looked at Sue, and somehow the awareness of who she was fell away from his mind. He looked at her, and suddenly she was no longer Ben Blake's daughter, but a flesh-and-blood woman, vital, beautiful, well-shaped, with inviting eyes and mouth....

He reached out and pulled her almost roughly to him. He tested that mouth, felt the body firm in his hands....

Sue caught her breath. She looked up at him, eyes serious. "Never like that before, Steve. Never like that—"

"I want you, Sue."

She nodded, her eyes unwavering.

"Now," he said. "Right now."

Again she nodded. "Yes." Her voice seemed almost crisp, but there was a faint trembling below the surface. He kissed her again, roughly.

She whispered, "I'll take Gretchen home. Mrs. Corpler's there. I'll get her keys for her office. I'll tell her it's a place for you to rest. I'll come back—"

Then she turned from him and was moving down the walk, a tall, lithe, handsome woman who knew as well as he what they both wanted.

"What time is it, Hillary?" Jack Kelty asked.

Hillary looked at his watch. "Twenty-two minutes after eleven."

Steve sat at the desk. A moment ago he had dialed Mrs. Corpler's office telephone. Sue was there, waiting. In a few minutes, he would be relieved by Rod, and then he would go up. He felt a pulsation of excitement. Then he glanced at Rod stretched out on the cot, at Harry Bell sitting resolutely in his chair, staying somewhere just between semi-sobriety and solid drunkenness. He listened to Mr. Potter still snoring in one of the cells. He was aware of the entire situation, but he tried to keep his mind totally on Sue, in an attempt to forget momentarily the worries he'd developed.

"Michaels," Jack Kelty said, his voice forcibly casual, "those punks in the pool hall—did you get any names? I mean, is there a blond one calls himself Teller? See, maybe I can tell you something about those guys. Maybe give you an advantage. I'm willing to help, see?"

It was the first time Kelty had made a direct reference to what amounted to his only hope now; he had not done it, finally, with much subtlety. A nervous tic had begun in his right eye. He smiled more frequently, but it was a nervous twitch of lips that did not indicate humor. The pressure was becoming too much, Steve was certain. If he had been dangerous before, he was ten times more so now.

"How about it, Michaels?" he said, voice rising. "Is that right? Is one of them Teller? What's the difference whether you tell me or not? I'm locked up. I'm only trying to help you out."

"Don't worry about it, Kelty," Steve said.

Kelty's face was a sudden mask of rage. "You bastard!"

Steve looked at him without answering.

Kelty began to pace, clenching and unclenching his hands. "You hick bastard. Screw you! You stink!"

"Take it easy, Kelty," Steve said softly.

"Goddamn hick cop! Why don't you come in here? Unlock the cell and come in here! Goddamn you, I'll kill you with my bare hands!"

Hillary now was looking at Kelty carefully, surprised by the outburst. What did he expect? Steve thought. Had he begun to believe his own copy? Then Hillary nodded faintly to himself, as though he understood finally that Kelty had reached that no-return point, so that if he didn't get free tonight he was going to wind up a screaming maniac.

"So help me," Kelty breathed viciously, "I'll kill you, Michaels!" Rod raised himself, looking at him. Kelty whirled. "You too, you sniveling bastard! Why don't you run home to your mamma?"

Rod's face darkened. He got up from the cot slowly. "I'll take you up on coming into that cell, Kelty. I'll—"

"Sit down, Rod," Steve said quietly.

"Yeah, sit down, stand up, go screw yourself on the ceiling, mamma's boy!" Kelty's voice had risen almost to a scream, then he turned and went to the far wall, leaning his head against the cool concrete, visibly trembling.

Rod finally looked at Steve. Steve met the boy's eyes. Frowning a little, Rod looked back at Kelty, then quietly sat down. In a moment, Kelty had control of himself. He turned around, his smile returning. Hillary, Steve noticed, had watched Kelty's entire performance with fascinated attention. Now he suddenly bent forward and began typing rapidly. Kelty came up to the bars, and thrust his hands through. "Out of cigarettes, Michaels. How about it?"

Steve opened a desk drawer, got out a new pack and tossed it to him. Kelty got a cigarette out, lit it and blew smoke at the ceiling.

"What time is it, Hillary?" he asked.

But this time Hillary was too busy recording what he had just seen and heard to answer.

In her bedroom on the second floor of the large white house, Gretchen listened to the hum of women's voices below. She had just showered, draped herself in a large white towel and now was sitting on her bed with a glass of brandy in her hand. The brandy was from a bottle picked up from the downstairs bar and sneaked upstairs as a matter of defiance for being left out of absolutely everything.

She swirled the liquid in the glass, gazing at it with her eyebrows arched in sophistication. Then she tossed it all down. Eyes stinging, she stood up and strode impatiently to a window. She could see the garage from here and had watched when Sue had left in her yellow convertible, hurried, flushed, excited. She'd heard her ask Mrs. Corpler for that office key. Something was going to happen, all right.

"Damn!" Gretchen said aloud.

She stood thoughtfully, remembering the keys she'd secretly had made in Parisville recently when Sue had let her borrow the convertible, an act committed just so that she could feel she owned a part of that car too; Daddy had promised her one of her own, but not until she was seventeen, the age Sue had gotten her first car.

She walked back to the vanity and got the keys from a drawer. Then she dug into another drawer and brought out a tissue-wrapped package. She opened the package and took out the black lingerie she'd bought when she'd gone with Daddy to the Agricultural Convention in Ashford six months ago. This possession was also a secret, because Mother had this thing about black and young girls, and moreover the bra had a striking uplift that would never pass inspection.

She got out her best stockings and began carefully dressing, examining her figure before she slipped a dusty blue cotton dress over her head. Then, finally, gazing at herself in the dress, she was satisfied. The blue brought out her tan magnificently, and the bra certainly didn't hurt anything.

She picked up the cars keys and opened her door. The hall was empty. She ran lightly down the back stairway.

At the small hallway between the kitchen and the back door, she looked into the kitchen. Mrs. Horvall, back turned, was pouring coffee; in the living room sounded a chatter of female voices.

Gretchen ran out the back door, then across the yard to the sidewalk. The street was silent; she moved very quickly. In no time, she had reached the courthouse.

She got into the convertible, nervously watching all doors. But nobody came out, even when she started the engine.

She didn't know what she wanted to do or where she wanted to go. She only knew that she had to do *something*. She kept thinking of Jack Kelty, and doing that sent her blood racing, even though she did not know exactly why. It was just that she knew he would be nothing like Rod, stumbling and inefficient. Jack Kelty had been around, and she wanted to know, really know, how she would affect Jack Kelty, who must know everything, if she were ever in a situation with him as she had been with Rod. That would prove something to her, beyond a doubt.

Mrs. Corpler's office was on the back side, so she couldn't see those windows now, but all the windows in the front were dark. The yellow bar-patterned light of the jail's windows showed plainly, but there was not a movement visible from where she sat, not a sound.

Frustration brewing, she put the car in gear and drove down the street, ready for anything.

Before Steve had gone upstairs to the office where Sue was waiting he'd told Rod to dial the number of Mrs. Corpler's telephone in case he was needed. But he had convinced himself by the time he got upstairs that he would not be needed.

Mrs. Corpler's office was bathed in bright ceiling light. The Venetian blinds on the three high windows were tilted shut. There were two desks, stacks of ledgers on a long table, an old leather couch that Mrs. Corpler used to rest her arthritic bones when business was slow, a water cooler, a typewriter on one of the desks, a telephone on the other. Sue, eyes dark, stood beside the desk that held the telephone, near the leather couch.

He came around the front counter, put the tommy gun beside the telephone and slipped his arms around her, looking at her. Her eyes met his for a moment, then she bent her head a little, closing her eyes, pressing close to him.

He'd seen something in her eyes in that moment. It was an intelligent surmise by an intelligent woman of a situation. She had, with her canny ability, realized that he was dulling the pressure with this, using this, the ultimate physical achievement between them, to quiet himself for a moment. Yet, he'd seen the judgment leave her eyes to be replaced by a look of purest desire. It meant only, he knew, that she loved him.

"Bright in here," he whispered.

She nodded against his chest. He reached across her shoulder and snapped off the ceiling lights. Then his mouth was on hers, feeling it open, her body shuddering as she turned herself over to him....

The sound of the telephone ringing was like something heard in a dream. It was far away, unreal. He was sure he was only imagining it, because he did not want to hear that or anything else. But it became louder in his ears, more insistent.

He finally picked it up. He held her with one arm and said, "Yes?"

Rod Newall said, "Steve, we're in real trouble now. Emil Dome killed one of those guys who was in the pool hall. Ben Blake phoned and said Emil Dome dropped one of them only they didn't know if he'd killed him. Then when I'd hung up, the phone rang again and it was this guy Teller, screaming wild. He said Dome fired for no reason and you've had it now. He said he's going to call back in one hour, and if you haven't let Kelty go by then, he said they're going to start tearing this town apart inch by inch …!"

Steve looked at Sue, knowing she had heard Rod's voice. He blinked, stunned. Then he said, "I'll be right down, Rod." He hung up and picked up the machine gun. "Stay here, Sue. Lock the door and don't leave this office under any circumstance." He strode out and down the marble steps, trying to control the wild anger surging in him....

Chapter 17

The volunteer guard on the pool hall had collapsed like a matchstick house.

Steve found this out the instant he telephoned Ben Blake's office from the jail. He got Ben Blake's voice immediately.

"Steve, this is a hell of a mess. Emil thinks he killed that kid."

"He did, Ben."

"Well, how do you know that?"

"Never mind now, Ben. I'll explain. Where's Dome?"

"Right here!"

"Well, who's watching the pool hall?"

"Nobody's watching the pool hall. Everything's gone wrong. Those rotten kids—when I went around to see what happened to Emil, they broke out the back way!"

Steve closed his eyes, opened them. "For God's sake, Ben."

"I don't like that tone, Steve! Let's get that straight right now!"

"All right, Ben. You'd better get down here. They might try to rush the jail. We're going to need everybody we can get."

"I'll bring everybody over there," Ben Blake snapped, and hung up.

Hillary stood beside the desk. "How did it happen?"

"I don't know. We'll find out pretty soon. There's one thing— Those kids, except for the one Dome killed, are on the loose now."

Kelty, who had been waiting tensely at the bars, smiled; but there was no humor whatever, nothing but a masklike fleeting grin.

"On the loose?" Hillary said.

"The guard on the pool hall fell apart. Where they are now is anybody's guess. What a hell of a sweet situation!"

A few minutes later Ben Blake led in Emil Dome, Si Metcomb, Bud Celt and Tim Crawford.

Tim Crawford spoke first: "That guard idea of yours was brilliant, wasn't it, Michaels?"

The interior of the jail was suddenly crowded. It had the sharp smell of sweat that could have only come from deep fear. It had that and the liquor smell of Harry Bell, who now carefully stood up with glazed eyes, trying to pose at attention. Mr. Potter had arisen and, in a half-fog of sleep, come stumbling out from his cell. Everyone ranged around Steve. Steve looked at Tim Crawford. "What got you out of your lock-up house, Crawford?"

Tim Crawford's eyes blazed. "The more I see of you, Michaels, the more I'm sure we should have closed the gate before you came back into town."

Steve started to answer, then did not. He looked at Emil Dome. "You shot and killed one of them."

Dome, quivering with excitement, grunted. "You're damn right."

"How did it happen?"

"The sonofabitch made a try for it."

"Try for what?"

"For breaking out."

"Did you warn him before you fired?"

"What do you mean did I warn him?"

"I told you that if one of them started out, to warn him. Is that the way you did it?"

"I'll tell you this, Michaels. Do you think anybody's paying any attention to what you say? Goddamn it, all that is stupid! Why am I going to start yelling around and shooting up in the air and give away where I'm hid!"

Steve's mouth had turned white. "In other words, you didn't give any warning at all. You just shot the first one who came outside."

Dome grinned meanly. "Right through the goddamn head!"

Steve stared at him, shaking inside, trying to control himself. "You stupid sonofabitch."

Dome stared back, astounded, all of his vast fat tissues quivering. "I'll knock you on your ass, Michaels!"

Steve continued to stare at Dome, his hand dropping to the machine gun lying in front of him.

"Why," Dome gasped, "you're crazy! You're pulling that tommy gun on me?"

"That's right. And I'm calling you a stupid sonofabitch. Worse! Don't you realize what you've done? You've just killed a human being in cold blood!"

"For good reason!" Dome yelled.

The telephone had started ringing again. The sound was enough to distract Steve and so allow him to pull his senses back together and control his anger again. He said to Rod, "Get it." He watched Ben Blake's face, already darkly angry, flush even more as Rod Newall stepped forward and picked up the telephone.

Rod said, "Yes, he's here." He put the telephone down and said to Ben Blake, "It's your wife."

Ben Blake picked up the telephone with a jerk, hating the youth with his eyes. "Hello, Kate! We've got more damn trouble in this town than it's seen in seventy-five years. Those kids are on the loose. Now you get things started there and tell everyone absolutely to stay inside, no questions. Call Alice and have her go to work from the switchboard. Get everyone to phone everyone else. Anybody wandering around out there right now could be in a hell of a fix!"

He stopped, frowning. He exploded, "What? She's *what?* Well, where the hell is she! Doesn't Sue know?" He turned toward Steve. "Down here? I'll phone you back, for Christ's sake!" He put down the telephone. "Gretchen's gone! Kate says Sue's here. Where is she?"

"In Mrs. Corpler's office. But I'm sure she doesn't know anything about Gretchen. Sue drove down alone."

"Well, I didn't see her car out there!"

Steve looked out a jail window and saw for the first time that the yellow convertible was gone. "Call Sue, Rod."

"Why don't we keep this goddamn kid out of it!" Ben Blake snapped.

"Go ahead, Rod," Steve said.

As Rod dialed, Emil Dome said, "Afraid to take your hand off that gun, Michaels, for fear I might knock your head off?"

Steve did not answer. In a moment Rod was saying, "Do you know anything about Gretchen being gone?" Then, in another moment, "Well, your car's gone and so is Gretchen." He looked at Steve, and Steve said, "Tell her just to stay up there." Rod did and hung up.

"Where the hell is she?" Ben Blake demanded.

"She was here once tonight, Ben."

"Here! In the jail, you mean?"

"I sent her home with Sue, but apparently she should have been sent home with an armed guard to keep her there."

Ben Blake swung toward Rodney Newall. "Is this your fault?"

"Maybe it's just Gretchen's fault, Ben," Steve said. "Did you ever think about that?"

Ben Blake turned to Steve. "You're really beginning to annoy me, Steve."

"I'm sorry about that, Ben. But we've got to look at facts. I'd guess Gretchen took Sue's convertible. I don't know why, but I know this situation has gotten steadily worse. Those kids are loose. A lot of people are in danger, including Gretchen. They've called in, Ben. They're furious, and they've given an ultimatum."

"An ultimatum?" Ben Blake said, frowning.

"They want Kelty released in what amounts to about thirty-five minutes from now. They're going to call then. If we haven't released Kelty, they're threatening to start making serious trouble. You can guess what kind of trouble."

Kelty had been standing attentively inside his cell. Now his hands came up and fitted around the bars tightly.

"Well, by God!" Ben Blake said. "With my daughter out there?"

"I'll tell you what we're going to do—!" Emil Dome began.

"Shut up, Emil," Ben Blake said; he turned, eyes thinning, pacing.

Steve looked at Dome, thinking that though he had made a deputy out of Dome by putting him on that guard, Dome had, by deliberately disregarding orders, committed a felony. When this was over, he was going to ask that Dome be charged with manslaughter. But this was not over, and there was not very much he could do about it right now....

Hillary, these last minutes, had watched and listened with great care, hiding his excitement with a casual exterior.

The situation had developed into potential far beyond his expectations. Most of it was already on paper; and as soon as communication was established with the outside world, Martin Hillary was going to be one of the most famous newspapermen in the United States.

But this was not over yet; there were still hours to go before daybreak, and anything could happen before then.

He watched Ben Blake pacing, then looked at Steve Michaels. He leaned back. Those kids wanted Kelty out in an hour. What, if he were not released, would happen?

Those kids were going to go wild. Innocent people in the village were going to be hurt. There might even be an attempt to rush the jail. Hillary did not much care about the welfare of the innocent people, nor did he once consider the fact that he could have prevented the entry of Kelty's fan club into town in the first place. He was only considering the threat to his own skin in the event of such a try.

But assume, of course, that such a try were unsuccessful—that the fan club could not break in. How, then, would it all end?

It would be a flat ending, in truth, if Kelty's fan club merely hurt two or three of the town's citizens and then, at daybreak, were rounded up and bundled undramatically with Kelty back to Ashford.

Hillary rubbed his chin. Turn it around. Assume Michaels actually let Kelty go. What then?

Then you really had something. Because what, if released, would Kelty do?

Would he join his fan club? No doubt. Then try to get off this island before the troopers poured in? No doubt.

There was no argument about what direction of action would provide the greatest drama and so offer the greatest advantage to Martin Hillary.

His palms pricked with perspiration. But he forcibly repressed his excitement, trying to halt his mind from writing a phase of this story that had not yet begun. The important thing now was to see if that phase could not be nudged into aliveness. It would, he realized, involve a certain amount of risk to himself. Kelty was over the line now, a fact you could detect merely by looking at his eyes. Kelty might turn on him. But the odds were against that, Hillary thought. He'd championed Kelty, and if he did not directly cross him, Kelty should leave him alone. It was a considered risk he would have to take.

He stood up casually and reseated himself on the corner of the packing crate. He smiled and said in a voice loaded with vibrancy, "Gentlemen, I don't think there's any debatable situation here."

Ben Blake stopped pacing. "There isn't? Oh, there isn't?"

"Of course we all wish for better things. But under the circumstances, there seems only one sensible thing to do here."

"And what would that be, Hillary?" Steve snapped.

Hillary looked at Steve, a faint smile at the corners of his mouth, a humorless chuckle escaping his lips. "Let Kelty go."

Chapter 18

Gretchen had driven to the west end of the village, pressing the accelerator down and leaving it down, tearing through Blue Valley at a speed she'd never been able to use within the town's limits before.

When she passed the road sign that said, *COME BACK TO BLUE VALLEY*, she kept going, wildly, the river smell strong now. When she saw the small orange light of a warning lantern resting beside the running board of a Model A Ford, she finally braked, the car skidding haphazardly on the gravel until she plowed to a stop, gravel flying, not twenty yards from where the water had come up.

Frank Dinkier, Blue Valley veteran of seventy-five, friend and cribbage companion of Abner Potter, stepped from his old car and made his way slowly to the convertible. Frank had been one of those put on his lonely vigil by Ben Blake; in case of a further rise of the river, he was to get into his Model A, rattle into town and say the word. But the river had been going down, not up; and Frank had just about gone to sleep when he'd heard the convertible.

Snowy hair ghostly in the light of a moon just appearing, he peered into the yellow car.

"What you doing out here anyways?"

"Leave me alone," Gretchen snapped.

"Well, what way is that to talk?"

"Leave me alone, can't you?"

Frank Dinkier peered at her for a moment longer, then made his tottering way back to his Model A. He looked back at her once, then climbed in his own car and slammed the door so hard the door almost bounced off its hinges. The car creaked as Frank got himself readjusted behind the wheel, then he began to semi-doze again.

Gretchen instantly forgot about Frank Dinkier. She looked through the night, seeing the glinting reflection of the freshly risen moon on the currents of the river, hearing the dull roar of the whirling water. The water was everywhere.

She shivered and looked up at the sweep of stars in the sky, yearning to become weightless and float free and clear straight to the heavens where she could breathe. This town, she thought. *This town*
...

She suddenly opened the glove compartment, remembering that Sue kept extra cigarettes there. She tore a pack open, put a cigarette between her lips and lit it from the dashboard lighter. *Damn!*

She smoked silently, the radio off now, listening to the water sweeping by. If it weren't for the water, she would go straight down the road, on and on, to all the places she wanted to see. This town was no place for her!

She inhaled her cigarette, remembering that talk she'd had with

Daddy, when he'd told her, "Baby, you and I are different, somehow. We kind of step ahead, and that's nothing to be ashamed of. The world has always got to have people who step ahead. Well, just remember that's okay, Baby. It makes us special, don't you see? Right here, in this town we love, we're special every minute of the day. People look up to us, and we have to get used to it. It's an obligation, Baby, and you have to take good care of it."

She'd known after that that she *was* special; but it didn't make her love this town and feel obligated to it. It made her dissatisfied, eager to get out, to test her real potential. If she was special, she had a right to that, didn't she? She had a right to anything she wanted, didn't she?

She thought of Jack Kelty again. The excitement returned, full blown. She could remember the way his eyes had looked at her, spelling out things she could not even imagine, but which she suddenly hungered for—because Kelty was not of this place, not of the routine and the dull and the colorless that had become Blue Valley in Gretchen's mind.

She ground out her cigarette, aware that she could barely feel the brandy she'd drunk earlier. She swore, angry that she had not brought some with her.

She suddenly got out of the car and walked over to the Model A. "Frank?"

Frank Dinkier came awake with a start, peering out at her. Gretchen opened the right-hand door. "Frank?"

"Thought you wanted to be left alone."

Gretchen crawled into the car. "Frank, have you got anything to drink?"

"Drink? There's a water bottle in the back seat. You sure change your tune when you want something. What you doing out here anyways? Ain't safe! Been told them kids are running around."

"Frank, be an old sweetie and tell me if you've got something to drink—I don't want any water."

"You ought to have your hind end tanned is what! Ben spoiled you, that's the trouble. Something to drink!"

"Frank, it's all right. Mother said I could have some at home."

"Then you go home and get some then."

"I don't want to. I want you to give me something."

"Ben'd raise a sweet bunch of hell if I did, I'll tell you that. I may be old, but I ain't addled yet."

"Frank," Gretchen said imploringly, "come on. I know you've got something. You always take something in your car when you go fishing. You must have brought something tonight."

"You're mighty danged nosy!"

"Come on, Frank."

"Come on nothing. I ain't going to give you nothing. I got some hard cider in back on the floor, but you ain't gettin' any of it."

"Frank, Daddy'll never know. What's the difference?"

"He'd skin me."

Gretchen was silent for a moment. "Maybe he'd skin you if he knew you were out here asleep. Maybe he'd get mad about that. I don't think he ever gives credit to people he's mad at."

Frank snorted angrily. "My daughter, I'd whack you black and blue!"

"Come on, Frank, just a little."

"No!"

"Just a little, please!"

"Oh, dadblame anyhow!" He jerked around and shakily pulled up a large jar. He unscrewed the cap. "I ain't got any glasses to drink out of anyhow. I think you better not."

Gretchen took the jar out of his hands. "I don't need a glass." She tipped the jar up and drank.

"Goldang a'mighty! That's enough!"

She handed him the jar. "Thank you, Frank. You're such a darling and awfully sweet."

"I'm a dang fool is what I am!"

"I won't forget it, Frank," she said, getting out of the car.

"You dang well better!" he yelled after her. But she didn't answer. In a moment, she'd turned the car around and was racing back into town.

Fury had sobered Norman Teller. In the time that had passed since Emil Dome's shot was fired from across the street from the pool hall, he'd kept seeing the look of Louie Harlan turning, arms flying out, then collapsing in a pitiful, jerking pile on the sidewalk beside the Mercury. Now, as he crouched by the front window of a house owned by John and Esther Pickering and situated directly across the street from the jail, he'd sobered and begun thinking more clearly than he ever had in his life. When Louie had gone out to the car to get more wine and was shot down in cold blood, he'd sobered very fast. He'd waited only long enough for Marcelli to drag Louie's body in and then lift it as he would a loved child, then he'd let them out the back way and into this random-picked house owned by the Pickerings.

John Pickering was on the other side of the river at Hampton Mill. Esther Pickering was presently talking furiously with the rest of the girls in the living room of the Blake house. Marcelli had merely kicked the back door once, and it had swung open. The fan club had marched in, led by Marcelli carrying the lifeless body of Louie Harlan. Marcelli had placed the body carefully on the couch and knelt beside it. Teller had tried the telephone by picking it up and listening to the dial tone, then, using the number found in the thin book beneath the telephone, had called the jail with his ultimatum.

Now he crouched by a front window, looking at the yellow light of the jail's windows.

"What now, Tell?" Richard Rajeski asked anxiously.

Teller rubbed a hand across his chin, eyes bright with hate. Gone was any memory of any wrong-doing committed: the entry into Blue Valley with the ambition of breaking Kelty free, the breaking into the pool hall, the destruction, the insulting, all of it was forgotten. All that remained in mind was a knowledge of having been wronged. The body lying on the couch was proof of how much they had been wronged. Louie Harlan, dead, provided cause, and neither Teller nor the others had ever owned a good, substantial cause before.

Teller looked at Nick Cowley, sitting in a chair in the dim light, slack and pale-faced, staring at the body of Louie Harlan. "You see where that broad you talked to went, Nick?"

"What broad?"

"How many broads you talked to in this dump? That broad who was all broke up and worried about her kid!"

"That broad! Yeah. Went in a house halfway down the next block."

"She said her husband was gone, right?"

Nick Cowley blinked, livening a little, taking his eyes from the corpse of Louie Harlan. "Yeah."

"You know where she lives, her old man's gone—you want a little fun, Nick?"

Nick stood up. "Yeah."

"You see what I mean, Nick?"

"I'm ahead of you, man."

"You ever had the measles, Nick?"

Nick's smile broke grotesquely. "I'm what you call—immune. All she's got around is measles, it ain't gonna hurt old Nick!"

Chapter 19

They had been arguing for a half hour. Steve could not believe he'd heard right when Hillary had said it; now Tim Crawford, Si Metcomb and the visitor to Blue Valley, Bud Celt, had agreed with it.

"Just let him out!" Tim Crawford said angrily. "Just open up the cell and let him out. To hell with him. To hell with all of them. Let them drown in the damn river, what do we care?"

"Shut up, Tim," Steve said wearily.

Tim Crawford turned angrily to Ben Blake. "Order him, Ben."

"Be still for a minute, Tim!" Ben Blake's face was a diagram of worry as he kept pacing the floor.

Martin Hillary looked at Steve with alert, shrewd eyes. "What, specifically, is your objection, Michaels?"

"You're not that stupid, Hillary," Steve said. "You're not even remotely stupid. What do you think my objections are? Let a killer go? You want me to list my objections to that?"

"Just for the record," Hillary said smoothly. "Just so we know exactly where you stand."

"All right. He's killed two people, almost a third—and that third, severely wounded, was wounded trying to capture him. If we let him go, we wipe out that effort. No doubt he'll kill more, if he can."

"How can you be sure of that?"

"Keeping him here is one way I'm sure he won't."

"But I mean, should you let him go, what makes you think he's going to kill more people?"

Kelty watched and listened from his cell as though he'd lost personal identity in the minds of everyone in that room, as though he had become, instead, simply the object of barter in the impending transaction.

Steve took a breath, trying to keep his voice steady. "His action is historic by now, wouldn't you say? But turn it around, Hillary. What makes you think he won't?"

"Because, despite your historic implication, he's not really a killer in the first place."

Everyone now looked at Hillary, including Ben Blake. Steve stared at him in fresh amazement, then laughed harshly. "Maybe I've been misinformed, Hillary."

"All right—yes, he has killed, but only in self-defense. If you've read my columns, you'll know that. The Ashford police put him in the hole, right from the beginning. But this boy—"

"How about the guard in the beginning, Hillary?" Steve said tightly. "Kelty didn't kill him? It was all an illusion, was it?"

"Again a former member of the Ashford force. You know that. Granted Jack should not have been attempting theft in that warehouse. This despite Jack's great need for money to pay for his mother's medical needs, despite his inability to get it from employment with the Hareford Grain Company, where, I will reiterate, his father was killed as the result of faulty equipment twenty years ago, and a company, I will also reiterate, controlled by Harold Hareford, police commissioner in Ashford. No, I'll be the first to admit Jack should not have attempted theft, ever. I'm certain Jack himself would agree with that. Am I right, Jack?"

All eyes turned to Kelty. With great and careful effort, Kelty removed his hands from the bars. He bent his head a little, a forlorn look flickering into his face. "I wish to God I'd never thought of trying to rob that warehouse—no matter if my Ma was sick or not! Yes! I made a mistake! I'm sorry for it!"

"Oh, for God's sake!" Steve exploded. "Listen, Hillary—"

"Let Hillary talk!" Tim Crawford snapped.

Hillary smiled politely at Crawford. "Jack admits to an initial error. And I'll swear to you no man has ever paid more heavily for an error. Jack, did you actually get anything from that warehouse before you were accosted by that armed guard and forced to shoot in order to save your life?"

Kelty shook his head. "Not a thing. I—" He paused. "I don't know why I did it. Once I got in there, I knew I didn't want to do it. If I hadn't run into that guard, I'd have just left. That's the God's truth, so help me!"

Hillary nodded, looking very serious. "That's for the record, gentlemen. Oh, yes. I've heard this desperate killer business before, but never with an ounce of personal understanding. Because the accusation has always been made by people like Albert Duggan, who—"

"Why not let Duggan rest, Hillary?" Steve snapped.

Hillary smiled faintly. "That's not our point now, anyway. The point is, I believe, what will happen if Kelty is allowed to go free?"

"If you want to make a hypothetical estimation, Hillary," Steve said tightly, "you can do it all night. But that's as far as it's going to go. How much time do we waste doing this? Those kids gave us an hour, and we've wasted a lot of it already. Regardless, how can we trust anything they say? They may or may not give us an hour, and Gretchen's running around out there somewhere, Ben. We've got to organize some kind of patrol so we can prevent—"

"Shut up, Michaels!" Tim Crawford exploded. "Go ahead, Hillary. What happens if we let Kelty out?"

"For one thing, you give those young friends of Jack's what they want. And sometimes, gentlemen, I assure you compromise is of the highest honor and necessity. Giving Jack's friends what they want would, I will estimate, avert any foolish tragedies that might occur if you *don't* give them what they want."

Tim Crawford nodded. "That's exactly right."

"Then what, Hillary?" Steve said, face flushing.

"Why, I would imagine that would be all of it, wouldn't it? Consider everything very carefully. How long is it before daybreak? A few hours?" Hillary smiled grimly. "I wouldn't want to be in Jack's shoes. I really wouldn't. But try to look at it from his angle. Let's assume, Michaels, you let him walk out of here—out until he disappears and makes contact with his friends. What then? You say he'll go on killing. But I say why? *Why?* This town is an island. Can he escape it, Michaels?"

"He can try."

"Yes, of course. But he's risking everything if he does. The odds on making a successful crossing are very slim indeed. And even if he did, then the odds on any secure escape after that are even more astronomically against him. All things considered, his being returned to stand trial in Ashford would seem to me a safer course. Jack has already proven he is not suicidal. So what then?"

"Yes," Steve said. "So what then?"

"Why, what better chance has Jack Kelty got to prove himself? If he's released and joins his friends, assume that he then turns himself back in, along with his friends, detouring all potential tragedy to everyone including the citizens of this town, and thereby proving once and for all he is not the savage monster the Ashford Police Department has been so eager to make him!"

"My God!" Steve breathed. "How can you stand there and mouth that kind of thing, Hillary!"

"Shut up, Michaels!" Tim Crawford said, nearly crazy with fright.

"My reasoning is false?" Hillary asked Steve.

Steve laughed harshly. "You try to sell that, Hillary, you can sell something even simpler. When the fan club calls, I'll give Kelty the telephone and he can do this good deed right from the cell. He can call it all off, right then and there. Tell them to turn themselves in. It's very simple, and there's no trouble whatever. That is, if he's the Boy Scout you're trying to make him."

Hillary carefully lit a cigarette. Kelty's eyes switched from Steve to Hillary, back and forth, fingers tightening at his sides.

"Now that's interesting, Michaels—because it illustrates very accurately the situation we've got here. I think you're failing to consider Mr. Dome."

Emil Dome blinked. He had been listening silently, his fleshy head tipped at an angle in an attempt to assimilate each word that was spoken and then fit it into some kind of reasonable order so that he knew, fairly well, what the hell was going on between Steve and Hillary. "What about me?"

"Well, now," Hillary said. "I have no doubt in my mind that as a citizen of this town you had every right to do what you did. That is, fire on one of those kids. You're not, after all, a trained police officer any more than Michaels is. I'm sure I might very well have done the same. If the boy happened to be killed, that is simply the result of one quick, chancy shot fired in an effort to defend one's own town—am I right?"

"I killed him, sure!"

Steve laughed bitterly. "I'd go over that 'chancy' business again, Hillary. Dome's an expert shot. He proves that every year during our coyote hunt."

"I take your word," Hillary said unperturbed. "But these are unusual circumstances. Now perhaps Mr. Dome thinks he was being very accurate. As it turned out, he was. But when, in the light of cool thinking, this thing is judged, I have no doubt whatever that that shot will be considered one fired under great tension and thus unreliably performed. Such, in fact, that the actual killing of that boy will be judged an unfortunate accident committed in the heat of desperate defense."

"Why, goddamn it—" Dome began, fat jouncing around his jowls.

"Just a moment, Mr. Dome," Hillary said quickly. "Let me finish, please, then we'll hear your side of it."

"Shut your mouth, Emil," Tim Crawford said. "Let him finish. Go on, Hillary!"

"All I'm saying is this: aside from circumstances, Jack's friends have lost a member as the result of a bullet fired from Mr. Dome's rifle. Aside from circumstances, one thing is very obvious—they are now feeling a definite hostility because of that, as well as a definite distrust. Am I right?"

"They goddamn well ought to feel something!" Emil Dome said proudly.

"Yes, and this is *precisely* what they feel right now. And so why, if you simply handed Jack the telephone, Michaels, would they believe anything, including any entreaty Jack might make to them to surrender? Wouldn't it be the most natural thing in the world for them to think it was simply a trick? After all, one of their own members has, only a few minutes ago, gone down with a bullet. But on the other hand, if Jack were able to meet them personally by going free, then, of course, they would follow his direction. I have no doubt of that. Am I right, Jack?"

"You're right, Mr. Hillary," Kelty said. "I could get them to—"

Steve was shaking his head. "You and I know damn well Kelty isn't going to turn himself back in. You and I know that it's going to be a bloody job to go get him, if he ever gets out of here, and that whoever has got to do it is very liable to get killed in the process. For God's sake, if he gets the help of those kids it's like turning a bunch of wild animals loose—"

"Wild animals?" Hillary said, his voice going up a notch. "Are you honestly serious, Michaels? Wild animals? Is that what you think of this boy behind those bars? Is that what you think of those children hiding out there somewhere in this town in deadly fright right now? Wild animals? I'm astounded, Michaels! Has the ghost of Duggan appeared and climbed into your skull? Why, this is preposterous!"

Steve frowned, shaking his head, amazed. "What are you trying to do, Hillary?"

"Why, to see the proper thing done! My God, man, to see some humanness somewhere, some ounce of decent behavior!" Hillary suddenly turned, pointing a finger at Emil Dome, his intensity making the finger tremble. "Take a look at this man, Michaels. Here's a man who had the stoutness of heart to pick up a gun and try to defend his little village!"

Emil Dome blinked, unprepared for this sudden attention. For the moment he was speechless.

"I ask you, Michaels!" Hillary said, his voice continuing to rise. "Is that not what he did? Did he not stand guard at your direction? Bravely? And now he's got blood on his hands! Why?"

"Because he elected to shoot instead of following orders!"

"All right! But does that make him a monster, a wild animal? Or does it just make him a human being, caught in the vise of tension brought about by unfortunate circumstances above and beyond the control of every man, woman and child in this little village? Good Lord, Michaels, this man is a hero! If he killed, he killed, yes! But he did so in the name of this town, his friends, his neighbors! He stood there and held the rifle in his hands and he thought I shall defend this town I love. And if his bullet struck the life from that poor, misdirected boy, whose fault is that? My God, we must look at it for what it is, Michaels! You say he should have followed orders! But is he a soldier, a professional peace officer? Or is he just a common citizen of this community who tried to do the best he could? Look at this man, Michaels. Look at your neighbor here, with the name of Emil Dome, and tell me, please tell me. Is he a human being who did the best he could? Or is he a wild animal? I ask you, Michaels!"

The attention given to Hillary during his speech was undivided and intense. Steve's mouth had whitened, knowing that Hillary had led them just where he wanted them.

Emil Dome blinked. He turned to Steve. "You going to call me an animal?"

Steve did not answer. He continued to stare at Hillary. "All right, Hillary. You've had a good, intellectual time. You're pointing your nose in the direction of as much bloody circus drama as you can incite, to make damn sure you get your money's worth of sensationalism out of this situation. You've spoken a good piece, and you may as well finish it, if you've got anything else to say."

Hillary relaxed a little. "Very little, as a matter of fact. I'll ignore your hysterical accusation. I'll say only that I'm certain everybody can draw his own conclusion now. Kelty, in my opinion, is no different than Mr. Emil Dome. They have both killed. They have both killed for what amounts, in my opinion, to very similar reasons. I can't see the difference in their actions, from a moral viewpoint, except that before this is over Mr. Dome is going to be a hero and Jack Kelty may very well die. Of course, that is, in a way, up to you, Michaels. It depends on what you do now. If you let Jack go, you'll give him a chance to prove himself—by allowing him to bring those kids in. If you don't, you are sending him back to the wild beast police jungle of Ashford, where they are waiting to tear him apart with ready fangs. You are also inciting those kids out there to do God knows what! To ruin their own lives by going hysterical and hurting some of the citizens of this town—perhaps brutally, perhaps in a manner that is deadly. Let us face it, Michaels, there is no law in this town tonight, only what ought to be a civilized and intelligent man's judgment of what should be done. Whether you like it or not, Michaels, you seem to have been elected God tonight in Blue Valley."

Hillary sat down, lighting a new cigarette, studying the end of it. Steve tried to control his anger. He spoke very quietly. "The argument's completely phony, Hillary, and you know it. I've made my choice. I'm not releasing Kelty."

For a moment, Emil Dome looked at Steve through narrow, dark eyes. He'd caught up with everything now and figured out just where Hillary had gone with all his words. A hero, Hillary had called him. Dome committed his push-pull rub of thumb across nose. A half hour ago he'd never have agreed to letting Jack Kelty go. But now he was sensing how things were going. Figure they let Kelty go. Figure that someone—someone named Emil Dome—was waiting out there in the bushes. Then figure that same someone, the minute Kelty got together with his trashy friends, started shooting. Save the state an electricity bill. Kill Kelty, kill the whole rotten bunch if he could. So, if he was a hero now, what would he be if he got the whole litter?

Emil Dome ducked his head a little farther into the fat folds of his neck. He said, "Maybe you'd better start listening to this Hillary, Michaels."

Steve shook his head, amazed. "Now you, Dome. One minute you're shooting one of them down, the next you want to do them the big favor!"

"Just a minute, Steve," Ben Blake said, seeming to shake himself from his worry with great effort. "Just a minute."

Steve looked at him, waiting, feeling a sudden flicker of apprehension; he did not, he told himself, want to have to oppose Ben Blake under any circumstance.

"We've got to give consideration to what Hillary's talking about."

"Ben, you can't mean that!"

"Steve, let me talk. I have no desire to aid a criminal. Who does? But as Hillary says, these are special circumstances. I've got a daughter out there right now!"

"Well, why don't you start looking for her, Ben!"

"I will, in about one minute. But first we're going to make sure those bastard kids out there don't start tearing this town up!"

"How are you going to do that, Ben?" Steve asked, voice going cold.

A muscle flickered in Ben Blake's cheek. "This whole thing has been a mess. The flood alone has hurt this town of ours, hurt a lot of people who live in and around it, killed some of them, in fact. I think that's the thing to think about. How much does any town deserve?" He motioned a hand angrily toward Kelty. "We talk so much about this one man standing behind those bars! How many people are dead with their heads stuck in four feet of muck in that flood, snuffed out, for no reason other than luck went bad? How can we spend time worrying about one man like this? Is that our responsibility? Or is our responsibility to our town, our own little community, our own group of people! If those kids out there start hurting anybody, it's not just bad luck, it's our own fault! Is that justice? How can that be justice!" He stopped, licked his lips, then walked to the bars where Kelty stood. "What happens if we let you go, Kelty?"

Kelty's head jerked in a spasm of pure nerves. He forced his best smile. "It's just like Hillary says, sir. It's my chance to prove I'm not what they say I am in Ashford. I'd talk to those guys and tell them just where they stood and bring them back in. I swear it!"

Steve looked at Ben Blake with amazement, listening to Kelty utter the very words Hillary had so skillfully suggested to him only minutes ago.

"All right," Ben Blake said, turning, looking at an astonished Steve. "That's good enough for me. When they call again, Steve, tell them we're ready to let him go."

"I'm for that," Emil Dome said, his eyes glittering.

"By God, yes!" Tim Crawford snapped.

Si Metcomb took a step forward. "That's all we can do."

Bud Celt put on his insincere smile. "I, of course, don't live here. But I have an idea what we'd do in Parisville. I think we'd do just what you gentlemen are deciding now."

Steve stood behind the desk, looking back at them, shifting his unbelieving stare from one pair of eyes to the next. "Are you all crazy? You think there's trouble now, what do you think it'll be if Kelty gets out? My God, he's free to grab anyone he wants as a hostage. He can—"

"I won't!" Kelty almost screamed. "I swear I won't. This is my only chance to prove myself! Why would I ruin that!"

They were, Steve realized, listening to Kelty, not to him. He stood looking at those faces in front of him, and it was suddenly as though he were a thousand miles away, seeing a film with these men as actors; he even felt a sharp, guilty audience appreciation for the way the best actor of them all, Martin Hillary, suave representative of a far more sophisticated society, had led the homely, town-loving sheep into the proper corral.

Steve looked at Ben Blake, and gone was the dream of the past; no longer was Ben Blake the admired, the ultimate, but only a small-focused man who had spoiled a daughter and would not admit his guilt, who would rather see a half dozen more people killed and blind himself to it by looking only at his own precious little village, saying to hell with everything else. Steve looked into Ben Blake's face and knew to what extent he had—unconsciously, perhaps, but done it anyway—licked the boots of this leading citizen in order to make clean his past and solid his future. He blinked once, hearing that voice again, *Don't let Kelty go....* Duggan was still talking, and if Steve listened, he was going to smash everything, including what he had with Sue, because she was her father's daughter as much as Gretchen....

"That's my decision, Steve," Ben Blake said meaningfully. Steve put his hand directly on the tommy gun again. "I'm afraid it's not yours to make, Ben."

Ben Blake blinked, a deep flush came into his face. "Now, wait a minute, Steve. I appointed you temporary sheriff. I did so as the mayor of this town. Now I'm telling you what we're going to do."

"I'm not letting him go," Steve said, his voice flat and cold.

"Now—I mean just wait a minute, Steve. I appointed you, I can take the job away from you."

"I don't think so, Ben."

Ben Blake had begun breathing hard in the stunned silence. "What do you mean you don't think so? By God, you're crossing me, Steve?"

"I'm sorry, Ben."

"You mean to say you're deliberately going to stand there and refuse to listen to what I'm telling you?"

"That's it."

"By God! By God, you're finished, Steve! Just step away from that desk, will you?"

"No, Ben."

Ben Blake sucked his breath in. "You've gone crazy! This is the rankest kind of disregard for authority. By God, this is an emergency! My word better be law, or we're really in trouble!"

"I'm sorry, Ben, but I don't think your word's any good right now. I don't think you're seeing anything very clearly at the moment. I'm continuing custody of Kelty, regardless. That's the way it is."

"I think the man's gone mad!" Hilary said extravagantly.

"Steve," Ben Blake said in a trembling voice, "I'm taking away the authority I gave you. Emil, I'm appointing you sheriff. Get away from the desk and that machine gun, Steve. You're through!"

"The only thing I can tell you, Ben, is to get out of here and take these men with you—you'd better start looking for Gretchen."

Ben Blake's face was crimson. "Take over, Emil!"

Steve brought the tommy gun up. "I'm asking you to leave."

"By God, I'll take that gun right out of your hands, Michaels!" Emil Dome grunted.

Behind him there was the sound of a safety being snapped off a shotgun. Emil Dome and Ben Blake turned. Rod Newall stood with the gun balanced in his hands.

"Now wait a minute, wait a minute!" Ben Blake shouted. "You put that gun down and get the hell out of here, Newall! I mean that!"

Holding the gun carefully, Rod Newall moved sideways until he stood by Steve's elbow.

"You don't have to do this, Rod," Steve said.

"I know that," Rod said.

"Why, that goddamned kid!" Ben Blake roared. "Get him out of here!"

Neither Rod nor Steve moved. Ben Blake turned around again, looking at Harry Bell. Harry Bell stepped over beside Rod Newall. "Me and Steve have been friends for a long time, Ben. And this Newall boy kind of reminds me of Steve when he was younger."

"You drunken fool, Harry!" Blake said.

"Well, I've heard that before, Ben. But if I were you, I'd stop talking and go out and look for that daughter of yours before she gets in real trouble. When you find her, you might paddle her hind side for the first time too."

"Shut the hell up, Harry!"

Harry Bell shrugged and stood very straight, swaying a little. Then Abner Potter made his slow way over to join Steve.

"By God!" Ben Blake cried. "You'll wish you'd thought better of this, Abner!"

"Yell away, Ben," Mr. Potter said. "I'm too damned old to worry much about your hollering."

Ben Blake shook his head with one violent movement, as though forcibly shaking his rage away enough to see clearly. "All right! The rest of you come with me! I swear you won't get away with this, Steve!"

Steve nodded grimly. "All right. But when you leave, don't try anything with me after that. I'll use this machine gun, I promise. If anybody tries anything with me or my prisoner, I'll kill him. Is that understood, Ben?"

Ben Blake jerked around and left the jail, followed by Tim Crawford, Emil Dome, Si Metcomb, Bud Celt. Hillary looked at Steve. "Am I still allowed my press privilege to be in here, Michaels?"

"I'd rather pull this trigger on you. But if you insist on staying, stay. Just keep out of my way."

Hillary nodded. "Thank you—Sheriff." He smiled as the door slammed behind the exiting group. "Very rare color in this room tonight."

"You helped make it that way, didn't you, Hillary?"

Suddenly Kelty was screaming from his cell, "You bastard, Michaels! You stupid, sonofabitching bastard!" Tears started in his eyes. "You rotten, stinking, no-good bastard, you!" Then he bent forward, his whole body shaking, his voice escaping in a high-pitched whining moan.

Hillary kept smiling, examining Steve with bright eyes. "You really hit something off, didn't you, Michaels? Do you think you can handle it?"

Steve stared back for a moment, then looked away. He felt a cold sensation deep in the pit of his stomach. Could he? He didn't know....

Chapter 20

Gretchen had driven haphazardly around town feeling a futile sense of indirection. Her ambition to do something was nearly overpowering, but the ambition was held in such a hopeless frustration that it made her very muscles hurt.

Like the insects drawn to the globes atop Blue Valley's street lamps, she finally drifted back toward the jail.

She approached tentatively on the back side, knowing that within that structure was the exciting compulsion that drew her here, knowing at the same time that she did not want to be caught and taken home to be locked up, this time, for the night. She turned the car onto the street directly bordering the jail, driving slowly. Then she saw her father's car parked at the curb ahead of a pickup that looked like Emil Dome's. Her tongue flickered nervously over her lips.

At the same moment, she noticed the Beechum drive directly across the street from the jail. A cottonwood tree and a weeping willow shielded the drive from the street lamps and even, at the moment, from the stars and the moon. Gretchen braked, shifted into reverse, and whipped the car back into the drive until she was in almost total darkness. Mrs. Howard Beechum, she knew, had gone over to her mother's with Mrs. Pickering; Howard Beechum was on the other side of the river.

There, the motor cut, she waited, heart pumping from the building excitement. She closed her eyes for a moment, picturing the hard, good-looking face of Jack Kelty, then opened them in time to see her father, followed by Tim Crawford, Si Metcomb, Emil Dome and someone she didn't know come trooping out of the jail. She watched carefully as they strode across the lawn. Her father, Si Metcomb, Tim Crawford and the other man got into her father's sedan. Emil Dome climbed into his pickup.

Her father's car roared down the block and turned left at the next intersection. But Emil Dome's pickup continued halfway down the next block, where it suddenly wheeled into the alley to the right.

Gretchen watched, puzzled, seeing the lights moving behind the row of houses opposite the front of the courthouse. Then the lights went out, midway, just behind Minna Slattery's house.

A few moments later Gretchen was certain she heard the faint slamming of a back screen door. She frowned, unconsciously nibbling at a cuticle of her right thumb, wondering what was going on now, sitting in that dark driveway, not two hundred yards away from where Kelty's fan club waited in the silence of the Pickering front room.

Minna Slattery, a life-long resident of Blue Valley, never married, active in a real estate and insurance business begun with her inheritance from her father and continued at a small profit for the past forty years, heard the sound of the pickup coming down the alley behind her house. She jumped visibly, then cut the kitchen lights and stood pressed to the kitchen door, seventy-year-old body atwitch.

Minna was a capable-looking woman with steel-gray hair and

snapping black eyes, seeming incapable to a casual eye of ever developing fear. But since she'd heard of the breakout of those hoodlums from the pool hall, she'd been remembering that young man she'd read about who had prowled the dark streets of San Francisco seeking out elderly ladies to rape.

She heard next the opening and closing of the door of the vehicle stopped just behind her house, then the solid footsteps coming up the back walk from the garage. She thought, in a wild moment of panic, she should scream, run to the telephone and call someone, then hide in a closet. She was prepared to do all of these things, when she heard the grunting voice of Emil Dome:

"Minna, you there?"

She edged to the right back window and finally saw his pickup gleaming in the moonlight just beyond her garage.

"Emil Dome, is that you?"

"Let me in, will you?"

"Why?"

"Minna, this is important!"

"Anybody with you?"

"Damn, no, Minna. Open this door, will you?"

"Don't swear at me," Minna said, opening the door.

"Just got by me, Minna," Emil said, coming in.

"What's that in your hand, Emil?"

"My rifle, Minna."

"I don't want any shooting in this house!"

"Take it easy, Minna. I'm on a patrol, see? I got to sit over here and guard that jail. This here's an emergency, Minna. Now, you just stay away from the front part of the house and you'll be all right. Now you're all right, ain't you, Minna?"

"I don't like this, Emil."

"Well, who does? But it's got to be done."

"Do you want some coffee, Emil?"

"I don't need none, Minna. You just let me be, that's all."

He strode by her into the living room.

"You close that door, Minna, and stay back there, will you?"

Minna did, listening. She heard the front door carefully opened. In a moment she heard the faint squeak of the glider on the front porch and knew that Emil had seated himself out there in the dark protection of the roof's overhang.

She listened some more and heard no more. She went over and put a pot of coffee on the stove. Suddenly she felt better. She didn't like anybody storming through her house like Emil Dome had just done. But then, on the other hand, Emil was near now. If anybody came sneaking up to her door with rape on his mind, there was one person in this world she was sure wouldn't hesitate to shoot that person's head off. She'd seen the look of Emil's face that last coyote hunt and heard it when he'd said, "I'd rather go out and find me something and shoot it and kill it and see it dead than eat, by God!"

In the triangular watch now being performed on the jail, the southeast vertex was being haphazardly filled by the four remaining members of Jack Kelty's fan club. There was no system; it was merely an on-and-off flurry of action, as the tension built.

Red-haired Nick Cowley was breathing hard. He'd refocused in his mind the image of Lou Ann Bordly, and in a way he was hoping that farmer cop was not going to let Jack Kelty go so he could hurry up and do what he knew how to do best.

"You think he will?" he asked Norman Teller.

"Shut up, Nick," Rajeski snapped. Rajeski's nerves were sawed sore by the tension. "How much more time, Tell?"

Norman Teller looked at his watch. "Three minutes." He looked out the window. The guard on the jail had been so erratic that no one had seen Gretchen come up the block, then swing backward into the Beechum drive. But they had heard the car, then looked out, only to see Ben Blake and the others march from the jail, get into the sedan and truck and drive away. They had not noticed that Emil Dome had cut off midway down the next block.

"I don't think he will," Nick Cowley pronounced, closing his eyes, wondering just how Lou Ann Bordly was going to act when he went to work.

"What do you know?" Rajeski said bitterly.

"Shut up, Cut," Teller snapped, peering out the window.

"What?" Rajeski almost yelled.

"I said shut up!"

"Screw you, Teller! Louie's had it! Goddamn Marcelli acts like he's dead himself." His voice had begun to tremble.

Teller turned around, going angry all of a sudden. "You're yellow, Cut! You're so stinking yellow you're about to crap, huh?"

Rajeski bent his head a little, putting his teeth together. "No, I'm not," he breathed.

"The hell you're not. You're chicken!"

"No, I'm not!" Rajeski almost screamed.

Teller gazed at him for a moment, then shrugged. He looked through the dim light at Marcelli sitting motionless on the floor beside the head of the couch where the corpse of Louie Harlan lay.

"Gives me the creeps!" Nick Cowley said. "You could bust him with the butt of your gun, he wouldn't move."

"He'll be all right," Teller said. "He'll wake up and move when we get Jack out."

"Tell?" Rajeski said in a moment. "What then?"

"What do you mean?"

"Say in two minutes, one, whatever it is, Jack comes walking out that door over there. What then?"

"What do you mean, what then? We signal, bring him over, and we done what we came to do!"

"Yeah, I know. But I mean where do we go from there?"

Teller frowned. He realized that he hadn't really thought about it. Get Kelty out. That was all that counted. Then they had to get off this stinking island of a town. But what then?

He shook his head, the thought making him even more nervous. To hell with it. Jack would know what to do next. So long as they were with Jack, everything was going to be all right. "Don't worry about it," he snapped.

"How long now?" Rajeski asked.

"One minute," Teller said, voice tight.

The minute, to Teller, Rajeski, Cowley, seemed an hour. When it ended, Jack Kelty had not walked out the jail door. Teller said, "All right."

Nick Cowley said, "I'll get going. I'm gonna show that little hick-town housewife some real city action!"

"Hold it, Nick," Teller said grimly. "Give me the phone."

Rajeski handed him the telephone, and Teller dialed swiftly. In a moment, Steve's voice sounded. "Who's this?" Teller demanded.

"Michaels."

"The cop with the chopper?"

"Is this Teller?"

"Teller. Right. So how about it? Is Kelty walking out of there?"

"Teller, I can't do that!"

"All right, cop. You just made a bad mistake. You're going to wish you hadn't!"

Chapter 21

Steve's eyes flickered to Kelty, then to Rod, Harry Bell, Mr. Potter. "Take it easy, Teller. I want to talk to you."

"Yeah? Well, you done enough talking already, wise boy. Your talking still rings in my ears. How was it now? I won't fire on a man who ain't doing anything! Ain't that what you said, cop? So we got one dead now, shot through the head! No warning, no nothing! You stink, cop! You really stink!"

"Listen to me, Teller. I gave an order—no shooting unless you were warned and refused the warning. The order was disobeyed."

"Does that make Louie alive? Who believes it anyway! I said it before, cop. You stink! Now I'm telling you for the last time. Let Kelty out of there, no tricks this time, nothing but Jack Kelty walking out of there free and clear!"

"I can't do that, Teller."

"All right. You're asking for it. You remember I told you about Nick Cowley? You remember that, cop? How old Nick likes his women? Well, he's got one all picked out—a nice, plump, juicy little housewife right here in squaresville. You say no to me, I say yes to Nick, and he goes over and says hello, ma'am; and that ain't all he's going to do."

Steve rubbed the back of his fingers across his forehead. "Teller, you're digging yourself in deeper. Can't you see that?"

"Teller!" Jack Kelty suddenly screamed from his cell. "Teller, listen—!"

But Steve had been looking at Kelty, expecting something. He brought the telephone away from his mouth with a snap, covering the mouthpiece with his palm. He jerked his head to Rod. "Put that shotgun on him. If he even breathes hard, shoot!"

Kelty, mouth quivering, stared at Steve silently with intense and bitter hate.

Steve brought the telephone up again. Teller said, "Was that Kelty yelling?"

"Never mind that, Teller. I want to make a deal with you."

"Deal? What are you talking about! I'm making the deal, man."

"It's going to be daylight in a few hours. This place is going to be swarming with troopers then! Think ahead a little! You've already lost one man trying to jump in with Kelty. Is he worth it?" Kelty grasped the bars, face strained, but Rod put the shotgun at his stomach; Kelty remained silent. "Teller, you're just a sucker for a man who's already in the chair. Why join him?"

This time Teller hesitated a moment, then said, louder than ever, "Words, cop. You're full of words, ain't you?"

"Listen—" Steve felt the sweat prickling on his forehead. He tried to make his mind work accurately. Teller, none of them, trusted him now—not since Dome's stupid shooting. But if he had their trust to some degree, he could, perhaps, talk them out of ruining everything. He rubbed his forehead again, hand coming away wet. "Teller, let me talk to you in person."

"You're nuts!"

"I want to prove to you that I mean this—that I'm willing to make a deal. You meet me anywhere you want. I'll come alone. I swear it. I'll bring the machine gun, I'll admit that. And I'll use it if you try to get me. I'll take one or as many as I can with me, if you try that. But you're going to have the advantage. You can watch me come. You can cover me all the way, all of you. I won't shoot unless I have a reason. I promise that. Teller, you're in real trouble if you don't listen to me. You're going to burn right along with Kelty, if you make that threat of yours good. Listen to me. How about it?"

Seconds went by, then Teller said, "We got just one thing in mind, cop—getting Kelty out."

"All right. But maybe you're going to get killed trying to do it. And if I don't kill you, then you're still going to die later if you keep looking for trouble. All I want now is to talk to you face to face. How about it?"

Again there was a long pause.

Steve said, "You've still got a chance, Teller. You still haven't gotten in so deep you can't get out."

Teller snapped, "How about that guy who knocked Louie off?"

"I told you, Teller—he disobeyed. I'm not using him now. If you'll let me talk to you, I'll explain."

Teller laughed bitterly, but was silent again. Then, "You try any tricks with us, cop, you're going to be the first to go, you know that, don't you?"

"I know that, Teller."

"Where you want to talk to me?"

"You name it."

Silence again. "I'll tell you, cop. You might just figure to set up a trap for us. I don't buy it."

"I swear I won't, Teller. You're going to have to believe in that, if you want to get off this hook. And the hook's on fire."

More silence. Finally, "Listen—you just walk out of that jail and out to the street that runs south in front of the crummy courthouse, see? You turn left at the corner and keep walking. We'll tell you when to stop. And if you try to cross us again, that'll be your last cross. Got that, cop? And do it right now!"

The connection was broken. Steve stood up, putting the telephone down. "Rod, it's up to you again. I'm going to try to talk to them. Lock the door when I leave. Under no circumstances, absolutely none, open that door to anyone. Hillary? You're staying right here."

Hillary looked at him. "I wish you luck, Michaels. You're going to need it."

Steve picked up the machine gun and moved swiftly to the door. Outside, he walked down the sidewalk to the first intersection south, then turned left, following Teller's instructions. He tried to keep his mind open and fair, thinking only about stopping that fan club and diverting further disaster.

But he was thinking, despite that good intention, that the fan club must be nearby, watching the courthouse. It was a logical place. Moreover Teller had called the instant the hour was up when Kelty was not released, proving that he had no doubt been watching the jail. And Teller was specific about his instructions, as though the street were right in front of his eyes and he would be able to observe Steve the instant he stepped outside the jail door. With this knowledge, Steve knew where they were based now, approximately, and so had a better advantage than he'd had a few minutes ago.

But I'm not going to try to outwit them, he promised himself. I'm going to play it straight....

Emil Dome snapped forward on Minna Slattery's glider. He carefully watched Steve stride down the sidewalk. Where the hell was Michaels going? Dome lifted his rifle, looking down the sights at Steve's head. Goddamn, why wouldn't he let Kelty go? Dome's finger drew up the play in the trigger. He remembered how that kid he'd killed earlier had looked in the sights. Goddamn, he would like to let go right now. Steve Michaels. Anybody!

Slowly he lowered the rifle, nervous now because Michaels was doing something that he didn't know about. He started to get up, to follow. Then he thought better of it. Kelty was what counted and Kelty was still in that jail.

Dome refitted his fat-covered muscles in the glider, eyes switching back to the front of the jail as Steve turned and went down the next block toward the main street. Come on out of there, Kelty! he thought. Come on, you sonofabitch, and I'll blow your head off!

In the Pickering house, Teller had forcibly pulled Tommy Marcelli from his vigil beside the body of Louie Harlan, to place him at the window looking out at the courthouse.

"Tommy, listen. Take this pistol, see? Take it in your hand and sit here and watch that jail, do you understand me?"

"Screw you, Teller," Marcelli said disinterestedly.

"Just watch that door," Teller said. "See? That's the cop walking down the sidewalk. We're going to talk to him. We're going to go talk to him, and we're leaving you here to watch that jail—right here with Louie, okay?"

Marcelli shrugged and gazed out on the Blue Valley evening.

"Now listen," Teller said. "It ain't going to happen, I figure. But if it does—if you see Jack come out of there—you holler at him, see? And shoot to signal us, see? Now remember, if Jack gets out of there, he's just the one to pay off these hick farmers for what they did to Louie, have you got that? But just take it easy, because I don't figure Jack's coming out of there for a while. Just sit tight, Tommy, and watch. Okay?"

Marcelli sat with the pistol in his great hand, stolidly looking out. "Screw you, Teller."

"That's the boy," Teller said, then straightened and hurried through the house, Rajeski and Nick Cowley behind him.

"I figure," Nick Cowley said, "I should have gone and seen that broad. Then they'd know we really meant business."

"You may get to yet," Teller said grimly.

They slipped swiftly and silently out the back way.

Teller instructed, "Cut, you get on the other side of the street. Come in down that alley back of the movie place, and be careful. Nick, you stay behind that cop. I'm going to cut him off when he hits that building back of the movie joint. If I yell to fire, cut loose. Cut him down. You got those guns set?"

Rajeski and Cowley gripped their pistols. "Yeah," Rajeski said.

"Let's go," Teller said thinly.

Moments later, Steve heard the sound of someone running across the street a half block behind him.

He did not turn around, but kept moving, hand tight around the machine gun. They had been hiding somewhere near, all right. In a moment he was going to be stopped. Take it easy, he told himself. Look calm. If you spook them, it's going to be like dropping a match in a large tank of gasoline. Easy now, easy …

"Cop?" a voice sounded from behind a clump of lilacs, just across the street. "That's good, cop. Right there, under that street lamp. Just stand like that, cop. Don't move an eyelid, you got that, cop?"

At the same second, Gretchen had gotten from Sue's yellow convertible and run across the street and up to the door of the jail. From the porch of Minna Slattery's house, Emil Dome watched her with quick eyes, surprised to see her, knowing that by now Ben Blake was driving up and down Blue Valley's streets searching desperately for her. But he did not get up and cross the street to get her. He did not want to give his position away.

Gretchen knocked on the door. "Rod?" she called plaintively, making it sound as though he were the only man in the world she'd ever thought about. "Rod? Please let me in. Hurry, Rod!"

Chapter 22

In a moment, Rod's voice sounded from inside the jail. "What are you doing, Gretchen?"

"I'm trying to get inside, Rod. Please open the door."

"Listen, Gretchen, your father's looking all over for you. You've driven nearly everyone crazy! Are you all right?"

"I will be if you'll let me in. Come on, Rod. I'm scared! Please, Rod!"

Suddenly the door opened. "Gretchen, I swear—come in, will you? And just sit down until I locate your father."

Gretchen came in, smiling brightly. "Thank you, Rod, dear." Now she could see Kelty again, see the quick flash of appreciation in his eyes as he looked at her. This was what, as soon as she'd seen Steve walk away from the jail, she'd wanted—to be near Jack Kelty again.

Rod was walking back to the desk, the door locked behind him. He picked up the telephone.

"What are you going to do now, Rod?" She walked toward him, using her body effectively, her eyes brushing Kelty's. Kelty was looking at her very carefully now, eyes dark and alert.

"Call your father, if he's at his office."

"Rod, why are you going to do that?"

"Because he's about to lose his mind worrying about you! Where have you been anyway?"

"Driving around. But don't call him, Rod. He'll be furious."

"He sure will. And for good reason."

Harry Bell stood up unsteadily. "Gonna get your bottom paddled, young lady. You'd better count on that." He lifted Hillary's bottle, saw that only a thin amount remained in the bottom.

"How about pouring me a drink, Harry?" Gretchen said sweetly. "Then I won't mind so much."

Hillary, sitting at his packing crate, smiled faintly. "Well," Harry Bell said, "I'll tell you, Gretchen, I hate to be selfish, but there's just about enough left here for me. Do you mind, Mr. Hillary?"

"At your service, sir," Hillary said smoothly. "By all means."

"Is Mr. Potter asleep again?" Gretchen asked.

"A difficult night, Miss Blake," Hillary said.

"Where did Steve go?"

"Out," Rod said, starting to dial.

Gretchen put her hand on his, stopping him. "Please don't, Rod."

"Take your hand away, Gretchen."

"You didn't say anything like that the other night, Rod."

Rod flushed deeply, and Kelty laughed; it was a raucous laugh, but it tended, at the end, to a high thinness.

"All right," Gretchen said, whirling away, tossing her head, "I thought you were some other kind of person than just a sissy informer."

She edged a look at Rod, and knew she'd struck a nerve. The accusation was childish, but Rod had always been sensitive about some of the most obvious things. In a way, she was sorry to embarrass him, because she liked him well enough and she'd felt awfully close to him the other night. But all she cared about now, really, was Jack Kelty; and she didn't want her father coming in here and ruining everything.

Rod sat down behind the desk, looked at the telephone for a moment, then said, "All right, Gretchen. It's up to you. I'm advising you to call your father and tell him where you are. Or call your mother. Or at least call Sue—she's up in Mrs. Corpler's office. But it's up to you. I guess Steve wouldn't want your father coming over here anyway."

"Why not?" Gretchen asked, surprised.

Hillary leaned forward, smiling. "It seems, Miss Blake, that your father and Mr. Michaels have come to a parting of the ways."

Gretchen looked at Jack Kelty, doing her best things with her eyes. "A parting of the ways?"

"More or less. Michaels sent your father and his friends out at gun point."

"Why?" She looked at Hillary now, very attentive.

"One reason was you, I suspect. Did you know that a gentleman named Emil Dome shot and killed one of those boys in the pool hall?"

Gretchen blinked. "No."

"Oh, yes. This angered those boys, who in turn went into hiding. They telephoned in that they might very well start causing serious trouble if Jack here was not released within an hour."

Gretchen looked back at Kelty.

"But as you see, Jack wasn't released. Michaels couldn't see his way clear, despite the opinions of your father and those with him. Then your young friend here, Mr. Newall, and Mr. Potter, and Mr. Bell all chose to align themselves with Michaels. The others, including your father, were sent out."

"But Daddy wanted him released?" She continued to stare at Kelty.

"That's pretty much the way I interpreted it. Wouldn't you agree, Newall?"

Rod rubbed a hand over his shirt. "He was upset about you, Gretchen. He thought, since you were outside somewhere, maybe those guys who were in the pool hall might … well, you know."

"Oh," Gretchen said softly. "Oh."

"Now," Hillary said cheerfully, "Michaels is attempting to bargain with those young gentlemen from the pool hall. In my opinion he's behaving rather foolishly."

"He is?" Gretchen asked, taking in everything very carefully.

Hillary nodded slightly, smiling. "Very sad, indeed."

Gretchen turned her eyes back to Kelty. "And Daddy wanted to let him go—?" she said very softly. She arched her back slightly, feeling Kelty's eyes travel over her body. Then his eyes came up to meet hers. She saw deep inside them, and realized, with a flicker of new excitement, he was trying to tell her something with his eyes.

Something very definite …

Steve, standing at the rear corner of the theater building, was motionless. He knew there was one of them behind him and one to his right; the third, Teller, was still behind the lilacs.

"Okay, cop. What now?"

"I want you to come in with me."

There was a second of silence. "You're a comic, huh, cop?"

"I'm not, Teller. I'm dead serious."

"Why do you think we're going to do anything like that? You think we're crazy?"

"I think you are if you don't. Figure it out—what chance have you got? I'm not turning Kelty loose. What can you gain?"

"I told you—we're going to start putting on the pressure."

"All right, Teller. Say you do. Say you send that boy of yours out and let him molest a woman. You've had it then. But right now, what have you done?"

"We had one of us killed by some goddamn nervous-fingered hick—"

"All right, Teller. I put a man across the street to guard that pool hall. I instructed him to use his rifle only if you disobeyed his command to stay there. He fired without asking questions. When this is over, I'm turning that information over to the authorities. I'll try to see that he's charged for that. As far as you're concerned, the only real thing you've got against you right now is breaking into the pool hall and threatening me to get Kelty loose. I'm telling you honestly—I'll forget both things if you'll turn yourselves in. I'll write it down as too much excitement and too much liquor. Damn it, Teller, listen to me! You're in no real trouble if you come in now! Forget about Kelty! Start thinking about yourselves!"

Now there was a very long silence. Steve waited, tense. Finally Teller, his voice giving away his fear, his willingness to get this over, said, "You sure about that, cop? You ain't selling us out?"

"I'm not selling you out, Teller—any of you."

There was another long silence, then Teller said, "Okay, take off, cop—go back to your jail. We'll talk it over. We'll let you know."

Steve knew that Teller was willing to quit this minute, but could not bring himself to do it without some show of final stubbornness.

"All right, Teller," Steve nodded.

"Take off, cop."

Steve turned and began walking back down the block, feeling the excitement of knowing that now, if Teller instructed them to turn themselves in, it was the end of trouble on this night in Blue Valley. In a few hours it would be daylight, and help would cross the flooded river. In a few hours it was going to be all over.

Then his mind turned back to his encounter with Ben Blake. Yes, the danger would be over. But he knew one thing: he was finished in Blue Valley. He thought of Sue, still waiting at Mrs. Corpler's. Sue, daughter of Ben Blake. He felt a cold chill of loss. He'd turned against Ben—how would Sue feel now? Always loyal, always loving; you could always, he'd thought, count on Sue. But could he now that he and Ben were finished with each other? How would it be when she no longer viewed him as the fair-haired, father-approved young man? Was Sue Blake any different, really, than anyone else in this town?

He tightened his hand around the grip of the machine gun, as he neared the end of the block. He thought of Al Duggan. He'd kept his promise to Duggan. He hadn't let Kelty go. But what had it cost? Maybe everything, he thought....

The sharp crack of the rifle snapped his head up.

He looked across the courthouse lawn and saw two running figures coming from the open jail door, outlined against the yellow light spilling out. He heard the rifle a second time, and then saw Emil Dome moving across the street, from the left, heading onto the lawn.

Someone on his right was yelling, "Kelty! This way, Kelty!"

Steve whirled to see the large figure of Thomas Marcelli dancing across one of the yards down the block. Then he realized that it was Gretchen who was coming out of the jail with Jack Kelty. He stood for a second, stunned.

Then he moved, realizing that Emil Dome was still running across the courthouse lawn, stopping once again to raise his rifle and fire at the two figures moving now at full tilt for the driveway beside the Howard Beechum house.

"Hold it, Dome!" Steve yelled. "Gretchen's with him!"

But Dome did not hear that. Jack Kelty, shotgun in one hand, the P38 pistol once owned by Roy Hawkins in the other, had turned and with great and deadly accuracy put a 9mm caliber bullet straight through Emil Dome's forehead.

Emil Dome's last thought was that he was going to kill again in a moment, really kill again, just as soon as he could steady his wild excitement long enough to get his shooting eye back.

But Emil Dome stumbled down to his knees and rolled over and lay very still, the rifle fallen from his hands, dead instantly, having killed all he was going to kill in this life, dead from a bullet fired by a man who was an even better killer than Emil Dome had ever hoped to be.

Chapter 23

Powerless to use the machine gun, Steve ducked and ran in the direction Kelty and Gretchen were taking. He saw the large figure of Marcelli pounding across a front lawn ahead of him. He realized instantly that Gretchen seemed to be moving with Kelty as though willing.

But before he'd gone half the block, he heard the sound of a car engine kicked into action, raced to an angry whine; then the yellow convertible squealed onto the street, turning in his direction and cut wide open. He saw Marcelli grab out, leap in as it passed, barely tumbling into the back seat in time.

A bullet whined just beside Steve's right ear. He threw himself sideways, behind the cover of an oak's trunk. Behind, he heard a sudden shouting and turned to see Richard Rajeski jump into the street, waving his arms desperately. "Jack!"

But the car driven by Jack Kelty, Gretchen ducking beside him, Marcelli digging for cover in the back seat, bore straight down on Richard Rajeski. At the last second, Rajeski screamed and threw himself sideways. The front bumper nicked him and sent him pitching up on the John Pickering lawn. A moment later the convertible screamed around the corner and was gone.

Steve rolled to his feet and trotted toward the fallen Rajeski. He stopped beside the boy and looked at the way Rajeski had fallen and drawn his legs up in a fetal position, palms pressed tightly against his face, shaking, moaning in a thin, inhuman way.

Suddenly appearing from between houses, looking strangely helpless and blinking with fright, were Norman Teller and Nicholas Cowley.

Steve looked at the pistol held forgotten in Teller's right hand.

"Put that down, Teller," he said.

"What?"

"The gun, Teller. Drop it." Teller dropped it. Steve looked at Cowley. "If you're armed, get rid of the gun, right now."

Cowley nodded dumbly and took a pistol from his jacket pocket and put it on the ground.

"Now stand over there and don't move."

Teller nodded faintly, and both of them walked over to the edge of the sidewalk and stood there unmoving. Steve bent beside Rajeski. "You look like you're just scratched up. Anything broken?"

Rajeski continued to sob in desperate fright.

"Come on! Straighten up. Let's see what's wrong with you."

Finally Rajeski removed his hands from his eyes. His eyes were wide and fixed. Testing his muscles, he slowly got to his feet. He swallowed, more moaning escaping his white lips.

"All right," Steve said. "You're lucky. If you're carrying a weapon, drop it."

Hand shaking, Rajeski pulled out a switch knife and a small caliber pistol and dropped them on the grass. "Now stand over there with your friends."

Rajeski stepped back beside Teller and Cowley.

Steve picked up the weapons. "What do you think of your hero now?" he asked thinly.

There was no reply. He nodded in the direction of the jail. "Let's go."

They hurried across the courthouse lawn until they reached the body of Emil Dome. Steve bent down and tested the pulse, knowing it was useless. Then he herded the trio into the jail, his stomach knotting in apprehension over what he would find.

They were not locked in a cell. A white-faced Martin Hillary was lighting a cigarette with a trembling hand, his aplomb gone for the moment. Mr. Potter stood with his face against the north wall, motionless. Harry Bell was sitting loosely on the cot beside Rod Newall, who was shaking his head slowly, looking groggy, touching the back of his scalp.

"Saw it from here," Hillary said, swiftly regaining his composure. "Dome's dead?"

"That's right," Steve said. He looked at Teller, Rajeski, Cowley. "Into that cell." They filed in, and he closed the door. He found the keys on the floor and locked the cell.

Rod kept wagging his head. "I can't believe she did it."

"What happened, Rod?"

"Gretchen—"

Hillary inhaled from his cigarette. "The girl hit him on the head with the bottle there. She picked up the shotgun and held it on us and got the keys out of the desk and released Kelty. They left in a hell of a hurry—didn't even take time to lock us up. Kelty just ordered us to face the wall and be quiet, then left. He wanted out, period."

Steve stood frowning. "You mean she's with him willingly?"

"That seems to be it," Hillary said.

Steve shook his head, astonished.

Hillary ground his cigarette out. "I think if I hadn't befriended him journalistically, he might have—" He shrugged.

"Killed all of you?" Steve finished thinly.

"Maybe so," Hillary said, eyes thin in thought. "But on the other hand, Dome obviously fired on him first."

"When are you going to give up on him?" Steve snapped. "He's got that girl out there now. And one of these kids." He jerked a hand toward the cell holding the remainder of Kelty's fan club. "Don't you have a conscience, Hillary? How many other people are going to get killed now?"

Hillary nodded, unruffled. "Somebody's going to have to bring him in."

"Well, who the hell is that going to be, Hillary? You?"

Hillary let an ironic smile show faintly on his lips. "I'm afraid that's not my line, Michaels."

Steve forcibly held his building temper under control. He looked at Rod. "You'd better get outside and get some air, Rod."

Rod nodded. "I'll be all right in a minute."

"Come on," Steve snapped. He looked at Harry Bell. Harry Bell spread his hands apologetically, more sober now than he'd been in hours. "Sorry I couldn't do anything, Steve."

"Apparently there wasn't anything that could have been done."

Then he noticed that Mr. Potter was still standing facing the wall.

"I think, Mr. Potter," Hillary said, "you can turn around now."

Mr. Potter turned around tentatively. "Mean bastard."

Steve nodded bitterly. "Yes, Mr. Potter. Yes, indeed."

Hillary motioned at the cell. "These boys just turned themselves over to you willingly?"

Steve looked at them, stripped of all bravado. "Kelty tried to run down one of them." He looked at Teller. "Who's the one who got away with Kelty?"

"Marcelli," Teller said numbly. "Tommy Marcelli."

"Is he armed?"

"The last time I saw him. I guess Louie's still in that house."

"Which house?"

"Across the street. The green one. Tommy carried him in there and put him on the sofa—" Suddenly Teller's eyes misted. He turned and moved to the back of the cell, trying to get control of himself.

Steve said to Harry Bell, "You'd better break the news to Mrs. Blake—tell her Gretchen's with Kelty." He rubbed his hand across his forehead. "What a sweet hell of a mess!" He looked at Hillary. "I take it you're still out of this, Hillary. You wanted Kelty out. Now he's out I take it you don't want to get involved in trying to bring him in."

Hillary shrugged. "My advice, Michaels, is to let it go. The girl did it willingly. It'll be daylight in a few hours. Let the police worry about it." He spoke smoothly, a faint smile on his mouth.

Steve nodded slowly, then switched the machine gun to his left hand, stepped forward, and hit Hillary squarely on the edge of the jaw.

Hillary stumbled backward, hands flying. He fell into the bars of the cell Jack Kelty had vacated, slipped down to the floor clumsily. He shook his head, sitting there, then slowly got to his feet. He looked at Steve, the smile flickered once more. "Feel better now?"

Steve turned abruptly. "Come on, Rod."

Rod followed him outside. He stood against the closed door in the night air, looking bewildered.

"It's all my fault, Steve."

"You let Gretchen in?"

Rod nodded. "My big error—my really big one." He touched his head again. "She—can get somebody to do what she wants just about any time. Me, anyway."

Steve shook his head angrily. "I can't believe she'd do a crazy thing like this! Why?"

Rod blinked. "I wasn't even looking at her. She was just sitting there. She'd been listening to Hillary explain about how her father wanted Kelty turned loose, and—"

"Oh," Steve breathed. "But why would she do a thing like this even if she thought Ben wanted him released? What kind of a thing would get into her brain to—"

"Steve," Rod said. "I think— I mean, maybe she went for Kelty. I don't know. I—" He shrugged. "I wasn't telling you the truth exactly when you asked what happened the other night. I mean, she's—kind of sophisticated about things."

Steve looked at him, frowning. "It was her idea that night. She told me to come over and said what she—well, wanted to do. I mean, I'd never—you know. Only she said she wanted to. And she said I ought to bring something—to protect us. So I did, and, well—" His face had flushed again, and he looked out over the lamplit courthouse lawn, a muscle flickering in his cheek. "I guess she doesn't give a damn who the hell she does what with!"

Steve nodded slowly. "Okay, Rod. I understand. But wild or not, she's just a kid. She doesn't know what she's gotten into. Ben can thank himself for half of it. The only thing that counts now is that I've got to go after Kelty and try to bring her back in one piece. I hope to God he doesn't hurt her."

Rod straightened forcibly. "I'll help, Steve." He turned. "I'll pick up a gun, and—" He sagged. Steve caught him. He looked at the scalp wound in the lamp light. "You were really hit. You'd better stay here, Rod."

"I'm all right."

"Don't argue with me, Rod. Take over in there and hold those kids. Have Harry and Mr. Potter bring in Dome's body. Call Sue in Mrs. Corpler's office and tell her what happened." He paused, eyes thinning. "He's going to try to get across that water— How many decent boats left in town?"

Rod rubbed his mouth. "Some rowboats. They took Ed Burnstead's big one over to Hampton Mill, I know. Ray Finch is the only one who's got a small boat with an outboard attached. I don't know if they took it over to Hampton Mill."

Steve nodded, thinking about Ray Finch, a middle-aged bachelor who worked at a service station and lived with his father on the east edge of town. "I've heard him talk about that boat. I guess everybody has, including Gretchen. If Gretchen knows about it, Kelty knows about it by now. Ray's on the other side of the river. How about his father?"

"The old man got sick a couple of weeks ago. I think he'd be at their house."

Steve walked swiftly back into the jail. He looked up the Finch number and dialed it. There was no answer. "Call Sue, Rod." He started for the door.

"Steve," Rod said. "I swear I can help you."

He shook his head.

"You're going after Kelty, Michaels?" Hillary asked.

"That's right, Hillary."

"Alone?"

"No, I've got a small army out there."

Hillary's usual smile did not appear. He sat down on the edge of the packing crate, looking down. "It's suicide. Michaels."

"Maybe."

"He's got Marcelli with him—I wouldn't do it, Michaels."

"I know you wouldn't, Hillary."

Hillary looked up, met his eyes. "You'd better get somebody to help you."

Steve smiled grimly. "Who, I wonder?"

Hillary continued to meet his eyes for a moment longer, then looked down again and sat there, unmoving.

Steve walked to the door, out, and moved down the sidewalk, glancing once at the sprawled corpse of Emil Dome, wondering if his own body would look as stiff and unreal in death....

Chapter 24

When Steve had reached his sedan, he heard the running footsteps behind him. He turned to see Sue hurrying toward him. She stopped in front of him, eyes frightened, face pale.

"Rod told you?" he said.

"Yes."

"I'm sorry, Sue. I hope I can get her back safely."

She nodded, looking at him. He paused, then said, "I've got to go, Sue."

She continued to stare at him. "Steve, you told me to stay in that office. I did. I heard the shooting and I couldn't see anything. I almost lost my mind. But I stayed there, because you told me to."

He nodded. "You're a good girl, Sue."

She stood, face drained of color. And then her hand came up and the palm cracked sharply across his cheek.

He blinked, bewildered.

"I've always been so good to you, because I love you," she said, voice tight and rising. "In turn, you treat me like something too damned precious to handle. I'm willing to sleep with you, whenever you want, because I love you. But the only way you'll buy that is when you're under tension and need it. When you're in real trouble, you leave me out of it. I'm just a pretty package, never really to be unwrapped. You don't love me, Steve! I've loved you with all my heart! But it's been a one-way proposition, hasn't it?"

"Sue, listen—I've got to go out and hunt a killer down, don't you understand that? I may not come back alive, don't you get that through your head?"

"Yes, I do! And my own sister may come back dead with you. But even more than my sister I'm frightened for you, Steve. You're the one I'm thinking about. Don't you understand that?"

"Yes," he said softly. "But, Sue—I've had it with Ben. He wanted Kelty released. I wouldn't release him. So—"

"So, Steve? What difference how it is with you and Daddy? Has it got anything to do with us, Steve?"

"But—"

"Damn you, Steve. Don't you understand anything? Don't you understand that I don't care about anything—my father, my sister, my mother, nobody—but you? Not if it means having only one thing. If that's you, that's all I want!"

He looked at her, then reached out suddenly. "Sue, you were wrong when you said I didn't love you. I do. I didn't really know for sure until tonight. Not really. But I do now."

Her lips were against his, wet, warm, her tears rubbing onto his face. "That's enough," she breathed. "That's enough."

"I've got to go, Sue."

"Don't, Steve. Let them do it when they cross the river."

"I can't."

"Yes," she said faintly. "I know that." She tipped her head back, looking at him in the pale light. "You'll come back, won't you? Won't you, Steve?"

He smiled thinly. "I'll try—I'll try."

Chapter 25

He'd driven three blocks when Ben Blake's car nosed ahead of him, engine roaring, and brought him to a stop.

Ben Blake got swiftly out of his car, shotgun in hand, came running back and got in beside Steve. His face was white. His whole body was trembling.

"I've got the story," he snapped. "Get moving."

Steve started up again, wheeling around Ben Blake's car and heading east.

"I'll kill Kelty myself, by God. I'll kill him myself!"

"Easy, Ben."

"My baby—my little baby!"

"I'm sorry, Ben."

"Goddamn Newall kid, letting her in there! When I get back I'll kill him too! Why did you leave that kid in charge of that jail?"

Steve glanced at him. "Did you know that Gretchen found out you wanted Kelty released before she let him out?"

Ben Blake turned his head, staring at Steve. He stared at him for perhaps three seconds, then something happened to his face; it seemed to change like a wax figure too close to heat. "It couldn't have been my fault!" he whispered. "I've loved her, loved her—" His voice choked away. He turned his head, looking forward, eyes filmed over, shoulders slumping. "Please. God—"

They saw the yellow convertible. It gleamed in the glare of the headlights at the end of skid marks where it had been brought to a wild stop just in front of the old Finch house.

"God Almighty," Ben Blake breathed.

Steve cut his lights and motor. He got a flashlight from his glove compartment. He looked at the small white house perched at the edge of town, lonely-looking, a small truck garden on one side, an old shack on the far side next to a field of corn. All of it looked ghostly in the moonlight.

Steve was motionless for a moment, getting used to the presence of that convertible. Kelty had made no attempt to hide his escape, partly, no doubt, because he was a maniac now and not thinking clearly, partly because he was city-bred and would not understand the fact that almost everybody in a small town like Blue Valley, including Steve, could learn quickly where a usable boat was located.

"Do you think that boat's still here?" Steve asked quietly. "It wasn't used in the flood?"

"No," Ben Blake said in a thin peculiar voice. "I know it wasn't. Ray told me it was too small for that kind of water."

Steve nodded. "Let's go, Ben. I don't think we'll find them here. But be very damn careful."

Silently they got out of the car and moved toward the house. The door of the screen front porch hung open. The smell of the flood, Steve noticed, was stronger. The house was absolutely silent. The door that let into the house proper was also open. Steve pointed his flashlight, machine gun ready, and turned the light on. The beam instantly fell on a figure lying on a worn, flower-patterned rug in the center of a collection of old-fashioned furniture.

They moved inside, quickly and silently. They looked down on Ray Finch's father, Homer, lying dead and mutilated from the direct blast of a shotgun, his blood soaking into the flowered rug; around the body scurried a loud-buzzing fly.

"Jesus!" Ben Blake said hoarsely and swayed as though he had been struck.

"Stay by the door," Steve said grimly. "I'll check the rest of the house."

He found nothing. He returned to Ben Blake. "How far is the water from here now?"

Woodenly, Ben Blake said, "Probably right over the knoll in back." He rubbed a fist harshly over his face, shaking his head. "Dead, Steve. I know it—she's dead!" A sob, a tearing sound so alien to Ben Blake that it was grotesque, came from his lips. "My fault—my fault!"

"Come on, Ben."

Steve walked out of the house, followed by a robot-moving Ben Blake. Carefully he looked at the shed, then approached it. He kicked the door open, machine gun ready. He waited, the light from the rising moon growing whiter, stronger. Finally he stepped inside. He moved the flash beam over unused chicken coops then saw, at the far end, the wheel marks of a trailer cut through the dusty dirt floor. Double doors at the far end were open. He started to go through the shed, when he heard the sound—soft, whimpering.

At the opposite end of the building was a section once used as a horse stall. He hurried to the wooden partition, followed by Ben Blake. He turned the flash on the figure lying on the floor.

She lay with her hands pressed against her face, dress torn as though ripped with a savage hand straight from the neck to the hem. Stockings askew, black lingerie in rags, she lay frozen, as though waiting to die in that position.

"Gretchen!" Steve said. But Ben Blake was past him, dropping to his knees beside her. "Baby—baby! Are you hurt? Christ don't let you be hurt—"

Gretchen shook her head slowly back and forth, not removing her hands from her face, and sobbed dryly. "Raped me … he raped me."

Ben Blake struggled with his jacket, putting it around her. "God forgive me." His voice was choked, and he put his face against the backs of her hands. "God forgive me—"

Steve stood silent a moment longer, then he said quietly, "Stay with her, Ben."

Ben Blake did not move, but only continued to kneel beside his daughter, his apology sounding again and again. Steve walked outside and looked at the trailer marks that had carried the boat along the edge of the field. They were manhandling the trailer, he thought, to get the boat to water. They couldn't be far ahead of him now.

Beyond the cornfield lay the thrust of a brown-grassed bluff. In the strong moonlight, Steve could see the glittering rush of flood water through a clump of elm trees to the south.

He trotted toward the bluff, moving up from the cornfield. When he reached the peak, he went flat moving to the edge.

There, the bluff was scooped away abruptly, running down to the flooded land in a rain-rivuleted series of small crevices. He saw the boat already in the moon-reflecting water, the prow swinging with the strong current. He saw Marcelli and Kelty climbing into it.

He half rose and yelled, "Kelty!"

He wanted only one thing. He wanted Kelty to turn, to stand upright, so that he could kill him cleanly and properly, without hurting Marcelli. But Kelty suddenly shoved the boat forward, ducking. The boat instantly bobbed wildly, pitching dangerously. As though sensing the futility of it, Kelty suddenly threw himself back, falling through the shallow water, gaining land.

Behind him, Marcelli screamed, "Kelty! Don't! Can't swim! I can't—!" The current tossed the boat over, and Marcelli screamed once more before he was sucked into the dirty water. Then the river ran swiftly, with no more sound than its whipping current made, as Kelty ran in a jagged line for a cluster of trees fifty feet downstream.

Steve came down the bluff. He stopped halfway, going to his knees, raising the machine gun. There was no other way, he knew, and once more he heard the tired voice of Al Duggan, *Don't let him go....*

He pulled the trigger, the machine gun jumped in his hands as bullets splattered after Kelty, shaking the fallen leaves and wild grass behind him, until the bullets caught up and sent him spinning.

Kelty gathered himself up, still holding his gun, screaming now with rage, trying to make his legs go, wrenching around to point his pistol in the direction of Steve.

Steve squeezed the trigger again. The bullets cut along the ground and again into Kelty. Suddenly Kelty twisted, fell sideways, then lay still, crumpled on the bullet-spattered moonlit earth.

Steve sat down backward, clumsily and heavily. His mouth watered and he closed his eyes. He was suddenly retching with sickness.

When that was over, he opened his eyes and stood up. He came down and looked at Kelty's body carefully. Then he turned and walked slowly back up the face of the bluff and down along the edge of the cornfield. He walked very slowly, the machine gun still in his hand....

Chapter 26

When the sun was high and bright, the first helicopters had landed and the water had begun to go down rapidly. Steve, in fresh clothes, Sue beside him, parked his car at the curb beside the Blue Valley Hospital, converted from a large old-fashioned house. Doctor Renley had been flown in and was busily engaged in medicine. The sheriff was also in town, once again in charge of the jail.

"You're sure she wants to talk to me?" Steve asked.

"Yes," Sue said.

"You want to come in?"

"I think she wants to see just you right now. We've already talked, Steve."

He nodded, got out and walked up to the front door. Ben Blake, he discovered, was sitting, tired-looking and drawn-faced, in the old-fashioned parlor of a waiting room. Steve looked at him, then went on down the hall where Katherine Blake came forward to meet him.

"This room, Steve."

"Thanks." He met her eyes. She reached out and touched him. "Thank you, Steve—for protecting all of us."

She opened the door for him, and he stepped inside. It was closed softly behind him, and he looked at Gretchen, her face pale even against the white of a pillow.

"Thanks for coming, Steve."

"Glad to."

"I was just lying here wondering if I'm pregnant. Would I breed a monster because it was Jack Kelty's, I wonder."

"Those are pretty grownup thoughts, aren't they?"

"It's necessary now, don't you think, Steve?"

"I guess it is."

"And about time."

"We all take a while."

"Even you, Steve?"

"Even me."

"That's good. I'm glad to hear that. I wanted you to come and see me so I could apologize to you for everything. Instead you give me something to go on. I'm glad to hear you're a little human too, Steve."

"Quite a little."

"But I'm still apologizing." She turned her head suddenly, looking out a window at a clear sky. "I'm so damned sorry, Steve. Not for myself. But for everything. Mr. Finch dying—" Her voice caught. Tears showed in her eyes.

"Maybe it really wasn't all your fault, Gretchen. A lot of people wanted Kelty turned loose. You've taken more punishment than any of them will."

"No," she said. "There's Daddy."

"I think," he said finally, "you have grown up."

She turned her head back to look at him. "I hope so. I think I have. I've sent word that I hope Rod will come and see me too. Do you think he will?"

"He might. He's quite a boy."

"You and Sue are leaving Blue Valley, Steve?"

"That's right. As soon as we can cross the creek. Maybe they can use me at the University."

She nodded again. "Good luck, Steve."

He bent over and touched her forehead lightly with his lips. "Same to you."

He left quietly. Katherine Blake was waiting for him in the hall. "Steve, stop and talk to Ben, won't you?"

He met her eyes. "I don't see any reason."

"Please, Steve."

He finally nodded. "All right." He moved down the hall. A bandaged Rodney Newall appeared and met him halfway.

"Get any sleep, Rod?"

Rod shrugged. "I'm young. I don't need it."

Steve grinned. "True. How's your mother?"

"She calmed down pretty well."

"And that crack on the head?"

"Like hitting a solid steel ball." He looked down the hall. "I thought I'd see how Gretchen's doing. You know. I mean, it's nothing personal to me anymore. But it must have been rough on her." He motioned a hand behind him. "Hillary's outside—he's been trying to find you."

"Maybe I can miss him if I have any luck." He walked down the hall and into the waiting room. Ben Blake looked up at him, then seemed to become suddenly more alert. He started to stand up.

"Sit down, Ben. Katherine asked me to speak to you. I frankly don't know why."

He nodded wearily. "I can understand how you feel, Steve. We let you down, didn't we? All of us, but particularly me."

Steve looked at him, and Ben Blake suddenly seemed much older, much less capable. "It wasn't just me you were letting down, Ben."

Ben Blake kept his eyes on the floor, very tired-looking. "No, not just you. Everyone and everything. People and principles." He shook his head. "Loved my family, loved this town. I let it all down trying to take the easy way." He looked up. "Steve, you've got to forgive people like Tim Crawford—they're no good in a situation like we had, and you can't expect them to be. But I was supposed to be leading this town, and you had to do it for me." He paused. "You and Sue are leaving?"

"That's right, Ben."

"Yes, I can see why, Steve. I don't blame you. But I wish you wouldn't. Not just so you and Sue would be around. Sure, I'd like that. But mostly because we need you here. I thought I was the big hub here, but we need someone like you, Steve. Someone personally strong, to help give this town some real fiber. I had it once, and I guess I got weak. I'll try to find it again. But it would be easier, loving this town the way I do, to know you were a part of it, Steve."

Steve met Ben Blake's eyes. "I don't think so, Ben."

"Think about it, won't you, Steve? I'm begging you to do that much."

He nodded finally. "I'll think about it."

He walked outside to the bright light of the day. Martin Hillary was waiting for him on the sidewalk. Hillary smiled broadly. "Been talking to your fiancée, Michaels. You're leaving?"

"What's the difference, Hillary? Your personal interest? Developed during our strong friendship last night?"

"Not at all, Michaels," Hillary said cheerfully. "I've never been one to develop a liking for someone who has hit me."

"You're lucky I didn't kill you, Hillary. I still might, you know."

"You hate my guts?"

"That's a fair description of it."

Hillary shrugged. "Do you think that bothers me, Michaels? As a matter of fact, I've grown to dislike you rather intensely. But that doesn't change anything now. My job on you, I mean."

"I don't follow you, Hillary."

Hillary shrugged again. "Very simple. Pretty soon there're going to be newsmen all over this place, but I've got the jump. I'm way ahead. And so the others are going to have to follow me. And what I'm going to do, Michaels, is make a hero out of you like the public has never seen before. You should like that. If not for ego reasons, then because you're going to be a bigger hero than Jack Kelty ever was. You see? Duggan would have liked that, the good winning out over bad. That's what's going to happen, Michaels. When I get done with you, every ounce of influence Kelty ever had on anybody is going to be wiped out and replaced ten times over by the symbol of one Steve Michaels. Get set for it, Michaels. It's going to be very big."

Steve examined him. "Personal advantage, Hillary? Or conscience?"

Hillary's smile flickered away. His bony face was serious in the bright sunlight. His eyes shifted beyond Steve, as though trying to search into space for the answer. Then he smiled again. "Either way, each man has his own soul. Yours is clean. Why worry about mine?"

He turned and walked briskly up to the hospital, paused, then called back, "I'd like to interview the Blake girl. Can you get me in, Michaels?"

Steve turned abruptly and walked to the waiting car. Behind, he could hear the soft laughter of Martin Hillary.

Inside the car, sitting beside Sue, he looked at her, the events of all the past hours flashing in his brain, like a quick-moving motion picture. The toughest part, he thought, perhaps had been the holding to a love firmly, never letting it be warped, true to it every minute and so clear with everything else, because it took a clear and whole spirit to love properly. He was certain, sitting here, looking at this woman, that he had now learned how to love properly.

"I was thinking," he said, "maybe we should stay in Blue Valley."

She looked at him, clear-eyed, and he knew she was seeing right through him. "I see."

"It's a thought anyway," he said, starting the engine. She nodded, smiling. "It's a thought."

THE END

BLUE MASCARA TEARS

James McKimmey

This book should be
dedicated to Ray Bradbury
and so it is.

Chapter I

The doctor motioned toward the room in the manner of a man overloaded with work, responsibility, and the intimate knowledge that people can die under his hands. But the doctor was young, Cummings thought, tougher now than he would ever be again. "Okay, Inspector. He's conscious. But he's dying."

Inspector Jack Cummings walked into the room. A nurse stood beside the gray-faced man lying in the bed, plasma dripping into him. The windows were night-black against the soft interior lighting. A girl was sitting in a corner, tight skirt high and showing her pretty knees. Her mink was slung carelessly over the chair back. She was blond and stupidly beautiful. Her blue-mascara eyes stared at Cummings without expression. The wedding and engagement rings on her finger flashed softly as she clenched and unclenched her left hand.

Cummings came up beside the bed opposite the nurse. She was twenty years older than the doctor, Cummings estimated; she didn't like the approach of death any more than he did. He looked down at the man whose name was Robert Lundstrom. Three bullet holes in his body, Cummings thought, and you could see that in his eyes; they rolled slowly toward him, staring out of a flaccid face. The blond-gray hair was askew against the pillow, but the last haircut had been expensive; Cumming's eyes flicked over the neatly manicured nails of the dead-lying hand outside the sheet.

"I'm Inspector Cummings, Mr. Lundstrom," he said quietly. "Can you tell me what happened?"

The voice wheezed distantly, "I'm a big man. A very big man."

Cummings nodded. "I'd like to know what happened."

"Holy God," Lundstrom whispered, "I want a priest."

The nurse looked at Cummings, then at Lundstrom's wife sitting in the corner. "Is he Catholic?" the nurse asked.

The girl's head swung back and forth. Her voice came out high and toneless. "Get him a priest!"

The nurse pressed the button that lit the bulb outside. A student nurse opened the door. The nurse beside the bed said, "Father Malley, in a hurry."

"Jesus," Lundstrom said, "I'm dying."

"Do you know who did it, Mr. Lundstrom?" Cummings asked.

"Dog barking," Lundstrom said.

"What?"

"When I was phoning Cutter. I had a dog when I was a little boy."

Cummings looked back at the girl. She sat motionless, staring ahead. He turned to Lundstrom again. "You were phoning Cutter?"

"To tell him I had the sixty-five G's. Lila was shopping."

"Mrs. Lundstrom?"

"I'm dying, Lila," Lundstrom said. Again Cummings looked at the girl. She didn't move.

"Knocko Cutter?" Cummings asked.

"Into him for sixty-five G's. He knew he was going to get it."

The etherous smell, the disinfectant smell, the smell of Mrs. Lundstrom's sweet and expensive perfume; the hushed motion outside the corridor; and now the priest walking in as if on sponge rubber. As young as the doctor, Cummings thought: lean, crew-cut hair, fair face, with smudges of darkness beneath the eyes.

He took Lundstrom's hand in his and looked across the room at the girl. "Bless you, child."

"He's not Catholic," the nurse said.

"I want to be absolved," Lundstrom said.

"I'm Inspector Cummings, Father. I'm trying to find out what happened."

Lundstrom stared at the priest from his putty face. "Get out, Priest. What can you do?"

"He said get out!" the girl called in her high, toneless voice.

Eyes weary, the priest left.

"You called Knocko?" Cummings asked.

"I'm a big man," Lundstrom said. "The best."

"You called Knocko to tell him you had sixty-five thousand dollars?"

"I said that," Lundstrom rasped.

"You had sixty-five thousand in your hotel room?"

"Cash."

Cummings shifted his heavy shoulders. The diffused light gentled his hard face, softened the scar across his cheekbone left by a ricocheting bullet years ago. "We didn't find the money."

"I know. It was in the bureau. That's why I'm here. I didn't want that priest, see?"

"Knocko knew you had the sixty-five thousand. Anybody else?"

"Not even Lila. I never tell her anything. Is it her business? Do you know how much that mink cost? Why should I tell her my business?

Christ, I wish I'd bought my mother a mink. But she's dead and I'm dying too."

"What happened then, Mr. Lundstrom?"

"I told Knocko I'd meet him at the hotel in two hours, but I had to pick up Lila. She can't find her way back even in a taxi. I left the hotel. Is the priest gone? I've got nothing against him or his religion. He can't help this. But he can't stop it either."

"What time did you leave the hotel?"

"About five in the afternoon. Holy God. Will I see my mother when I die?"

The nurse looked at Cummings. Cummings shifted his shoulders again. "You left at five?"

"Yeah," Lundstrom gasped. "But I forgot my wallet. I was halfway to meet Lila at Beck's, and I didn't even have the cab fare. So I had the cabbie go back to the hotel. The drapes were pulled in the room. It was dark in there. I started to turn the switch. I heard a whip crack and felt it in the back. Then two more. Heard somebody running out. Lay there and passed out. Can't anybody help? Lila?"

The young doctor returned and motioned Cummings aside. Cummings looked at Lundstrom's wife, who stared steadily ahead. The doctor bent over the man in the bed. Lundstrom said, "Is that you, Priest? I'm glad you're back. Get me up there, please. Where my mother is?" The voice was a distant whisper. Finally the doctor straightened.

Cummings looked at the now silent man in the bed, then at the girl. Two tears ran down in small blue-streaked streams over her young cheeks. She didn't move. She said nothing. Cummings walked out of the room and took an elevator down, thinking that death was like a once-familiar song you'd forgotten the lyrics to. It made you think of the other deaths you'd known. You felt them all again; then you wondered what the song was about. When the song was sung for you, he thought, maybe you would find out.

He went to the car where Mandell was sitting behind the wheel. It was raining lightly. There were a few droplets across the dark fabric of Cumming's suit jacket; they were beaded lightly over his hatless steel-gray hair. Mandell shoved the car into gear with pushing energy, bull neck bulging. "He conk out?"

"Yeah."

"Say anything?"

Cummings told him.

"Where now?" Mandell asked.

"Knocko Cutter."

"You want to phone that in to the captain?"

"No."

The one-way radio spoke softly. Mandell jammed the car forward, swinging it fast out the curving hospital drive. The streets were darkly shiny. Lights flared.

"After Knocko, we go to the hotel," Cummings said. "You don't want to call the captain before you tag Knocko?"

"I'm not going to tag him; I'm going to talk to him."

"Right," Mandell said.

Cummings was silent as the car sped downtown, nosing into the heavy night traffic of the Tenderloin District. He watched the familiar store fronts, hotels, small restaurants, the wealth of bars. He was thinking of the way that blue mascara had run down Mrs. Lundstrum's face. Mandell ran the car into a red zone beside a newsstand, ahead of a small lunch counter.

"Ask him about Vinni," Mandell said brightly.

"Who's Vinni?"

"The most beautiful hooker in the world! Ask him."

Cummings got out of the car. Before he closed the door he said, "You're going to phone the captain while I'm in there. But don't do it for ten minutes. You phone him before then, I'll cut off that chicken feed you're getting from the Palms. I might even put you back on the street."

Mandell's face lost its brightness. "Who do you think you are, Cummings, some kind of god?"

Cummings snapped the door shut. The owner of the newsstand waited for him, weather-browned face broken by a fat-lipped smile. "How's it go, Inspector? You working on that shooting in the Danway Hotel?"

"I might be."

"Sixty-five grand, I hear. Gone like a breeze."

"It came to you fast, didn't it, Solly?"

"It always does. And everybody knows."

"That's right," Cummings said. "Everybody knows."

"You want to see a new one?" Solly said, his grin turning satyric.

"I've got half a minute."

"You'll want to give it more." His hooded yellow slicker squeaked as a hand dived under a pile of newspapers and withdrew a large brown envelope. Eyes gleaming, he slid a glossy photograph out and turned it judiciously toward Cummings. "Come in close. Don't let the rain hit it."

Cummings shook his head. "Who took it?"

"Ernest. Ain't that the goddamnedest? I mean, look at that."

"I am," Cummings said.

"How does he do it? How's he get them to do that, with him and his camera right there? Ain't that the end of them?"

"How much?"

Solly looked surprised. "You want to buy?"

"I just want to know what the going price is these days."

"Ten'll take it."

"We've got inflation, all right." He walked into the small counter restaurant. The light was bright and the air steamy, flavored with the odor of heated grease. He was thinking about the dying of a flaccid- and gray-faced man he'd never seen before who wanted to go to heaven and join his mother. Three small .22 bullets pumped in the back in exchange for sixty-five thousand dollars. Money and death, and sometimes you couldn't separate the material from the spirit. Even the girl was money to Lundstrom, he thought; that almost had to be, because she'd been expensive for him. Then came the reaper, and somebody had been killed; and the only tears that were shed were blue mascara.

"Hi, there, Inspector!"

He nodded to a stalk-thin counterman. "How are you, Charlie? Knocko in?"

"I'll tell him you're here."

"You don't have to." Cummings walked on back past the counter stools, opened a door, then moved through a short hallway to rap twice on a second door.

"Who?" came a foggy, high-pitched voice.

"Cummings."

"Jack!" He heard the man walking quickly; then the door swung open. Knocko grinned at him, ducking his round, balding head. He was a foot shorter than Cummings, but as wide. His suit hung flawlessly. The office, unlike the counter section in front, was richly paneled and furnished with good leather and wood. "I figured you'd be coming, Jack."

"I figured you'd figure that."

"Captain Blaine sent you, right?"

Cummings didn't answer.

"Well," Knocko said swiftly. "Sit down. You want a drink?"

"What have you got?"

"Everything. How about Black Label?"

"That'll do. Where's Bernie? Abner?"

"They've got to sleep. They bug me anyway. Two slobs. They were smart like you, I'd keep them around all night, just to get an education." He poured the Scotch neat and put the glass in front of Cummings. "How's it go, baby?"

Cummings leaned back in the comfortable leather chair, looking at the paneling, smelling the aroma of good whisky. He could also smell Knocko's after-shave; it went for maybe double the price of the liquor, he thought. And why didn't he take some of all of that? Not just the lousy shot, but enough to keep himself in complete stock, always, in good amounts. Because, he thought, then you became a part of the sea, instead of swimming through it. "Up and down, Knocko. That's the way it goes. Always."

He tasted the Scotch carefully, then put the glass back on the desk. He said, "You know what happened?"

The light on Knocko's face faded sadly. "Lundstrom."

"Three times in the back."

"Maybe he'll live."

"He's dead."

"When?"

"Fifteen minutes ago."

Knocko's face tipped slightly sideways. The eyes slanted toward Cummings. "He wake up?"

Cummings got out his pipe, ran a finger lightly around the rim of the caked bowl, then filled it with tobacco. He watched the flame of his match as it fired the tobacco, letting the silence hang. Then he looked at Knocko and thought of what his muscles, Bernie and Abner, had done six months ago to the girl who'd held out a fee from a trick. She'd called headquarters with a voice nearly gone from screaming against a towel. Then she'd lain flat on her back on the bed, spreadeagled, arms outstretched flat on the bloody sheet, unclothed, waiting for them to answer her call. When Cummings had got there with the ambulance people, she'd said, "Look, for God's sake, what they did." But Knocko's disclaimer had been accepted up the line. A sadistic customer had been blamed. They'd never found him.

"Well, tell me, Jack," Knocko said.

"He woke up."

"What did he say?"

Cummings repeated it. "And so now he's dead."

"Yeah," Knocko said mournfully. His face tipped sideways again. "You wanted to check with me because Lundstrom owed me the money, right?"

"Tell me about him, Knocko."

Knocko shrugged. "Two-bit gambler. Had it one month, lost it the next. Worked Nevada, then this state, where he could find the action."

"You gave him some."

"A couple of shots at blackjack. Friendly."

"Sixty-five thousand is friendly, Knocko?"

"You're not going to read me the Bible now, are you, Jack? I thought you understood."

"I understand all. Someday the Federal people are going to swing you by the neck."

"Oh, baby, listen. You want another shot?"

"I want to know when Lundstrom called you."

"About five o'clock? Yeah."

"What did you do then?"

"What did I do? I went down to the Palms for a drink. Five in the afternoon. I always do."

"Who saw you there?"

Knocko straightened. His eyes, Cummings thought, were like pale, translucent marbles, shifting in appearance as such marbles would with changing light. He saw fire in them now. He was thinking of Knocko's large home in the Oak Forest section. His wife, a former stripper, had achieved the pale, unencumbered look of the socially chic. He had two children, a boy seven, a girl nine. Both had advanced I.Q.'s, by some curious genetic phenomenon. They were properly mannered, coolly polite, and would, someday, find a leading place in society, so long as Knocko was able to keep his operation going. If he did, they were going to be placed on the market rich. And someday no one would remember how Knocko had given them their start. Certainly not the hooker who'd held back the fee, because she'd died of internal hemorrhaging forty-one hours after Bernie and Abner had fixed her. He didn't blame the children, but he might if they developed tendencies toward snobbism later on.

"I don't think I like that, Jack."

"I don't give a goddamn, Knocko. Who saw you?"

"I think you'd better give a goddamn, Cummings. Did the captain send you around for this?"

"Forget the captain."

"I'm not going to." He put his hand on the telephone.

"I wouldn't phone him, Knocko."

"You're telling me that?"

"Don't lift it."

The sun was shining in Knocko's eyes now. Corner muscles of his mouth tightened. He lifted the telephone.

Cummings bent over the desk. His fist smashed the telephone out of Knocko's hand. With his other hand he took a handful of jacket and drew the man to his feet, then sent him stumbling backward against the wall. Knocko's face whitened. His eyes turned cloudy. Cummings took three steps after him and slapped him across the mouth, bouncing his head back against the rich paneling. He grasped the jacket again as breath hissed through Knocko's lips. He snapped him against the wood three times, then lifted him back into his chair. Finally he replaced the telephone on the holder. Then he reseated himself. His pipe was still in his mouth. He puffed at it gently, watching Knocko.

"You bastard," Knocko whispered.

"Keep it up. I'll do it again."

"You'll never get away with that. I promise you."

"Who saw you at the Palms?"

"A dozen people." A small trickle of blood ran down from Knocko's mouth; he wiped at it with a handkerchief.

"You could have sent somebody else. Bernie. Abner."

"They were with me! I can prove it. What's the matter with you? Lundstrom owed me the money. He was going to give it to me in two hours. Why would I want to see him killed? Jesus, Cummings. You're going crazy tonight!"

"So somebody else did it. And you lost the money. You didn't look like you were in grief when I came in here, Knocko."

"Why should I? I figured *you* found the money. I figured you were coming to give it to me."

Cummings laughed, his teeth biting the stem of the pipe. "Funny, Knocko. Even Solly outside knows better than that. You knew the money disappeared."

"All right, I had the word. So what?"

"Lundstrom said nobody knew about the money except you and

him, remember? Not even his wife."

Knocko dabbed at the blood still trickling from his mouth, head shoved low. "You've been waiting to get me for a long time, haven't you? Why?"

"For one thing, how about that hooker you had fixed?"

"That's a lie."

"All right. It's because you smell. How's that?"

"You know what's the matter with you? You're bitter. You have been ever since that alky wife of yours tumbled down the hill, and—"

"Shut up, Knocko."

"If you didn't have the god complex, you'd be on the other side of it. You'd be with me. That's what they cut you out for the day you were born. But you—"

Cummings doubled a hand and put it on the desk. "You want more?"

"If I had Bernie and Abner …"

"You haven't. So it was only you and Lundstrom who knew about the money. Lundstrom's dead and the money's gone."

Knocko stared at Cummings' doubled fist, then put away his handkerchief because the bleeding had stopped. "Jack, listen. Why? I mean *why?*"

"You wanted the money."

"I told you I was at the Palms, with Bernie and Abner. A dozen people know that. Check it. Besides, Lundstrom was *giving* me the money he owed me. Why would I chop him when it was coming anyway?"

"You never trusted a nickel in somebody's else's hands in your life."

"Jack, listen—"

"You wanted to make certain you really got it. It's simple."

"No, baby. Never. Lundstrom was a cheapie, but he wasn't a fink. He was good for it. He had to be, to get the action. How long would he have lasted if he'd finked anywhere? He got into you; then he paid back when he had it. He had it. Only somebody else knew and chopped him. Now I'm out the sixty-five thousand."

"Who knew he had it, Knocko?"

"How do I know? Maybe the guy he won it from. Followed him here and took it back. How do I know? His wife?"

"I keep telling you Lundstrom said she didn't know."

Fire showed in Knocko's marble eyes again. "That broad? Two steps from a hooker? Money, that's all that talks to her. I ought to know. I introduced her to Lundstrom. She was putting out for the fat cats around this town, and I handed her to Lundstrom. He was crazy enough to marry her. Why? Now look what's happened. All screw, no brains. But she'd have enough to find out he had the money; because she could smell it. Bust her around, why don't you? Break her nose, and you got the money. Then maybe I get it back."

Cummings looked at his pipe and thought: No, Knocko did not like women. His wife was the necessary ornament, to breed his kind, to model his phony legitimacy. But the others he hated. Viciously.

"Maybe I'll work her over, Knocko," he said. "While she's in grief."

"Grief!"

The telephone rang. Cummings looked at his watch. He stood up.

"Is that all?" Knocko asked, surprised.

"For now."

"I didn't like that pushing around. The captain won't either."

Cummings nodded. "Don't bother calling him. Just lift the phone. He's calling you."

Chapter 2

Cummings stepped into the captain's office, a simple room with light-gray walls; there were two pictures on the captain's desk: one of his family—a plump wife and two daughters—and one of the mayor inscribed, "To my dear friend, Captain of Detectives Otto Blaine."

Blaine looked up, his eyes hurt and condemning. Hands white and very clean beneath starched cuffs, he put down a report he had been reading with care. He had installed a sink in one corner of the room and washed his hands perhaps two hundred times a night. Cummings wondered what the impulse and significance were. Perhaps there were none. He sat down in front of the desk. The captain swung his chair sideways, gazing away at a blank wall. Coolly, Cummings thought. In pain. He wore no jacket. That was carefully fitted over a hanger on an old-fashioned wooden rack. His tie was knotted neatly against his collar. His hair was gray and trimmed in military shortness at the temples. He had been a first lieutenant in Washington, D.C., during World War II. Cummings had been an infantry major in the European combat.

"Mandell said you wanted me back here. Right away."

The captain continued to stare in grief at the wall. "Why did you do it, Jack?"

"The Lundstrom case happened in my district. I have it. I'm working on it."

"Why did you push him around? Why didn't you tell me you were going to see him?"

There was an electric percolator on a small table in a corner; the sergeant had just set it up for the captain. It started bubbling with a rhythmic, liquid sound. "I've been an inspector on this force for twelve years, Captain. I don't usually ask permission to talk to scum."

"You know what I mean, Jack. You know damn well what I mean."

"Yes," Cummings said. "I know what you mean."

The captain turned, his face turning pink. "Why this one-man crusade to get Knocko Cutter? Why?"

"Because he works my district. I don't care what kind of influence he has at city hall. He's an illegal gambler. He's an illegal moneylender. He runs the prostitution. He's a killer. Is that enough?"

"None of that's been proven."

"Otto, do you want me to take you over there and get you in a quick game of fan-tan? You want a loan at one hundred per cent compounded interest? You want to get laid?"

Blaine's face turned pinker. "Don't talk to me that way, Jack. Don't ever talk to me that way."

Cummings put a hand in his jacket pocket and put his fingers tightly around his pipe to hold his temper. It was not really Blaine, he thought. It was above Blaine, in the mysterious but real area which you could never, as an inspector, quite put the light on clearly. But it was there above, sucking up part of Knocko's profits. It was a corrupt administration that had put on the fix, and Blaine was merely in the middle, protecting himself, holding on to his job like a frightened rabbit, pretending that he had no part of it when he strengthened the fix by attempting to protect Knocko Cutter. He was perhaps a good man, but without guts, who had marred himself irreparably by looking the other way. He was perhaps a good man who had become a hypocrite without admitting it to himself, becoming as well the official protector of the fix. But perhaps, Cummings thought, his crime was only a matter of degree. Because the fix was everywhere, in some form, large and small, no matter the endeavor. But this was a very large fix.

"I'm a Mason," Blaine said. "An Elk. A member of the American Legion and the Chamber of Commerce, I am a Presbyterian. I am the father of two girls. I don't smoke. I don't drink. Don't talk to me about getting laid, Jack. Don't ever do that again."

His world, Cummings thought, had become a fantasy, despite the reality surrounding him. That was what reality sometimes did when it was too strong. Because of his job, and the way he handled it, he was up to his neck in filth; yet he could sit in the sanctity of his grey-walled room with the pictures of his family and the mayor, the aroma of brewing coffee in the air, and let the garbage pass by, unseeing, unsmelling. But did he feel? Just before sleep perhaps? "All right, Otto. I'll be very careful in the future."

"All right, Jack. And I'll ask you again. Why did you push Knocko Cutter around?"

Why, he thought, had he done this? The reason was simple. The job had become his life's blood, and he couldn't bring himself to sever his existence from that nourishment. He might starve to death. And why did Captain Otto Blaine, or even the chief, or even higher, allow him to continue? Because he knew every river, every stream, every rivulet in his district. He knew, and was known, and could perform what nobody else could there. Perhaps more important, and because he knew a lot, it was best to hold on to a man who knew that much. "I still remember that girl he had killed six months ago. I couldn't touch him. Not even lightly. Because the fix is on."

"God damn it, Jack," the captain exploded. "I don't like sacrilegious swearing, but I don't like your inferences either. There was no evidence. Nothing. Do you think I'm on the take? Are you going to tell me that?" His voice had sharpened and gone louder.

"I don't think you're on the take. But somebody is."

"Who? Have you got any evidence of that?"

Cummings laughed softly. "All right, Captain."

"That girl. What was she, anyway? A whore. What could she have expected? Sooner or later."

Cummings looked into Captain Otto Blaine's eyes and was certain of one thing: his rationalization was real, in his mind. There was no status in whoring. You could pronounce negative judgment on the profession. Therefore the simple crime of torture and murder could be forgotten.

"Working for Knocko, palming a fee, that's right—that's all she could expect."

"No evidence," the captain repeated. "None."

"They tore her apart, Otto. You should have gone down and looked at her."

The captain's lips thinned. He turned his chair again and stared at the wall. "I'm going to tell you something, Jack. No man under my command goes anywhere and works over anybody. No matter who it is. I don't want that to happen ever again."

Cummings nodded bitterly, thinking that what he meant was: Rough up anybody in the district, but don't touch Knocko Cutter.

"Do you get that, Jack?"

"I think you've made it clear."

"Mandell told me what happened with Lundstrom."

"When he phoned you about my seeing Knocko?"

The captain swung back to face him again. "Why in the world would you think Knocko would have killed Lundstrom to pick up the money he was going to get anyway?"

"I check everything, Captain."

"Then let's see some action on this then. He said he was at the Palms."

"Sure, with Bernie and Abner and a dozen other people. And he's got that bar fixed like everything else."

"How about a little less personal vendetta, Jack? How about thinking about Lundstrom's wife?"

"He said she was waiting at Beck's department store for him. I'll check it tomorrow."

"She could have hired somebody."

"Sure."

"Where'd Lundstrom get the sixty-five thousand?"

"Gambling, I suppose."

"Where?"

"The hotel told me he'd said he just came up from L.A."

"Somebody may have followed him to get it back."

"I've heard that before tonight. It happened to cross my own mind."

"I'll put it on the teletype and have them check down there. Find out who he was playing with."

"That could help."

"How much have you checked at the hotel?"

"Not much. I followed Lundstrom to the hospital. I wanted to get as much out of him before he died, if he did. He did. And I didn't get much."

"You'd better question his wife, Jack."

"I figured I'd give her ten or fifteen minutes for mourning before I did."

"When you get smart, Jack, I can overlook it. But when you're causing trouble and getting smart at the same time, it annoys me."

"All right, Otto. I just don't like to see somebody die. I did, not too many minutes ago."

"He was a cheap gambler."

"He was a human being."

The telephone rang softly atop the captain's desk. He lifted it and spoke quickly, then put it down. "You'd better get over to that hotel, Jack. That's quite a place in that rotten district you feel such a holy father about. Now they've had a rape there. Take care of it."

Chapter 3

The Danway Hotel was two blocks from Knocko Cutter's lunch counter, in the heart of the district. Cummings, accompanied by Mandell, left the car in a parking zone in front and walked through the still-wet evening. Ten years ago, under another city administration, the lobby had offered a musty rundown front to a cheap collection of shoddy rooms used by small-pension oldsters and in-and-out customers of five-dollar hustlers. That administration had raided the hotel three times and finally closed it.

It was then purchased by a man named Irving Levi. He owned part interests in three Nevada casinos and had brought in the roving gambling trade, such as Lundstrom. He had cleaned it up and redecorated it, including the lobby, which now offered pale plastic furniture and two rather ornately framed mirrors. Men who could afford better came here, and there was no prostitution. Even Knocko, Cummings thought, had not been able to penetrate the Danway with his operation; the gambling performed was private, among customers only.

Franklin, the night manager, was waiting for them in front of the small mahogany desk. He jerked his thin shoulders nervously, stretching his long neck. "This is a bad night for the Danway, Inspector," he said. Cummings noticed a slight tic in his right eye. "Terrible. Mr. Levi himself came down. He's in my office now. He wants to talk to you."

"I'll give him a minute."

Cummings strode with Mandell to the office. Franklin trotted ahead of them, swinging open the door to the small office. "Here they are, Mr. Levi!"

"All right, Franklin. Don't cry, please. Just leave us alone a little." Levi was small and smooth-faced and wore a white tie beneath a dark-blue suit.

"Yes, sir," Franklin said, and left.

"Inspector," Levi said to Cummings, getting up behind the desk. "Assistant inspector?"

"That's right," Mandell said.

"Sit down, Mr. Levi," Cummings said. "We're not staying."

"Murder," Levi said, sitting down wearily. "I called headquarters. They told me he died. Now rape. What else?"

"It's your night."

"I'll tell you, Inspector! Sit down and I'll tell you. Just a little. I want you to hear."

Cummings sat down. Mandell backed to a wall and leaned there.

"What makes it happen?" Levi asked. "I know it all my life. I believe in it. But what makes it?"

"That's the puzzle," Cummings said.

"It's like I sit down to play twenty-one. It comes to me. Irving, it says to me, play twenty-one tonight. I play twenty-one, with a feeling. It's like some voice coming down to me from the sky, saying, Irving, play. But I don't hear it. I feel it. It's like music I can't hear, but I feel it, in the blood, running along like a beautiful melody I couldn't hum to you. And what happens?"

"You're a winner," Cummings said.

"Every time. Other times I hear another music I couldn't hum to you. Bad music. I feel that in the blood too. Like what? Like it says, Irving, don't touch nothing. But the brain, it says something else. It says play, Irving. Take the action; it's all right. But the music is wrong. And I play. What happens?"

"You lose."

"Every time. Why?"

"I don't know, Mr. Levi. They call it occult, I think."

"Occult, sure. But I don't care what it's called. I care what it is. And I had it this morning. The bad music. My brain, it says, Irving, it's all right; you're doing fine. But the music I feel and couldn't hum to you if I lived a thousand years says no. It says, Turn in your chips, Irving. Cash in and sit back. Enjoy your grandkids, a good cigar now and then, a little good bourbon maybe. But get out of it. That's what the music said I felt in my blood. And what happens?"

"Somebody shoots Lundstrom."

"Now some little girl up there. Fourteen years old. She comes screaming home and tells her parents she's been raped by a Negro. Oh, God, Inspector. Why?"

Yes, Cummings thought, why? What brought it together, one thing, then another, and you could feel them coming before they came? You knew that they were taking you somewhere, somewhere, as Levi has just said, where you had to consider cashing all the chips or getting ruined in the game. He felt that now, but why? How many murders had he covered? How many rapes? So why the feeling now? But he'd felt it, as Irving Levi had felt it. And it was true: you couldn't hear it, but you could feel it. The music was real and it never lied.

"I've got to get up there, Mr. Levi."

"Sure. But let me say it. The little girl. Raped out in the streets. Not here, thank God. But Lundstrom. What do you think about that, Inspector?"

"I haven't had much time."

"Just one thing. You think maybe Irving Levi is in it just for the money, right?"

"Maybe most of the world is."

"Maybe. All but a few. Maybe you're not, Inspector. I've heard things about you."

"We've got to get upstairs," Cummings said.

"Only remember, Inspector: Lundstrom I wouldn't have hurt a hair on his head. Why? Sixty-five thousand dollars? I can give you that much, Inspector. Cash, right now. Maybe it's true I'm in it for the money. But I do it clean. I wouldn't've hurt Lundstrom."

"You can't now."

"Ah, God, yes. But I do it clean, Inspector. I don't hurt them, like Knocko."

Cummings nodded. "I believe that, Mr. Levi. But I'm just starting."

Cummings rapped lightly on a door numbered 510. A medium-tall man in an undershirt opened the door. "Mr. Joplin?" Cummings said. "Inspector Cummings. This is Assistant Inspector Mandell."

"You took a hell of a long time coming," Joplin said in a flat, nasal accent.

"Sergeant Brooks is already on the street checking this." He moved inside with Mandell, looking at the hunched but muscular white shoulders of the man. His hands and face were tanned.

"I don't want sergeants in uniform," Joplin said. "I want detectives. Is that what you are?"

Cummings' eyes switched, examining the room. A plump woman in a worn housecoat sat silently in a chair, her face raw-red, as if it had been scrubbed with a too-strong soap. There was an empty, untidy bed. In a studio couch along one wall the pale face of a pretty girl appeared above a blanket, large brown eyes watching Cummings. The room was crowded and stifling with steam heat. "We're detectives, yes."

"Time you got here then."

There was a whisky bottle on a nightstand; a glass, partly filled, was beside it. Cummings could smell the whisky and the man's sweat. Joplin sat down on the bed beside the table and propped his elbows on his knees with the glass in his hands. He'd had enough for rare courage, Cummings thought. So had the woman, he decided, except that it had not given her courage but only stupefaction. She had enough Puritan in her to have hidden her glass before they came in; he could see the bottom of it beneath a drape. There were two unused chairs, but Joplin did not make an invitation. Cummings and Mandell stood.

"We've got the sergeant's report," Cummings said. "But I'd like to hear it again, so we get it right." Repetition, he thought, was the great advantage. Get enough of it, and you often found the truth.

"She come in here." Joplin nodded toward the girl beneath the blanket. "She was walking down the street, coming back from a show, and this nigra grabs her into an alley and rapes her." He shook a cigarette out of a pack from the night table and put the filter between his yellowed teeth. He looked at Cummings with hazy, hating eyes.

The girl watched Cummings. Her mother sniffed mournfully. A closet door was open and Cummings could see what was apparently all of their clothing stuffed into it: cheap, shabby garments. But the bottle on the nightstand, he thought, contained the best. He looked at his watch. It had been exactly twenty-one minutes since Captain Blaine had delivered the news of the rape. The phoned report from Sergeant Brooks had indicated that the girl had come directly home after it had happened. She was perhaps less than thirty minutes away from the disaster, and Cummings could not find it in her eyes; there was no shock visible, no horror, no self-hating for having been the unwilling instrument for a man gone savage. But you could never tell, he thought, and it was never the same.

"That's what happened?" Cummings asked the girl.

"Yeah," she said.

"We come up from Norman," Joplin said. "We was down in Saint Pete, and we come up through Savannah, then over to New Orleans, then up to Norman. Now we come here. I'm in construction, see? I can run any kind of heavy equipment you want. I can get a job anywhere. Only we should've stayed in Norman instead of coming to this town. You know the price of renting a house here? That's why we're staying in this place. So now the only daughter I got has got some nigra putting that black—"

"Jess!" the woman said.

"Truth!" the man said. "Just like she said it. That's what happened, didn't it, Tina?"

"Yeah," Tina said.

"Where did it happen?" Cummings asked the girl.

"We told the other one," Joplin said.

"I want to get it right."

"Where was it?" the man asked his daughter.

"Down the street two blocks. Where the alley is."

"That would be where the health food counter is?"

"That's where it was."

"Where did this colored man come from?"

"He was in the alley."

"Then what?" Cummings asked.

"He jumped out and grabbed a-holt of me and dragged me in there and did it."

Cummings looked at Mandell, who was staring at the girl in fascination. She had an extraordinarily beautiful complexion. But there was no animation in her face or eyes. Cummings pictured the place the girl had named. The street there was well-lighted and, until very early in the morning, usually busy with people. The alley was relatively dark, but not secluded. Three bars had rear doors opening to it, and customers sometimes used the back entrances. To have accomplished his mission, the attacker must have been fast.

"Nobody was near on the sidewalk when he grabbed you?" Cummings asked.

The girl rolled her head slowly against the pillow.

"Did you cry out when he grabbed you?"

"I was too scairt. Niggers always scairt me."

"Did you fight him? Scratch him?"

"What the hell's the difference?" Joplin said. "Scratching ain't going to be what that nigra's going to get. I find him, I cut them right off him."

"If we're looking for a man who might be marked, it helps," Cummings said quietly.

"I didn't do nothing," the girl said. "He scairt the hell out of me."

"Don't say 'hell,'" her mother said and looked thirstily at the drape where she'd hidden her glass.

"Well, he did," the girl said.

"Don't argue with your ma!" the man snapped. He poured his glass half full again. "Every nigra in the world ought to be castrated. Be some worth then. Use 'em like jackasses, then, and they don't breed. What if he knocked her up?"

How many people in the country thought that way? Cummings wondered. The minority object of hatred, a balm to defective personal confidence, anxieties, fears—a balm like the booze. This man, he thought, didn't drink for pleasure but for courage. He hated for the same reason. And why had the daughter of such a man been the object of hatred on the other side? No man raped for pleasure any more than this man drank for pleasure. He raped out of hatred. Was that it? Or was it something else?

"Don't say that," the woman said.

"Black-blooded bastard."

"Where, exactly, did it happen?" Cummings asked the girl.

The girl brought a pink hand from beneath the blanket and rubbed her nose. "'Bout halfway down the alley. Put me up against the wall and did it that way."

Tears showed in the woman's eyes. The man said, "Christ Almighty!" He got up and retrieved her glass from behind the drape and put it in her hands. "They never seen a woman take a drink? You got a damn good enough reason." He sat down again on the bed and said to Cummings, "You in what? Vice squad?"

"We're in a special division. We handle all of it."

"You better handle this, then. Or I'm taking it clear up to the mayor."

"Sergeant Brooks said you couldn't describe the man," Cummings said to the girl.

"Nothing but he was a nigger."

"Tall, short?"

"Tall enough to do what he did."

"I mean, was he large, small, fat, lean?"

"Big, I guess. He was big."

"Beard? Clean-shaven?"

"I don't think he had a beard."

"What was he wearing?"

"I don't remember."

"It was raining. Did he have a raincoat?"

"Some kind of raincoat. Yeah. When he got me up against the wall, he opened it up and—"

"You don't have to tell them that," her father snapped.

"Did you call a doctor, Mr. Joplin?" Cummings said.

"What for?"

"She should be examined."

"It's done, ain't it? What good is that? If she's knocked up, it's too late now. If she is, I kill that kid the day it's born."

"Don't talk like that," his wife said, and she was drinking now too.

"I think she should be examined," Cummings said. "There might be a possibility of infection."

"Oh," Joplin said. "Well, where do we get a doctor this time of night?"

"We could take her over to City Hospital."

"All right," Joplin said.

"If one of you wants to come along ..."

"Ain't any reason," Joplin said. "Just make damn sure nothing else happens to her. And deliver her back safe. How long's it take?"

"It shouldn't take long."

"I'll be looking at my watch."

No, Cummings thought, he wouldn't. He would be looking into the bottom of his glass.

"Get dressed," Joplin ordered the girl.

She pushed the blanket aside and swung her legs over the side of the bed. She was dressed in nothing but a slip. She walked to the closet, demonstrating a completely matured body with large, thrusting breasts and ample, swinging hips. She squeezed into a tight purple skirt, then drew on an equally tight orange sweater. She pushed at her hair and looked at Cummings, then at Mandell; she smiled at Mandell.

"What are you going to do to get him?" Joplin asked.

"I'll have the vice squad start picking up men who've got this kind of record, are known to be in the district, and who match the description. We'll be working on it too. I know this section. A Negro—somebody should remember seeing him."

The man refilled his glass and his wife's, eyes moist and red. His speech was thickening. "When you get him, I want ten minutes with him. Alone."

"Are you ready?" Cummings asked the girl.

The girl pulled a cheap raincoat from a closet hook and nodded. Her father motioned a hand distantly and tipped his glass up. "Jesus," he whispered, then stared ahead, letting his hatred warm him along with his liquor.

They went out into the hall and followed the girl toward the elevator. She was carrying her raincoat, and her behind switched extravagantly in the tight skirt. Mandell, Cummings noticed, watched with dedication. Maybe, Cummings thought, it wasn't rape for hatred at all, but that rare one for pleasure. Which meant that maybe it hadn't been rape at all, beyond the statutory kind. But whatever it had been, he thought, watching that motion, he could see how it might have got started.

Cummings stood in a small anteroom of the hospital. The doctor, who was not the one who had attended Lundstrom's death, had poured coffee for them. He was large with a black mustache. He propped one very big-shoed foot on a chair and sipped the coffee contentedly.

"Somebody had her then?" Cummings asked.

"Oh, yes."

"First time, you think?"

"No. I gave her a shot. Told her when to come back. I sent her out to the cashier, so they know where to bill her old man." He shook his head reflectively. "You know what I think about that rape, Inspector?"

"What's that?"

"I think maybe she liked it."

Mandell had driven around the building to park in the front lot of the hospital. Cummings saw the girl at the cashier's window; Mandell was waiting in the lobby. "Set?" he asked the girl.

"That doctor was real handsome, wasn't he?" she said, as they walked toward the lobby. "I mean doctors are something. Niggers I hate. I'm scairt of them. But I like doctors. White ones."

Mandell joined them. As they started through the lobby, Cummings saw her in a corner of the room.

"Did you see her?" he asked Mandell.

"No."

"Take the girl out to the car."

Mandell and the girl went out. Cummings walked to the corner. "Mrs. Lundstrom?" he asked softly.

She looked up at him. She had repaired her make-up, but her eyes were pink and swollen.

"Inspector Cummings."

"I remember."

"Is everything all right?"

"They took him away."

"I'm sorry."

"So am I."

"Are you waiting for someone?"

"No."

"Could we help? A ride back to the hotel?"

"I'd never stay in that hotel again."

What, he thought, did she really feel? He could tell nothing from her voice or face. "Isn't there somebody I could call for you? A friend?"

"I've got no friends in this town. I've got no friends anywhere."

"Do you want to go to another hotel, then?"

She looked up at him again, sitting in expensive clothes topped by the mink. "I haven't got any money."

"You mean you can't get it tonight?"

"I couldn't get it any time."

"If there was something in your husband's effects, I could—"

"Three dollars. They gave it to me. That's cab fare. But I've got no place to go in a cab. I won't go back to that hotel. I don't have money for any other. He worked on credit, see? What he had was the sixty-five thousand. He set up charge accounts for me. Only he never gave me any money. He'd even come around and pick me up, when I was out somewhere. So I never needed any. He was going to get into a game tonight. They'd give him credit. Only now he's dead."

She looked away from him. She felt something, all right. It was perhaps nothing more than desolation for her own plight. But she was feeling at least that.

He walked to a public telephone booth. A few moments later he returned and held out a twenty-dollar bill. "I phoned a cab for you. It'll be along in a few minutes, so you won't have to ride in our car. Tell the driver you want to go to the Bay View Motel. It's a nice place. I made a reservation for you. See if you can get some rest. I'll have your things sent over to you. Then I have got a few questions, but they won't be tough. Say tomorrow afternoon, about five-thirty. All right?"

She looked at the bill, then took it and held it carefully. The mascara was running again. "Thank you," she said.

Chapter 4

When they got back to the Danway Hotel, Mandell pleaded hunger. Cummings sent him down the street to a lunch counter. He rode with the girl up to her floor. When she went inside, he saw that the room was dark. He returned downstairs and found the night manager, Franklin.

"An honestly horrible night, Inspector," Franklin said. "How's the girl?"

"She'll be all right."

"Mrs. Lundstrom hasn't come back. I mean, we could put her in another room. Not in the one where it happened." Franklin shuddered. "Blood's so terrible to clean up. But do you think she'll be coming back? It isn't that we're overly concerned. But with Mr. Lundstrom out of commission, as it were, I'm not certain about her means of support, if you know what I mean. With all of that money stolen—well, she could sell something, I suppose. That mink—"

"Maybe that'll bury him," Cummings said flatly.

"Well, that's an idea. It's just that we're familiar with the fact that Mr. Lundstrom often walked the financial tightwire, as it were, and—"

"Is this your worry, or Mr. Levi's?"

"Oh, Mr. Levi has nothing to do with it. But as night manager—"

"She won't be coming back, Franklin. Just collect her things. One of our cars will pick them up. You can stop worrying. I'd like to see the switchboard."

"Certainly, Inspector."

He led him behind the registration desk. A clerk looked at them sullenly. "Let's look alive, Mitchley!" Franklin snapped. "It's Inspector Cummings!"

Mitchley failed to look alive. Franklin drew in his breath in disgust, then pointed through an open Dutch door to a small switchboard room. On one side of the board was a turn rack containing check-in cards. On the other was a small desk.

"Who runs it this time of night?"

"Actually the calls are quite sparse during the night, so when a call comes in we have it set on buzzer. Mitchley just skips in here—well, he doesn't skip, he's really quite dull, that fellow—and handles the call. During the day we have our regular operator."

"Who's that?"

"Laureen Beggs. She's been with the hotel ever since Mr. Levi acquired it."

"What hours does she work?"

"Eight to five. Forty minutes off for lunch. Mr. Dudley, the day manager, steps in on her lunchtime and takes over. He grouches about it, but after all, that's the hotel business. I have to relieve Mitchley in the same way nights. None of us has everything, do we?"

"She would have been on the switchboard at five this afternoon then?"

"Yes. When I came on duty a few minutes before five, I recall coming in and saying a few words with her. A minute or two after five, when Mitchley got on the desk, she left."

"Where does she live?"

"In the hotel. I'd rather imagine she'd be asleep now. But if you want to talk to her—"

"I'll catch her tomorrow. Leave a note for her that I'd like to talk to her in the afternoon, will you?"

"I certainly will, Inspector. In fact, anything I can do. You're going to crack this, aren't you?"

"We'll try."

"And that little girl who was raped. Awful!" He shuddered again. "I hope you get the devil who did that."

"We'll try that too, Franklin."

"I just know you will. There's something about you, Inspector. Something that commands instant respect. It's your demeanor. I think maybe it's the way you're built, too." His eyelids squeezed down. "You're built awfully well, Inspector."

"Well, thank you, Franklin," Cummings said. "That's truly lovely of you."

When Cummings moved back through the lobby, he saw that Mandell had not yet returned to the car. Mandell, he thought, was a screw-off, an informer, interested in getting deeper in on the take, and consistently disloyal to his wife; additionally, he was probably a lousy father to his three kids, because he seemingly spent as little free time at home as possible. But as a cop he was strong, could take and carry out a forceful order, had unflagging nerve in a clutch, and could fire the service pistol carried beneath his jacket with hairline accuracy. He was useful.

Then Cummings saw a man standing up from one of the lobby chairs. He walked over, and the man grinned shyly. "How are you, Jack? I've been tailing around after you for an hour."

"It's been a night."

"Got a couple of minutes?"

"I think so."

He sat down with him, feeling easy in his presence. Mike Hawley was a columnist for a morning daily; but he looked, Cummings had always thought, as a novelist should. He was tall, lean, a bit stoop-shouldered, though he was not yet forty. He wore old, expensive suits and similar shoes, and had attended Princeton. There was a folded trench coat and a tweed hat resting on the chair beside him. Most of the columnists on the paper, Cummings thought, kept their readership either by playing to tight mass prejudices, or by deliberately insulting sacred cows, but doing it with no other motive than the desire for strengthening readership. Hawley, however, wrote his column—on any and all subjects—with a rare honesty. His power was in truth, and Cummings had liked him ever since Hawley had been a workaday police reporter.

"Maybe the cleanest hotel in the district," Hawley said, "and now look at it."

"You going to do a little crime reporting, Mike?"

"If it has social implication."

"Crime always has social implication. What else?"

Hawley nodded. "Murder. Rape. High drama and the implication, especially rape."

"You're interested in that—especially."

"Especially, since miscegenation is involved. She was raped?"

"Somebody banged her."

"She give you anything to work on?"

"Not much."

Hawley leaned back, gray eyes reflective. "We have the big colored revolution, and something like this is certain to happen. Three days ago the mayor and a collection of leading citizens assured the Negroes of improved conditions. Now a man with dark skin takes it upon himself to demonstrate his authority by using his ultimate weapon. What's the girl like?"

"Pretty. Built. Fairly stupid, I'd say. Her parents are also stupid, boozers, and fresh out of Florida, Georgia, and Oklahoma."

"That'll give Negroes a chance to scream foul, won't it?"

"Maybe they'll be right. Maybe not. It wouldn't be the first white girl to be raped by a colored man. But I'm sick of racial bearings, religious bearings, or any other ethnic bearings. If we had a touch of individual morality in the first place we wouldn't have that."

"Ah, but we don't, and we do."

"The mayor, you said. He gives a racial group assurance of improved conditions. Lip service. You know it. And I know it. You say revolution. There is no revolution unless it turns violent. It's wishful thinking, something to believe in, to make the conditions seem better. People always need something to believe in, to live for, to die for. But look down the history of cultures, and you'll find that what people have lived for and died for is generally as long-lasting as an ice-cream cone on a hot day."

"What do *you* believe in then, Jack?"

He filled his pipe and lit the tobacco, thinking: What do I believe in? Swimming through the sea, always working never to become a part of it, because the contamination would be fatal. But could you keep from being a part of it? Could you escape the contamination in the end?

He worked in the system of the fix, and tried not to become a part of it. Was it possible? Or was he only fooling himself, being Christ-like within his own mind and heart, but deceiving himself that he was achieving the attitude? Was, he thought, Christ really fallible or, as they said, infallible? Could anything, less than God, ever achieve anything that approached infallibility? Perhaps, he thought. But perhaps not, if the anything were human. Perhaps Christ was purely human, after all. Perhaps his was a reasonably successful swim through the sea, no more, with the contamination slighter than most men achieved. But to do it he would have had to have known he was Christ, wouldn't he? Maybe he had been God, in that form, after all.

"I don't know. Myself, I guess. That's what I believe in. And maybe not so much in that."

"If every man believed in himself, we'd have it, wouldn't we?"

"Maybe not. Because when a man starts believing in himself

enough, he wants other people to believe in him too. Then he inflicts his attitudes on others. Maybe he's full of self-delusions. If he gets enough power he turns out to be a deadly charlatan. He doesn't know it, and nobody else foolish enough to believe in his beliefs knows it either."

"Most people want to follow power. To believe in someone. Sometimes they don't care if the object of attention is a charlatan, or his beliefs a deception."

"It's a hell of a lot easier than unscrewing the top of one's head and trying to see what's really inside—without relying on some kind of god. Easier not to ask personal questions, easier to follow the leader."

"Who may be corrupt."

Cummings nodded. "Large and small scale. But it always comes down to the same thing: the individual. And if the individual is as safe as he can be from delusions, then I think, in the end, it's all right. And I'd better get the hell to work."

Hawley smiled. "Always a pleasure to talk to a philosopher, Jack."

"One of my self-delusions, too. But mostly I'm a cop, And maybe that's all I want."

"Maybe," Hawley said, "that's enough."

Cummings drove his own car home wearily. He and Mandell had questioned half a dozen Negroes known to be in the area at the time of the girl's rape. Three of them had provable alibis. None of the remaining three had sex records, but the vice squad would stay on them. Tomorrow, he thought, he would arrange a lineup and give the girl a crack at it. The Lundstrom shooting, he thought, was a blind alley. Knocko's alibi of the Palms seemed tight—but he could have, as Cummings had told the captain, fixed it. It appeared to be a simple murder for money, with no other motivation obvious. And when the motivation was simple, it was always the toughest to solve.

He drove the winding, climbing streets as dawn touched the sky. The rain had stopped now, and there was a reddish look to the wet streets. He parked in front of his house, the lights of the city dimming as daylight increased. He sat for a moment, looking at the steep steps running up to the small white house. It stood among the others, silent, dark-windowed, and lonely-looking. And it was lonely, he thought; it had been ever since Delle had tumbled down those steps in an alcoholic haze, breaking her neck. Five years ago, and the memory of it was as sharp and biting as it had been when it happened.

That, he thought, was when he'd really become a cop, because the work was all that was left then. But, no, he thought; it had really happened before that, when Delle had started down the dark road of too much drinking, moving away from him in her fog, coming back only briefly to shriek and shout condemnations, never remembering later what she'd said. It started then, because there seemed nothing he could do to stop her destruction, so that he had moved away from her and all the good they'd known the half-dozen years before that, to find solace in the work. Now she was dead. And he'd found nothing to replace her—nothing but the work.

He got out and moved heavily up the steps. A drink, he thought. Some reading. Then a sandwich. And the sleep: four, maybe five hours, because that was all he could ever manage. Then back to the work, blessing it for its consuming quality.

He brushed his soles against the doormat; then, with his left hand, he turned the knob against the pressure of the night lock, key ready in his right hand. But the knob turned beyond the accustomed pressure. He tensed with practiced alertness.

Silently, he returned the key ring to his pocket, holding his left hand on the knob. Then he slid his right hand inside his jacket to the grip of his pistol. He paused, then turned the knob, kicked the door open, and went in fast, free hand moving instinctively toward the light switch. He heard the whirring sound of something coming at him. But he was diving sideways, rolling in the sudden flare of interior light. The gun was out of its holster. He pointed it as he lay on the floor. "That's it," he snapped, and looked at the unhandsome, chagrined faces of Abner and Bernie.

Abner, wearing a black, conservative topcoat over his huge frame, held a pistol by the barrel in one giant hand. He was half crouched, shoulders tipped, the frustration of his missed swing etched into his broad, flat face. Bernie, similarly coated, stood nearly a foot and a half shorter than Abner, his silencer-equipped revolver held in his small, crab-like hand, pointed at Cummings. His small eyes were measuring, his jockey-lean body upright and tense.

Neither moved. Cummings concentrated on Bernie, whose gun was in firing position. Three seconds went by. Four. Cummings' gun was held steadily, muzzle pointing at Bernie.

"You'd better put it down, Bernie," he said.

Neither answered. Neither moved.

"Look at it this way," Cummings said. "You came to work me over.

Now you're going to have to kill me if you don't put that down. You're going to get killed in return. You lost your choice when Abner missed."

"What'll we do?" Abner finally said in his thick, froggy voice.

"What would *Knocko* do, if you got into murder?" Cummings said.

"Maybe you better," Abner said.

"I'll decide," Bernie said.

His voice, Cummings thought, was like the sound of a fly buzzing. But he was a fly who had a deadly sting. Abner straightened slightly.

"Don't move again, Abner," he said. "Or it'll be you." He grinned without humor at Bernie. "How long, Bernie?"

"I could get you three times in the gut before you got the trigger pulled, Cummings," Bernie said.

"Maybe. Maybe not. Even so, you'll have killed a cop. Step over to the telephone and call Knocko. Ask if he wants a dead cop on him."

"Maybe you better," Abner said to Bernie.

"Shut up," Bernie said.

"I think maybe you'd better too, Bernie," Cummings said. "I'm getting tired. Maybe I'll squeeze first. Who'd care if you die?"

"Knocko."

"That's a pleasant thought. But I don't think so."

The brain inside Bernie's head was working, he thought, like an old lady walking through mud.

"I'm putting it down," Bernie said finally.

"Do it," Cummings said.

Bernie put the gun down tenderly and straightened with regret.

"Kick it over," Cummings said.

Bernie touched it with the narrow toe of a black shoe. Then he carefully sent it across the rug. He did not want, Cummings thought, to abuse that gun.

"All right, Abner."

Abner put his gun down clumsily and kicked it over to Cummings. Cummings picked up both guns and put them on a table. Then he lifted the telephone. He looked at his watch. Knocko never deviated from his schedule; he was more reliable than a machine. He called his home and in a few moments heard a voice fuzzy with sleep: "What?"

"It's Jack, baby."

"Oh, Jack! How'd it go?"

"Not like you figured."

"Who? What? I don't understand."

"I'll help. You ever try anything like that again, I'll close it out for you. I'll push all of it clear up to a grand jury investigation. It won't make any difference where you've got the fix then. Because I can do it alone that way. Now do you understand?"

He heard nothing but the angry breathing of the man. Grand jury, yes—he could do it that way. And Knocko knew it. It would ruin his own situation. But it would ruin Knocko too. It was the final trick. He put his own gun down and picked up Bernie's. Bernie had thumbed the safety on before he'd put it on the floor. Cummings switched it off. He pointed it at Bernie.

"So you understand," he said to Knocko. "And I've got something else for you. Bernie's gun's in my hand. I'm going to send him back to you—dead." He moved the receiver closer to the muzzle of the pistol. He stared at Bernie's wary eyes; the corners of them tensed. He squeezed the play out of the trigger, then gave it the final pressure, switching his aim at the last fraction of a second. The gun made a soft, exploding sound. The bullet ripped into his sofa. Bernie stood motionlessly; only his fingers moved—they curled into his palms, then straightened. Cummings hung up.

He unloaded both guns, then threw one and then the other onto the sofa. They would, he thought, replace them anyway.

"Pick them up and get the hell out of here. Only leave twenty bucks on that sofa, so I can get it repaired."

They moved swiftly to reclaim the guns. Bernie extracted a twenty-dollar bill from an expensive wallet. Cummings saw with satisfaction that his hand was trembling—but more from the indignity of having failed, he knew, than from fear. Bernie, he'd decided long ago, did the real work; he'd been the one who'd personally worked that hustler over, he was certain, while Abner had provided only the necessary physical help. Bernie was a loner, a man who must, Cummings thought, slide into the gutter at the end of his work and disappear in that dark region until Knocko needed him again.

But Abner was less complex. His strength was singular: physical. He was simple, and his mind moved along one narrow road at a time. He was foolishly and hopelessly in love with his wife, who had once worked for Knocko as a prostitute, worshipping her as some did saints. His devotion to her was a consuming passion, and some day reality would smash it for him. Cummings did not want to be around when that happened.

"Out," he snapped.

And they left.

Chapter 5

He came slowly awake in the shade-drawn bedroom, with no sense of time or place. He had been walking along a pine-needled path past giant-trunked trees, golden sunlight coming down in an angled shaft, warming him. There was no sound. But he could see the black shapes of birds floating high in a sky as golden as the sunlight. A small squirrel ran nimbly across the path, leaped onto a tree and disappeared around its trunk. But he heard no rustle of needles, no whisper of breeze, no chatter from the squirrel.

He was not really walking. His movement was an effortless shift of one leg, then another, as if floating. He could not feel the earth. He breathed but found no scents, no smells. He simply moved, looking; and the path turned and curled, taking him on in that golden, silent world.

Until finally sound crashed at him: the sound of the forest, the sound of animals—a cat roaring, birds singing. He heard the wind blowing through the upper reaches of the tall trees. It came as suddenly as if a vast loudspeaker had become alive with current. He could smell pine now, and somewhere something had died; he could smell the putrefaction.

The noise grew, the smells, the feel of the wind coming down from the trees. He shivered and began running, feeling his feet jolting against the needled path harshly. Sweat poured from him. And suddenly he was frightened. He ran desperately as the claws of the brush tore at his clothes. The golden light had become gray, frosted. Then it turned yellow and heated. The sounds became louder. The path disappeared and became, ahead, a funnel of blackness. He stopped, whirling desperately, feeling the forest tightening about him. And he saw it: the squirrel, inching around a tree trunk, ten times larger than it had been, a terrible face, chattering horribly. The chattering turned into a hideous buzzing sound. The animal gray, setting its giant rat's feet against the bark, springing at him, teeth ready …

He sat up, finally awake. He wiped a large hand across his eyes, then looked at his watch. He'd been asleep not over an hour. The buzzing sounded again. Now he knew that it was his door buzzer. But in the dream the buzzing had been Bernie's voice, the squirrel's face Bernie's feral features.

He got up and put on a robe and slippers. He walked through the neat, small house into the book-lined living room. "Who is it?"

"Me." The voice was feminine, bright, cheerful-sounding.

He opened the door. A girl with dark hair and a pale, archly beautiful face smiled at him. Her hair shone in the morning sun. Her make-up had been applied with ultimate skill. She wore a full-length beaver with a careless correctness. Her legs were finely shaped. "Can I help you?" he asked.

"Turn it round," she said. "Can I?"

"It would depend, I suspect."

"Ask me in and we'll see what it depends on."

He swung the door open and closed it behind her. She turned slowly and gracefully, looking at the room. Then she unbuttoned the coat, spreading it, inviting him with the motion to take it. Her dress was a simple blue sheath, showing her good body perfectly. She turned again. "I thought so."

"Thought so what?"

"You're smart. It's written on your face. I knew you'd be reading all these books."

"Maybe I just buy them. Maybe I'm dumb. I think I am, because I don't know you."

She smiled again, blue eyes merry. "Vinni."

He held her coat. He nodded slowly. "I see."

"Don't say it that way. Are you going to make me leave?"

"I'm not going to make you do anything."

"I love it here. It's so quiet and peaceful."

"It isn't always. It wasn't a couple of hours ago."

She sighed. "Knocko felt terrible about that."

"I know. He's sensitive."

"I just knew you'd be that way. How do you say it? Sardonic? It's cute. I love it."

"So Knocko sent you. Because he felt terrible about what almost happened."

"Don't you have a cigarette?"

"Sorry."

"I have." She'd dropped her handbag on the sofa. She picked it up and got out a holder and put a cigarette between her lips. She waited until he struck a match for her and held her fingers against him.

"Won't you ask me to sit down?"

"The sofa's been damaged. That chair is all right."

He sat down a little way from her. She simply sat there smiling, but she created an emotional impact. She moved her hand with the cigarette, and even that was sensual. She'd learned her business well, he thought, or she'd been born knowing it. Either way, he could feel her attraction strongly.

"This is the time I love best," she said. "In the morning, with the sun shining outside, the shades drawn. You think of everybody else busy in offices and things. And you're not. Do you have something to drink?"

"I don't think you're going to stay."

"For one drink? I'd love a Scotch, rough. Will you have one with me?"

He walked to the kitchen and made two drinks. He came back and handed hers to her and sat down again. It was bizarre, he thought, and typical of Knocko. The grand jury threat had reached him. He studied her, and decided that she probably was, as Mandell had stated, the most beautiful hooker in the world. She created an illusion of the elite. Her cosmetics were quiet. She wore a single bloodstone ring on her right ring finger. She wore no other jewelry. The simplicity was effective, because all you thought about was her.

"Cheers, luck, and all things lovely," she said.

"All right. All things lovely."

"I've seen you. Several times. Everybody knows you in the district."

"It's that kind of district."

"I thought I'd like you. I do. Honestly."

"That's nice to hear."

"What do you think of me?"

"You're beautiful."

"I can call you Jack, can't I?"

"Why not?"

"Sure. Why not? This is wonderful, being here." She knew her way, all right, he thought. Completely. "Did I wake you?"

"I don't know," he said. "You or a dream. I was about to be eaten alive by a giant squirrel. He looked like Bernie."

She put her drink down. "I don't want to talk about Bernie."

He could understand that. She must have heard what had been done to another of Knocko's girls six months ago, and known who was responsible. How had she gotten into this? he wondered. What was in the brain, the emotions, that sent her, with her fragile and regal beauty, into the racket of whoring?

"I know what you're thinking," she said.

"I guess it's inevitable."

"A lot of them ask." She shrugged. Her smile was gone, and she was even more beautiful. "It's what I am, I guess. I like money. Lots of it. I have no acting talent, no show business talent of any kind. I could model. But I wouldn't make as much. I'm the best Knocko has. I can pick and choose, most of the time. I don't mind, most of the time. The only thing—it's lonesome. You're in what I am, you're alone. That's why I like this. You should see my apartment. It's marvelous. But I like this better. Much better."

She was good, he thought, because she was convincing. That, next to her physical beauty, would have to be the most important thing about her. For false love, gotten with money on the barrelhead, you had to have the illusion of conviction. No man, except the perverted or the too-young, really wanted any kind of love without the conviction that it was true. Without that, you were making love to the mechanical vessel, or to yourself.

"But you don't believe me, do you?" she said. "That I like this … that I like you?"

"I don't know."

"Don't you like me?"

"Yes." He nodded. "But I don't like the situation."

"What I do, you mean?"

"I don't mean that."

"But you're a detective."

"That's right."

"I'm illegal. You could jail me, couldn't you?"

"You know better."

"Because Knocko's got it fixed."

"And somebody's got Knocko fixed. We're all fixed. So we work around it."

"That's what I do," she said. "Work around it. I get what I can, when I can. That's what I'm doing now."

"I'd like to believe that, but I don't."

"Why not?"

"Because you're too expensive. I can't afford Lincoln Continentals. I can't afford two-hundred-dollar suits. I can't afford African safaris. And I can't afford you either. The only reason you're here is because I scared hell out of Knocko with a grand jury threat."

She looked thoughtful. "Could you hurt him that way?"

"Maybe."

"That would ruin me too then, wouldn't it?"

"You could go somewhere else where it's fixed."

"I guess so. Do you want me to go somewhere else right now?"

She was the God-created epitome of properly molded flesh, so clear-eyed and beautiful that it was hard to believe that she was also the symbol of Knocko's evil, of, perhaps, all evil, everywhere at all times. You didn't want to think of that. You only wanted to think of having her, and of how it would be. It would be good, he thought, because she was physically perfect and convincing and all-knowing about the business of physical love. "Of course not," he said. "But I'm going to ask you to."

"Why?"

"Knocko."

"Can't we forget him?"

"I never forget him."

"Why not? This morning? Let's make an island. Just you and me. I want to forget Knocko too. Honestly I do."

"But you can't. Because that's why you're here."

"As of now, no more. For me and for you. A little while. Why not? I'll tell Knocko you threw me out."

He shook his head slowly. She got up and came to him.

"No?"

Her dress came off with a slick, sliding sound. She shook her hair and smiled at him. She was, he thought, made of rough steel inside. But outside she was silken-smooth and as soft as clouds. She moved to him.

"You do what you want with me," she whispered, "because that's what I'm going to do with you."

Chapter 6

Rain had stopped late the next afternoon, but the sky was bleak. Traffic rolled ceaselessly through the streets between tall, grime-dulled buildings. In one upper room of the Danway Hotel a man in his mid-forties with a sallow face lay on a bed and contemplated suicide. He would never do it. In another, a small, wizened man in a white shirt dealt himself a hand of poker with a smooth, fast motion. He looked at his watch, then at the cards. He took three more from the deck. He uttered a short oath and dealt himself another hand. In a third room an elderly woman sat in a rocker that inched forward then backward in a slow, funereal rhythm. She stared out her window across the tops of other buildings, wondering if the sun would shine before it set, her single concern.

Mandell swung the department car into the red zone in front of the hotel. He and Cummings walked inside. It was a quarter to five, and Cummings had not slept much. But he had not minded that, he thought; not at all. Franklin was already on duty. Cummings had him take them into the switchboard room, where Franklin introduced them to Laureen Beggs, the operator, then left.

She sat before the board in pristine silence until Cummings said, "They tell me you've been here since Mr. Levi took the hotel over."

She nodded abruptly and rested the tips of her fingers in readiness against the surface of the board in front of her. She was, he estimated, in her late twenties; but there was an older look in her eyes. She was not pretty. She somehow reminded him of girls he'd seen in Salvation Army uniforms, plain, with no make-up except lipstick, staring in repose as the mouth shaped the words of the song, which no longer had personal meaning. She might fit with that, he thought.

"I'd like," he said, "to check your records on a call that was made from the hotel yesterday afternoon."

She turned her chair and brought down a report sheet attached to a clipboard. "Yes?" Her voice sounded crisply efficient.

"This was near five o'clock."

"You mean Mr. Lundstrom, don't you? The gentleman who was murdered?"

"That's the one."

She ran a finger along an entry and nodded abruptly again. "Mr. Lundstrom never out-dialed. You can do that here, you know. You dial zero to get the tone, then you phone straight out. But Mr. Lundstrom always had me do that for him. Several gentlemen do that. It's part of our service."

"So you dialed for him?"

"Yes. 144-6689."

Knocko's office number, he thought, as Lundstrom had said. "What was the time?"

"Exactly one minute to five."

Cummings studied the board. "I wonder, Miss Beggs, if you'd show me exactly how you handled the call? Just explain and go through the motions, if you don't mind."

She touched a small light indicator. "Well, that's 802, the room Mr. and Mrs. Lundstrom were using. The light went on. I never use the buzzer when I'm on the board. I put the plug in like this and turned this key, which connected me to Mr. Lundstrom. He asked for his number. I dialed, like this. He had his connection."

"What then, Miss Beggs?"

"That's all. As soon as I'd got Mr. Lundstrom's party I closed the key."

"I see. And how do you know when the parties have hung up?"

"The light goes out."

"But you could switch in on the call, couldn't you?"

Her lips pressed together. Her pale eyes darkened. "I consider that a personal insult, Inspector."

"I'm merely talking about a theoretical possibility, Miss Beggs. I don't mean to insult you. It is possible to switch in on a call?"

"Of course! There's this monitoring switch—this one, with the white handle. But that's used simply to make certain disconnections have been made. It is absolutely against the law to monitor any call, and I am not a lawbreaker, Inspector."

He was remembering Lundstrom's final words: that no one but Knocko knew that he was in possession of that kind of money. He looked at Laureen Beggs, at her lusterless face, at her guileless eyes. She had a room in the hotel. She'd gone off duty three minutes after the call had been made. In his initial quick questioning, as Lundstrom was being rushed to the hospital, he'd found that neither of the two bellmen on duty had seen anyone on Lundstrom's floor. Neither had the maids. The elevator had not been in operation except to deliver Lundstrom back to his room when he returned for his wallet. But there was a back emergency stairway. Anyone could have gone up that unseen and entered Lundstrom's room—especially a hotel employee who would have known exactly where it was along the hallways and who might have had access to a master key. He looked at his watch again. "I'm sorry to inconvenience you, Miss Beggs, but we'd like to talk to you a little more. I understand you have a room in the hotel. Perhaps Mr. Franklin could let you off a few minutes early, and we could talk to you there. Inspector Mandell will go with you. I'll be along in a few minutes."

"I don't know where in the world you're going, Inspector. But it's like I said. I'm not a lawbreaker. And if you wish to talk to me, that is perfectly all right."

When Mandell had disappeared with her, Cummings spoke to Franklin: "Does Miss Beggs ever listen to calls?"

Franklin's eyelids fluttered. "That is absolutely not allowed in this hotel, Inspector! Ever!"

"But *does* she?"

"Mr. Levi," he said indignantly, "would fire her straight out of her pants if she ever did such a thing. Our guests' privacies are protected with absolute zeal, Inspector."

"How about the master keys? Who has them?"

"The maids. The bellman."

"Anyone else?"

"I do, of course. And the day manager. But surely, Inspector, you're not going to infer that I—"

"I'm not inferring anything, Franklin. How about extras?"

"We keep them there, behind the desk."

Cummings looked at a row of keys hanging just to the side of the door leading to the switchboard room. "One that could have opened Lundstrom's door?"

"There're two." They moved to the rack. "Right here."

Cummings looked at the slim keys; there was not enough surface to have collected fingerprints.

"But my goodness, Inspector. Whatever—"

"Were there two last night, after Lundstrom was killed?"

"Last night?" His eyelids fluttered again. "Heavens, I don't know. I would guess so."

"But you don't know for sure. Someone could have picked up one, then returned it later."

"Well, yes. But honestly, Inspector—"

"It's all right, Franklin. Relax."

Laureen Beggs had modified the hotel's standard furnishings in her room by replacing the drapes with frilled blue curtains. There was a matching spread on the bed. Everything was spotless and in its place. She sat primly, as Mandell stood, his eyes roving lazily, searching the room. Cummings brought out his pipe. "Do you mind, Miss Beggs?"

"Yes," she said.

He put the pipe back in his pocket. "I don't want you to feel we're trying to implicate any wrongdoing on your part, Miss Beggs. That's true, isn't it, Inspector?"

Mandell nodded, smiling at Cummings' approach. "That's true."

"What we're doing, Miss Beggs, is simply checking everything we can about this."

"It's routine. I know. I've heard that on television."

"That's right, Miss Beggs. It's routine. Now you got off duty a couple of minutes after five yesterday afternoon. Then what did you do?"

"I came in here. Why?"

"We just want to place everything and everybody. What did you do then?"

"I don't see that it's any of your business." She clasped her hands in her lap as if, he thought, protecting her virginity, if she had retained it to protect.

"I mean, how long were you here?"

She took a breath; and he realized that she was a little more tense now than when they'd started this, though she still maintained poise. "Until six o'clock."

"Then what did you do?"

"I went out and down the street to the Cruthers Cafeteria for dinner, just like I always do."

"I see."

He smiled at her gently. His mind, over the years, had taken on a certain sensitivity. The sensitivity had the fallibility of a lie-detection machine: the absolute achievement was that he knew when a subject was nervous or not nervous—which seemed to be the sole attribute of the machine. Laureen Beggs did not seem to be honestly nervous, though she obviously resented this. But then, he thought, quite probably she resented a lot of things in her life.

"Did that take very long?"

"No longer than usual," she said crisply.

"Then you came back here?"

"Of course."

"Miss Beggs," he said softly, "do you own any kind of firearm?"

She began blinking rapidly, jaw muscles working beneath her white and fragile skin. "What is the meaning of that supposed to be?"

"Just what I asked."

"Why don't you guess whether I do or not?"

He nodded, thinking that she was tougher than she looked. With the exposure to the Danway's ebb and flow of varied guests, she might have to be, after a time. "I don't believe I'll have to guess, Miss Beggs. We can obtain a search warrant."

"Get it then."

"I'd hoped you'd be more cooperative."

"I don't care what you'd hoped."

"I can understand that this is an inconvenience for you. But if you're not a lawbreaker, then I don't see what you would have to hide from us, do you?"

"I'm not hiding anything."

"Do you own a firearm?"

"Of course I do. A single woman, living in a hotel? Not that we don't have excellent guests, but you can't screen them all."

"Do you mind if we have a look?"

"This is ridiculous."

"Of course it is, Miss Beggs. Where do you keep it?"

"In the third drawer of the bureau."

Cummings nodded to Mandell, who walked over and slid open a drawer. He lifted a stack of light-blue lingerie.

"Third drawer *down!*" Laureen Beggs said loudly.

Mandell smiled and opened the next drawer. He lifted a compact .22 pistol by its trigger guard and handed it to Cummings. Cummings held it in the same fashion. The handle was probably the single place that might hold a fingerprint or a palm print, but he held the gun with care anyway.

"It is loaded, Miss Beggs?"

"Naturally. What good would it be otherwise?"

Using a fingernail, Cummings put the safety on. "Do you always keep the safety off?"

"I keep it on."

"I see." He opened the chamber and, using light from a window, looked down the barrel. "Do you fire it often, Miss Beggs?"

"That is quite stupid. I've never fired it in all my life."

He examined the fine metallic trailings left by an escaping slug— or three slugs, he thought. "How long have you had the pistol?"

"Five years."

"And it's never been fired?"

"That is right."

"Miss Beggs," he said, "I'm afraid you're going to have to come along with us."

Chapter 7

They sat in the gray-walled office of Captain Blaine; they had been there for two hours. Mandell slouched indolently in a corner chair, looking sleepy. Light had gone outside, and the ceiling tubes of neon shone down on Blame's short gray hair as he looked at Laureen Beggs sitting squarely before his desk in an armless straight chair. As was his habit, Blaine had questioned her steadily, insistently, with the slow ease and quiet of a cat moving toward a quarry. He was honestly and truly happy about this, Cummings thought, because he had Laureen Beggs, not Knocko, in his sights now.

"Why don't you tell us the truth?" Blaine sighed. "It would be so much easier for all of us, Miss Beggs."

"I've told you the truth," she said resolutely. But now she had lost whatever poise she had once commanded, Cummings saw. She did look honestly nervous. She kept turning a cheap ring with a pink glass setting so steadily that the skin beneath had reddened.

Blaine's telephone rang. He lifted it and nodded, listening for a time, then returned it to its cradle. "Well, now. I would say that would just about do it, Miss Beggs. That surely must just about do it."

Her lids lowered defensively. "This is so ridiculous."

"Let me go over it again, please. Then I'll add what I've just learned."

"It won't make any difference. The whole thing is absolutely ridiculous."

"Let's see if it is, shall we?" He touched one fresh-scrubbed finger with another. "Robert Lundstrom was shot three times with a twenty-two-caliber pistol. Yours is a twenty-two-caliber pistol."

Her voice came out shrilly. "You think I don't know that?"

"You say you've never fired the pistol. Yet there is no doubt whatever that the pistol has been recently fired. The magazine contains identically the same brand of cartridges as the ejected casings found in Robert Lundstrom's room. This is hopeless of you, Miss Beggs."

"I know exactly what you're trying to do! You're trying to frame me because you don't know who did it!"

"There are, in the magazine, exactly three cartridges short of the full number it will hold."

"I never shot that!" she shouted. "It had all the bullets it would hold when your muscle men took it! I know what you've done. *You've* gone and had it shot. Now you're trying to frame me."

"Ah, yes," he said quietly. "But now I've had the report from ballistics, Miss Beggs. As you probably know from the viewing of television you've told us about, no pistol creates the same marking on a slug as another as it's propelled along the rifling of a barrel."

Cummings looked at him. The call he'd just received might have been concerning any number of things, but it had not been that call from ballistics; there hadn't been time for them to have completed a thorough and accurate testing. He was faking now, demonstrating his absolute hunger to slip the noose around this woman's neck, thereby absolving Knocko. Cummings turned back toward Laureen Beggs, to see that her eyes now looked like those of a small animal trapped and waiting for the death blow.

"I'm sure you understand, Miss Beggs. So now I've been informed by our ballistics people that slugs fired out of your pistol have the identical rifling marks made on those slugs which were removed from the deceased, Mr. Lundstrom. The roll photography has been completed, and it's always truthful. Also the grooves of the bullet, the turn direction, and the rate of twist have all been confirmed. Finally, the marks on those ejected casings found in the hotel room provide exactly the same marks achieved from our test firing—the markings from the breech lock, firing pin, ejector, and extractor all match. There really isn't any point in going on with this, is there, Miss Beggs? Why won't you please tell us just what happened. Will you do that?"

Again she was blinking rapidly. But now, Cummings thought, she seemed bewildered and surprised. Blaine was faking, all right, but he seemed to be striking home with it.

"Shall we give it up, Miss Beggs?" Blaine asked gently but insistently. "Shall we just give it up?"

"All right," she said, and her body seemed to go limp.

Cummings frowned, watching her.

"Tell us what happened, Miss Beggs," Blaine said, unable to hide the note of victory in his voice.

"I listened in on the call. I heard Mr. Lundstrom telling this Cutter person that he had all that money in his room. When he hung up, it was time for me to quit. I took one of the master keys. Then I went to my room and got the pistol and went up to Mr. Lundstrom's room. I've never had money. Not in my whole life. I found it, and then Mr. Lundstrom was coming back. I heard his key in the door, and I got behind it. When he came in, I knew he'd find me and I couldn't keep the money. So I shot him. Then I ran out and downstairs. Nobody saw me. I put the pistol back in the bureau. When I went back on duty I put the master key back. That's all there is, and there isn't any more."

She stared at the rug, face pale. She had stopped turning the ring on her finger; instead, she was gripping it tightly with two fingers white at the knuckles.

"Where did you find the money?" Cummings asked.

"I've said all I'm going to say. Throw me in a cell."

"You'll be booked, of course, Miss Beggs," Blaine said. "But we won't do any throwing. You'll be allowed to phone a lawyer, just as we said you could do the instant we brought you here. I think it might be very advisable. But now we would like to know where you put the money."

"Look for it," she said.

"It might go a whole lot more comfortable for you if you would please tell us where the money is now."

"Get yourself a crystal ball," she said, but her voice was quivering; her eyes had misted.

"You won't tell us?" Blaine asked softly.

Her shoulders began shaking. She made no reply.

Blaine sighed, but there was a smile of satisfaction turning his mouth. "All right, Jack."

Cummings stood up as Mandell came slowly to his feet. He guided her out of the room, thinking that there was just one thing seriously wrong about this: it had been far too easy.

Chapter 8

Mandell stopped the car in front of the Bay View Motel. Cummings was still thinking of Laureen Beggs. Because of her refusal to give information about the location of the money, she had been informed that she would have no hope of release on bail. She didn't seem to care, and she refused to phone a lawyer.

Cummings looked at the line of motel units, forming an L—clean, white, modern units—though the motel's name bore no relationship to reality: there was no view of the Bay.

"What do you think, Mandell?"

"I'm thinking about getting me some."

"Why don't you? You're married."

"I don't mean that. You know what I mean. I woke up this afternoon thinking about that."

"Well, what I mean is Laureen Beggs."

"Oh." Mandell shrugged. "What's to think?"

"It was easy, wasn't it?"

"They should all be happy that way."

"Knocko'll be happy."

"Sure."

"Captain Blaine's happy. Everybody's happy."

"Except you. What's the matter?"

"For one thing, she looked surprised when Blaine delivered that fake ballistics report."

"They've got it good now. It's turning out anyway, isn't it? Just like he faked it. They got the roll photography on the slugs checked out. Same gun killed Lundstrom. You saw me take it out of her bureau. She said she did it. What do you want?"

Cummings nodded. "All her life she walks the straight. Then she climbs off her chair, goes upstairs, and kills a man."

"Figure it. She looks like everybody's unmarried aunt, right? She keeps her mouth shut and they don't hear her swear, cries a little, a good lawyer pleads temporary insanity … What's she going to get? And time off for good behavior? Nobody knows where the sixty-five thousand is except her. She gets out; she's got it made. Who's dumb?"

"Simple as that."

"Right."

"Only Lundstrom's dead and his wife is crapped up."

"We all got problems."

"I love you for your heart, Mandell."

"I know you do, Jack. Want me to go in with you?"

"I'll get it."

Cummings stepped into the night air. If the motel did not possess a view of the Bay, it was close enough to get the fresh, pure breeze blowing off the water. The sky was clear now, and the stars were brighter than they had been in some time. He walked into the small office, where a lean, smiling man appeared behind the desk.

"Hello, Inspector."

For years he'd directed people he knew—friends and relatives who came to the city—to this motel. The times had become scarce lately.

Relatives had died, and he hadn't kept in contact with those who were left. Friends had thinned, too, since Delle was gone. Well, he thought, you had your life and fixed it the way you received it, most of the time. If he'd begun traveling more and more alone, then it was probably because he wanted it that way. "Mrs. Lundstrom. I sent her over last night."

"Oh yes. Is she the one? I mean, the wife of the one I read about?"

"Yes."

"She's in Six-A. Downstairs, Inspector."

He went along the walk running in front of the units. He stopped at the door marked 6-A and rapped on it. There was a light inside shining against the drape and under the door. There was no answer. He tried again. Then he returned to the car.

"No?" Mandell asked.

"Probably having dinner or something. I'll try her tomorrow. When did you get the lineup set for?" Now he was forgetting Mrs. Lundstrom, and Laureen Beggs too, concentrating again on the Joplin girl.

"How about eleven? Johnson said he'll show then. He's a good boy, Johnson. Some of them didn't like his getting inspector. But when they put him on the vice squad, I figured that's all right, you know? That's a good place for Johnson. Vice? Give it to an expert."

"You mean sex."

"Sure. Johnson's got to be an expert."

"I figured that's what you'd figure."

"Well, I don't think he thinks you're the hottest torch was ever lit either."

"I don't really give a damn, Mandell. Who've you got?"

"Creep named Singer."

"Likes playgrounds."

"Correct. Another one named Jones."

"Which Jones?"

"Albert K."

"Little boys, usually."

"And one vice picked up."

"Record?"

"Just unemployed. Matches the description. Was in the district. No alibi."

"All right. Only we'd better let Joplin know now, or he'll be out of his head on the booze by that time."

"Yeah, but he'll give her to us again anyway. And it's like I said. I've been thinking about it ever since I woke up this morning. That girl's ripe. What do you think?"

"I'll say one thing about you, Mandell—you've got a whoring attitude."

Mandell looked at him swiftly, with a look that Cummings could not figure out. "Don't we all, Inspector?"

As Mandell had predicted, Joplin turned the girl over to them alone. They drove her to headquarters, and now they were seated in the room with its hard floodlights bathing the small step-up stage with whiteness. There were four men standing against the light, all Negroes. They'd been questioned briefly, and now they stood silently, eyes tightened belligerently against the unceasing glare. One of them was small and fragile with a fancy white shirt and tight black slacks. One was squat with a thick neck and wore a ragged sweater. One was of medium build and dressed neatly if inexpensively in a conservatively styled gray suit. The fourth was tall and athletically built, with a smooth, handsome face, dressed in blue jeans and an ancient sport jacket over a shabby golf shirt.

"What do you think?" Cummings asked the girl quietly.

"Well ..." The girl hesitated. "I'm almost sure."

"Which one?"

"The big one. On the right."

Cummings picked up a raincoat from the seat beside him and handed it past the girl to Mandell. "Tell him to put it on."

Mandell walked into the light and handed the coat to the tallest Negro. "On."

The man looked at him with dark, impenetrable eyes. He put the coat on.

"That's him," the girl said.

"You're certain?"

"It's the one who did it."

Outside, the girl smiled at Cummings. She was wearing what was apparently a new outfit of a flame-red dress and a bright blue coat. (He had not seen the clothing in the Joplins' closet the night before.) It was a cheap and gaudy demonstration, but apparently it pleased her. So did having fingered the tall one on the lineup, he thought.

"You're glad, huh?" she said. "That I could pick him out?"

He said to Mandell, "Take her back, will you? Then pick me up here."

Mandell's eyes brightened. "Sure."

"It's tough when somebody does a thing like this," Cummings said to the girl. "They can get the book." He looked again at Mandell, who shrugged and sighed, saying, "Okay, Inspector. Take her back and pick you up."

Cummings walked into a small locker room with its soap-and-sweat smell. The tall Negro had stripped off the jeans, sport jacket and shirt. His dark, muscular body gleamed under the ceiling lights. He looked at Cummings briefly, then drew on a pair of well-fitting suit slacks. "What'd she say?"

"Said you were it. How come, Johnson? I thought you were happily married with three kids."

"Very funny, Cummings."

Cummings stepped close to a wide mirror and examined the beginnings of a fast beard. "You don't like me, do you, Johnson?"

"Have I said so?"

"I have the feeling."

"Would it bother you?"

"We all want to be liked, don't we?"

"Only it doesn't always work out, does it?"

Yes, he thought, there was an attempt at revolution. But still it was as he'd told Mike Hawley: there was no real revolution until it got violent. And maybe this one, whatever it was called, would become violent, all right—perhaps it was already. Then you had an honest revolution. Maybe it had to come to that. Because there would be, and for a long time to come, this feeling that existed between a capable and intelligent Negro named Johnson and himself, simply because he was white and Johnson was black. You couldn't wipe away environment, even by law. But perhaps, as in the case of all laws, the law was necessary and deserving, because there was no better way that had been demonstrated without it. Still, the tension was there, and there was no use believing that it wasn't.

"Do you want to be liked, Johnson?"

"I want to be loved, Cummings. Just like my mother loved me."

"That would be sweet, wouldn't it?"

"What's with the girl?"

"Canard. Only I've got to prove it."

"I'll help you."

Cummings turned around, looking at the man adjust his shoulder holster against a white shirt. "If she'd accused a white man?"

Johnson shrugged. "She didn't."

"No," he said. "She didn't."

"So I'll help a little harder."

Cummings nodded. "I can understand that."

"I'm surprised, Cummings. I didn't think you cared."

Cummings laughed softly. "I'm a bastard, in other words."

"Maybe you wouldn't have to be."

"Maybe I'm not. Maybe it's just what you think."

Johnson looked at him closely, then drew on a tailored jacket, looking now like a handsome, successful lawyer or physician, Cummings thought. "I'll tell you the truth, Cummings. I don't know what to think about you. Except you're a good cop. That I know. So does everybody else. I'd like to be as good a cop as you."

"A compliment. Maybe we'll work it out, after all. You're a good cop too. I told Blaine that before you made inspector."

A dark eyebrow arched faintly in surprise. "I didn't know that."

"Well, you didn't need it."

Johnson's mouth moved in a slow, hard smile. "A man who wants to be loved like his mother loved him? Sure I needed it. Why didn't you tell me?"

"You didn't ask."

Johnson nodded and buttoned his jacket. "That's true, isn't it? So now I'll ask. You really don't care, do you, Cummings? Whether I'm black or not?"

He felt a quick discomfort by that swift, unexpected, naked question. Then that faded as quickly as it had come.

"No."

"Well, I'll tell you, Cummings. I'll take a hater faster than I will a hypocrite. But I don't think you're either. We may make it, after all. That *would* be sweet, wouldn't it?"

"It really would."

"So, back to the alleys. Do you really think it was a canard?"

"Sure, but let's prove it. Oh, her father wants ten minutes with you, by the way. Alone."

Johnson stopped by the door and nodded. "Any time."

Chapter 9

He was still thinking of Johnson that next late afternoon as he scouted through the district, trying to find something that would lead to the truth of what had really happened to the Joplin girl. Mandell was further down the block, checking a drugstore refreshment counter, where the girl might have gone. He was seated at one of four stools of an outside health food counter, waiting while the proprietor, a fat, bearded young man, served one of his concoctions to a tiny woman wearing a coat that might have been made, Cummings thought, from the skin of a polar bear.

He was thinking that Johnson, like himself, had grown up in this city—but in the Negro district. Right now he would be sifting through the human sands of that area, trying to find the same thing he was looking for, in order to help purify the Negro race by proving that the girl had pulled the canard. It was a noble effort, he thought; and at the same time it was also a selfish, personal effort. But you couldn't blame him for that. Perhaps that was not the fault, at all—the selfish, personal aspect of it. Perhaps the fault was that Johnson was attempting to improve his level and his lot, by his effort, and perhaps by so doing improve the level and lot of others of his color; but he was still operating within the fix, the fix high above them, demonstrated always by the being of Knocko Cutter. He was, like Cummings, attempting to swim through the sea without becoming a part of it. But then, he thought, maybe Johnson could get away with it, and maybe he could too. It was something nice to think about, no matter whether it would become true or not....

The woman in the polar bear coat drained the glass of whatever it was she had been served. She did it in the manner of a drunk consuming a desperately needed glass of whisky. She even shuddered when she had finished, Cummings saw. Then she placed the glass on the marble counter with a soft click and moved down the sidewalk as if restored to youth.

"What was it, Rudy?"

"Rattlesnake meat and piss from a tiger."

"I thought it might have been carrot juice."

"That's what she thought too."

"Do you believe in this stuff, Rudy?"

"She'd be better off chewing weeds off the ground."

"Why do you sell it?"

"To prove the utter inanity of this existence we live in."

"You're a cynic, aren't you, Rudy?"

"The other way around. I am real. It's the world that's false, because *it* is cynical. Where has love gone, Inspector?"

"I suppose there're some people who could tell us. Maybe they've got the market on it. And that's why we have so much trouble finding it."

"Tell me where. I'd like to know that. Truly I would."

"Maybe we don't look hard enough."

"Why should we? It's gone! Like rain on the desert. This world *is* a desert. The water is love. And the water disappears."

"I wonder why, Rudy?"

"Because the human heart has been squeezed dry of its juices by false prophets and Judases posing in the guise of saints. That's why!"

"That's cutting a broad path."

"Ah, but true. Where do we look? Tell me, Inspector! Gaze out on this humanity making its miserable way before us. Is there one splinter of love or kindness or nobility before your eyes?"

"That's hard to tell."

"Not for me. That's why I do this, you see? Here, behind this counter, I stand apart. Let them pass before me, one by hopeless one. I am not part of them. I throw dung on them. Oh—not you, Inspector. You are a noble and wise exception."

"Thanks, Rudy."

"I mean it. Truly. You wouldn't want any of this crap, would you?"

"I'd like some information, if you've got it."

"One of the first responsibilities of an honest and real individual in this horse's-ear world is to cooperate with the law. I'm at your service, Inspector."

"Ever see a girl, blond, fourteen, but looks older?"

"Lots of them come along like that."

"Large brown eyes. She might have been wearing a tight purple skirt and an orange sweater most of the time. A blue raincoat too. She's living at the Danway."

"Yeah. Listen—that wouldn't be the one I read about in the paper this morning? This girl was got right down the alley?"

"I didn't know it was in the papers."

"Little item, no name. You know. To protect the young and female."

"It might be, Rudy. Her name's Joplin. Do you know her?"

"I don't know her. I've seen her. Stacked, right?"

"She's stacked, all right. She comes by?"

"Now and then. Never bought any of this. But I remember her."

"Ever see her with anyone?"

"Male?"

"Male."

"One. I've seen them come along fast. Not too often. Like they didn't want to be seen together."

"Know his name?"

"World's full of finks. I forget names. What's his, anyway? He works at the Danway, I know that. Comes by in the bellboy uniform, most of the time. Tall, skinny, blond kid. Maybe twenty-three, twenty-four. I wouldn't give him the time of day. One look at him, I know what he is. Ten to one he pimps. Now he's trying to score with a fourteen-year-old girl. He stops once in a while and buys some of this crud. Maybe he thinks it'll make him pretty. How can you make somebody pretty when his soul is false? He told me his name once. I remember now. Norman something. Bellboy. Fink. I tell you, Inspector, the world's full of them."

"Maybe you're right, Rudy. But then I'm not a saint like you. Who am I to make the judgment? Maybe you helped the world a little today. Who knows?"

"Well, remember, Inspector. I'm pure. That's the one thing I am. I'm pure."

Cummings stood beside the desk in the Danway Hotel as Mandell lit a cigarette and threw the match on the floor. Mitchley, the deskman, followed the trajectory with surprise, then shock; and finally he stared at Mandell with ill-disguised disdain. Franklin, the night manager, motioned his hand agitatedly.

"It's all right, Franklin," Cummings said. "Don't get excited."

"But you ask me about Norman, and what else can you expect, Inspector? He is virtually my albatross. I cannot tell you how the man irritates me. He's a snot, that's what he is. An absolute snot!"

"He's a snot then. Does he live here?"

"Oh, no! I wouldn't take him for a guest. That's the truth, Inspector."

"What is so disgusting about him, Franklin?"

"His attitude. Start with that, Inspector! Conceited and snotty."

"That's why you wouldn't let him live here?"

"It isn't up to me. It's up to Mr. Levi. It was also up to Mr. Levi to hire him. Because God knows I wouldn't have. He's a dirty thing, too."

"In what way?"

"Sex," Franklin sniffed. "He talks about it, all the time. I believe that is an animal thing to do. Sex is a private, personal matter, isn't it? Why should one have to listen to someone spewing about it all the time? I say it's a matter of personal morality, and nobody else's business. But he spews and spews about what he's done or what he's going to do with this woman or that." Cummings saw a faint shudder move Franklin's shoulders. "That is truly animal, isn't it, Inspector?"

"I don't think animals talk a whole lot about sex, Franklin. Where does he live?"

"Oh, let's see now," Franklin said angrily. "Where does he live, Mitchley?"

Mitchley opened a card file and ran his finger along the cards. "Five fifty-seven Walsh Street."

"Two blocks away, Inspector," Franklin said. "And not far enough."

"Have you seen him with any of the hotel guests?"

"He's a bellman. He's with them all the time, naturally."

"In his off-time. Female guests."

"He'd better not! That is strictly forbidden! Can you imagine what would happen if we didn't have rules of that nature? A man with an animal attitude like that? Why, before you know it you'd have something atrocious. Like rape, or …" Franklin stopped and his lids began fluttering. "Oh, surely, Inspector. First Laureen Beggs. And now Norman? *Surely* this doesn't mean that—"

"This doesn't mean anything, Franklin. And I want both you and Mitchley to understand that this is private. I don't expect it to go any further. Is that understood?"

"Certainly, Inspector! There's never been any doubt about that. But do you actually mean that—"

"I don't actually mean anything. Now tell me what else you don't like about Norman."

Franklin, he saw, had already made his determination about what this meant; now there was a look of happy malice in his eyes. He narrowed them spitefully and said, "I don't think he's remotely honest, Inspector. I truly don't."

"What do you base that on?"

"Well, he's been out two days now, counting today, and I *sincerely* doubt that he'll show up tomorrow. He says he's sick. I wonder from what? Tell him, Mitchley. Tell him what you saw yesterday afternoon.

Before you came on duty."

Mitchley said with noticeable savor, "I saw him in a bar down the street. Sitting right there."

"Isn't that nerve, Inspector? Does he have no concept of the burden he creates on others?" Franklin's eyes narrowed again. "I'll tell you something else. I know for a fact that he's a thief."

"You mean he steals from the rooms?"

"Nothing so obvious as that, or he'd be out of here, pop, right on his fanny. But he's been stealing food from the kitchen. Do you know why?"

"Tell me, Franklin."

"His dog! Can you imagine that? Threatening one's position by actually stealing for a dog?" Franklin shuddered again. "God, how I hate animals! But that's not the point. The point is that it's a perfect example of what kind of person it is who would actually be so cheap and dishonest, and stupid, if you will, to steal for a dog!"

Cummings' mind was reaching back now, trying to separate something from all that was stored there. "The address where he lives is an apartment house. Is that where he keeps the dog?"

"Little thing, apparently. Disgusting little yippity-yap, I suppose. God. *Living* with it. I suppose it drools and dirties on the floor and everything."

Now he had it sorted. Lundstrom, speaking from his dying bed: "Dog barking." The question: "When?" And the answer: "When I was phoning Cutter." He felt his chemistry quickening—which always happened when he'd found a glimmering of light. "Let's take another look at the switchboard, shall we, Franklin?"

"Of course, Inspector. But I'm terribly confused, if I do say so. I just don't know where you're going."

"Don't worry about it."

"Oh! We had to get this new girl so quickly when the shocking news about Laureen came to us—*how* could she have done it?" His voice lowered to a stage whisper as they proceeded toward the switchboard. "Anyway, this girl is terribly dumb, Inspector. I don't know how we're going to manage! Mitchley! Come along with us. Mitchley can possibly answer any further questions you want to know, Inspector, if he'll just try to come alive. I'll try to help too."

The girl hired to replace Laureen Beggs was a pretty girl not much over twenty-one, Cummings guessed. She smiled warmly when Franklin introduced him to her.

"I'd like you to tell me something, Miss Collins. Say you've got one call up. Say you're talking to someone."

"Yes, sir?"

"Say another call comes in. You want to hold the first call and take care of the second."

"That happens all the time."

"How do you do it?"

She demonstrated efficiently.

"But now," Cummings went on. "Say you forgot to close that key to cut out the first call. You'd have a three-way connection, wouldn't you?"

"Of course."

"And if you were monitoring a call, Miss Collins?" Cummings said.

"Inspector Cummings," Franklin protested, "we absolutely don't allow that, here at the Danway."

"Miss Beggs admitted it, Franklin."

"That *woman!*" Franklin said in outrage.

"With the monitoring key open, Miss Collins, you take a second call, or you've already got one going: the first party could hear what you were hearing with the monitoring key open, couldn't he?"

"Certainly, Inspector," the girl said.

"Thanks very much."

When they had left the room, Cummings said, "I don't think she's so dumb, Franklin."

"Well, she put on a good show for *you*, but that doesn't fool anybody." Franklin drew in his breath. "Whatever are you doing, Inspector?"

"Right now, I'm going upstairs. But I warn you, Franklin: if you let any of this out, I'll have you in a cell—with a dog."

"Oh, God, Inspector! That isn't even funny!"

Chapter 10

"All right," Joplin said loosely. "Where is the son of a bitch? I want to get my hands on him!" His bottle was nearby; his words were slurred.

Mandell smiled and looked at the girl, who was sitting on the studio couch in her slip. Her mother was drunker than she'd been the first night. She looked blankly ahead with moist eyes.

Cummings said, "What son of a bitch are you talking about?"

"The one who did it. Show me that nigra!"

"She was lying."

Joplin paled with anger. "What?"

"I said she was lying."

Cummings looked at the girl, who stared back at him, looking frightened now. He turned toward the closet and saw the new outfit hanging there. No, it had not been there the first night.

"You're saying that about my daughter?" Joplin rose unsteadily. Mandell touched his chest. He sat down. "Get your hands off of me!"

"You can stop yelling, Joplin," Cummings said.

"I'll do anything I want in my own room!"

"You're disturbing the peace. You want us to take you in for disturbing the peace?"

"What's going on, anyway?" Joplin said, but his voice was reduced in volume.

"That's what I want to find out. Why did you lie at the lineup?" he asked the girl.

The girl didn't answer. Her father said, "What do you mean? She picked out the nigra, didn't she?"

"She picked out a Negro who happens to be one of our inspectors."

"I don't give a damn what he does."

"He was on duty when whatever was supposed to have happened to your daughter happened—if it did. Do you give her an allowance, Joplin?"

"What's that got to do with anything?"

"Does she buy her clothes or do you?"

"I do!"

"When did you buy her the new dress and coat?"

"What new dress and coat?"

And, Cummings thought, he had not noticed in his alcoholic daze. He motioned toward the closet. "The red dress. Blue coat."

"I never saw them before. You buy them?" Joplin asked his wife.

"I got no money for that."

"Where'd you get that stuff?" Joplin asked his daughter loudly.

The girl looked down at her lap, and she still appeared frightened, Cummings saw.

"I want to know!"

"I bought them," she said stiffly.

"Where'd you get the money?"

"I got it."

"From *where?*"

The girl sat silently.

"Did somebody give you the money?" Cummings asked crisply.

"*Give* her the money!" Joplin said. "She don't know nobody in this town. Who's going to give her money?"

"I think she might know somebody."

The girl looked up at Cummings and blinked slowly.

"How about a bellman in the hotel?" he asked. "Is that where you got it?"

"What bellman?" the girl asked, now sullen.

"His name's Norman Phillips."

"I don't know any bellman."

"What are you trying to get away with?" her father said.

"She's been seen with him," Cummings said.

"Who says?"

"I do."

"You been with some bellman?" he asked her belligerently.

"No," she said, but her voice was almost inaudible.

"He lives in an apartment two blocks from here," Cummings said. "You've been seen going there with him."

It was a dark shot; and it got response from Joplin: "That's a lie!"

"I'm afraid not." He stared at the girl. "Why did he give you the money?"

"He didn't."

"Shall I bring him up?"

"Did he say he gave it to me?"

"I want to hear your version."

The girl was silent. Her father watched her, face pale again. "Well?" he shouted.

"He just gave it to me."

Joplin's head swiveled back and forth in disbelief.

"You met in the hotel?" Cummings asked.

The girl stared down at her slip-covered thighs, silently.

"How long have you known him?"

"Since about three or four days after we moved in."

"You've been going to his apartment?"

"By God," Joplin said, "you'd better not say that!"

"She'd better if it's the truth. Why don't you just keep quiet for a bit, Joplin. Just shut up."

Joplin hunched his bare white shoulders and wiped a hand roughly across his mouth. He was silent.

"You've been going to his apartment?" Cummings repeated.

"Yes," the girl said quietly.

"The Negro business was a lie, wasn't it?"

"No."

"We'll find out everything anyway. We're just trying to give you the advantage of telling us yourself. Have you been intimate with this bellman?"

"I ain't going to allow—" her father began.

"I told you to shut up, Joplin!" He nodded to the girl and decided to use her first name. "Tina?"

"Yes," she said softly.

Joplin started to rise again, but Mandell pushed him gently back into his chair.

"Tell us," Cummings said.

"Well," she said, "we been doing it." She sniffed and rubbed her nose. She looked up finally, her eyes switching fleetingly toward her mother, then her father. She looked down again.

"I'll kill her," her father breathed.

"Go ahead, Tina," Cummings said.

"Only Monday, after supper, it was different."

"How?"

"Norman was all excited. I don't know about what. He gave me this money and said go buy some pretty clothes. Then we did it. Only he was so all-excited he didn't take no time …" She shrugged. "You know."

"To use a contraceptive?"

"I heard enough!" Joplin roared.

"Is that right?" Cummings asked.

She nodded.

"So you dreamed up the story about the Negro attacking you in the alley, because you were afraid you might have gotten pregnant?"

"Well," she said, "it could have happened the way I said it did. Some nigger in the alley. They always scairt hell out of me. It *could* have happened."

"I'm going to skin her alive!" Joplin shouted.

But, Cummings thought, his fury was more for his frustration in knowing that he could not blame this on a Negro than for the frank confession of his daughter's sexual experience with a white bellman named Norman Phillips. Joplin, or his wife, could not have failed to realize the risk involved in their complete failure to chaperone the girl's time.

"I'll tell you what you're going to do, Joplin. You punish her any way you want to, except by pushing her around. You hurt her, I'm going to make you wish you'd never been born. We'll take care of Norman Phillips. You're going to do something else too. You're going to quit looking down that bottle and start paying attention to what she does with her time. Otherwise, she's going to go into the hands of the juvenile court. I'm talking to you too, Mrs. Joplin."

He looked at both of them and knew that his words would have little or no effect and that quite probably it would be how the matter would wind up: the girl would eventually go into the jurisdiction of the juvenile court. There were some, he thought, who ought to be parents and some who ought not to be; then they'd hurt only themselves. But there was little he could do about that, because the act of reproduction was the simplest and easiest of performances for almost any of the species. It was its consequence that created the complexity. He hoped one thing: that the girl had not gotten pregnant—which might start a series of events such as this all over again.

"Remember what I told you," Cummings said.

Equipped with a search warrant, Cummings got out of the car after Mandell had parked it in front of the apartment house. "You're picking up a scent, aren't you, Jack?"

"You don't need to be a bird dog to do it."

"What are we looking for?"

"Norman Phillips and some money."

"Like sixty-five grand?"

"Like sixty-five grand."

Mandell pressed the button beside Phillips' name in the dusty foyer and got no response.

"Get a key from the manager," Cummings said.

Minutes later, Cummings opened the door of Norman Phillips' apartment. A small dog darted into the living room as they stepped in and started barking at them furiously.

"What the hell is he, anyway?" Mandell asked. "What kind?"

"The loud kind," Cummings said.

They moved through the small apartment, the dog complaining hysterically. There were three rooms furnished in surprisingly good taste.

"I'll take the living room," Cummings said. "You start on the bedroom."

He began a careful search of the room, opening drawers, moving pictures, lifting cushions. The dog trailed him, never coming too close, but never ceasing his ear-shattering barking either.

Mandell came in carrying a thick roll of currency. "Bathroom. He had it wired into the water closet."

Feeling a quick satisfaction, Cummings took the money as the door opened. A tall, lean youth wearing black slacks, a soft white shirt, and an expensive yellow alpaca sweater stood there.

"What's going on?" he said.

He saw the money in Cummings' hand. Fright and dismay changed the look in his eyes.

"Come in, Phillips," Cummings said.

The youth hesitated, as if ready to spring sideways.

"I wouldn't," Cummings said. His hand was inside his jacket, touching his pistol. "Come in now."

Norman Phillips moved slowly into the room. Mandell stepped behind him and ran his hands skillfully over the sweater.

"Where'd you get this, Phillips?" Cummings asked.

"Who are you anyway?" the youth asked bitterly.

"Detectives. Where'd you get the money?"

"I never saw it before. Where'd *you* get it?"

"In the water closet."

"I don't know anything about it."

Cummings nodded. "Okay, Mandell."

Chapter 11

Norman Phillips sat at a small table in an interrogation room. Cummings was seated across from him. Mandell watched with his back to the closed door. This time, Cummings thought, he was going to finish before turning it over to Captain Otto Blaine.

"I don't know anything you're talking about," Phillips insisted. "I can get a lawyer."

"Your privilege."

"I don't need one. Because I don't know anything about this. Nothing."

"You didn't know Robert Lundstrom was shot in the Danway and died from it?"

"Who doesn't?"

"That sixty-five thousand dollars was stolen from his room?"

"All right."

"There's a total of sixty-three thousand in that roll we found in your apartment."

"So?"

"You haven't got a prayer, Phillips."

"I don't know how that money got there, and neither do you. What can you prove?"

"That it was found in your room. That's enough. Nobody's that stupid, including a jury."

"I don't know how it got there."

"You know we arrested Laureen Beggs?"

He blinked nervously. "I read about it."

"Know her?"

"Sure I know her."

"How well?"

"She works at the Danway. I work there. I know her."

"Do you like women, Phillips?"

"Don't mix me up with Franklin."

"You like the dog too, don't you?"

"Is that a crime?"

"It's a barker, isn't it?"

"Are you going to arrest him too?"

Cummings drew out his pipe, loaded it, and fired the tobacco, watching the youth steadily. "How about a girl named Tina Joplin?"

Phillips pulled a forefinger slowly across his upper lip. "Who?"

"Tina Joplin," Cummings repeated quietly.

"That's the girl in the hotel, isn't it?"

"She's fourteen years old. You're in trouble every way you turn, aren't you, Phillips?"

"Now what?"

"Statutory rape."

Phillips looked at the table. Strength seemed to drain from him. "What did she say?"

"That you'd been intimate with her several times. Including Monday night. She started by blowing the whistle on a Negro she said raped her. She gave up, finally, and said she'd had relations with you that night. Only you didn't use a contraceptive. She was afraid of being pregnant. What happened, Phillips?"

Phillips remained silent, staring at the table, face drawn now.

"You were too excited, right? Why were you excited?"

The youth continued to be silent.

"Why did you give her the money?"

Cummings watched him, puffing slowly on the pipe. Finally he said, "No? All right. I'll tell you. You worked it with Laureen Beggs. She was on the switchboard Monday afternoon. She had you on a line when she plugged in Lundstrom's call. You heard Lundstrom say he had sixty-five thousand in his room. You hung up and went to the hotel. Two blocks, and you could do it fast. By that time Laureen Beggs was off duty. She gave you her gun. You went up to the room and got the money. When Lundstrom came back, you killed him. You gave the gun back to Laureen Beggs, took the money home, and celebrated by banging a fourteen-year-old. Now Laureen Beggs is taking it by herself. You must be beautiful with women, Phillips. But you're also a son of a bitch."

The youth wagged his head hopelessly. "Not true."

"Before Lundstrom died, he remembered hearing a dog barking. He heard it on the phone. It was your dog."

Norman Phillips' hands closed on the surface of the table. His head dropped and wagged back and forth. "Laureen didn't have anything to do with it," he said, in a defeated voice.

Cummings nodded, surprised. "Let's hear it."

"I was talking to her on the phone from my place. She and I, we get together now and then, you know what I mean? She isn't so hot-looking, but … I don't know. Anyway, she always cut me off when she got another call and I was talking to her. Only she must have forgotten this time or accidentally hit the switch and cut me in again. But she was listening in on the call Lundstrom was making. She always listens to calls. I heard it too. Lundstrom said he had the money in his room. I figured he might leave it there. So I hustled over to the hotel, like you figured. Laureen still wasn't in her room. I knew about her pistol, and I got it. I went up the stairs and found the cash in Lundstrom's bureau. When he came back, I panicked. I shot him. I put the gun back in Laureen's room later."

Cummings' tobacco had gone out. He tapped it out of the pipe bowl. "Laureen Beggs and the Joplin girl. At the same time. Then you shot Lundstrom and stole sixty-five thousand dollars. Why the gallantry now, with Laureen Beggs?"

"She must have figured it had to be me. So she was covering. She didn't have anything to do with it."

And, Cummings thought, it was simply that Phillips realized that Laureen Beggs had been willing to sacrifice herself for him, or it was an unexpected streak of honor that he could not understand and never would.

"You'd better phone a lawyer, Phillips. You're going to need one."

As Mandell drove back to the district, Laureen Beggs sitting silently in the back seat, Cummings was thinking that the confession by Norman Phillips had slightly hurt the ego of Captain Otto Blaine—finding out that the story he had so skillfully extracted from the woman had been false. But the major thing was that Knocko Cutter was still out of it, and that was all that finally counted.

Mandell parked in front of the Danway. Cummings got out to help Laureen Beggs from the back. As she stepped to the curbing, she twisted her body away from him.

"Get your hands off me!"

"We're sorry, Miss Beggs. But you really gave us no choice when you confessed to it."

"Don't you understand?" she said shrilly. "I *wanted* to do it. I *loved* him. And you had to ..." Her voice broke. Tears rolled down her cheeks. "*Why did you have to spoil it?*" she shrieked and ran blindly toward the hotel.

"Now?" Mandell asked.

"Bay View Motel. Maybe it'll help her a little—knowing we've sure got the one who killed him. Maybe there's a chance she can get a piece of that money too, before Knocko claims it all."

Mandell nodded agreeably. "Finally came together, didn't it? Lundstrom. The Joplin girl. One and two, and you got the whole thing. Simple."

Cummings watched the night street as Mandell drove swiftly through thinning traffic. Yes, he thought, one and two, and you got the whole thing. Simple enough, and now there were no more doubts. Yet he had a strong feeling that he was heading somewhere definitely now, simply because there had been a lot of ones and twos to get the whole thing. Everything was coming together, to create the large answer. But what was it? he wondered. Whatever it was, it had come about as the result of his own inclination toward the direction a long time ago. A man had to take what he found along the way, and do the best he could with each part of it; but the way he went, the direction he followed, was the way he had started when the choice was still his....

He got out and walked quickly to the door marked 6-A. Once again he saw light shining against the drape and under the door. There was no response to his knock. He tried again, harder. He waited a few seconds; then he went to the office. The lean manager appeared, looking sleepy.

"Watching television, Inspector. Fell asleep. Be awake in a second."

"I still don't get an answer from Mrs. Lundstrom."

"It's a funny thing. I haven't had a glimpse of her since she checked in."

"Have you cleaned the unit?"

"Well, you know. We've got the kitchens. It's semi-housekeeping. We just lay in enough towels, that sort of thing, so the customer can take care of himself."

"I remember now."

"We like to make it homey, but, naturally, if they want anything—"

"Have you seen anybody go in?"

"Marge thought she did. She was up to get a glass of water yesterday morning, and it was about, oh, seven-thirty. Something like that. She thought she saw a couple of men at her door. She was half asleep. She went back to bed then. She mentioned it when I told her you'd been here."

"Let's take a look."

"Certainly, Inspector. I'll get a key."

Moments later they stepped into the unit. The living room was square and compactly furnished with modern furniture over a dark-blue carpet. A studio couch had been made into a bed, and the covers were turned back. The pillow looked as if someone had slept on it. Her bag, containing the things he'd had sent here from the Danway the night Lundstrom had died, was resting on a suitcase rack. Her cosmetics case was on the nightstand. The lighted lamp on the stand created the illumination he'd seen outside. The small kitchen adjoining the room looked untouched. The bathroom door was closed. Cummings opened it.

He looked at her nude body in a tub half-filled with bloodied water. Both knees were above the water, and her head was resting face up against the back portion of the porcelain. Her face had been scrubbed, and she looked much younger than she had when the mascara had been there. Her eyes opened upward. Cummings heard the manager gasp and saw him backing from the room. He knelt to examine her without touching her. Finally he put a hand into the blood-reddened water and lifted her forearm. Her inner wrist was slashed, as if by a razor.

He walked outside, where he found the manager leaning against the outer wall of the unit. The man shook his head slowly, with a sick, uncertain smile. "Sorry, Inspector. But I never before …" He suddenly leaned forward and put a handkerchief to his mouth. He straightened, eyes watering. "I'm really sorry, Inspector."

"It's all right," Cummings said shortly, feeling anger going through him. He put a hand around the man's arm and helped him toward the office.

"I tell you that hit me, Inspector," the manager said weakly. "She was such a beautiful girl."

"Yes," Cummings said harshly. "She was such a beautiful girl."

Chapter 12

Afternoon shadows were running longer from the trees in the small park across from the ancient headquarters downtown. A few old men sat in statuesque immobility, mirroring the death that would soon come to all of them, as pigeons waddled hopefully along the crosswalks in search of feeders. A light wind was coming in from the bay, sending a single sheet from a newspaper fluttering across the tended grass. Cummings sat beside Mandell at a small short-order counter half a block from headquarters watching the paper blow against a tree trunk and stay there. Life, he thought distantly. You blew with the wind, haphazardly; then you wound up pinned against the tree that was waiting for you. Then you were finished. What you stood for was history, like that sheet of newspaper. Then they pronged you on the end of a stick and sent you off to the refuse collection, where you were burned with the rest of the old news.

Mandell tapped his coffee cup and said loudly, "Let's fill it up, shall we, Oscar?"

A short Chinese came up with a sour look on his normally cheerful face and splashed coffee in both of their cups. Oscar was in a lousy mood, Cummings thought. So was Mandell. And so was he. He'd chosen eggs and ham, and it had been too much; somehow they had not been prepared well either.

"Furguson get much done yet?" Mandell asked. He lit a cigarette, and, Cummings thought, not only was he in a lousy mood, but he seemed nervous.

"I'll check with him when we get done."

"It figures, doesn't it?"

Mandell's voice was rough, and he was speaking very rapidly. He was bothered, all right; and that surprised Cummings.

"Somehow it doesn't."

"You always swim upstream, don't you, Cummings?"

He looked at him with hard eyes. "Maybe that's why I'm an inspector and you're an assistant, Mandell."

Mandell blew smoke out and stared grimly at his coffee. "Her checkbook was Lundstrom. Lundstrom died." He shrugged.

"You want it that easy, Mandell?"

"If it was suicide, why not call it that?"

"You say Lundstrom was her checkbook. With her looks, she could have found a dozen other checkbooks soon enough."

"She was in grief."

"I don't buy it."

"Jesus, Cummings." He lifted the coffee cup finally, then put the cup down hard. "Goddamned rotten crap. I'm tired of coming here."

"Did you think she was in grief?"

"I barely saw her. How would I know?"

"She was sorry for herself, but I don't think she was feeling bad enough about Lundstrom that she tried to follow him."

"All right," Mandell snapped. "The blade she used came out of the razor she had in her cosmetics kit."

"Probably."

"It's simple."

"Everything's simple to you, Mandell. It's a happy state you live in."

"If she didn't do it, who did? And why?"

"You're the one who's worrying about it."

"Nobody knew where she was except you and me." Mandell's left hand jerked up and his fingernails scratched rapidly at the skin in front of his ear.

Cummings watched that quick motion. "Unless she told somebody before she checked in. She apparently didn't leave, once she got there. There're no telephones there."

"That's right," Mandell said quickly. "Maybe she told somebody before she checked in." He seemed to relax.

"You like that, Mandell?" Cummings asked, feeling himself tensing.

"It's an idea."

"How come you like it?"

Mandell would not look at him. "What's the difference?"

"I don't think she told anybody, Mandell. I think she went straight from the hospital to the motel, and she didn't go out again until we carried her out."

"You're God again."

"What's bothering you?"

"You. Because you're always looking down from the heavens on us poor slobs."

Cummings closed his large hands tightly on top of the counter. "When did you tell Knocko where she was, Mandell?"

Mandell visibly tensed. "You're dreaming."

"The motel manager's wife said she thought she saw two men at her door on Tuesday morning."

"She couldn't identify anyone, could she?"

"You dumb, stupid son of a bitch!" Cummings said. "When did you tell him? And why? To protect that scrummy little take you're getting from the Palms?"

"I don't have to take that from you. I can—"

"You can tell me when you told him."

Once again Mandell was scratching himself. "You got a vendetta with Knocko, that's not my business."

"I'm going to break your arm off, Mandell, if you don't tell me."

"All right! He asked a simple question. I told him."

"When!"

"He called me up at home, after we went off duty Tuesday morning. What's the difference?"

Cummings could feel his heart pumping. Tuesday morning. She probably died while he was with Vinni, the most beautiful hooker in the world.

"That's blood you're going to have on your hands the rest of your life, Mandell."

"Now wait a minute, Cummings," he said, a whining note going into his voice.

Cummings got up and walked swiftly out the door into the late sunshine. The anger blinded him for a moment. Then he moved on, toward headquarters.

Mike Hawley smiled as he came in. "You look like you could push the columns apart and send the temple tumbling, Jack."

"I might have reason."

"Anything I can use?"

"It's not funny, Mike."

"Sorry." Hawley's smile disappeared.

"You get a story out of the Joplin thing?"

"Not the way it turned out."

"That's right. It didn't turn out, did it? The miscegenation part of it."

"Well, you solved the Lundstrom shooting with it. But nothing else now. And the Lundstrom shooting was pure crime, the way it wound up."

"I told you before, Mike. It always has social implication."

"How does this one?"

"How about the system? Is the system social?"

"I'd say so."

"What is the system?"

"You tell me, Jack."

"Ever hear of a fix?"

"Big or small?"

"Big."

"Like in this town?"

"Like in this town."

"I've heard."

"That's material you can work on, isn't it?"

"Sure."

"How'd you like to help break it?"

Hawley looked at him questioningly. "Break it?"

"That's right—break it."

He nodded. "That would be agreeable."

"Don't use anything until I say so."

"All right, Jack."

He could see the excitement in Hawley's eyes.

"You want to come along and see what the medical examiner's got?"

"With Mrs. Lundstrom?"

"That's right."

"Is that where this starts?"

"It started a long time ago, Mike, but maybe this is where it'll end."

The body lay beneath a sheet in the spotless room. The medical examiner was a slight man wearing black-rimmed glasses. They made him look bookish and intellectual; but they did not hide the reality of his eyes, which reflected too much death.

"She bled to death?" Cummings asked.

"That's right."

"Time?"

"She's still in a state of rigor. I checked the temperature. Tuesday morning."

"Anything else?"

The examiner nodded grimly. He turned the sheet back from the lower part of her body. "Internal damage. Severe."

Cummings felt the anger all over again. "Like the hooker six months ago?"

"No hemorrhaging. But it must have been painful. I don't know what kind of animal—"

"I do," Cummings said shortly.

The examiner covered the body again. Hawley looked at Cummings closely.

Cummings said, "Torture."

"It had to be that."

"She might have cut her own wrists to stop the pain?"

"That could be too."

Cummings walked out of the room, accompanied by Hawley. His neck felt stiff.

"Murder?" Hawley asked.

Cummings took a breath. "Give me a little more time, Mike. Then I'll hand it to you."

Cummings sat in the gray-walled office of Captain Otto Blaine, watching the man scrub his hands with the vigor that came from extreme nervousness. His own anger now had been cooled by the knowledge that Mrs. Lundstrom may have been the sacrifice, but that he was going to make it count.

"It doesn't make any sense," Blaine said, rubbing his hands together. "Why doesn't it, Otto?"

"Because I don't think he'd do such a stupid thing." Blaine walked back to his desk, his face showing his resentment for this.

"Knocko is stupid about some things, Otto. This was one of them."

"Who knows what could happen to a cheap bit of business like that?"

"I don't give a damn whether Mrs. Lundstrom was a cheap bit of business or not. Knocko hates women. He figured she was the one who got Lundstrom's money. So he sent Bernie and Abner to work her over. They did. Now she's in the morgue."

"Anybody could have done it," Blaine said, shaking his head. "Anybody."

"It's Knocko's trademark."

"There isn't proof, is there? Where is the proof? I say it's a suicide until there's proof of something."

Cummings watched him with hard, steady eyes. "I'm going to get him, Captain. I'm going to use every piece of information I've got, every knowledge I own, every instinct, and all the energy I've got, to get him. And when I do, it'll knock the structure apart from bottom to top. It'll kill the fix, Captain. Once and for all."

Blaine stared back at him for a moment; then, without seemingly realizing what he was doing, he got up and started washing his hands all over again.

Chapter 13

Knocko sat at his expensive desk and smiled at Cummings. He'd just been shaved, and the smell of lotion was more noticeable than ever. His fingernails gleamed from a fresh manicure. What hair remained had been trimmed expertly.

"The captain tell you I was coming?" Cummings asked.

"Yes."

"You don't look worried, Knocko."

"Why should I be?"

"Murder's something to worry about."

"What murder, Jack?"

"Didn't the captain tell you?"

"About what?"

"Mrs. Lundstrom."

"Suicide."

"Maybe. After somebody worked on her. That'd make it forced suicide. That's murder in my book."

"Do you think I did something like that, Jack?"

"What do you have against women, Knocko?"

Knocko's smile evaporated. "What does that mean?"

"I don't think you like women."

"You're crazy."

Touch a primitive nerve, he thought, and the poise was gone. "You finished yourself with this, Knocko."

"Why don't you bust me or get the hell out of here, Cummings."

"I'm going to get rid of you this time, all the way."

Knocko's eyes turned cloudy. "You hypocritical bastard. Do you think you're better than I am?"

"Why not?"

"I'll give you a reason—Vinni."

And he finally realized the real meaning of Vinni. The symbol of all evil, more specifically Knocko's evil, with her clear-eyed beauty. It had meant nothing at all, except the purpose of carrying out Knocko's orders. She'd been sent as a balm but, more importantly, to make sure that he was occupied while Bernie and Abner worked over Mrs. Lundstrom. That was a taint, he thought, that he might never escape.

"Maybe it takes the same breed of animal to destroy another, Knocko. In that case, I'd start worrying."

"I'm trembling, Jack."

In the night air, he found his mind searching to find the real beginning of Knocko's destruction. He saw Solly beside his newsstand. He remembered the picture Solly had shown him the night Lundstrom was killed. Bernie, he thought. Abner, the start was there. Then he remembered something he'd stored away: Abner and his prostitute wife, whom he worshipped. The something was there....

He walked back to the car, where Mandell waited grimly. "Day off tomorrow."

"It ought to be now." Mandell would not look at him, and had not since he'd confessed his part in Mrs. Lundstrom's fate.

"Take off. I'll cover for you."

"You want to get rid of me."

"That's right. I want to get rid of you."

"That isn't going to break my heart, Cummings."

"Take off then."

Mandell slid out of the car and walked away stiffly. Cummings got behind the wheel and drove fast and expertly, feeling a pulsation of excitement. He could smell it coming, he thought. A small thing. But it might be enough to throw open the door all the way....

He stopped the car in front of a vintage storage building in the warehouse district. There was a musky smell of fowl as he opened a battered door. He walked up a plank stairway, using light from a street lamp shining through a dusty window. At the top was a door painted a violent red. He rapped his knuckles against it.

In a few moments it opened to show him a small, delicate man wearing huge, thick spectacles. His equally huge eyes appeared distorted behind the lenses.

"Inspector?"

It was a voice that sounded as if it came from a throat that had been permanently bruised.

"You want to let me in, Ernest?"

Ernest backed away from the door, waving a hand with a sparrow-quick movement. "What's wrong?"

"Nothing's wrong, Ernest."

"I got out of the district a long time ago."

"Sure you did."

He looked around the high-ceilinged room. There was a dirty unmade bed. A splattered kitchen stove stood precariously on rusting legs across the room. In the center of the room was a round modeling platform draped with a fading blue velvet cover. To the right was a tripod-mounted camera. To the left was a film projector and a rolled-up screen.

"I ain't lived there in three years, Inspector."

"I know that, Ernest."

"So what's the beef?"

"Who said there's a beef?" He smiled and tried to decide among a collection of spindly, near-collapsed chairs. He decided to stand. "How's it go, Ernest?"

Ernest jerked his shoulders nervously. "You know."

"If I knew, I wouldn't ask, would I?"

"Listen, Inspector. I swear—"

"So how's it going?"

"I eat."

"That's something, isn't it? That's better than not eating, isn't it?"

"What's the matter, Inspector?"

"Nothing's the matter, Ernest. Relax."

"How can I relax?" he whined.

"Get any good ones lately?"

"Good ones?"

"Come on, Ernest."

"I take passport stuff. You know that. That's all."

"That's passport stuff, all right. But passport to where?"

"I don't know what's wrong, Inspector."

"I saw the latest. It's a beauty."

"Where?"

"Solly."

The small man wagged his head forlornly. "He wasn't supposed to be showing that to nobody. That was just between me and him."

"And anybody else willing to pay ten bucks for a copy. That ought to be a good profit, Ernest. Ten bucks a shot."

"I never gave him no right to try to sell that. That's the truth, Inspector."

Again Cummings smiled.

"I wish you wouldn't do that, Inspector. It makes me nervous. What can I do for you?"

"Well, I was thinking about something Solly told me about a few weeks back. A party. At the Chambers Hotel. Knocko Cutter threw it. Abner wasn't there, but his wife was. You remember that party, Ernest?"

"Me?" His eyes were large and bulging behind the thick lenses.

"Solly said you took some film for Knocko."

"Well, you can't believe nothing he says anymore! What kind of a thing was that for him to say! I never took no film at that party!"

"See if you can't remember. Knocko sent Abner out of town; then he threw the party. Bernie was there too."

He waited patiently. With the flash floods out, the room was lit solely by a lone bulb hanging from the center of the high ceiling. It put Ernest's face in deep shadows and harsh light, reflecting against his glasses so that he could not see the bulging eyes. The sea was the district and Knocko and Solly and everyone else connected with it. It was the whole city. The sea ran and he was swimming in it. He was within a last-burst distance from the shore now. But the air was still foggy and he did not know if he approached reef or beach. A buoy sounded vacantly, from beyond the city's edge, in the real and honest sea. It was a lonely sound, but a sound of beckoning.

"Don't you remember, Ernest?"

"No," Ernest said unconvincingly. "I never took no film at that party."

"How much income did you report in April, Ernest?"

"That's a private matter, ain't it?"

"Between you and the government it is. But they like to get it accurate."

"You ain't with the government, Inspector."

"City government."

"That ain't the same as Federal."

"What if I tipped a Federal revenue officer I know that you were picking up a good take on what Solly sells for you?"

"Listen, Inspector. He ain't telling the truth about that."

"It doesn't make any difference, does it? Solly's in my district. I can close him. He'll say what I tell him to. I'm going to tell him what to say—unless you tell me about that party."

Ernest drew a ragged handkerchief from a rear pocket and dabbed regretfully at the corners of his mouth. "Well, it was just a party, see? You ain't going to tell Knocko I told you, are you?"

"I don't think that'll be necessary, Ernest."

"He'd kill me."

"I'll see it doesn't happen."

"Well … it was Knocko. Bernie. Couple of other guys Knocko keeps around."

"And Abner's wife."

"Ruth's her name."

"A nice name."

Ernest dabbed at his mouth again. "Knocko told me bring the movie camera, see? Then they got Ruth drunk." He shrugged.

"What then, Ernest?"

"She got kind of wild. I mean, not kind of wild. She got wild. So they started fooling around with her, you know what I mean? They took it along like that."

"How far?"

"Well," Ernest said defensively, "how far can you take it?"

"You took movies of it?"

"I gave Knocko the film after. I don't know what he wanted to do with it. But he paid, I gave it to him."

"Have you got a copy, Ernest?"

"Me?"

"Did you keep a copy for yourself?"

"What would I do with a thing like that?"

"I can call that revenue man, Ernest."

"Listen, Inspector …"

"Come on, Ernest. Let's get it into the projector."

The soft whirring of the machine stopped, and Ernest turned on the ceiling light. Cummings stood thoughtfully, remembering each sordid scene he'd viewed. They'd used the girl like animals, Bernie included. There was something primeval within her nature, and she'd responded to the call. But the ultimate sickness had been Knocko's, he thought, the single member of the party who had not touched her. He was the one who'd arranged it; he'd instigated the final action that had taken place and thoughtfully had Ernest there to film it. His sickness was demonstrated in his desire to tear down what Abner, in his simple but passionate devotion to the girl, owned and he could not own. He hated Abner's passion because he was not capable of it. So it had come to this.

"All right, Ernest," he said. "Let's pack up the projector and roll up the screen. I'm going to borrow them and the film."

"Inspector, you can't do that! If Knocko ever—"

"Come on, Ernest. Hurry up!"

Grimly, Ernest got the equipment ready and helped him carry it down to the car. As Cummings got behind the wheel, Ernest put his face close to the window, large eyes bulging.

"He'll kill me, Inspector. I swear it! I told him he had the only copy."

"Relax, Ernest," he said, and pulled away swiftly.

When his shift ended, he transferred the equipment to his own car and drove home. In his living room he set up the screen and fitted the film into the projector. Then he walked to the telephone and dialed. Moments later he heard a sleepy voice.

"You awake, Abner?"

"Who's this?"

"Cummings. How would you like to come over to my house?"

"Me?"

"Why not?"

"What do I want to go there for?"

"I've got something you'll want to see."

"What?"

"A film."

"What kind of film?"

"Taken at a party Knocko threw a few weeks ago, while you were out of town."

"Film? What kind of film is it?"

"Ask Ruth. I'll be waiting for you."

He hung up, remembering how he'd thought that one day reality would smash Abner's consuming passion for his wife, and that he did not want to be around when that happened. Now it was going to happen, and he was going to be around when it did. But there was no helping that now, because it was the way to the shore, once for all.

Chapter 14

He opened the door to the giant man, whose broad face encased bewildered, stupid eyes. He wore no coat, and his shirt, beneath a suit jacket, was tieless. His hair was rumpled. "What is this, Cummings?" he asked in his thick froggy voice. He looked as if he were ready for a fury he could not understand—but confusion was keeping it in control.

"Come in, Abner."

Abner stepped inside and looked at the projector and screen. His ham hands came out in a motion of perplexity. "What is this?" he repeated.

"You tell Ruth?"

"I told her you called, what you said."

"What did she say?"

"Nothing, except she was thirsty. She went out to the kitchen to get a glass of water. She didn't come back. When I went to look, she wasn't there. She went out the back way. I ..." He shook his head in the manner of a bull who smells his enemy but cannot find him.

"Sit down, Abner."

He was thinking of how the body of Mrs. Lundstrom had looked in that bathtub, and he felt no remorse for this.

Bernie, he was certain, had done the real work. But Abner had been there. Abner had helped. Now Abner was going to get hurt; and maybe it was going to hurt him as much as they'd hurt Mrs. Lundstrom.

He started the projector, leaving a single lamp on. Abner sat watching the screen like a child preparing to see a potentially exciting western that had been vaguely described to him but about which he was yet unfamiliar. Cummings watched him, not the screen. He noticed for the first time how Abner's dark, coarse hair was cut in the back: artlessly, straight across with the shaved skin below the line of the cutting showing whitely. His neck was thick and ran straight down from the bottom of his ears to the enclosure of his white shirt. There was a small X-shaped scar at the back of his right ear. Stiff hair bristles came from both ears; the ears were oddly shaped, with almost no lobes.

A man, Cummings thought, shaped his own course, all right. But some did it with less control than others. Abner was such a man, because he had less mental capacity to make his choices. Still there were those with no more intellectual ability, and they had not chosen this way. Abner was responsible for that, and there was no way to know why he had made the original choice. The only fact was that he had. So he had gone somewhere. Now, on that screen, he was seeing where somewhere was.

The man gave a short grunt. Thick muscles of his neck visibly tensed. His shoulders beneath the dark jacket lumped and showed it through expensive cloth. Cummings could hear him breathing. He could smell sudden sweating.

Then Abner came off the chair as if starting a somersault. He straightened and his great hands flailed ahead. The screen was thrown against a wall. He wheeled, eyes widened in rage, flashing in the light from the projector. Cummings reached for him as he plunged back. But he went through Cummings' hands with the strength of the insane, to lift the projector and send it into another wall, glass smashing. He wheeled drunkenly, mouth open, gasping, "Kill them! Kill them!"

He stared at Cummings, then his legs churned as he pitched toward the door. Cummings dived at him to hook one arm beneath one of his, the other crossing in front of the man's chest. They slammed together into the door. Then they crashed down against the already damaged sofa, cracking its middle. Rolling to the floor with him, Cummings bent one of the large man's arms backward and pinned his head tightly against the rug.

Abner gasped, "Kill them! Knocko! Bernie!"

"I've got a better way," Cummings said hoarsely.

"They'll die!" Abner said in a half-scream.

"My way, Abner. Do it my way!"

Abner had got his gun from the holster inside his jacket. Cummings struck sideways with a flat hand, and it spun across the floor. Then he pinned the man's head against the rug again.

"My way and they're both finished!"

"My gun!" the man said desperately.

"You'll never get a chance."

"Gun!" Abner pleaded.

"Don't you know where she went? Straight to Knocko. They know you'll be gunning for them. They'll be gunning for you first."

He moaned pitifully against the floor.

"Don't you understand, Abner? You walk out the door, you're a dead man."

He could feel the man's body going limp. He pushed himself to his feet. Abner lay staring ahead, not moving.

"Come on," Cummings said softly, and lifted the man to his feet. Abner took a blind step, sagged; then Cummings guided him to a chair, where he collapsed limply, head rolling back.

"Why?" Abner breathed.

"Knocko's sick," Cummings said. "You loved her, and he hated you for it."

"But her? Why?"

"You started loving her too late, Abner. It was all too late."

"I loved her."

"Sometimes it's one way."

"She said she loved me."

Yes, he thought, and perhaps she had. But probably she'd loved only the escape from the work she'd done for Knocko—and the money Abner got for his work. They lived in an animal world, but Abner did not know that. Like any animal, he had no comparisons to make, because he could not see beyond his own life. "She's gone to Knocko, Abner."

Abner was drawing in his breath through an open mouth, his head lolling against the back of the chair. "We can fix him now," Cummings said softly.

"I got nothing," Abner said. "Nothing."

"What happened to Mrs. Lundstrom?"

"I'm already dead."

"Abner, listen to me. What happened to Mrs. Lundstrom?"

"Bury me," Abner moaned.

"You've got a chance to make him pay for it, Abner. What happened to Mrs. Lundstrom?"

"I don't care anymore."

"Then tell me."

"Knocko thought she had the money."

"So he sent you and Bernie to her motel."

"I don't care."

"What happened, Abner?"

"She wouldn't say she had it. We couldn't find it."

"So you worked her over."

"Bernie did."

Now, he thought, he was getting all that he'd needed. "How did she die?"

"Bernie."

"Bernie. But how?"

"She asked to. Bernie was working on her. Towel against her mouth. He had me get her razor, hold it out to her. She was in the tub. She took it. Cut her own wrists."

A cloud of fresh fury blinded him for a moment. The fingers of his large hands flexed. He would like, now, to kill this man, this great, childish brute of a man, for his part in it. But he was only the paid instrument of the assigner. And it was the assigner he was after.

Suddenly the man was bending forward, putting his face against his palms. His huge shoulders jerked. He cried steadily, making a strange sound. And, Cummings thought, as Mrs. Lundstrom's grief had been for herself, Abner's grief was also for himself. He cried for the loss of a love that had been one way, all within himself and nowhere else. He cried for his simple soul, not for the girl who had died by the slash of her own motion to escape the torture of Bernie. He cried as a hurt dog whimpered, uncomprehending, only feeling.

"I'm going to take you in, Abner," Cummings said carefully. "You're going to repeat exactly what happened. You're going to name Knocko. You're going to name Bernie. It'll go easier with you if you do it that way, Abner."

"I don't care anymore," he sobbed.

"Think what they did to Ruth, Abner."

"No." He was whimpering like a child. "I don't want to!"

"You've got to. You've got to pay them back for that."

"Kill them!"

"Just come with me. Tell the story."

Tears streamed against his palms. "Kill them!"

"There's a small room at the prison, Abner. Round. Two chairs in it. They'll gas them there, side by side. It's certain. Just do what I say."

Abner brought his palms from his face and lifted his head to look at Cummings with reddened eyes. "Will they die?"

"That's right, Abner."

Abner nodded slowly, face wet and wrenched with childish anguish. "All right."

Chapter 15

Cummings sat in Captain Otto Blaine's office, feeling the exhausted satisfaction of having completed a long journey he'd been certain, at times, would never be completed. Blaine's face was sadly grim. He sat without his usual military straightness. He looked defeated and frightened.

"End of it, Captain," Cummings said.

"It was a stupid thing," the captain said. "A stupid, stupid thing."

"It's going to finish Knocko. This'll tear the whole thing apart. The fix is off. Without Knocko, you've got no fix. They'll have to start over, only this time it can be stopped."

"I never was a part of any fix, Jack."

"I'm not saying that. It just happened. Little by little. From hand to hand. Until Knocko was it. But now we've got him. Abner's singing now. When Brough and Abramson get done with him, we'll have it."

"You look tired, Jack. Why don't you go home, get some rest?"

Cummings nodded. "Only let him talk until he's washed out. The more the better. When it's official, I want to be the one, Captain. I want to pick him up myself."

"We'll get it, Jack. So it's certain. I just can't believe he could have been so stupid."

"Read it, when Abner's done, Otto. You'll know how stupid he was."

"We'll phone you, Jack."

Cummings stood up. "Don't let anybody see or touch him, Otto. He's our ticket."

"I know, Jack. You go get some rest."

He parked his car on a high hill, weary but not sleepy. He stepped out in the chilled, clean air and walked to a guardrail to look down on the sweep of lights scattered across the city. Dawn would come shortly, and now there was the darkness, with the wind coming in cold gusts. He stood picking out the section that was the district, thinking that Brough and Abramson would be working on Abner steadily, inchingly, scalpeling every shred they could get from him. And when it was done, and they had accomplished their expert surgery, he would go get Knocko to end it.

Something small and dark moved along below the guardrail. It came slowly, uncertainly; then he saw that it was a small black kitten. He sat down on the rail and tapped the metal lightly. The kitten hesitated, then leaped up beside him. He put a hand on its soft fur and heard the instant purring. One small kitten, he thought, in the sea that was a city of a million people. Defenseless, unknowing, unblemished. The way they had been in the beginning. But, he thought, looking again at the scattered lights below, the apple had been eaten. And now what did it mean?

People, he thought; that was all it meant, finally. Human beings, in the moving waves, all of them trapped into life without having asked for it. He had not asked for it either, any more than anyone else had. But he had it. And what was he doing with it? The best he could, he thought. Protecting himself, but squeezing the system now, in his own way. You got one piece of evil destroyed, he thought, and you cleaned up a little. That meant something, didn't it?

The kitten moved onto his lap, searching for warmth and protection. His fingers touched the slim furry neck tenderly. Again his eye swept over the expanse of city below. The fixed system, he thought. And yet so few of them knew: only those who fixed and those who felt the fixing directly. A cop could feel it directly—make a wrong arrest and you were fired. And if the work was your life, then they cut off your life for having fooled with the fix. But most, no—they didn't know.

More lights flickered on as he watched. They were getting up now. Women with curlers in their hair would be moving about kitchens. And soon the men would come and sit down to tables. Eggs would be fried or scrambled or boiled. Bacon or ham would be cooked in spitting skillets. The smell of freshly brewed coffee would float through the houses. Newspapers would be unrolled and propped and read. Children would eat hungrily from cereal bowls, awake instantly, chattering loudly and excitedly with the freshness and enthusiasm they perhaps would never find again. It was the beginning of a routine, and the routine would continue through the day and end at night and resume the next day.

But, he thought, how many of them cared for nothing but themselves and those close to them? The answer was the vast, middle majority, he thought. They were the ones who failed to care. They went along with the routine, unquestioning, letting it happen. And there was the fault. If enough cared, it would be impossible to fix any system, large or small.

And so somebody, he thought, had to care, and to act. He had cared, he knew, and now he had acted—for the majority who didn't care.

The kitten, he discovered, had gone to sleep in his lap as dawn started its first light. It slept in a curl, with its nose tucked beneath a paw. He could feel its warmth, exchanged for his. He sat there for a time longer, thinking that he had a good feeling for this cat, because it could not be blamed for anything. A cat was incorruptible because its will was unthinking. It went the course of the sun, and only fate took care of it—or man did. Man could not yet control the sun. But he could change the course of a cat's life. Or a city's life.

Carefully, he put the kitten on the pavement. The animal stretched, then arched its back and looked up at him, crying. Good luck, cat, he thought. Then he got back into his car and drove home, feeling very tired.

He slept hard and dreamlessly. When he awakened he had slept longer than he had intended. He walked to the telephone, coming wholly awake with the motion. He dialed. Moments later, he listened to the voice on the other end, disbelievingly.

"Well, where's Blaine?" he exploded.

"He just went home," the brisk voice stated.

He swore and slammed the phone into its cradle. He dressed swiftly, then went down to his car outside, the redness of anger filming his eyes.

Chapter 16

Captain Otto Blaine's home was a typically handsome middle-class house in the Westridge section, one in a row of other typically handsome middle-class houses, all of them looking uniformly precise and well-tended. The lawn—two squares of grass on either side of the straight walk leading to the door—had been watered the night before; and the droplets on the green blades shone in the morning sunlight. He pressed the button beside the door and heard chimes inside. In a moment, a woman opened the door. She was plump, with a pretty face that seemed much younger than her years. She had smooth, fair skin, and her graying dark hair was carefully arranged. She wore a crisp yellow house dress and smiled at Cummings with bright, dark eyes.

"Well, Inspector."

"I'd like to see the captain, Mrs. Blaine."

"Surely. He's in the living room, having his nightcap. Come right in."

He followed her into the immaculate interior, through a short hall into an Early American living room.

"Otto," Mrs. Blaine said, "it's Inspector Cummings."

Blaine sat in a maple cricket chair, wearing baby-blue pajamas and leather slippers. There was a glass of milk on a small table before him. He looked up with nervous eyes.

"I'll just leave you two to discuss business or whatever," Mrs. Blaine said cheerfully. "Would you like coffee, Inspector?"

"Thank you, no," Cummings said, and with a sense of detachment he realized that Blaine had all the trappings of the typical, happy-appearing family. His wife had the same look that magazine editors searched for to sell products in national magazines, the same look advertising agencies sought to create as the typical image on television screens. His children had that same look. And Blaine himself in neat blue pajamas and slippers, with his nightcap glass of milk, looked like a typical head of any household.

Mrs. Blaine left. Captain Otto Blaine bent forward to run his finger around the mouth of his glass. "Jack, you know that I dislike being rude, especially off duty. This is your day off. I just got here. But you know I don't like to bring things home."

He stood looking at the man, feeling his jaw muscles working. "*Why?*" he asked.

"There really wasn't any other way open." Blaine lifted the glass, drank, then put it down, carefully.

"What happened?" Cummings said, his mouth feeling dry.

"Brough and Abramson questioned him thoroughly. There just wasn't enough."

"I can't believe that," Cummings said, holding his mounting anger. "What do you mean, there wasn't enough?"

"I'm not going to lie to you, Jack. If you don't believe what I'm telling you, then—"

"He said Bernie tortured her, didn't he?"

"If you could believe that."

"And why couldn't you believe that?"

"He talked at length about some sort of film you'd shown to him."

"Well?"

"He seemed to be in a severe state of agitation. He rambled thoroughly. I just don't feel that a clear line of testimony on his part was accomplished. That film—where did you get it, Jack?"

"Does it make any difference, Otto?"

"Just curious."

"I got it from a man named Ernest, a pornographer Knocko hired to shoot it at a party."

"And it depicted what?"

"A few things you wouldn't want to hear, Otto."

"Now please don't use that tone, Jack. I don't like it." He lifted the glass and sipped the milk again. "It involved Abner's wife, didn't it?"

"That's right."

"I gather you had prior knowledge of this film, didn't you, Jack? You didn't just happen to run across it last night. You'd known about it, hadn't you?"

"I'd heard about it, yes."

"Don't you see, Jack?"

"I'm afraid not."

"Why don't you sit down? Please? I want to be absolutely honest about this, just as honest as I can be. And I don't want any misinterpretations whatever. Please sit down."

He sat down slowly.

"Jack," Captain Otto Blaine said, "you're a tough man. A very tough man. Do you know that?"

"I am what I am, Otto."

"Yes, and that's very admirable in almost every way. Every man should be what he is."

"I still don't know what happened down there, Otto. I'd like to. Did he walk out alone?"

"We'll get to that, Jack. But I want to say all of this as carefully and as precisely as I can. Even though I'm now off duty and normally would be on my way to bed just now. You can light up your pipe, if you like, Jack. Mary has no objection whatever. As a matter of fact, she likes the smell of a pipe being smoked now and then. She's often wondered why I didn't get into that habit. She says there's something distinguished about it."

Abner was free, he thought, and now the captain was talking as if he had come here on a relaxed, social visit. It was another habit of Blaine's, to escape the reality of a situation. How good was Blaine, anyway? he wondered. With his inclination toward dodging the uncomfortable action, was he not too weak for his job, after all? And did he not know that? So that he was constantly frightened for his position and security—so that he could not afford to let the fix collapse? Perhaps no one handed him sealed envelopes. But perhaps his job relied wholly on those who did pass those envelopes. Because it was entirely possible that he couldn't meet an honest competition.

"It's all right, Otto," he said coldly. "What is it you're getting at?"

"Well, now, this film again. What happened, Jack? How did Abner come about seeing it?"

"I showed it to him. You know that."

Blaine smiled slightly and nodded and lifted his milk glass. "Don't you see what's happened?"

"I'm trying to, Otto. I'm trying very hard."

"This fixation you have on destroying Knocko Cutter. It's a vendetta, isn't it?"

"Shouldn't it be?"

"As long as we work within the rules, I should say not. But vendettas are still dangerous. They tend to lead to extreme emotionalism, so that now and then a man is susceptible to forcing what he believes to be a fact into existence, whether or not it's justified."

"Go on, Otto."

"All right. And please try to remain calm, Jack. Because I'm going to be honest with you. Because I respect and like you."

"Let's be honest then."

"You showed this film to Abner." He nodded, and his voice became softer. "A despicable film, showing indescribable things being done to this woman, who is, I understand, a former prostitute. And you did this knowing that Abner is married to her."

"Yes."

"And still you don't see the significance?"

"I think you're trying to defend Knocko. I think that's the significance. Remember, Otto, it was his party. He was the one who wanted the film."

"I don't care about that," Blaine snapped. "I'm talking about you now."

"What about me?"

"You made up your mind that this Mrs. Lundstrom's death was

Knocko Cutter's responsibility. You did so on grounds that would not hold up in a court of law. I think you knew that then and know it now. So … this film. You sent for Abner and deliberately showed it to him, knowing that such a thing would incite him to the point of doing and saying anything."

"I see." Cummings looked at his own large hands with stubbed, thick fingers crossing each other in his lap. He had been foolishly unreasonable with the buoyancy, the relief, that resulted from thinking he had accomplished it. Buoyancy could color and cloud and make optimistic the worst kind of dirty reality, because you always, in that condition, tended to believe what you wanted to believe.

"You think I incited him and told him what to say, so he could pay back Knocko and Bernie for that party." His voice was steady and toneless

"I think you saw the device, yes, and then got a little overeager. Perhaps 'overvindictive' would be better."

"How did he get out, Captain?"

"He was questioned thoroughly, as I said. Then his lawyers appeared."

He looked up at the man, feeling the skin at the edges of his eyes tightened. "Did he send for them?"

"I believe Knocko Cutter sent them for him."

"How did Knocko know he was there?"

"Well, I really couldn't say, Jack. I thought perhaps you might have told him, in your overeagerness."

His mouth stretched back; his teeth were held tightly together. A vicious lie, he thought, from one of the bastard hypocrites of all time. Blaine had made the call, he knew, and made easy the entire path it has taken. "What then?"

"The substance of his co-called confession was examined most completely. It was terribly rambling and disjointed, Jack. Some of it made no sense at all. The main thing that seemed to come through was that he was highly inflamed for having seen that film. Now, I'm not making judgment on the conditions depicted by that film. That is not at all the point here. The only point was that it was sufficient incitement for this rather stupid, pathetic man to attempt to carry out vengeance on Knocko Cutter and this person called Bernie."

"And I was the one who incited him. Purposely. To get a false conviction."

"Jack, I don't really think you meant anything to be false. I'm not saying that. It's simply as I said. I believe you became overvindictive."

"What then?"

"This morning he was released on bail." The captain tapped his glass gently. "That is all that has happened. Naturally, we'll proceed along with this. Through proper channels."

Cummings nodded, his mind distant now. Where had Abner been taken? Was he already dead? "Who was the judge?" he asked quietly.

"Curtiz."

"What was the bail?"

"Five thousand."

He began laughing, with no humor, harshly, the sound ringing through the room.

"Jack, I don't like that."

He stood up. "I'm laughing for a dead man, Captain. I'm laughing because he was a loser from the time he was born, and he deserved to die—but not this way. That's the twist. He should have taken them with him. Only now he's dying alone, and they're getting away with it."

For a moment, the captain looked bewildered, as if the exact meaning of it all was becoming clear to him, driven through to his brain that wanted to believe in nothing but the reasonability of the peculiar justice he sought—justice that was corroded on all its edges by the taint of corruption.

"He's a dead man, Captain."

Captain Otto Blaine's face lost its composure entirely. He flushed deeply. "Cummings, you see nothing but black and white. You care nothing for what goes on in between. To you, Knocko Cutter is black. Therefore he's your obsession. Destroy him, because he's black."

He nodded stiffly, looking through the man. "Thanks for the time, Captain."

"What are you going to do now?"

"I'm going to waste my time looking for him."

"And if you find him?"

"What's the difference, Captain?"

Blaine shrugged and dismissed him with that motion. "It's your day off."

"That's right," Cummings said bitterly, moving toward the hall. "It's my day off."

Chapter 17

"Early for you, Inspector." She was a cherubic old lady in a spotless white sweater standing beside a small flower stand. "Time off?"

He nodded. "How's the granddaughter?"

"Oh, she'll graduate this June. Bachelor of Science." The merry eyes the color of a pale sea gleamed proudly. "Here." She took a small white rose from its holder and carefully fitted it in Cummings' lapel.

"You've done well by her, Alice." He got out a fifty-cent piece and handed it to her.

"That was a present, Inspector."

"Goes to a good cause."

"Well," she said warmly, "it's been easier with you in charge of the district, Inspector. Makes an old lady feel safer."

"It's what I've always told you, Alice. Any trouble, you tell me."

"Everyone knows that. That's why I never have any trouble. But I guess you've had enough of your own lately. Lundstrom. The girl who was raped. Now Lundstrom's wife."

He nodded. "Keeps a man busy. But that's what they pay me for. You haven't seen Abner around today, have you?"

"Abner? The big one?"

"That's the one."

"Not today."

"Well, I'm interested, Alice. Pass it along."

"I sure will, Inspector. Anything for you."

He walked down the street, wanting to go over the district, not only for the task he was certain was hopeless—finding Abner—but because it just might be the last time he would walk it, this way.

Abner's apartment was in a slate-colored building six stories high near downtown. He stepped into the building warily, without hope. Moments later he pressed the button beside a black door. Finally, he tried the handle. Surprised, he felt it turn. He opened the door and stepped inside, thinking that Abner, after his telephone call in the middle of the night, had left so swiftly that he'd failed to turn on the night lock—and obviously he would not have been back.

The walls of the living room were chocolate, and the furniture was a blazing display of garishness: new and expensive and chosen with absolute bad taste. Two fashion magazines lay open on a white rug. A half-finished drink stood on an end table; he could smell the Scotch. Ashes flicked from cigarettes were visible on the rug in a dozen scattered places. What kind of life had it been here? he wondered. What had they talked about? What, truly, had interested them? He remembered that Abner had had a childish interest in ships and often went down to the docks along the waterfront to watch the liners come in and leave their berths. But what had been his life here, with the woman he'd loved so passionately?

He opened the door to the kitchen and looked at a litter of unwashed dishes stacked over a counter. He walked through and tried the back door, which led to a rear stairway. That was unlocked too. No, he thought: neither of them had returned after he had delivered the bomb in the form of that call about the movie.

He returned to the living room and opened the door leading to a single bedroom. The wide bed was unmade, and black lingerie, a yellow negligee, and a pink bath towel were scattered over the sheets and electric blanket. Women's shoes were displayed around the floor, perhaps a dozen pairs, left as they'd been kicked off. A vanity table supported a giant collection of cosmetics, each bottle and case surrounded by spilled facial powder. She was sloppy and primeval, he thought. But he had loved her, and that had probably been the final error of his life.

He left the apartment and returned to the street. It was nearing noon. He walked down to a small bar called The Get-Away. He sat down on a stool, down from the other three patrons. The bartender, a heavy dark man, came over. "Drinking on duty, Inspector?"

"Off duty, Harry."

"Oh, yeah. This'd be the day, wouldn't it? Only you don't take many of them."

"I guess that's right."

"You want a Pabst or whisky?"

"Pabst."

He opened the bottle and put it before Cummings with a glass. "Pretty good hops flavor the brand."

"Better than some."

"They ought to make it like they used to."

"They started selling it in supermarkets to women. They figured women wouldn't like it if it tasted like beer."

"How do they know?"

"They don't, Harry."

"Listen, Inspector. You got a minute?"

"I wouldn't be here otherwise."

Harry leaned closer, convivially. "I got a problem."

"Okay."

"Money."

Cummings nodded slowly. "Money."

"No, listen. I don't mean it that way. I'm not going to bite you, Inspector. Just a problem in general. See, my sister-in-law, who got busted up with this musician she married, remember? The guitarist? Blew guitar. That's what he always said. I knew that wasn't going to work."

"I remember."

"Well, anyway, she landed in the hospital after they split, and the medics took out her gall bladder."

"I didn't know that, Harry."

"Well, it just came on, and there she is; they're taking it out, only she don't have the medical insurance or money, see? So my wife, she said we got to take care of it for her. They want a thousand. I take it out of the bank, every last nickel we had in there, and it's gone. See?"

"That's pretty generous of you, Harry."

"That's what I told my wife. That's pretty damned generous! A full grand, just like that! But now look what's happened."

"What's that, Harry?"

"Well, we been buying a lot of furniture on credit, see? They got this revolving thing. We got behind on payments. It just seemed to happen. And the further we get behind, the deeper in we get. It's a losing thing, Inspector."

"How deep?"

"Six hundred. And I think about the grand I had in the bank. What do I do?"

"How's your credit?"

"Nothing, now. I mean, we're behind, see? Who's going to give credit now?"

"Have any life insurance?"

Harry shook his head. "I had the G.I. Only I let it lapse after I was into it with a loan."

"How about the Cadillac?"

"The Cadillac?" He looked at Cummings in astonishment. "That's what I live for, Inspector. I couldn't get rid of that."

"You've got it paid for, haven't you?"

"Sure, and that's what it's all about. I love that car. I couldn't do anything with that, Inspector. All my life I wanted a Caddie."

"Get a chattel mortgage on it."

"Which?"

"Borrow against it."

Harry blinked rapidly. "With my credit?"

"You don't need credit. If you don't pay, they take the car. You love the car. You'll pay. Just like you were still making payments. You clear up the rest of the stuff."

Harry nodded gratefully. "That's beautiful, Inspector. I been worrying my gut out all week. I feel like a free man again. How about another beer, on the house?"

"No, thanks, Harry."

"Well …" He bent closer. "I heard, Inspector. But I haven't seen him."

"Okay, Harry."

"I do, you'll find it out."

"Thanks."

He walked down the street in the midday sunshine, the air cleanly cool. A slight young man with a thin, nervous face came up from behind and grasped his arm. Cummings stopped. "Hello, Ritchie," he said softly.

The young man hitched his shoulders. "I got something for you, Inspector." He jerked his head toward an alley.

Cummings followed him away from the sidewalk traffic. "What have you got?"

The youth stared at him with dark, contracted eyes, shoulders jerking again. "Abner."

"Where?"

"Well … I've been out of work, Inspector."

"I know, Ritchie."

"I want to help. But … you know what I mean?"

"How much?"

"Twenty-five."

Cummings shook his head.

"There isn't much time, Inspector!"

And, he thought, the time he was referring to did not concern Abner, but the satiation of his habit. "I haven't got it, Ritchie."

"Don't you want him? I saw him! Not five minutes ago!"

"Too much."

"Twenty?"

And, he thought, maybe this was the last time he'd be talking to Ritchie in the district too, in this capacity. He knew what, if he gave him the money, would be done with it. But Ritchie was beyond help now, until he helped himself. "Fifteen," he said, and thought at least it would give him a time of escape from his torments.

"Okay, Inspector," the youth said swiftly. "Fifteen."

He got out a five and a ten and handed them to him. "Where?"

"Blink's Donut. Saw him sitting in there big as life five minutes ago. You better hurry, Inspector."

The youth moved down the alley swiftly, disappearing at the same speed with which he was ruining his life. Cummings walked two blocks and stepped into a small doughnut shop. He looked at the three booths and the counter. All seats were taken. There was no Abner.

He stepped to the counter and said to a tall man behind it who wore a white uniform with a chef's cap, "Abner, Blink?"

Blink shook his head. "Not in maybe a week."

He left the district in his car and drove down to the long line of pier buildings. The air was cooler here, and would turn very cold when the sun had set, as it would do shortly, with bright red-yellow flaming on the water, then the quick-plunging disappearance. He parked wearily, frustrated by the hopelessness of his search. He walked down the sidewalk, slowly, and stopped finally where he could see the decks of a passenger liner, empty of passengers now as its insides were being refurnished and restocked for the next sailing.

He looked down at the dark water rolling in light waves in the slip. The real sea, he thought: brooding and vast and incomprehensible. Enemy or friend, he thought, depending upon your position. To Abner, it had probably appeared a friend. Childlike, Abner had come here and stood as he was standing now, to watch with awe these ships, this water. A giant fool of a man with a boy's brain, capable of watching killings, helping. Now where was he?

Dead, he thought bitterly. Most certainly he was dead now. Perhaps he was in this sea, bound and weighted and plunged into the black depths. And who had killed him? All of them. He had, with that call and the showing of the film. And Captain Otto Blaine had, when he'd allowed him the freedom of meeting death. And Bernie. And finally and most certainly Knocko. But it had been Abner himself, in the beginning, who had kindled his own destruction by the direction he'd sent himself. But he was not mourning Abner, he thought; he was simply mourning the loss of him, because now he was going to have to give up and hand in his work, which had become his life.

He moved abruptly to a telephone booth. The voice responded. "Hello?"

"Cummings, Mike. Can you get over to my house?"

"Right now?"

"Right now."

Chapter 18

"You mean," Mike Hawley said in disbelief, "they let him go?"

Cummings sat in the familiar living room, nodding.

"I can't believe it."

"That's the way it is."

"You couldn't find a trace of him?"

"I didn't figure to."

"What happens now?"

Cummings shrugged. "I'll resign. And then depend on you."

"How?"

"I'll tell you everything I know. You start writing the stories. The public's got to react. When it reacts hard enough, there'll be an investigation. It should have been done a long time ago."

Hawley watched him closely. "How much do you know, Jack?"

"Abner's enough, isn't it? For a start?"

"And what else?"

"I know the district. What goes on there. I'll give it all to you. If you start at the bottom, the fire begins. It'll spread and take the top with it." He looked at Hawley. "It'll take guts."

Hawley got up and paced slowly around the room, looking at the books abstractedly. "How long, Jack? How long have you been giving all you've got to this?"

"Seems like my life."

"And now you're willing to tear it up and yourself with it."

"I've got a responsibility," he said harshly. "There're people out there. Human beings. The fix is a cancer. Somebody's got to cure it. Who else will, if I don't? If you don't?"

"Guts, you say. Do you know what they'll do to you?"

"What's the difference, if it has to be?"

"They'll crucify you."

"It's happened to others—Christ included."

Mike Hawley turned, looking at him. "You're not Christ, Jack."

Cummings stared ahead, seeing nothing now. He could feel his pulse beating, knowing that it was coming to a finish now. Realizing the finality of it, he felt strangely above it.

He had given his life to the work, and now he was going to give that up. But if he took with him enough information to accomplish breaking the fix, then that alone had been worth it. Crucified? Maybe crucifixion was a privilege, and not everybody could earn it. It meant that you counted, and because you counted you had become dangerous. Yes, he thought, Christ—and thousands of others. And all of them must have felt, to some degree, what he was feeling now. You had to have accomplished something, to be worth a crucifixion.

"If we had him," Hawley said angrily.

"Yes," Cummings said. "But we don't."

"He would have been a perfect wedge. Absolute living proof."

"They knew that."

"Are you sure, Jack, you want to do it this way?"

"I am. How about you?"

"Naturally."

"The newspaper?"

"That isn't fixed."

"They'll try to shut you up, any way they can—Knocko and everybody else involved."

"Okay. You can be my bodyguard while you're talking and I'm writing. We'll get it done."

"That's all I want," Cummings said softly.

"When do we start?"

"Any time. Now. I'll talk all night."

"Let's start now then."

"How will you do it?"

"Questions. In the form of the facts you'll give me."

"Names?"

"They can stop us that way. But I can still point in the general direction."

Cummings nodded. He felt numbly remote now, as if it were no longer necessary to swim, but merely to float along with the existing currents.

"You have a typewriter, Jack?"

"I'll get it."

He walked to the bedroom, where he got a small, old portable typewriter and paper. Even the house, he thought, was no longer the familiar but lonely place he had known these last years. It was merely the structure against the elements now. The familiarity was gone, because the change of events had brought him into a strange and new position. The rhythm of routine was suddenly broken, cracked by the reality of circumstances. He was no longer Inspector Jack Cummings. He was a man who had created his new role: the breaker of the fix, the man they would crucify for it. But as a cop, he thought, he was through. Yet now it didn't matter. It didn't matter at all.

"You want a drink, Mike?"

"You go ahead."

He fixed himself one in the kitchen, then came back to sit down. "Where do I start?"

"Anywhere."

He began talking softly and precisely. His life, he thought—and he was turning it in doing this. He felt, for a brief interval, a deep reluctance returning. He'd been so close, with Abner, to getting away with it without ruining everything. But now …

Then the reluctance left; and he talked, word after word, sentence after sentence, as Hawley's fingers darted over the keys, pages accumulating. Then, breaking harshly into his concentration, he heard the telephone ringing.

He got up to answer it. "Yes?"

"Cummings?"

He could not believe the reality of the strained, froglike voice. "Abner!" he breathed.

Mike Hawley looked up quickly. Cummings listened, hearing the man's breath.

"It's me," Abner said.

"Are you all right?"

"I'm all right." The voice sounded nervously unsteady.

"Where are you?"

"I took off, see? Right after they let me go. Got into the car with those lawyers Knocko sent. When we got around the first corner, I busted out and took off. Bernie's car down the street. Saw it. You had it right, Cummings. They're gunning for me."

"They don't know where you are?"

"I been ducking all day, trying to get it straight. I wanted to call you before they let me go. Only they wouldn't let me, see?"

"I see," Cummings said.

"I figured it was like you said. I go out, and they'll finish me. So when I got loose, I busted. I been out of sight all day. Now—"

"Where are you, Abner?" Cummings repeated.

"The apartment. She didn't come back, Cummings. She won't ever come back, will she?"

"No," Cummings said. "That's over, Abner. But you've got to—"

"I've been trying to figure it out. Why did they let me go?"

"Because Knocko wanted it that way, Abner. So they could get a chance at you outside."

"Yeah," Abner said. "That's what I thought. So I decided. I decided to come back here and maybe she'd be here. But she isn't. Then I thought I better call you."

"You did the right thing. I'm going to come and get you, see?" He was coming wholly alive again, finding the hope once more, the hope that he could save all that he wanted to save and still break the fix.

"I got to make them pay," Abner said plaintively.

"You will, Abner. Just stay right there."

"If I go back to headquarters—"

"We'll do it another way. Just stay there. I'll be right down."

"You got to do it, Cummings. You got to."

"I will. Just hold on now."

He hung up and turned to Mike Hawley, feeling fresh energy going through him.

"He's all right?" Hawley asked.

Cummings nodded, fitting on his gun, then his jacket. "He's been hiding all day. He's back at his apartment. I'm going to go get him. We're going to keep him for ourselves this time, Mike. You're going to explode it in the paper while we've got him where nobody can touch him."

Hawley stood up. "Right."

"Get a room at the Bellstair Hotel, on Wentworth. Use another name. Frank Hawkins. I'll phone you for the room number after I pick him up. Then I'll get him in from the back."

"I'll be there, Jack."

Chapter 19

He drove the night street with a hard knot of tension in his middle. A reprieve, he thought. With Abner alive and put away safely, he could meet them head on. He could come through it with the department shaken apart and the commission hurt and the entire administration bleeding, but with himself intact, still a cop, surviving the breaking of the system. The work that had become his life would continue, and he could keep on breathing.

He stopped his car in front of the slate-colored apartment house. He saw, in the vestibule, that the self-operating elevator was at the top floor. He went up the steps quickly to the second floor and pressed the button beside the black door. He waited. He heard nothing. He tried again, feeling apprehensive. Then he tested the handle; this time the door was locked.

He ran down the steps, remembering the rear stairway. He rounded the building outside to find that the back door, facing a narrow, empty alley, was ajar; the area was dimly lit by a small bulb above the door. He stepped inside. The steps were rough concrete, with a metal handrail following them. He started up fast, then saw the dark stain of what was obviously blood in the concrete halfway up. He touched it; it was moistly sticky. He continued, then grasped the knob of the door that opened to Abner's kitchen. It turned, and he threw the door open.

He stared with mounting anger at what had once been litter and was now shambles. The dirty dishes had been swept to the floor to smash against the linoleum. A chair was overturned. He went through to the living room, which also had been wrecked. Knowing that it was no use, he opened the bedroom door; the room remained as he'd seen it earlier. He turned around, thinking that Abner hadn't gone easy—but they'd got him.

There was a loud knocking. He walked across the room, putting a hand inside his jacket. He opened the door to a large, ruddy-faced patrolman. The man blinked in surprise. "Inspector Cummings?"

"What is it?" he said shortly.

"Had a complaint by the superintendent here. Lot of noise up here."

"When did he make it?"

"Few minutes ago. I got here as fast as I could."

"Get down and find out if he saw anybody leaving by the back way. Hurry up."

"Yes, sir."

Cummings turned back to the demolished apartment, looking at a splash of blood on the white rug. He moved slowly between tumbled pieces of furniture, then savagely kicked a table lamp lying on the floor, shattering it. With another kick, he righted a chair and sat down, rubbing his palms across his eyes.

When Abner had slipped them that morning, Knocko had probably put somebody on this building, to wait and to watch. After Abner had phoned him, they had come in. Was he dead now, for sure? Or were they going to give him that slowly?

He looked up as the patrolman returned.

"Didn't see anything. Just heard the noise up here. What happened, anyway, Inspector?"

Cummings was silent, staring again at the splotch of blood on the white rug. What did it matter now? Abner was desired dead, by both sides. And the sides were in collusion. There was nothing to do about it. He stood up slowly.

"Do you know what happened here, Inspector?" the patrolman asked.

"Yes."

"I've got to turn in a report."

"That's right. You've got to turn in a report."

The man saw the red on the rug for the first time. "Blood, Inspector?"

"Put it in your report. Make a note that it should reach Captain Otto Blaine immediately. Say it was a bloody party. Say Inspector Cummings arrived too late. Say the party is over now. Say that Inspector Cummings has just resigned."

The man shook his head in bewilderment. "I don't understand, Inspector."

He walked past him into the hall, saying, "Try to keep it that way. It'll be healthier for you."

He parked his car again, this time in front of Solly's newsstand. The weathered man came over quickly, fat lips set in concern.

"Inspector!"

"I've got no time, Solly," he said harshly.

"Ernest told me. You ain't going to get us in trouble, are you? I mean, about those pictures?"

"I'm not going to get you in trouble, Solly."

He walked briskly toward the small counter restaurant, Solly trotting beside him.

"Ernest give me hell, he really did. Said you might close me up, I don't do what you say."

"Forget it, Solly."

"It ain't going to happen?"

Cummings tried the door of the restaurant, but it was locked. He rapped sharply against the glass, looking through the steamed window at the thin counterman scrubbing the surface of the counter. The counterman looked frightened.

"Inspector?" Solly whined.

"I told you to forget it, Solly!" he snapped.

Solly ducked his head obsequiously. "Anything you say, Inspector." He hurried back to his stand, and Cummings cracked his fist against the glass again.

The counterman came around the counter and said through the glass, "Closed, Inspector."

"Open the door, Charlie!"

The man hesitated, then unlocked the door. Cummings shoved past him.

"All closed, Inspector," Charlie pleaded.

But Cummings was moving along the counter.

"He's gone, Inspector!" the man called after him.

He pounded against the door in the small hallway. "You want to open it, Knocko, or do I shoot the lock off?"

He waited.

"All right, Knocko."

He slipped his gun from its holster, then heard the sound of moving on the other side. The door opened. Knocko's balding head was beaded with sweat. There was a small pistol in his hand.

"Put it away," Cummings said.

"I'm warning you, Cummings."

"I said put it away!"

Reluctantly, he slid the small gun into a pocket of his well-tailored jacket.

"Sit down," Cummings' voice was sharp.

Knocko rounded his desk backward, watching him, and sat down.

"I'm going to kill you, Knocko," he whispered.

A muscle twitched inside Knocko's right cheek. His hand moved toward his pocket.

"No," Cummings said. "The hard way, the slow way, the long way—the way I'm figuring you're doing it to Abner. Put your hands on the desk. Keep them there."

Knocko's fingers, with their manicured nails, came to the desk surface and rested there. The sweating of his head increased. A small rivulet started running down the side of his face. He didn't wipe at it.

"Where did you take him?" Cummings asked.

"Him? Who?"

"Abner."

"I don't know a thing."

"Who did you get to replace him—to help Bernie?"

Knocko shook his head, his eyes cloudy. "You're off the track, Cummings."

"I'm on the track. A one-way track now. And you're tied to it. I'm going to run right over you, Knocko."

"You don't learn, do you? You just don't learn."

"Yes," he nodded. "I learn. Slow. But I learn."

Another trickle started down the other side of Knocko's face. A hand moved from the desk toward the handkerchief in his breast pocket. Then it stopped midway and returned to the wood.

"You can't touch me, Cummings," he whispered. "Haven't you found that out yet?"

Cummings smiled, hating him. "As a cop, no. Yes, I found that out. But as a former cop, I'm going to finish you."

Knocko's face tipped sideways. "Former?"

"I'm done with that. But I'm just starting on you. I'm talking, Knocko. Everything I know, and that's enough."

"It won't go anywhere."

"It'll go to the people."

"What are you talking about?"

"I've got a newsman. He'll print it. Inch by inch. And pretty soon the people'll start screaming for blood. They'll get the blood. Yours."

Fire showed in Knocko's pale, translucent eyes.

"This time," Cummings said, "you can't fix it."

Finally a smile touched Knocko's mouth. He moved a hand toward his handkerchief again, paused questioningly, watching Cummings' eyes, then took it out and wiped at his face.

"Jack," he said softly, "don't be a fool."

"Know it," Cummings said. "It's over for you."

"I told you before. You were cut out to be on my side. You say you're going to finish me. You'll be finishing yourself. *Why?*"

"You know all the answers, Knocko."

"I don't! I swear to God I don't. Not where you're concerned. I don't understand you at all!"

"You will before this is over."

"Look at it. Stop being God for a minute. Who are you, anyway? *What* are you?"

"Jack Cummings," he said quietly.

"But no longer *Inspector* Jack Cummings. No longer anything. Just a man looking for blood. You said you were better than I am. Lusting for blood makes you that?"

"You'd know about the blood lust, wouldn't you, Knocko?"

"Look," Knocko said, leaning forward, wiping his face again. "You say you're out of the department. All right. You should have a long time ago, because you and I, Jack, you and I are brothers."

"In that case, it's going to be the kind of brotherhood Cain and Abel had."

"Get on my side, Jack. Forget the rest of it. Get on my side!"

Cummings laughed softly, bitterly.

"Nobody I'd rather have," Knocko said, a pleading note going into his voice. "Who could I get better? What have you been making as a cop? Do you know what I'll do for you? I'll guarantee fifty thousand the first year. I swear it to you. And you can—"

"Put your hands back on the desk, Knocko," he said. He stood up and watched the sweating man obey swiftly. "Keep them there."

He backed to the door, watching Knocko's eyes. He went out and strode the length of the small restaurant as the counterman ran ahead of him to get the door open.

Again he climbed the steep steps running up to the small white house: silent, dark-windowed, ever lonely-looking. Deliberately and certainly, he thought, he'd given up everything but the work. And now he was going to give that up too. To kill the fix. To finish Knocko. And what would he have when that was over? Where would he start again? What would he do?

Tiredly, he opened the door and stepped inside. Then he

remembered Mike Hawley. He was reaching for the telephone when it rang.

"Yes?"

The voice was distant, whispered, but he knew the froglike quality: "Cummings?"

"Abner?" The tiredness left instantly. He became wholly alert, his large body tensing.

The man coughed, then whispered, "Cummings?"

"Where are you, Abner?"

"Got away from them. Bernie. The other one. Think I killed him. Maybe Bernie too."

Cummings listened, hope igniting again. Knocko had been nervous, all right. Now he knew why. He hadn't owned the control after all. "Are you hurt, Abner?"

"Shot. Lost some blood. But I'm all right. It isn't bad." His voice wavered raggedly. "You got to come and get me, Cummings. I've got to pay Knocko back, see?"

"All right, Abner. Tell me where. I'll come right away."

"Pier Forty-eight. In an office at the back, inside. Had a key the janitor gave me, long time ago." He was coughing again.

"Abner?"

"I'm all right. Just tired. Make it fast, Cummings."

"We'll get you to a doctor."

"Main thing—I want to make him pay, Cummings."

"He'll pay, Abner."

Chapter 20

Cummings drove swiftly down the Embarcadero street, passing the high fronts of the pier buildings. Hope was aflame again. He'd missed one reprieve, but found a second. If Abner had killed one, maybe both, they couldn't let him go now. The collapse was coming from the fault in the structure itself. Knocko had pulled the beams apart himself, finally.

He came to a rocking stop and got out. He tried a small door to the side of the giant loading entrance; it opened. The high-ceilinged room was dark except for illumination at the far end. It came from an office walled on two sides by paneling and frosted glass; it was not ceilinged, only partitioned, and the light flared upward.

Cummings trotted along a set of rails used for loading carts. There was a fish smell, and the air was cold and moist from the wind now whipping off the water outside. He had been going somewhere, he thought, and now he was going toward it on the run: he was reaching it.

A door with frosted-glass panes was closed. He put his hand on the handle, turned it, and threw the door open. He stared into the bright glare of a goose-necked lamp, the neck bent so that the light poured at him in the doorway. He blinked against the light, trying to see clearly what lay behind the desk on the plank floor.

"Jesus," he whispered, stepping forward.

Abner's eyes stared unseeing into the light from the lamp. Blood stained his jacket. His tongue was visible between teeth set in a death grin. Cummings looked along his legs to the large-shoed feet, each turned at a peculiar angle. They'd broken his ankles, he thought. Then he saw the equally peculiar position of the giant hands. Wrists too. Tortured him, because …

He looked up suddenly, into the blackness above the partitions of the office. *Tortured him to make the call*, he thought wildly.

He reached for a metal folding chair with a cat's speed, his other hand going into his jacket for the pistol. He started to throw the chair at the lamp, but the soft explosions sounded above as he was making the move. He felt the slugs hitting him, surprised, but understanding, at the same moment. The chair flew into a glass pane, smashing it. In the light of the still-burning lamp he wheeled, metal tearing into him. Then he fell hard and clumsily, at the feet of the broken and dead Abner.

He lay with his face against the worn planks, his pistol resting perhaps three feet from his outstretched hand, where it had stopped after he'd fallen. Blackness took him and washed him away; then he came back, opening his eyes slightly. He could hear the faint sounds of someone coming down from an upper ramp, swiftly: tiny cat's feet sounds echoing through the building.

He looked against the light through slitted eyes and saw the body of Abner at his sprawled feet. Hit twice, maybe three times, he thought. The wetness was from his left shoulder and somewhere at his middle; that was the bad one, he thought, the one in the middle.

The cat's feet sound was closer now. It stopped somewhere near the doorway. Cummings steeled his will. He lay motionless. He stared through nearly closed lids. He waited. The sound resumed; then he saw the small, shined shoes with their pointed toes. He saw a fraction of black socks. He saw narrow tailored slacks and the lower part of a dark fitted topcoat.

Cummings stopped breathing. His eyes didn't move. One of the pointed shoes whipped into his cheek. His head bounced with the impact, then rolled back into position, the eyes staring ahead through slits, gleaming in the merciless lamplight.

Finally the gloved, jockey-lean man bent and carefully fitted a silencer-equipped pistol into the dead hand of Abner. Cummings saw the squirrel features briefly; then the man straightened. The small shoes moved from his vision. The cat's feet sound carried him away, until the soft echoing stopped.

Cummings lay unmoving for a long time; then at last he shifted his head slowly. He saw his gun still on the floor. Yes, he thought distantly, he'd finally scared Knocko badly—to this. But Knocko was making it very good. An easy case now, one that could be fitted together perfectly, with the desired conclusion.

Working for breath, he inched his knees up, moved sideways, then pressed his palms downward to push himself up. He got to hands and knees, and dizziness struck him. He rolled his head slowly, staring at the blood on the wood that had soaked through his clothing. Through blurred eyes, he looked at the telephone on the desk. If he could get Mike Hawley …

But, he thought, it was too late for Mike Hawley. Mike couldn't help him. He was dying now. Like Lundstrom in that hospital bed, he could feel it coming, knew it, and so who else? Nobody else, he thought.

He remained on knees and palms, feeling life flow. The blood was seeping out of him, he thought, and with that went everything else. But he hadn't finished yet …

Gasping, he got himself up and staggered blindly into the desk, to fall against the outstretched Abner. He swore, teeth biting together, and pushed himself from the lifeless figure. He reached his feet again, holding to the edge of the desk. *Have to*, he thought desperately. The blackness hit him, and he sagged. Then it passed, and he pushed forward, holding to his balance, walking like a drunk until he reached his gun. He bent to retrieve it, and lost his vision with the motion. He forced himself back up, teeth gritting. Then, with the gun shoved back into the holster, he started toward the door.

Lurching, falling, pushing himself up, his own hands stained now from the blood leaving his body, he went along the track rails through the darkness. Shock, he thought, was helping keep the pain from his senses. But his brain wanted to let loose, to give up, because it was inevitable now, he thought. Yes, he had gone somewhere, and it was all the way.

He fell again, a little way from the small door that led outside. He lay there in the dark, listening to his breath wheezing. He could taste blood now. He had either wiped a hand across his mouth and got it that way, or it was coming through inside. Give up, he thought. Let it go now.

But he could not.

He got up and again fell toward the door to hold to it. Slowly, he got it open and looked at his car shining softly in the light from a street lamp. A dozen feet, he estimated dimly, and a thousand miles. He started slowly, fighting the blackness that kept dimming his brain, and weaved, off balance, making the thousand-mile trip. Finally he caught hold of the cold chrome of the door handle. He opened the door and pitched sideways into the seat behind the wheel to half lie there.

The blackness came again, and he could not escape it. When he came awake, he could hear the sucking sound of his breathing. Laboriously he brought himself upright, holding to the steering wheel. Then, watching his hand with the detachment of watching another's slow motion, he switched on the ignition, feeling and hearing the engine come alive. He switched on the headlights, seeing them play against the building that had been, he thought, his personal Armageddon.

He shifted to reverse and backed the car, then moved it forward, to take the rounding curve of the Embarcadero street. Stay out of heavy traffic, he thought, and looked away from the pavement at his watch. The car veered, and an on-coming truck swerved out of his way, horn blaring. He righted the direction and drove on, thinking: not too fast, not too slow. If they picked him up …

He made the curve around the water side of the downtown district, then got onto an avenue that would lead him across town. The street kept wavering in his vision, and he had to correct the wheel abruptly when he tried to follow the deceit of his eyes. Another car sounded its horn at him. He stared ahead, hanging to the wheel, fighting for clarity.

Finally he turned off the avenue and moved into a broad street that took him into the fashionably styled Oak Forest section. As he did that, he saw headlights behind him. Dizziness disconnected his response. He felt the car swinging over, bumping over a curbing, then coming down again. A red light switched on and flashed behind him. A patrol car passed him and swung in front of his car. He braked and shifted to neutral and sat there, summoning up what little he had left.

A young face with hard eyes appeared dimly in his sight. "You want to get out and show your license?" The voice was tough and brittle.

Cummings wiped his blood-stained hands in the darkness of his lap. His words came out thick and slurred: "Who the hell you think you are?"

"I'd just take it easy and not cause us any trouble."

"Who the hell are you?"

"I'm asking you that."

"Doesn't make any difference who you are. Got your license number. You want to know who I am?"

"I think you're a driver who's going to be in trouble if you don't do what I'm asking you."

"Inspector Cummings."

The patrolman lifted a flash and turned it on his face. "Shut that off!"

The light disappeared. The young man's voice changed tone. "Sorry, Inspector. I—"

"Now leave me alone."

The youth looked hesitant. "Have a little too much to drink, Inspector?"

"I had a little too much to drink. And I had a fight with someone. I'm going to have another if you don't take off."

"What do you say we just follow you home, Inspector, and then—"

"I'll tell you once more. Get the hell out of here. You don't, I'll make you wish you'd listened."

The youth stood there for a moment longer. Then he said uncertainly, "You take it easy now, Inspector. Just take it slow and easy."

He walked ahead to the patrol car. Cummings waited, tasting blood. The car in front of him moved down the street. Its lights disappeared when it reached the next intersection. Slowly, Cummings put his car in gear again. Two more blocks, he thought, just two more
…

He stopped again, when he'd driven those two blocks, in the darkness created by a tree shading light from a street lamp farther up the block, front wheel bumping into the curbing as he switched off the ignition. The light was just beyond a large white house with a sloping, beautifully tended terrace. The wide garage entrance was to the right of it, with a broad, short drive leading in. Cummings looked at his watch and turned off the headlights.

Darkness reached for him again, but he fought it, drawing in his breath with effort. End of the line, he thought, and now he could hear the music of death. It was playing faster and stronger, moment by moment. Hang on, he thought, just hang on.

At last he saw the flare of headlights at the end of the block. He leaned sideways to lie against the seat with his eyes watching the light of the approaching beams growing brighter, then swinging away. Like clockwork, he thought; he always did everything by clockwork.

He pushed himself upright again, to see the large glistening car stop in the broad drive. The driver waited behind the wheel as the garage door lifted. Cummings drew the pistol from his holster, as the short, wide man stepped nimbly from the back and walked confidently along the curving path leading to the front door of the large house.

It had to mean something, Cummings thought, balancing the pistol against the door frame, pointing it through the open car window. It had to, he thought with a last moment of clear reasoning.

Then, in the last section of clarity, he thought: Wrong. I should have stopped it long ago. With the law, not the man.

But the pistol pointed, and clarity dissolved. He followed the target, forcing himself with his last strength to keep the gun steady. His lips moved back, teeth showing. His eyes raged with the expression of an animal wounded and cornered, incapable of reason.

"Goodby, Knocko," he whispered, and squeezed the trigger.

THE END

www.ingramcontent.com/pod-product-compliance
Lightning Source LLC
Chambersburg PA
CBHW050325160726
48002CB00001B/185